THE
WOUNDED
MUSE

THE WOUNDED MUSE

A NOVEL

BY ROBERT F. DELANEY

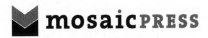 mosaicPRESS

Library and Archives Canada Cataloguing in Publication

Delaney, Robert F., 1968-, author
    The wounded muse : a novel / Robert F. Delaney.

Issued in print and electronic formats.
ISBN 978-1-77161-327-9 (softcover).--ISBN 978-1-77161-328-6 (HTML).--
ISBN 978-1-77161-373-6 (Kindle).--ISBN 978-1-77161-329-3 (PDF)

    I. Title.

PS3604.E5435W68 2018   813'.6   C2018-903077-1
                                                 C2018-903078-X

Published by Mosaic Press, Oakville, Ontario, Canada, 2018.
MOSAIC PRESS, Publishers
Copyright © Robert F. Delaney 2018
Cover Design by PolyStudio
Design By

ONTARIO ARTS COUNCIL
CONSEIL DES ARTS DE L'ONTARIO
an Ontario government agency
un organisme du gouvernement de l'Ontario

We acknowledge the Ontario Arts Council
for their support of our publishing program
We acknowledge the Ontario Media Development Corporation
for their support of our publishing program

Funded by the   Financé par le
Government   gouvernement   Canada
of Canada   du Canada

MOSAIC PRESS
1252 Speers Road, Units 1 & 2
Oakville, Ontario L6L 5N9
phone: (905) 825-2130

info@mosaic-press.com

To Klemens

"Who wants honey
As long as there's some money"

- William Patrick Corgan

BEIJING
June, 2006

Qiang squints as he checks the framing on the display of a camera resting on Jake's head. Facing a condemned housing block with just a few units still inhabited, Jake is a tripod. Qiang wants the right balance of human activity and dying daylight, divided about one-third from the top of the frame by the building's roofline. Lampposts along the footpath and light fixtures around the entrance have already been harvested for scrap metal, leaving holes and gnarled wires springing out like petrified eels. Trucks roll along the street behind them, heading to or from an onramp to the Third Ring or the neighbourhoods on the other side where more five-storey walk-ups   await the wrecking ball. There's no stopping anymore in this area, now a dark patch slated to rejoin the fabric of the sprawling city in a year or two when glass towers will rise from the mulch of recent history.

Several hundred metres away, another building like the one Qiang and Jake are facing is now rubble. A jackhammer sends shock waves through the air like artillery fire as workers decimate the last piece of foundation. The air is a fog of diesel fumes and concrete smashed into an ultra-fine powder.

A breeze picks up. Hot and dry from the Gobi Desert many miles to the northwest, it pushes through the city, a reminder that Beijing, despite its large and ever-growing scale, is just a small, man-made interruption in a vast, arid plain. Jake can feel desert dust mixed with minerals from the demolition site accumulate around the hairs in his nostrils and scrunches his face, which does nothing to loosen the invasive material. In the meantime, he will focus on other cravings. Perhaps a mojito tonight instead of red wine when he and Qiang head to one of the bars in the Embassy District. Summer has kicked in and it's the season for other avenues to intoxication. Besides, the only way to make red wine enjoyable in this heat is to drop an ice cube into it. That's what his Aunt Tracy, back in Kentucky, would have done. So Jake won't.

"How's it look?" he asks.

"Getting there," Qiang says quietly as he makes micro-adjustments.

Jake senses Qiang's concentration, as tangible as the camera on his head, so he focuses on the institutional blues and greens inside the still-inhabited apartments in case Qiang needs help remembering what was where. White, pastel blue and mint green had been the only colours available for interior walls until about a decade ago when wealth sprouted in the form of brighter hues that stand out in a cityscape coated in soot and desert dust. Restaurants began dressing their walls with large format photos of tropical coves, English gardens or North American autumnal landscapes. Standard issue water thermoses and washbasins churned out since the Cultural Revolution in dour maroon-tinged metal and white enamel gave way to colours inspired by new wave British pop from the 1980s.

By the time saturated colours began to re-appear in Beijing, like desert flowers after a once-in-a-generation rainstorm, the residents of the building Qiang is now documenting knew there was no point in repainting. The neighbourhood was marked for demolition. Just inside the Third Ring, the area would surely go to the most well-connected developer. It was just a matter of time before a work crew would make its way to this district to paint the character 拆 onto the walls. *Demolish.*

Wherever it appears, the character serves notice that residents have about a month to take their subsidy for an apartment somewhere beyond the Fourth or Fifth Rings. And so most of them do just that, leaving behind the street life that had teemed there for decades, if not centuries, where the business of eateries and shops housed in rough plaster and brick structures spilled onto the sidewalks where kitchen workers washed cookware and plates, peddlers sold everything from plastic combs to alarm clocks to mobile phone cases and barbers equipped with scissors, a wooden chair and a dented metal basin trimmed hair.

City planners have been doing much to make the migration more palatable. Giant machines are burrowing under the city, grinding out a dozen new subway lines to make life beyond the Fourth ring more livable. So, drawn to new residential towers with elevators, reliable heat and running water, few of the residents would have felt much fondness for the rigged and ramshackle lives they abandoned. Felt even less for neighbours, the troubled minority, who were left surrounded by darkness, satisfied enough with the work unit housing that had defined their lives.

Jake now wonders about Qiang's documentary subjects. Each unit still inhabited its own little diorama containing the story of a retired bureaucrat or state worker, each one a decision to defy authority. They remind Jake about the combination of choices, determination and luck that landed him here in Beijing, living his own life of resistance half a world away from his roots.

Qiang's lens has brought this understanding into focus. For more than a decade, Jake had watched with detachment as these communities disappeared, wondering only what gleaming structures would take their place. What new dining option would open its doors to a population that's come to expect nothing but new. Nearly twenty years after 1989, the last spasm of a very bad century, the chaos has dissolved into perfect, modern buildings. Each a promise of comfort and beauty in exchange for dreams of things less tangible.

Jake met Qiang a year earlier. A friend gave him a heads up that a newbie was relocating to Beijing and asked if Jake would be kind enough to introduce Qiang to some friends, maybe a place where he'd get a chance to talk to some reporters? Jake obliged and took him, literally and figuratively, to the centre of the city's expat social scene, the semi-annual soiree at the penthouse apartment of a Swiss banker.

"This is history," Qiang said to Jake as they looked down from the terrace at a pile of rubble that would eventually become the third stage of the China World Center. "Usually, you need a load of academics to make the calls on what constitutes a new era but anyone with eyes knows this is a new world."

The first two China World Towers, flanking the five-star China World Hotel, had marked the easternmost extent of central Beijing. Developers have since moved further out, jumping the Third Ring and pushing more residents out beyond the Fourth.

"Someone needs to document this with the right lens," Qiang said. "To the Western press, this is like Mordor. To the state press, this is the rebirth of civilization."

Qiang's conviction moved Jake. Others might have seen it as righteous self-possession but Jake took Qiang's declaration as a sort of grounding. He saw someone so embedded in a cause that everything else about a wealthy banker's party on a Saturday night, atop a building in the centre of the most important city in the world, meant nothing. The quips about a moronic U.S. president, the ironic phrases emblazoned on t-shirts, "The Revolution's Children Now Run the Show", paired with fine linen blazers and converse sneakers, the puffs of hash and Blondie's Heart of Glass thumping through the sound system all seemed trite.

Qiang had made sense of the economic growth and industrial output numbers, always orders of magnitude ahead of anywhere else in the world, that Jake had been writing about every day. He apparently didn't have eyes or, maybe, as he has told himself since he met Qiang, he's just been in China too long to grasp the enormity of the story he was covering. Jake hadn't been back to the U.S. since he left more than a decade ago.

With his lens on these few, soon to be extinguished, lonely rectangles of florescent light in front of them, Qiang is now zooming in on the details of this historical shift, this upheaval, in a way that Jake never has.

Jake has asked Qiang a few times whether he's concerned about the authorities, whether he's stepping over a line with this documentary. Qiang always brushes away the warnings as though Jake was suggesting sunscreen on an overcast day.

Still, he's taken some precautions to make them less visible. He has left everything but the camera at home so they wouldn't look like a film crew. And Jake is happy to serve as the tripod. He's getting a drink out of this but that's not why he agreed to come along. He'll be getting time with Qiang, the first person Jake has met in this city who's not chasing money.

Qiang abandoned that pursuit a few months earlier when he chose to ditch his corner office in Silicon Valley. He arrived in Beijing with nothing but a computer loaded with editing software, the camera that's on Jake's head and the tripod that's lying in the foyer of Qiang's sparsely furnished apartment just outside the East Third Ring.

"Can you hold the stance a bit more steadily?" Qiang asks.

Jake spreads his feet slightly and moves one foot behind to give him a wider base. Qiang then steadies the camera further by resting his elbows on Jake's shoulders while he pans across the length of the building. Enlisted in an effort that blends art and politics, Jake's shoulders now support a different kind of utility. Jake can, for a few moments, take pride in them without feeling vain.

His transformation from a clueless pre-teen in a coal mining town to foreign correspondent in China started with these assets when his Aunt Tracy told him how "broad shoulders make the man." She made the comment at a backyard barbecue, an event arranged by Tracy because some cousin or niece finished grade school. Slurring her words and gesturing with a cigarette in one hand, Aunt Tracy told Jake his shoulders were sturdy enough to get him into any life he wanted. In the other hand, she gripped a plastic tumbler full of red wine on ice.

With a head of permed red hair dyed even redder, Tracy stood out. As usual, everyone else was drinking beer or bourbon, or both and she would have made sangria if she knew what that was. Before she was too drunk to make any sense, Tracy took Jake aside and told him to "get out of this white trash heap and don't let anyone put you down."

As an eleven-year-old, Jake didn't understand what his aunt meant about white trash or shoulders. It wasn't until a few years later when he saw the James Bond film *A View to a Kill* with the blonde and buff Dolph Lundgren as a KGB henchman and the martini sipping Roger Moore that Jake got the idea to accentuate his best asset. Shoulder presses, bench presses, squats and crunches a couple times a week built up a body that stopped the tough kids from making fun of his pronounced buck-teeth. His shoulders gave Jake the courage he needed to leave Kentucky just a week after graduating high school. He left his mother and her live-in boyfriend a note: "I'm off and I'll get in touch when I'm settled."

Aunt Tracy, the only relative he ever felt close to, had passed away from lung cancer just a few months earlier. There was no one else he cared for in Magnet Hill, Kentucky.

"I think I got the shot," Qiang says as he takes his elbows off Jake's shoulders and begins examining the footage through the camera's display.

"Want to get some footage of the others?" Jake asks.

"Nah, the light behind the building is gone," Qiang says. "The shot will be too flat." He reviews more of the footage. "And you must be very thirsty," he adds, looking up with a satisfied expression. "Ten o'clock on a Thursday night. I know you want to get an early start on the weekend."

Jake squints his eyes and smiles. "You know me so well."

In fact, Jake wouldn't mind spending another hour roaming the condemned neighbourhood looking for artifacts.

YONGFU VILLAGE, HEILONGJIANG PROVINCE, CHINA
March, 1993

Dawei watched snowflakes the size of chestnuts fall outside the classroom window. Electricity to the two-room school would surely cut out soon and all of the students would be sent home. The wiring was shoddy, his father had told him when the building was constructed a few years earlier, shoddy like everything in Yongfu.

Snowstorms used to bring joy. Dawei once loved to clear the front of his house with the shovel his father fashioned by lashing half a cooking oil canister to a tree branch with bolts and thick twine. He would watch the blanket of snow thicken and drag the old shovel out every half hour. It was a contest, Dawei against the snow.

But the snow, on this late winter day when the lengthening days had Dawei hoping for the warmth of spring, made him brood. A clearer understanding about the difference between work and play emerged as suddenly as the hair that had recently sprouted in his armpits and around his groin. Clearing snow was a task, not a game. And this storm brought more than a new set of responsibilities. It drew a dividing line between childhood and adulthood.

The snow had been accumulating for hours and the students became more restless as they waited for the dismissal they knew would come at any moment. And then white flakes began falling on Dawei's desk.

When they hit, Dawei and his desk mate looked at each other. Falling with the weight of pebbles, the flakes were small and solid. Like sleet, but dry. This wasn't snow. A loud creak then interrupted the teacher's lesson as everyone in the classroom looked up to watch a crack tear across the white ceiling like footage of a lightning bolt in negative. The students sat, transfixed, trying to make sense of what was happening until the sound of rending metal joints – alternating screeches and snaps – prompted them to crouch and grab the sides of their desks.

Dawei jumped up from his bench and ran to the other side of the room just as the lights died. Amid yelps and screams, broad chunks of plaster from each side of the crack fell on a few of his classmates, exposing a matrix of struts and corrugated metal all bending inward.

Students began tripping over debris and running into each other as they scrambled to the sides of the room. With the lights cut and some of the windows now covered by panels dangling from the corners of the ceiling, it was difficult to separate the sounds of structural collapse from the abrupt movement of desks as students tried to make their way to the exit.

Dawei struggled to get his bearings. Xiao Bei, a classmate one year younger than Dawei, lay dazed and bleeding after being knocked off her bench by a chunk of plaster. She looked at Dawei as if to ask for guidance. Her expression kept him from fleeing even as the metal struts began straining the wall behind him, shattering banks of casement windows.

Dawei thought of the heroes in the stories they'd listened to in class: The Outlaws of the Marsh and The Journey of Meng. When someone needs help, the only honourable response is to ignore the danger. This is what it means to be an adult and a hero. And Xiao Bei was one of the few students who had never taunted Dawei about his stutter. They'd always played together during recess, often building simple structures with stones and twigs in the schoolyard while the other boys played soccer with the school's one ratty ball and the girls played tag.

"Dawei and Xiao Bei are getting married!" the other kids would sometimes yell. "Look, they're building their house!"

Xiao Bei would sometimes blush, but she had never stopped playing with Dawei.

As debris fell around him, Dawei understood that stories of courage and character aren't merely a means to fill class time. They're meant to help children learn to recognize when a door to adulthood opens. And Dawei wanted to jump through the door between him and his injured friend.

The teacher was trying to help two students on the other side of the room by forcing open the window behind them. She lifted them, one by one, onto the windowsill, allowing them to jump out while screaming at the students already outside to move away from the building.

As the other students ran towards the door, Dawei crouched down behind Xiao Bei, putting his arms underneath her back and wrapping them up through her armpits. He began dragging her backwards as more plaster fell and the wall next to him cracked from the pull of the metal struts now folding under the weight of the snow. Just a few feet from the door, part of the wall fell in on Dawei, hitting him on the back of his head and his shoulder.

A moment later, Dawei felt the strong grip of an adult, probably his teacher, pull him by the ankle. Then, the shock of snow on his cheek and in the background, more yelps and screams mixed with loud cracks and shattering sounds. He was hoisted up by someone who threw Dawei's arm around the back of his neck and grabbed his wrist as it flopped onto the other side. The man hustled Dawei through the heavy snow towards the local clinic. The cold air and the jostling began to revive Dawei. Once his wits reconnected, he planted his feet firmly on the ground and stopped. Panting and bent over with his hands on his knees, Dawei asked about Xiao Bei.

"Who?" the man asked.

"Xiao Bei. I… almost had her… out of the building," Dawei said between breaths.

"I don't know. They're trying to move the debris. If you're okay, I'm going back to help them. You should get yourself to the clinic."

"No. I'm coming to help them," Dawei said before the white colour all over the ground suddenly swelled to consume everything in his field of vision. Then everything went black.

Dawei woke with a searing headache sometime after the weather settled into silence. The first light of day defined the edges of the window's heavy cotton curtains made from old quilts. Dawei remembered his mother waking him in the middle of the night to change the rags wrapped around his head and ask him his name, the day of the week. There was just enough light to make out the time on the wind-up clock that sat on a shelf over the foot of his bed, next to the rest of his belongings: A mug holding his toothbrush and comb, some school notebooks and a stack of glossy magazines featuring Hong Kong movie stars.

Only a hint of warmth remained under Dawei's bed, a wooden platform on adobe blocks heated by a pipe connected to the stove just outside the faded sheet he had hung from the ceiling to separate his bed from the rest of the one-room house. The coal had burned out a while earlier and the blocks had almost completely lost their heat.

Dawei heard his parents mumble and manoeuver their way out of their bed against the opposite wall. He stood up, pulled his pants over his long johns, changed into a sweater and pushed aside the sheet. He looked out one of the grimy windowpanes on the front door as he put on a heavy jacket and slid his feet into a pair of boots by the door while his mother, Tieying, made a bed of kindling under a coal brick in the stove.

"You need to stay in bed," she said. "At least let me change the bandage."

Dawei pulled the rag from his head, wincing in pain as the blood-dried hair glued to the bandage separated from the fabric. He looked at the purple and black stains on the rag. Knowing that his mother would want to boil and hang it to re-use, he crumpled the rag into a ball and shoved it in his pocket.

"It's fine," Dawei said. "I need to find out what happened to Xiao Bei. Do you know what happened to her or any of the others?"

"A couple of them died on the way to the hospital," Tieying said. "I haven't heard anything about Xiao Bei."

With a lit cigarette dangling from his mouth, Dawei's father routed through a toolbox at the foot of his bed. He was looking for plastic bags that he'd need to pull over his socks so the holes in his boots wouldn't leave him with soggy feet. He needed to get to the toilet about 50 metres up the lane and would surely curse the whole way.

Dawei forced the door open against the snow that had blown into a slope that ran about a third of the way up the side of the house. He jumped outside and trudged through the snow in the soft pink light of dawn until he was far enough down the lane to see the roofless schoolhouse. The snow drifts around the walls, which had fallen inward along jagged and irregular breaks above the shattered windows, made the structure look like a geological formation.

Pushing through several metres of snowdrifts left Dawei out of breath and made the wound at the back of his head throb. The temperature began to drop and the frigid air stung his nose. He hopped back to the house where, a few feet from the door, he saw yellow stains left by his father. Dawei kicked his feet against the doorjamb to knock the snow off, ducked inside, pulled the door shut and slid out of his boots.

No school. Free for the day, or maybe for weeks or months. But the emerging adult in him knew this wasn't liberation. With the spring thaw still a month away, what would he do besides help his parents with more chores? Sorting corn and sorghum seeds. Stacking coal and firewood. Repairing tools and cracks in the walls of their home. He listened to the crackling of wood in the stove and waited for the diatribe that his father would surely spew.

His mother poured water from a thermos into a large pot on the stove.

"It's a curse to live here anymore," Dawei's father said in a gravelly voice bubbling with mucus. "Bastards. That was the only project here in years and they couldn't build it to withstand snow."

His mother ladled some water into a smaller pot and dropped in three eggs.

His father stood up, walked to the door and stormed out, slamming the door behind him.

With a pained expression, his mother marched to the door and jerked it open. "Get in here," she snapped. "No jacket. Are you crazy?"

But father just stood in the snow.

"Crazy," mother said as she smoothed her hair and her sweater. Then she turned the eggs in the pot as the water began to boil.

Father walked back inside. "Now the young will be just as helpless as the old," he yelled. He took a last drag from his cigarette and flicked it into the kitchen sink.

"We need to get him to Harbin," mother said. "We need my sister's help."

Dawei eyes opened but he didn't see the soot-stained ceiling. He looked right through it and saw Harbin instead, the exciting city hundreds of kilometres away. Dawei's trips to Harbin had only ever been annual events, at the New Year, lasting several days. They had always been the highlight of his year.

Aunt Dongmei, six years younger than Dawei's mother, finished her degree at a Harbin teachers college. Within a year, she married Uncle Yiming, a chemical engineer whose research into corn processing was driving a new division at his company. "Starch, a food additive," he explained, "was an especially sweet syrup that would soon be used in soft drinks.

The state-owned firm placed Yiming and Dongmei in a two-room apartment. The comfortable accommodations, the television programs, the reliable indoor heat and the variety of foods weren't the only things that made Harbin delightful for Dawei. Uncle Yiming taught him how to play badminton and ping pong and played the latest pop music from Hong Kong and Taiwan, often singing along in a booming voice that sounded like the stars on television. He always shared the seat of his bike, allowing Dawei to ring the bell and sometimes steer. Every trip outside, every errand run, every destination, was an adventure.

Twice a year, Uncle Yiming travelled to Hong Kong where he bought the magazines, portals to worlds full of beautiful women and handsome, heroic men, that he then gave to Dawei as New Year's gifts. The stories and advertisements within featured modern cities with buildings that reached into the clouds and were even more magical than Harbin. Sometimes there were tropical beaches with palm trees reaching out over blue water.

"This is no place for him," his mother concluded, shaking her head as she lifted the eggs from the boiling water. If their son didn't make it to university, she reasoned, at least his child, their grandchild, would have a chance. Something about the collapse of his school's roof strengthened his mother's spine. Her husband didn't argue.

A week later, Dawei and his parents were at the bus depot.

"We're lucky Uncle is good enough to make room for you," mother told him as she refastened the buttons on his coat. She wiped each of her eyes with the tips of her fingers, then ran them through her dry hair to make the tears disappear. "Be careful with the jars in your bag," she said. "Make sure they make it safely."

Father looked at Dawei directly. He hadn't ever seen the man's eyes straight on. "Don't spoil this opportunity," his father said. "You don't want to come back."

Qiang moves the bounce umbrella to balance the daylight flooding in from a window to the side of his interview subject. He needs subdued lighting because the old man's complexion is ashen, drained of moisture by regular infusions of chemicals that have never managed to shrink the tumors in his pancreas. His face will look even worse once rendered into video so Qiang brings the light levels down.

A sparse, gray fuzz wraps around the sides and back of the man's head in place of the standard black coif required for China's top leaders. Just this once, Qiang thinks, an interview subject might need some foundation. It might even be disrespectful to broadcast the image of this diminished man who once sat uniformed and shoulder-to-shoulder with other members of the Standing Committee, who used to project a strength gained through political struggles that saw him purged, rehabilitated, and purged again, as he appears now in front of Qiang's camera. But there's no time for makeup.

The old man's home is furnished with spartan wooden furniture from decades earlier. A square table with one leg that's been repaired with screws and a metal bracket sits against the far wall. One block-framed chair with frayed cotton velvet upholstery the colour of blood – the kind that used to crowd "soft sleeper" waiting rooms in train stations – sits in front of the man's television which is tuned to a CCTV-2 morning news segment touting the success of an irrigation project in Guizhou Province.

Qiang has set the TV's volume high enough to keep his interview subject's comments indecipherable through the bugs that are almost certainly in the apartment walls. Low enough, he hopes, to keep the responses clear enough in the final sound mix.

Qiang clips the mic onto the old man's shirt placket. The mic had arrived a few days before, a Sennheiser professional model that screens out background noise better than most models on the market.

"Can you count from one to ten?" Qiang asks.

"What?"

"I'm testing the sound, so I need to hear you speak."

"Ok. The one thing you need to know…"

"Sorry Mr. Zhou," Qiang says softly, like a parent coaxing a child about to get a dose of medicine. Qiang's not sure if Mr. is appropriate. There's also Uncle. In Zhou's day, he would have been called Comrade.

"I'm just testing the sound. Please save what you want to say until I start recording. Just one more moment and I'll be able to start recording. Please just count to ten."

Zhou sighs. "One, two, three …"

Qiang brings up the sound levels. After a few more adjustments to the light and a final rotation of the camera's lens, Qiang says, "Ok, Mr. Zhou. Thank you for your patience. I'm recording now." He hits record as he says the last word.

Zhou inhales slowly, summoning strength. "I don't know what has gotten out but one thing that must be understood is that we let Comrade Hu die," the old man says. His eyes dart between the lens and Qiang even though Qiang had told him to ignore the camera. It doesn't matter. No one will expect high production value, Qiang tells himself. He keeps the camera rolling.

"No one dared to put the orders on paper but they were clear. I delivered them to the clinic. I told the doctors face-to-face."

"What were the orders?" Qiang asks quietly, hoping he doesn't need to repeat the question.

"Don't you understand? Just as I said. The orders were to withhold any treatment. Let him die. He was dangerous."

Qiang drops his notepad and pen, then scrambles to recover them. This is more than he had expected. He figured he'd get more details about how the moderates in the government sided with the students, some key quotes that stayed with him over the years and how much resistance they put up against the plan to send tanks to the Square. Maybe even how they were too afraid to oppose the final solution, how they rationalized a decision that would reverberate across a generation.

Yet here is Zhou Xiaoyue, a revolutionary and then a reactionary, providing a detail that, if made public in 1989, might have led to a different outcome. The demonstrators wouldn't have been limited to students. Many more might have concluded that the government had lost its legitimacy. The earth in and around Beijing and every other city in China might have rumbled with anger and demands for political reform.

"Comrade Hu's ideas might have been risky, bold perhaps, but I don't think they were dangerous. I didn't think so at the time, either. But the chaos in the Square seemed to threaten everything."

The old man expels a slow, tired sigh.

"Who issued that order?" Qiang asks.

"It came from the Standing Committee. No signatures. Just a chop. You can look at the records to see who was in control at the time, who had the upper hand. But as far as I'm concerned, we were all responsible. The ones who disagreed didn't disagree with enough force. I just can't go to the grave with this secret."

Qiang wants to ask more questions but he can't afford to leave any more evidence that he's conducting this interview.

"Something changed in the air when I left the clinic on that day." Zhou says. "We were the generation that... We were supposed to have thrown out all of that superstition, but..."

His milky eyes look past the camera and through walls, in the direction of Tiananmen Square and Zhongnanhai, as though he's looking at ghosts.

"With that decision, with that directive, we ran afoul of the universe. All of the bloodshed could have been prevented if we had just showed a bit of compassion towards Hu."

Zhou goes quiet and Qiang glances at his watch, wondering if he should cut.

"There's a resonance between our actions on this earth and the cosmos. The cosmos was telling us to let go of some of the controls but we grabbed them more tightly."

Zhou then names the officials who wanted mercy for Hu Yaobang, those who later found themselves marginalized, and those on the other side, including himself, who insisted on burying reforms along with Comrade Hu.

"Hu wanted the best for China. He was an honest man. And we let him die. And we wonder why we need to, year after year after year, launch anti-corruption campaigns."

Qiang stops recording and removes the SD card from his camera.

"Let's take a break for a minute, Mr. Zhou," Qiang says as he slides the card into a space between two layers of the sole on his left shoe, a separation Qiang created by digging into the rubber with a razor blade. He erases the temporary file that saved automatically on the camera and then slides in another SD card. An empty one.

Qiang walks over to the television and turns it off. There's no need to mask the next part of the interview. He turns off the space heater, leaving the room silent except for the sound of neighbours going about their morning business. A door slams a few floors up, or down. A ration of garbage ricochets down a chute. A pipe rattles.

"Ok, Mr. Zhou. How about you now tell me what you think about all of the changes you've seen around Beijing as the city prepares for the Olympics."

Turning to look out the window, Zhou ponders the question.

"I think it's time," he says. "These buildings served their purpose. They provided a degree of comfort and dignity, enough for their time. But they weren't built well enough to meet the needs of today's citizens. No elevators. You know how long it takes me to get up one flight?"

Zhou leans forward, looking at Qiang, and gesticulates with an open hand as he asks the question.

"How can you realize the value of a neighbourhood near the centre of Beijing if you can only build up five storeys? You see the skyscrapers they have now from one end of Shanghai to the other? I believe this city should also reach the sky."

Settling back into his chair with a grimace, Zhou runs through his argument about how economic reforms can't proceed without a physical transformation.

A van with official plates pulls up outside of his building, stopping in the bicycle path. Inside the van, two officers listen to the conversation. It's clear enough to hear every word since Qiang silenced the television. Three men in nondescript suits step out of the van, leaving the driver and another officer in the passenger side front seat inside. A police car pulls up behind the van with two police officers who stay in their car.

"I know some people complain about having to move but there's no way to completely avoid disruption in some areas as this country re-engineers," Zhou says before he's interrupted by someone pounding on the front door.

Qiang's heart jumps into a full sprint. He had prepared for a bust-up, placing the odds somewhere around fifty percent. Kendra, his collaborator in Washington, warned him to make contingency plans. In their correspondence, Kendra gave Qiang the directions, suggesting that he shoot the questions about the death of Hu Yaobang first, obscure the sound, and then hide the video file as soon as he got the answers. She warned him to keep the sensitive part of the interview short. Better to get a few comments that make it out of Beijing than an hour's worth of thoughts that get confiscated. Months of safe-channel communication prepared Qiang for this moment. But the preparation means nothing now that the Public Security Bureau has arrived and the hypothetical becomes a meaty fist pounding on a door. Qiang surveys the room, wondering if there's a way out.

With a deep breath, Qiang regains his composure. He looks down at the side of his shoe sole and uses the point of his pen to push the SD card in further. They can't detain him if they don't find it. Or can they?

"Who is it?" Zhou calls out.

"We've received a complaint," snaps one of the men just outside the door. "You need to open the door now."

Qiang shakes his head. Complaint, maybe. But not from anyone living in this building.

6:00 p.m.

The officer sits across from Qiang handling the SD card they took from his camera, flipping it from side-to-side like it's a new discovery, as though he hadn't spent the last five hours viewing the clips it holds and deliberating with officers who had interrogated the old official.

He scrunches up his face while reading the details on the card, reciting the specifications in heavily accented English. Qiang notices the stains on his teeth, yellowed from the smoke of 10,000 cigarettes, matching the colour of the walls and ceiling. The walls were also pure white at one time. Scuff marks on the floor and on the walls where the chair backs have rubbed also mar the interior of the windowless room in which he sits.

Qiang hasn't seen daylight since the officers escorted him to the van outside of Zhou's building. He's not sure if it's late afternoon, midnight or morning.

"What are you doing here in Beijing, Sun Qiang?" the officer asks.

"I'm filming a documentary about the changes taking place in Beijing in the run-up to the Olympics."

The officer smiles sarcastically, like a bit character in a bad crime film. This one must be lower-ranking, Qiang thinks.

"I know about Zhao Xiaoyue's history," Qiang says. "That's why I wanted to talk to him. To prove what I'm trying to point out in my project."

"What are you trying to point out in your project?"

Too tired to mind his manners, Qiang snorts. "I don't know how many times I've explained this to your colleagues already."

"Explain it again," the officer spits back, his smile gone.

"The Chinese people support redevelopment. We all know the world will be watching. We all know that thousands of foreigners will flood our streets and avenues. Most people don't want to stand in the way of progress." Qiang pauses. He knows he can get carried away and he doesn't want to pontificate.

"Someone like Zhao, who emerged as a critic of the government in many areas, is an interesting subject to discuss this, don't you think?"

The officer is expressionless. In the absence of any other cues, and with a surge of enthusiasm blinding him to the reality of his predicament, Qiang chooses to try to create a convert.

"Someone who was with the Party from the earliest days, who was on the Long March, who's been at the centre of every phase of the growth of this country. Even after all of that, and having been rejected for speaking out, he's voicing his support for these changes."

The officer cocks his head, encouraging Qiang to continue.

"But here's what I've learned about those people speaking out about this. They're supportive too. Almost all of them. They're just asking for some kind of arrangement. We're talking about loans given with favourable rates, just like all of the state-owned enterprises get so they can be part of the redevelopment, to buy into the new Beijing. Don't you see? This solution addresses every problem we have. Rebalancing the economy away from bloated industries, developing the consumer sector, communities working with government. Don't you see the slogan written everywhere in this city? "Harmonious Society." None of us can walk ten metres without seeing it draped over a wall. Why don't we do this, embrace harmony, for real in Beijing?"

Silence ensues and Qiang wonders if his delivery was too hackneyed. He knows his zeal can sometimes overtake his ability to arrange thoughts clearly. Another officer walks into the room and sits next to his colleague. He may have been the one in the van's front passenger seat. Qiang isn't sure because he didn't get a good look at the guy.

"Here's what you're going to do in Beijing, Sun Qiang," the new arrival says. Qiang surmises that he's higher-ranking. "You're going to stop this foolishness or else you're going to find yourself in a lot more trouble." He grabs Qiang's wrist.

"Zhao is a fool and so are you. I don't care what message you're trying to get across in this project you speak of. The fact is that you have no business exploring this. Clearly, you've been in the U.S. for too long. Let me tell you right now, you're just slightly luckier than you are foolish because we're letting you go now. Your so-called project is over and we better not catch you conducting any more interviews."

Qiang clenches his jaw to trap the insults he wants to spew back "Could you at least give me back my camera?"

He knows this is a ridiculous question but he can't hold it back. A detention without charges. A requisitioning without justification. Does nothing in this country ever change? And this was barely a provocation. They know nothing of the interview buried in the sole of his shoe, the one that he will mail to Kendra in Washington to complete her film commemorating the twentieth anniversary of the crackdown.

"What camera?" the officer asks.

9:00 p.m.

Opening night at Destination and the drinks are half price until midnight. Gin and tonics in hand, Jake and Pierre stand together, backs to the bar, allowing them to survey the newly renovated décor. Floor and walls finished in polished grey concrete emit the clean scent of minerals. Laughing and taunting each other, the evening's first wave of patrons stand around heavy, stainless steel high tables filling a corner of the bar area, their spiky, Japanese anime-inspired hair spotlighted by halogen lamps embedded in the ceiling. Jake is acquainted with some of them but not well enough to say hello or even acknowledge their presence.

"This place could be New York or Paris," Jake shouts to Pierre over the booming sound system. "They really invested. It's not just a string of fairy lights and a sad mirror ball."

"They made the right decision," Pierre replies, keeping his sight trained on the slow procession through the entrance. "A city of ten million? A flood of new expats? I'd invest in a place like this if I had the connections."

"Is it me or are the Mainlanders getting hotter? I mean, look around," Jake says, pointing to the first bunch of guys congregating on the dance floor, swaying tentatively, with drinks in hand, to a Kylie Minogue mix. "They kind of get the rhythm now. They can't all be from Tokyo or Hong Kong, right?"

Pierre looks at Jake's light blue t-shirt emblazoned with the words "porn star" in a colourful bubble font from the 1970s, the fabric just tight enough to show the pecs that Jake works to maintain. Pierre points at the words and chuckles.

"You think that's going to get you laid?"

"I can't be sure, Pierre, but there's one thing I know for sure. It wouldn't get you laid because it's size small and you'd look lousy in it," Jake says, poking a protruding belly that Pierre hides under an untucked, white Ermenegildo Zegna shirt with a black floral design that crawls from one shoulder and spreads across the back. Pierre smacks Jake's hand away.

Jake pulls out his phone to check the time, wondering whether Qiang will pull himself away from his editing long enough to join them. The odds are fifty-fifty, based on past pledges to come out, so Jake tries to re-focus. He scans the dance floor like a cat stalking prey and notices a white guy looking back at him with a smile. He has thinning, light-brown hair and a somewhat bulbous nose but a friendly expression so unlike the distant, the non-committal and vacant demeanours Jake usually needs to break through to start a conversation and get things on course for the evening's eventual climax. Jake doesn't recognize him. A newcomer, which raises the likelihood of success because they're generally more open to new experiences.

As Jake smiles back, he sees Qiang just a few feet away from the white guy, pushing through a group of people he recognizes, each ranked and categorized by profession, ethnic preference, social circle.

"Sorry," Qiang mouths with an apologetic look as he approaches them. "There's a long queue out there. It's mayhem."

Pierre hands Qiang a gin and tonic. "Drink up. It's impossible to get an order in, so we got a couple of extras."

"Thanks. How much?"

Pierre waves away the suggestion. "Let's get out on the floor before there's no room."

A remixed Leslie Cheung song trails off into a stripped-down house beat and, after a few measures, the opening chords of Madonna's *Hung Up* bubble to the surface. Jake and Pierre look at each other, wide-eyed.

"Madonnnnaaaaa!" they shout, grabbing Qiang. They weave their way through the bar area and squeeze to the centre of the dance floor, moving like amoebae through gyrating duos grinding crotch-to-crotch, legs interlocked. The air is infused with alcohol, evaporating up from drinks that have been sloshed and spilled. Sweaty backs push against each other to open up enough room to pull t-shirts off, rock back and forth and pump fists by the time Madonna belts out the first chorus.

Pierre begins to unbutton Qiang's shirt, getting down far enough to reveal the small tattoo over his heart. 洋. Ocean. Qiang cups Pierre's hands in his own and, with the smile of a good sport, pulls them away from his shirt. Ironic, Jake thinks, looking at the only ocean he can't swim in.

Barely halfway to the first chorus, Jake notices half of the patrons look toward an area somewhere near the entrance. The energy on the dance floor changes. Smiles and laughter turn to wary expressions. Some guys begin to put their shirts back on. Others move from the dance floor, slowly.

Policemen, six of them, have filed into the bar. Two officers continue through to the back and disappear, presumably into the management's quarters. The four others stay close to the entrance that everyone seems to know not to rush toward. Two guards on each side.

Uniformed men in China have become abstractions for Jake because they're everywhere, representing the power structures he rarely sees. He writes about economics and finance so reports of detentions, harassment and other extra-judicial abuses of power are as remote for him in Beijing as they are for someone reading about them in New York City or Rio de Janeiro.

Qiang grabs Jake's wrist and slowly leads him back into the crowd around the bar. Something about Qiang's reaction to these officers sparks a pang of fear in Jake's gut, or perhaps it's just the reality of these officers up close in the refracted light. Madonna continues belting out her frustration about some sexual infatuation over a driving beat and flanging kaleidoscopic melodies which seem discordant against a backdrop of stone-faced police officers in olive drab uniforms and their wary prey.

"They'll be gone soon," Jake whispers into Qiang's ear. "They're just making sure the owners know who's in charge, right?"

"Are they looking for bribes?" Pierre asks, leaning in.

"They wouldn't be this obvious," Qiang says. "That's already been taken care of in some form or another. That's why I'm not so sure this is nothing."

"This place is heaving," Jake says. "There's too much opportunity for future bribes to scare anyone away, at least for the time being."

"Hung Up" fades into a Li Yuchun hit as the two officers emerge from the back. With a path cleared ahead of them, they walk straight toward the main entrance. They march through the doors and the other four follow in a precise, seemingly choreographed retreat.

"See," Jake says. "Sha ji jing hou, right?" Jake says. Kill the chicken to scare the monkey. Jake wonders if the proverb fits the scenario well enough. He doesn't want to sound stupid.

The music gets louder, helping to revive the energy. Pierre is now dancing with the couple he and Jake were eyeing before Qiang arrived. Pierre slides his hand down the back of the one with the red shirt and into the guy's back pocket. Jake points at him and looks at Qiang.

"How does he manage that?"

"The French accent and the million or so bucks a year he makes helps," Qiang says.

Jake has no response. He just nods and smiles. He wants to kill the conversation and turn this into the moment he's been trying to create since he first met Qiang a year earlier. Drawing on what must be the full capacity of the neighbourhood's power grid, the music gets even louder. This moment is crucial. Jake's heart pounds so powerfully that it rattles his ribs more than the seismic bass notes. He moves closer to Qiang, making his intention clear. But Qiang takes a step back and shakes his head slightly with a pained expression. The reaction suffocates Jake like a wrestler who's suddenly subdued.

"Let's talk outside," Qiang says as he puts a hand on Jake's shoulder.

The taxis slow down and honk as Jake and Qiang walk toward the curb. The muted thud of dance music vibrates up through the pavement and the treble rises each time the club's door swings open to let in more patrons. Two of three police vehicles, beacons flashing, pull away from the curb and the cars coming up behind them veer towards the far curb.

"Look," Qiang says, "my life right now is nothing but this project."

Jake nods silently, looking at the taxis congregating and honking like geese expecting to be fed. Hammering from the new towers under construction next to the dance club adds another layer to the cacophony. Jake can't speak. He wants to open a vein to let the humiliation and sorrow drain out and run down a gutter.

"I'm just unavailable until I get this done," Qiang says.

Jake wonders whether that means there's still a chance, sometime later on, months from now, perhaps, when Qiang's accepting an award at a film festival. But he knows not to ask. Now that he's been knocked off balance, Jake's thoughts fire randomly. He wonders why this consumes him so much. He's a journalist in the middle of one of the world's most important stories. China is no longer just a quirky, post-communist wonderland. It's no longer just any "developing market" beat. This is no place for someone distracted by heartache. He should be consumed by this work. Perhaps he's been here too long.

"Sorry, I don't mean to make things complicated for you."

Jake feels something catch in his throat as he speaks, something that will turn into a loss of control, something that might drive Qiang further away. So he looks down and coughs, turning the emotion into a meaningless physical reflex. Then he shakes his head and laughs.

"Where the hell is my head, anyway. We're here at Destination, like, watching the birth of, something. I don't know, like a gay renaissance in China. I should be documenting this for a story, right? One day someone needs to write a book about this. Let's get back in there, you know? Back in the thick of it."

Qiang puts a hand on Jake's shoulder. "Hey listen, I don't want to leave you high and dry but I'm really under the gun at the moment," Qiang says. "I need to get back to editing."

"Ok, anything I should know about? Anything I can help you with?"

Jake knows the answer will be no and that this embarrassing scene will now come to an end provide some relief.

"I need to work quickly now. Things got a bit dicey for me today."

The comment yanks Jake out of self-pity.

"All right, now you're scaring me. Things don't just 'get dicey,' Qiang. I might not cover the political stuff here but I know enough to know that any trouble is big trouble."

"Jake, if I were in big trouble, I wouldn't be here right now, would I?"

"Well then, can you please tell me exactly what happened?"

"I got a warning. It's that simple."

"And?"

"And they took my camera. So I need to borrow yours."

Jake looks at Qiang and then leans in closer.

"You've been warned and yet you want to continue with your interviews? Are you fucking crazy?"

"One interview. I have one left. You know I co-ordinate everything through an untraceable, pre-paid number."

"Well, if you're so good at staying under the radar, how did you get a warning?"

"I was at the wrong place. They didn't trace me through any of my communication."

Qiang sighs and looks down. "Jake, look. I've worked... we've worked too hard on this to let it go."

"You know they've changed the rules on the pre-pays, right? You need to leave ID to get them now."

"I know. As I said, I have one interview left. My pre-pay has just enough credit to get this done."

Jake looks around. The last police car pulls out into the traffic, the officer firing the siren in short bursts to clear a wide berth. He lifts a hand, signaling to several oncoming taxis. Three of them veer towards the curb coming within millimeters of each other. Two stay at the curb, waving Jake and Qiang into their vehicles. The taxi furthest from them swerves and accelerates back into the traffic.

"You've got me worried, my friend," Jake says as he opens the door of the closest taxi.

"Friend" sounds awkward because he's never called Qiang that before. Jake has chosen the word consciously, as a reassurance.

"Don't stay out too late. Sundays are better when you're not nursing a hangover," Qiang says as he shuts the car door.

Jake watches the cab drive away. A minute later, the car turns east and it's as if Qiang was never with him this evening, and Jake hadn't so carelessly miscalculated. Standing amid the chaos of construction noise, flashing neon signs and club music next to a busy street filled with aggressive, honking drivers, it's easier to bury a painful moment. Like throwing garbage into a raging river. The current will suck the trash under and no one needs to reflect on the offence.

Jake allows the rambunctious, accelerated energy of Saturday night in Beijing to absorb what just happened so he doesn't need to. It's just that easy, he thinks, and it occurs to him that he might still be in China even if Qiang had never appeared on the scene. It's not so much the glory of a scoop or the credibility accorded to "China hands" that keeps him there. It's the nebulosity of everything.

Looking at the bar entrance, Jake wonders if the white guy he was looking at earlier is still on the dance floor. Then he remembers Qiang's warning about hungover Sundays and finds himself running through possible scenarios that will play out if he returns to the bar. All of them involve enough alcohol to keep awkward conversations intact through the distractions of dance music at 100 decibels and the beguiling majesty of new, handsome faces on those who turn out to be no different from everyone else in the bar. This pathos has never stopped Jake before. A drink in a crowded, noisy bar may at least lead to an encounter that allows him to tune out all other uncertainties about himself and the world. Jake's been away from his family, from his hometown and from his adolescence long enough to know why he fled. Long enough to know that his invisibility growing up bred an unhealthy need for attention as an adult. So, he thinks, maybe turning his back on Saturday night at Destination could be his first step towards a stronger sort of self-confidence.

He's a good forty-five minutes away from his apartment on foot but the mild air of spring feels refreshing even if the halos of haze and construction dust around the streetlights reveal the pollutants he'll inhale on the way. No matter. He's been breathing this concoction for years and is convinced his body has reached a physiological accommodation, much the way skin thickens in the cold.

Jake heads south towards Jianguo Avenue through the narrow hutongs lined with low-rise housing blocks that were built sometime in the 80s. Clad in white tile now weathered to the colour of slate but not yet ripe for demolition, their overall uniformity is broken up by ground-level tuck shops selling beer, snacks and packets of shampoo hanging down like streamers. These shops stay open late but not so much for the revenue since there's less business to be had since more supermarkets are opening throughout the city. These shops are Beijing's public sphere. The owners sit on small stools with their friends, discussing whatever they've most recently learned about the world, perhaps from a relative with a daughter or nephew studying in Boston or Melbourne or Manchester.

Jake understands only some of their chatter because of the local accent that makes them sound as though their tongues are swollen. But their certitude is clear to Jake. With no illusions about their own government or anyone else's, they speak with authority, spitting truth like bullets between drags on their cigarettes as they rock back and forth on their stools, relaxed, legs crossed and not caring who might disagree. Their loud banter, punctuated with the occasional hacking up of mucous, is the life blood of a city whose main features are either unremarkably drab and utilitarian or grand and imposing.

The residential hutongs lead to Jianguo Avenue's diplomatic compound just outside the Second Ring. A cross between Miami Art Deco and communist block utility, this compound surrounded by high walls and guarded gates had served for decades as the only place foreigners could live. As China opened up, the half-dozen or so buildings making up the compound became required quarters for only diplomats and journalists. After the turn of the millennium, when the authorities had the technical wherewithal to spy on anyone, anywhere in Beijing, the compound was no longer assigned housing and became an option for those looking for high ceilings and an intriguing backstory. The government gave the exterior a brighter finish and installed modern window casings to bring them up to the standards of the many new developments throughout the city. Inside, they removed bugs from behind the wallpaper and cornice mouldings.

Heading east, Jake follows the broad sidewalk past other uninviting structures from an earlier era now festooned with Olympic Games motifs and slogans about national unity. Traffic crawls so slowly that Jake makes better time than any taxi he might have jumped into. Very few others bother walking down the avenue, especially at this time of night. Everything is spaced too far apart, separated by large manicured knolls filled with thousands of potted plants arranged into swirls and other geometric patterns that look more impressive from many floors up, like from the China World Centre just ahead. The latest China World Tower now dominates the northwest corner of the intersection of Jianguo and the Third Ring. The Yintai Centre, a skyscraper topped with modernized imperial motifs glowing red from the inside has just opened on the southwest corner, setting the area a world apart from the modest tuck shops and lively conversations they attract just a few hundred metres off the city's main axis.

The vast range of life he's just walked through and the rate of its change reminds Jake of why Qiang's work is so important. He's now as sure that the documentary will be a success as he is that Jianguo Avenue is becoming a new centre of global power. A sense of confidence swells within Jake, one that offsets any disappointment that he happens to be sober and alone on a Saturday night.

SUNDAY, March 24, 2007
10:23 p.m.

Qiang's one-bedroom flat in Progress Park faces east, allowing him to capture the changes taking place across the street and the entire surrounding neighbourhood. A camera fixed to his window with tape snaps a photo every day at noon. The time-lapse sequences shot here and in other locations throughout the city will capture the simultaneous demolition and reconstruction. Qiang will insert these sequences throughout his film, a technique that he hopes will keep his audience's attention when he's narrating some of the details.

The vast new property across the street is coalescing into grade-A office towers and a Four Seasons hotel. It's all built on what will be a shopping mall formed from beams radiating outward from the ground as if the fortress of grey metal was planted by extraterrestrials as a monstrous seed and sprang from the earth to commandeer the city. Growing outward and upward, the structure will soon deprive Progress Park's east-facing residents from a key selling point, the morning sunlight.

The new homeowners moved in a year earlier, assuming the low-slung brick housing blocks across the street would remain for a while. The old neighbourhood of squat worker housing blocks had been a town unto itself with ground-floor shops selling shampoo, cheap mobile phones and steamed buns. Behind the old buildings, a wet market strewn with plastic bags and Styrofoam had teemed with farmers selling produce from the backs of grimy pickups and butchers dangling scales from their fingers to weigh bloody hunks of pork while they haggled with customers.

That's all gone now. Demolition will start in a matter of weeks. The harbinger of abrupt change appeared on the old brick walls shortly after Progress Park's elevators started ferrying new sofas and bedroom sets skyward. A red character 拆, demolish, had been painted on the buildings sometime in the dead of night about a year earlier, just before the wrecking balls and earthmovers mobilized to pulverize the neighbourhood and make way for luxury. Grimy interior walls decorated with red Lunar New Year wishes and calendar pages were torn open to face the sunlight like freshly shucked oysters.

Qiang's phone rings, showing Kendra as the caller.

"Hey."

"Qiang, what's the deal with this number?"

Qiang emailed Kendra the number using an address he'd generated on a VPN that put his location outside of China.

"It's safe. It's a pre-paid account, the last one I picked up before they started requiring ID."

He hears Kendra sigh.

"Qiang, I just saw the footage you uploaded. Holy shit."

"So you didn't know that was coming?" Qiang asks.

"No. What I thought was coming was, I don't know, I figured he was going to denounce the hardliners. No surprises. It was going to help back up the theme, not... um... I didn't expect something that completely re-frames this project, Qiang."

"How do you mean?"

"Well, I wonder if Zhao's not just completely delusional. All of the documentary evidence suggests the opposite, that Hu refused medical care because he didn't want to be a bother. He had ideological enemies, but I don't think the leadership would have let him die."

"So maybe he's delusional, or maybe he just wants to settle scores before he's gone."

"Whatever the case, I'm going to need more time to figure out what's what. No matter, though. I'll figure out how to do that. I'm just glad we have this."

"You have this, Kendra, not me. It's intriguing stuff but, you know, it's not my project."

"Right, but I just want you to know I'm very grateful."

"It's the least I can do for your help with mine. It's just best we keep me as far away as possible from yours."

"Yeah, I hear you. I just want so much to give you credit for a very risky move. This is the kind of thing that wins awards."

"Well...," Qiang says before Kendra cuts him off.

"I know, I know what you're going to say. It's not about the awards," she says. "So tell me, you think you pulled it off without the PSB noticing? Not even any black sedans outside when you left?"

Qiang looks at the time display on his monitor. It's late and he wants to focus on preparations for tomorrow's interview, his last one. He'll be stuck on the phone for another twenty minutes if he brings up the events of the past for forty-eight hours. Kendra will want a detailed account of the PSB's intervention.

"Yeah, no issues," he says. "I wrapped things up quickly and got out."

Qiang knows what Kendra will say if he tells her about the warning. He's come too far to give up on the interview with his key subject. A community organizer, also an entrepreneur. A strange combination, which attracted Qiang's attention. The man founded a glass distribution company that transformed into a solar panel producer, one that exports millions of dollars worth of the products to Europe. Some of the organizer's investors hold senior positions in the municipal government. The money that comes in probably enriches enough people to have kept the entrepreneur safe. He started petitioning the Beijing Municipal Committee to consider a proposal that would keep communities intact. Especially the community he was focusing on, Jianguo Avenue just outside of the Third Ring, an area many thousands of people will see when the fireworks open the 2008 Olympics. Not an inch of this strip escapes the attention of the city's planners. Every other neigbourhood along Jianguo has either been renovated or replaced with new gleaming structures that would stand just as proudly in central Tokyo, Dubai or Paris.

If the organizer can get an audience with just a few members of the Municipal Committee, he'll agree to drop a lawsuit he's filed to stop the relocation of residents.

Qiang had watched the organizer make the case on YouTube, a presentation that tied together investment, community and solidarity. It concluded with the slogan seen on banners hanging everywhere in the city: "Building a Harmonious Society". With this, Qiang heard a political pitch that offered a plausible solution, not just a slogan, and, in that moment, resolved to make a documentary around this man and his idea.

Qiang made contact through the organizer's blog, got his cell phone number and, two weeks earlier, set a date for the interview. When he arrived at the organizer's home, no one answered. The man's phone was switched off. Then, his presentation on YouTube was blocked, fueling Qiang's determination. He found the lawyer preparing the suit against the municipality but his phone also went dead. Then two other sources went silent. The organizer resurfaced yesterday by sending a text, apologizing for the silence and suggesting 11:00 a.m. the next day for the interview.

It's almost 3:00 a.m. and Qiang has been editing footage since sundown. He gathers the final handful of raisins meant to tie him over until a dinner break he never bothered to take. A heavy rainstorm is starting to taper off. It passed through in waves, building to a crescendo powerful enough to push the last of winter from the air and usher in spring. The raging weather hadn't stopped the construction work across the street, though, as the pounding of steel prevailing over diminishing booms of thunder.

Billie Holiday has been singing through Qiang's tinny computer speakers to keep him company. Playful and then forlorn, her voice softens the rage of thunder above and the pounding of steel across the street. And then Nina Simone. These and other jazz legends accompany Qiang often as he edits through the night, the squelched trumpets and cascading piano chords creating counterpoints to the rampaging newness of China, he says.

"You might like the music," Jake once said to Qiang. "But I don't think you'd like the music as much without the artists' back stories. They're victims, just like the residents you're championing in your documentary."

"Wrong," Qiang responded. "The voices would be just as compelling for me whether or not I knew about their lives."

And with that exchange, over drinks and hours of discussion about the direction China's taken, Qiang and Jake became friends.

The thunder is now so distant and delicate, it sounds like a lullaby and Qiang has trouble keeping his eyes open. By the time he saves his work, strips down to his briefs, stuffs a pair of Styrofoam plugs in his ears and settles into bed, the pounding of steel stops. Perhaps a change of shift or a break to recalibrate the machinery.

He texts Jake.

```
last interview, i promise. set for tomorrow at
11:00am >

!!!! where? I'm going with you. >

you don't need to, but if you insist meet me on the
northeast corner of Jianguo and Dawang at 10:55. >
```

Amid the stillness, two unmarked vans bearing official plates – the letter A followed by only three numbers – pull up in front Qiang's building, stopping illegally. After a few moments, their engines and lights shut off.

MONDAY, March 25, 2007

The buzzing vibration of a text message wakes Qiang. He rubs his eyes, grabs his glasses and reaches for the cell phone on his nightstand. He's slept through his alarm which sounded an hour earlier. The organizer wants to do the interview at 10:00 a.m instead of 11:00. It's now 9:10.

"Shit."

Qiang runs through his questions as he showers. He wants them to come out naturally, not from a piece of paper. Nothing should interfere with an open exchange. Only amateurs use written prompts.

Qiang towels his cropped hair in front of a mirror on the wall, squeezes out a dab of molding paste and works it around the back of his head. He then pulls his hair forward and shapes the front into a bank of spiky tips. He buttons his shirt and pulls on a pair of jeans.

A reminder from Qiang's cell phone chirps. He yanks open a desk drawer and routes through a tangle of wires, pulling out a pack of blank mini discs. He grabs one, unwraps it and peels the enclosed sticker from its backing. After affixing the sticker to the disc, he scribbles some characters on it.

Outside, Qiang slides his backpack full of lenses, batteries and lighting equipment off one shoulder and swings it into a waiting taxi amid a chorus of honks from drivers behind them, commuters diverted into other lanes. He slides into the rear seat and tells the driver to head to the northeast Fourth Ring. As the taxi pulls away, one of the two vans that have been parked illegally since before sunrise pulls out into the traffic, following Qiang's cab.

```
Interviewee needs to move it up to 10:00. I need to
head over there now. Don't worry.>
```

The message had come through a half hour earlier, when Jake was covering a press conference. He sees the message at 9:45 a.m., just as he enters the subway at Wangfujing.

```
!!! Exact address?>
```

The doors shut as he hits send and the signal drops from one bar to none. Jake hits send three more times as the subway car starts moving east. He clenches his teeth, hoping the strength of his concentration will somehow blow a channel through the twenty metres of earth and concrete above him and bring one of the signal bars back. He's seen his signal flicker in and out on the subway, never long enough to make a call, but sometimes he's able to squeeze off a text message. But, of course, this doesn't happen now.

Jake can only stew as the subway car trundles beneath the city. He volunteered to proof the subtitles for Qiang, partly because he also wants to wrench himself out of a career that has become more corporate than planned. Qiang's documentary is the kind of project Jake expected to tackle himself when he arrived in China years earlier but, instead, he covers CEOs and Central Bank officials and Finance Ministry directors in Beijing. And no amount of coverage is ever near enough.

The size of China's economy has just surpassed Germany's and is now set to overtake Japan's. The pressure to whip out business stories, to stay on top of the great economic disruption, makes it impossible to focus on anything that would let Jake switch to a more meaningful track. At least that's what he tells Qiang, and himself.

Qiang's project didn't seem provocative at first. On-the-ground reflections of the physical transformation of Beijing. Spontaneous interviews on what the changes mean to the man on the street. If anything, the approach was pro-China. Show the naysayers that people in Beijing want reliable hot water, elevators and Wi-Fi. There will be disruptions. The people most affected will speak and the audience can make up its mind.

In the first interviews, Qiang got equal parts support and indifference, with many subjects wondering why someone would spend time examining the obvious. Then, chat by chat, as he focused the questions more on dislocations, he learned that some residents were trying to formalize a proposal that would allow them to stay in the area.

"We want a modern neighbourhood, of course," said an older woman who reminded Qiang of his mother. "But we want it for us ordinary Chinese folk, not for people coming to Beijing, spending 5,000 kuai a night on a luxury hotel room and then leaving,"

And then the direction of his project began to change.

Jake comes up from the Andingmen subway station and calls Qiang. The phone rings but Qiang doesn't answer. Why? Why can't he just pick up? Jake's respect for Qiang's tenacity turns to fury. Why didn't he send the exact address? He could have sent the exact address in a text.

10:57 a.m.

Standing in front of a bank of housing blocks somewhere in the vicinity of Qiang's interview, Jake has lost track of the number of times he's called his mobile. Each time, the line rings through to the message. That damn message.

> "The phone you are calling has been switched off. Please try again later."

He's heard it hundreds of times, a message he knows is coming even before the voice starts because of a distinctive, split-second click followed by an electronic chirp. Frustrating enough to hear under normal circumstances like when a source gets tired of Jake's attempts to confirm something for a story.

Later isn't an option. He'd take a thousand click-chirps later, when trying to report a story, in exchange for a direct connection to Qiang's voice right now. He wants to plead with every person passing by. Have they seen a thirty-something Chinese guy with a camera? He wants to stop the traffic and look in every vehicle. Each one that passes carries away a shred of hope.

Jake needs to stop this torture so he focuses on the buildings in front of him to anchor his thoughts. They're mostly empty and condemned, like the ones he helped Qiang film many months ago. All of them made uglier by their haphazard inconsistencies: window renovations done at different periods, some with aluminum frames, some in white vinyl, others with original iron casings bleeding rust tracks down the brick walls. Scores of power cables, now cut from the grid, wrapped around rusted metal brackets. The lack of life in these buildings is as present as the buzzing in one's ears in the dead of night and their silence feels like a distress signal.

Jake calls Qiang's number again. This time there's no ring. Just solid nothing.

11:42 a.m.

Jake bangs on Qiang's door and waits a few seconds, hearing only his own laboured breathing. He pounds again, this time so hard the doorframe rattles. Straining to detect anything other than the whisper of a nearby HVAC register and the low hum of electrical currents powering the corridor's light fixtures, he clenches his fists. Jake pulls Qiang's spare key out of his pocket. The lock is sticky, or maybe he just needs to calm down and finesse it. Jake jiggles the key, up and down and side to side, until something clicks. The door opens. With the curtains drawn, the sparsely furnished living room is dim. Jake hits a switch, lighting two lamps, one on each of the white cubes that bookend a tan sofa facing a television that sits on a low-slung, white stand. A recent issue of *The New Yorker* lies on the floor, splayed open, front and back cover facing up with about half of its pages turned underneath.

"Qiang? Are you here? Please say you're here."

The bedroom door is ajar and there is no light on in the room. Jake pushes the door open and flips the switch on the wall just inside. Qiang's desk is bare except for his printer. His computer is gone. Each of its drawers is open and empty.

"Those fuckers."

Jake pulls his phone out of his pocket. He dials nine of ten digits, pausing before the last one because he can't bear to hear the line go dead again. He sits at Qiang's desk, numb.

He thinks about the organizer that Qiang was planning to interview, a business innovator Jake heard about in the course of his business reporting. Something about solar panels. Qiang had suggested to Jake that the guy is worthy of a feature story for anyone covering business in China. Jake logged the story idea into his news agenda for the upcoming quarter. If the editors like the story enough, Jake might have been able to work in a side note about the financial arrangement he has been proposing for displaced residents. It was a financial story after all. But, as always, rumours about currency policy and interest rate changes kept the story about Qiang's hero, and the proposal to give existing residents a chance to buy into the new developments, perpetually in planning mode. If Jake had written that story, though, giving the organizer a higher profile among investors worldwide, perhaps his proposal would have an audience within the government. Perhaps the organizer wouldn't have disappeared. And Qiang would have wrapped up the interview weeks ago, before he wound up on the PSB's watch list. And Jake wouldn't be sitting in an empty apartment, staring helplessly at a wall.

"Why didn't I just write the story?"

Jake asks the question out loud to let it go. The question that has lodged itself inside him, pressing against his heart.

The pounding of steel across the street rattles the living room windowpane. Jake stands up, walks to the window and surveys the construction, noting how much it's grown since the last time he'd been at Qiang's place just a few days earlier. Perhaps the speed of the construction helped to drive Qiang's determination. Every new floor constructed spurred him to move faster.

Jake raises his head and scans the walls and ceiling and yells as loudly as he can.

"You fucking goons!"

He doesn't care who hears him: the neighbours, whoever is on the other end of whatever device is monitoring the apartment or the security guards downstairs who probably looked the other way as unidentifiable men marched Qiang and his belongings out of the building.

MACAU
July, 2004

Holding an empty plastic tub, Dawei kicks the door open, pulling a blast of the dining room's cool air around him. The sweat on his forehead and temples suddenly feels frigid. He heads toward the evening's last table. Another group of well connected Mainlanders throwing money around. Money flows to China from everywhere it seems. He's seen the news broadcasts about how China is rising. Americans and Europeans buy more and more goods made in China. Goods get shipped out on gigantic ships and, sometimes, Dawei can see the hulking silhouettes, looking impossibly top-heavy on the water as they move into the South China Sea. And then money returns to China. Money that winds up in the pockets of people who come here to Macau where they order expensive meals and gamble.

Yiming, his uncle in Harbin, works for one of these companies. He's an engineer at a state-owned firm that exports things to North America and Australia. He's not rich – not like the ones who drive black cars imported from Germany with windows tinted completely black – but Uncle Yiming and Aunt Dongmei have a nice apartment, one with hot water 24 hours a day. They told Dawei that if he worked hard to catch up with the other students in Harbin, he might also have a chance to work in a big state-owned enterprise.

That didn't happen, though, because he was stupid. Not stupid like his teachers said. It wasn't about the trouble he had writing characters and sentences the way the other students in Harbin could. It wasn't even about his persistent stutter. It was the lapse of reason that derailed his life in Harbin, his second chance, so abruptly and so soon after it started.

He was stupid to think a few hundred kuai would go unnoticed. He was only borrowing the money he used to buy tickets to a film. Just a few kuai. Easy to replace. But it was the book that caught his attention, a glossy hardback volume showcasing all of the most popular Hong Kong films over a decade and his common sense disappeared like a drop of water evaporating on a sun-baked pavement.

The book stood upright on top of a display case, guarded by an expressionless attendant. The case held an assortment of paperback books and other magazines, many of which Dawei would have paged through, month in and month out, until they were rags. The cost of admission and a magazine wouldn't have been so bad. But this hefty book of at least 200 pages, drenched with sharp cinematic colour, diminished all of the other books and magazines. Its cover was a collage of countless movie scenes that magnified the importance of each story, turning them into a universe of intrigue. It was almost as good as a private cinema, one that could be carried around in a backpack.

Dawei stopped and glanced at the book as he headed into the darkened theatre. The employee behind the counter, a middle-aged woman with a frizzy perm and a drab uniform, lay the book down, opened it and fanned through the pages, slowly enough for Dawei to recognize some of the faces flashing by, each one heightening his excitement. The price tag though – 110 kuai – left him no option but to continue into the theatre.

As he watched the film, a rags-to-riches story about a woman who works her way up from the factory floor to take over the management of a manufacturer in Guangdong, using her smarts to outwit incapable cohorts bent on padding their paycheques, Dawei saw himself as the hero, standing up against corruption and injustice. Dawei would always play this role in real life, so why shouldn't he be able to own a book documenting so many stories about good characters. No one else could be as moved by stories about justice as himself. It could become a talisman of sorts, a constant reminder of the importance of prudence and decency.

He would buy the book and replace the money. His parents were supposed to arrive from Yongfu Village a day later. They would bring with them a few hundred kuai, something for Dawei to start the New Year off right.

But whenever he thinks back on that decision, Dawei wonders what gave him the idea that his parents would give him so much. Spent wisely, that amount would have fed them for a month back in Yongfu.

His parents did arrive the following day, with nothing but pickled beets and a few heads of cabbage. They had nothing else because they had to pay for repairs to their house, repairs that they might have been able to manage themselves had Dawei been around to help.

He only realized later how it all looked. Later, after he stuffed his belongings in his backpack and left to find a job on a construction site.

Many years on, Dawei's not much closer to his dream of returning to his family as a success, ready to explain himself, apologize and make amends. He doesn't know how many more tables he can clear here in Macau before he will try a new plan.

As Dawei approaches the table with his plastic tub in one arm and the bill tucked in the crook of his other arm, Zhihong and his colleagues are dislodging remnants of curried squid from their teeth. Dawei starts putting plates and chopsticks in the tub, making room to set it down, and then pulls out the bill. Unsure who will pay, he places the bill dead centre. The other waiters have gone home, leaving Dawei and the restaurant manager to close. Zhihong's division head throws down several hundred Hong Kong dollars. The others slide into their suit jackets, grab their attachés and chatter about good luck while Dawei begins clearing the dishes. Zhihong tells his colleagues that he won't join them, that he'll call his wife in Beijing and then turn in for the night. He grabs an unfinished bottle of *baijiu* from the centre of the table and fills his glass while the others leave.

The restaurant manager, a wiry man with wispy hair dyed black and combed over a shiny scalp, switches some lights off and squawks in Cantonese about the late hour.

The dining room smells like cigarettes, seared garlic, curry and baijiu. Zhihong sits under the only set of fluorescent ceiling fixtures still on, lights that create an electric bluish haze above him and make him stand out from the rest of a dining room defined only by shadows. Dawei continues clearing. He looks at the money and then at Zhihong. He can't tell if the man is drunk, lost in thought or both. Zhihong pours the remaining few ounces of *baijiu* into his glass, which he empties as Dawei puts the last of the table's plates into his bin.

"Sir, can I take this for you?" Dawei asks in Mandarin, while gesturing toward the money. Dawei knows from the dark suit worn over a polo-style shirt and file-sized black leather clutch that Zhihong and his group are from the Mainland.

The manager switches off the pop tunes that play from speakers rigged precariously into two corners of the ceiling, leaving the hum of air conditioning units and the sound from an occasional car passing just outside to fill the room.

Zhihong looks up at Dawei, holding his stare. "Sorry," he says, picking up the cash and presenting it with two hands, a move that Dawei finds uncomfortably ceremonious because he isn't sure if Zhihong is mocking him. "Keep the change," Zhihong says.

Taken off guard, Dawei begins to stammer. The change is probably more than 50 Hong Kong dollars, but Zhihong overrides the refusal by waving him off. Attempting to stand, Zhihong lurches forward and puts his hands on the edge of the table to push back his chair. He loses his balance and lands on his ass as the chair's metal frame smacks against the tile.

"Are you okay?" Dawei asks as he helps Zhihong to his feet, handing him the file clutch. Giving his head a quick shake to refocus, Zhihong takes it.

"I guess I had more than I thought," he says with an embarrassed chuckle.

Dawei takes the cash to the manager, who pulls 45 Macanese patacas in change out of a pouch in the cash register for Dawei to return to their intoxicated patron. Dawei doesn't shove the money into his pocket right away. He's annoyed that the boss is making change in the local currency when Zhihong paid in Hong Kong dollars. Zhihong has treated Dawei with respect and now he must repay with change in a currency that's worthless anywhere else. He wants to say something to the boss but knows he will just wave off anything Dawei has to say. The old man has doled out these sleights for decades, small measures that have kept him in business while establishments run by more conscientious managers have closed. They're as ingrained as the wrinkles on his forehead and around his eyes. The manager tells Dawei to walk with the intoxicated patron until he's inside a cab.

"I don't want to have to answer questions from the police," he mutters.

Dawei grabs a small backpack from behind the register and unbuttons his white shirt, speckled on the front with curry sauce. The oily mess on the final dishes he's just plonked into the sink will solidify overnight, adding to tomorrow morning's work. The manager won't care. Dawei puts a hand on Zhihong's shoulder and leads him to the door.

Outside in the humid night air, Zhihong steps unevenly as they walk through the stillness of Macau's Coloane Village, alongside the walls of weathered yellow mortar streaked with mould. The gnarled root system of a Banyan tree that's probably been growing for a century has broken up the old sidewalk. Bunches of filament vines hang down.

Dawei puts his arm around Zhihong's back and holds his waist. Zhihong lays his arm across Dawei's shoulders. A cat jumps from the darkness of an alley into the street where it hesitates for a split second before darting over to a shadowy corner ahead of them.

With his free hand, Zhihong roots through his pocket, pulls out a 100 Hong Kong dollar note, and slides it into the pocket of Dawei's stained shirt.

"For your trouble," he says.

Dawei reaches for the note. "Mister, you're too kind. Th... th... this isn't necessary," he says.

Zhihong grabs Dawei's hand with a tight grip. He stares at Dawei as though the money is a burden. "Take it," Zhihong says. "And don't call me sir. I can't be that much older than you. My name is Zhihong."

"I'm Dawei."

They walk in silence as Dawei looks ahead and behind for a cab.

"Where are you staying?" Dawei asks.

"We're supposed to be staying in Hong Kong but my colleagues and I came over here for some business," he says, raising an index finger in front of his mouth and looking at Dawei. "Shhhhh...Business."

Dawei looks at him, puzzled.

"We're not supposed to be gambling," Zhihong explains. "But our division head always finds some extra in the budget to get a couple of cheap rooms here." He laughs. "I'm usually the one who ends up sleeping on the floor when we take these side trips and I don't even like gambling. So, I figured I'd let them go ahead. They'll be there for hours. I'll be in the bed tonight."

Zhihong stops. His expression suddenly becomes contorted. Putting a hand to his mouth, Zhihong wheels around and hurries to a nearby alley where he crouches, arches his back and lets a stream of vomit spill out against a wall.

Dawei walks over to Zhihong, pulls a half-empty bottle of mineral water out of his backpack and hands it to him. Zhihong guzzles the rest of the water and wipes his mouth with the back of his hand. A mangy dog rushes over to inspect the regurgitated seafood which has been marinating in forty-proof baijiu and bile. After a tentative lick, the dog runs away.

"I'll walk you to the roundabout. There should be cabs there," Dawei says, helping Zhihong up.

"Walk me to the embankment. My head will clear up if I just get some fresh air."

The embankment in Coloane Village runs along an inlet that separates Macau from Mainland China, a strip of water leading to the South China Sea. It's just wide enough to soften the constant clanging of construction noise coming from the new developments on the other side.

Dawei had worked on some of them before he figured out how to find an agent who could get him a job in Macau washing dishes. Twelve-hour shifts, seven days a week, but at least no backbreaking work. No risk of falling.

Sometimes, after his shift in the restaurant, Dawei is too tired to sleep so he goes to the embankment to look at the construction lights from Zhuhai. Staring at them and the reflections they cast on the water, Dawei can feel some pride about his improved circumstances and gathers some inspiration to continue towards something even better. He doesn't know what form "better" will take, or how he will get there, but looking across the water at Zhuhai helps him put things into perspective. It's better to look at construction sites he's escaped from at a distance than to look at dishes he must clean and floors he must mop.

Zhihong has obviously been to the embankment before. Maybe he's also looking to escape the Mainland. But why? He obviously has a good job. At least he has enough money to tip well.

At the railing, just above the small waves lapping at the stones, Zhihong pulls out two cigarettes.

"You have the look of a monk, my friend, forlorn and serious," he says, handing a cigarette to Dawei.

Dawei runs a hand through the stubble covering his head and then takes the cigarette. It feels odd, Dawei thinks, to want to stroll through this silent corner of Macau with someone he barely knows. The long hours in the restaurant always leave him with sore feet, ready to return reluctantly to the dormitory he shares with seven other workers. He flops onto his bunk, smelling his own stale sweat, and the peace he gathers on the embankment pulls him to sleep, unaffected by the chatter among the other roommates.

"What kind of work do you do in Hong Kong?" Dawei asks.

"I'm an advisor to some film production companies there," Zhihong says, exhaling a puff of smoke.

The idea of film production shifts Dawei's thoughts. What started as a vague appreciation of this random stranger's generosity becomes a focused curiosity.

"Really? Film production? Does that mean you work in movies?"

Zhihong chuckles.

"I'm no director. I have barely anything to do with production. I just compile research on what the domestic broadcasters are looking for, what audiences want, what sort of policies are in force."

Dawei doesn't absorb much beyond the fact that Zhihong works with film producers, with a direct connection to films made in Hong Kong. He imagines Zhihong on the set of a Tang Dynasty drama, with actors dressed as regents, generals and concubines. Dawei has dreamed of being on a set, any set, yet has rarely had the opportunity to be part of an audience.

"I... wound up here to be closer to movies," Dawei says. "I was inspired by them when my parents took me to Harbin to visit my aunt and uncle every New Year. Everything about the city was exciting. So many good things in the city but nothing was as exciting as the movies."

He pauses, catching himself, wondering if he sounds silly. Will Zhihong see him for the fool he is, like the teachers and classmates in Harbin, the ones who never bothered to help him catch up? He steels himself for that judgement, ready to walk away because… because he doesn't need to be out this late. Not when he needs rest.

But Zhihong is smiling genuinely. He wants to hear more.

"My uncle would take me to see movies. He told me they were filmed in Hong Kong. When I watched them, I got so excited that my hands would clench the armrests for two hours and my fingers always hurt the next day."

Zhihong laughs and Dawei feels even more at ease.

"When things went bad for me in the northeast, all I thought about were the m…m…movies I saw there and I headed this way."

Memories of the times Dawei spent in cinemas with Uncle Yiming lead to another: a warm, autumn day in Harbin's Stalin Park along the Songhua River, where he and uncle played badminton after watching a film. The park was full of families and couples bringing their kids to eat grilled corn and fly kites. Dawei and Uncle had settled onto a bench to eat the steamed buns and poached eggs Aunt Dongmei packed for them. Yiming reclined, head back, looking skyward as he smoked a cigarette. Fulfilled by another cinematic adventure and confident after beating Uncle for the first time, Dawei lay on his back, letting the dancing kites above coax him to sleep. Dawei had, for many years, recognized that moment on the bench along a river running through Harbin as his last carefree moment. He'd often run through that afternoon whenever the heat and humidity of Macau kept him awake in his bunk.

"I don't understand how being here, in Macau, would help you," Zhihong says.

This comment, so sensible, stings Dawei. It highlights his naïveté. He'd left Harbin abruptly, and with nothing, after trying to make it on his own as an unskilled construction worker. He'd wake before dawn and work well into the night. Dawei's only break from work was during the Lunar New Year when the others would leave to visit their families and he'd stay in the grimy, unheated barracks.

Memories of movies made in Hong Kong had sustained him for a while, standing in for all other forms of hope. Honest, strong and handsome leading men succeed; villains are vanquished; justice prevails. The stories and characters loomed so large in his mind, crowding out the reality of his life so completely that he saw no other option but to head south, to Hong Kong, where those much better realities were produced.

On a rare day off, Dawei sold some construction tools that he pilfered from his site and bought a hard-seat train ticket for Zhuhai.

"I was stupid," Dawei finally says. "I thought that if I could find a way to Hong Kong, I could get a job on a set. I would figure things out from there." He pauses. "I never even made it to Hong Kong. I made it to a kitchen in Macau. Stupid."

"You're not stupid," Zhihong says. "You're...determined. You have more guts than I ever had."

"But I'm s...s...still washing dishes," Dawei says. "I...I..." Memories and regret become entangled in his head, making him stutter more than usual. He bangs a fist on the railing to unblock his words. "What good is determination when you're stupid?"

Zhihong is quiet. He reaches out slowly and puts his hand on Dawei's shoulder. "You're not stupid. I wanted to be in movies too. I thought I'd make a good director but now I'm just a bureaucrat taking orders."

Dawei leans more heavily on the railing because Zhihong's soft grip incapacitates him. No one has touched him since his schoolmates in Yongfu would huddle, arms across shoulders, for warmth or when sharing a secret, or just because that's what school kids do.

Zhihong's touch is different. It liquefies Dawei's every muscle and sinew so that the only thing holding him up is the railing. Dawei closes his eyes to immerse himself in the vibration that's taken over. He sees rich colours – midnight blues, blood maroons and forest greens – undulating in velvety textures. And underneath this wash of physical sensations and visions, he feels reassurance. Fearing any move he makes will interrupt this energy, Dawei resists the urge to look at Zhihong. A look might clarify what's happening between them and that's a risk he doesn't want to take. Eye contact might pull them into unfamiliar territory that can't be navigated. So he remains silent, trapped in ecstatic torture, and looks over the inlet.

The water represents hope because it's never fixed. He looked at it for hours when he arrived in southern China, this water that could take him away from the construction sites of the Mainland and the kitchens of Macau. It could take him even further from Yongfu village in the far northeast, where a collapsed roof on the local schoolhouse years ago started a chain of events that led him to a dead end here, on a speck of land full of casinos, mashed-up Chinese and colonial history and people looking to spend great quantities of money that seem to bubble up from invisible springs that Dawei has yet to find.

"You're hard working and forthright, Dawei," Zhihong says. He's now looking out into the distance. "If I were a director, you'd be my inspiration for the best martial arts saga ever filmed. You'd be my... muse."

Zhihong said muse in English. He knows that Dawei wouldn't know about the mythological beings who, according to Western literary lore, inspire artists. "A muse is like a source of inspiration for artists. A muse helps them produce their best work."

The comment comforts Dawei as he keeps his gaze fixed on the water's surface. He wants to freeze the moment and possess it, to save it inside some solid form that he can wrap up and put in this backpack.

TUESDAY, March 26, 2007

Jake wakes up in Qiang's bed, alone and still in his clothes from the previous day. The sight of Qiang's desk stripped of everything except a printer and a coating of dust just barely visible in the first light of dawn suffocates any hope that Qiang was taken in only for a warning. He doesn't know how he's going to pull himself up, go home to change and then head to the newsroom for another day chasing stories about currency policy rumours.

Feeling the vibration of a city shifting into a morning rush, Jake lies under the covers of Qiang's bed, a place where he had often imagined himself waking. But under very different circumstances. Irony weighs on him more heavily than the bed's thick quilt. Outcomes are never what he wants or expects them to be. Perhaps everything he hopes for is unrealistic.

The clattering of construction across the street reminds Jake that he can't stay in bed all day. In a last attempt to escape the reality of what's happened in the past 24 hours, Jake pulls his knees into a fetal position and buries his head in the pillow, smelling the bitter cocoa scent of unwashed hair. He puts his arms around the pillow and clutches it.

*****

Pacing the newsroom with a cell phone to his ear, Jake is trying to find someone who's heard from Qiang in the past day or so. "Call back if you hear anything."

"I don't know anything else at the moment."

"He's been working on this documentary. The subject matter is a bit controversial."

"I'll get back to you if I hear anything."

After all the dead ends, he sits, elbows on knees, hands clutching the phone, looking at the device with senseless anger over how much it has betrayed him over the past two days.

Frustrated, Jake searches for the email address of a former Beijing journalist named Kendra Monahan who Qiang mentioned was acting as a collaborator on his documentary. Qiang was also assisting on a documentary Kendra is working on about the 1989 crackdown.

Jake remembers watching Kendra at press conferences. When he started as a reporter in Beijing a decade earlier, Jake was warned to keep her in his sights and follow her as closely as the newsmakers. She filed the fastest headlines and always got exclusives from corporate executives and government officials in attendance.

Finding Kendra's email address at the human rights advocacy group she now works for, Baseline Monitor, he copies the address and pastes it into a new email.

```
Dear Kendra,

I'm a Beijing-based journalist, who you may or may
not remember when you worked here. I'm also a good
friend of Qiang, who I understand you have been men-
toring on a documentary about property development
in China. His phone has been switched off ever since
he interviewed a subject for the film. That was two
days ago. I've just come from his apartment to check
in on him and he wasn't there. I let myself in with
a spare key he gave me and found that his computer
and external drives have been removed. Anyway, I was
wondering if you could offer some advice.
Best regards,

Jake Bradley, Toeler News, Beijing
+86 13696548973
```

Jake reviews his email and sends it at 5:30 p.m. Kendra is twelve hours earlier in Washington, DC. He sighs and leans back in his chair, rubbing his eyes as he wonders how quickly she might respond, if at all. Perhaps the work she's done with

Qiang is over. Who's to say whether she wants anything to do with him anymore?

Flat screen monitors hanging from the newsroom's ceiling show shaky footage of a suicide bomb that has just been detonated in a Baghdad market, bloodying dozens of people. It's the top story on every network. Framed with different graphics. The BBC, GlobeCast, Al Jazeera, each one shows the same scenes of carnage with varying in and out points, zoomed in by slightly different degrees, all of them cutting away just before the debris becomes clear enough for viewers to discern lacerated body parts among the pieces of blackened and twisted debris. Local police and U.S. military vehicles kick up clouds of dust. Women in black chadors scream at the sky. With the volume turned down on all of the screens, the hum of the newsroom's hard drives is the only sound.

An email from Kendra arrives, breaking the silence with its ping. Jake does a double take when he sees Kendra's name in his inbox, bold and unread, full of promise, like a Christmas gift.

```
Jake,

This is horrifying. Thank you for letting me know.
I'm looking into this now, checking with my sources,
and will call you as soon as I have more informa-
tion. In the meantime, please check with everyone
there who knows him (if you haven't already). Do you
have contact details for any of his family members?

Kendra
```

WEDNESDAY, March 27, 2007
2:00 a.m.

Jake snaps awake, thinking about an email from a year earlier. The email address. Qiang's sister's email address. It's in the chain. He remembers the subject line: "Super low airfares!" Qiang forwarded the email about promotional airfares to second and third-tier cities like Xining, places stuck behind the development curve where little has changed since Jake first arrived in China in the early 1990s.

Jake had taken occasional trips to places like Xining and Lanzhou to re-live, in controlled doses, the China that existed in every city when he first arrived. Places where a dozen lamb skewers seasoned with hot pepper and cumin costs only five kuai; where barbers work on the street amid hawkers selling transistor radios and alarm clocks; where shop owners in the back of their stores watch the evening news on jumpy black and white television screens and where the sprawling, state-run guest hotels have broken elevators and six metre wide corridors, threadbare carpets that buckle into tripping hazards, baijiu fumes mix with stale cigarette smoke and where and clocks behind the reception desk that show impossible times like 7:00 a.m. in New York, 3:00 p.m. in London and 3:27 p.m. in Moscow. Threatening and haunted when Jake first stayed in them years ago, these kinds of places no longer exist in Beijing and Shanghai.

Jake took these trips as a form of time travel. Qiang had accompanied him sometimes, before he became engrossed in his documentary work. Qiang shared Jake's fascination with China's not-so-distant past although he viewed it through the lens of someone who had lived there. And so, he encouraged Jake to travel to the past, to take photos and come back with ideas for more documentaries.

```
"Book within 24 hours and travel within two weeks
and you can enjoy a round-trip airfare of only 400
kuai!"
```

Jake remembers the sentence completely, as though some spirit floating above him in the dead silence of nethertime dropped it into his mind.

Not bothering to put on boxers or a robe, Jake lumbers over to his computer in the spare bedroom, sits on the rough synthetic fabric of his office chair and shakes the mouse to bring the screen to life. He types "Super low fares!" in the search window.

"Bingo," he whispers as the email shows up.

He copies the address and hits "COMPOSE."

```
"Dear Diane, 我是你弟弟的一个朋友… I'm a friend of your
brother…"
```

October, 2004

"We've decided that the project isn't commercially viable."
The first line of the email punctures Zhihong. He doesn't bother to read any further. He should have expected this outcome. The production company seemed interested so Zhihong plied the executives with information about what their competitors are planning, the latest data on what's playing well on the Mainland's networks and the mood within the party.

The production company gave Zhihong a small advance for the script. Its subplots hinted at official corruption but were subtle enough. The story runs out of sequence, requiring the viewer to put the pieces together. It wraps science fiction and history around a love story, creating an entirely new genre. Creativity that's genuinely Chinese. Audiences are ready for this. Zhihong assured them that the project would test the broadcast bureau's boundaries but that he could steer it through his supervisors.

Zhihong bet that, if treated right, the story would draw an audience large enough to keep the money flowing, sponsors beckoning and the ideologues at bay. Full payment for the screenplay was supposed to follow but that wasn't the main goal. Zhihong was supposed to get a role as consultant and production assistant once production began. He would cut his ties to the bureau and eventually sit in a director's chair.

But the entire plan has dissolved. After clinching a mini-series deal with CCTV-5, the production company promptly lost interest in Zhihong's project.

He doesn't tell Yue Tao. She's already angry. Just off the phone with a colleague, his wife has just learned that the Education Ministry plans to cut bonuses in exchange for more annual leave. She squeezes white lotion onto her hands and rubs it into her shoulders and neck as if what counters the dry Beijing air will also be a salve for her indignation.

"They're giving us only half of the bonus we've gotten in previous years," she tells Zhihong. "We can't plan for anything if they're not consistent."

Yue Tao snaps the lotion cap shut. She then brushes her hair aggressively, puts it up in a red plastic clip and strategically arranges a few ringlets that fall to her shoulders. She buttons up a white blouse with eggplant polka dots and slips into a black skirt. The skirt and blouse bunch together under her belt, exaggerating the frailty of her build.

"What do you expect?" Zhihong asks, placing some clothes into a small suitcase which sits on a chair by their bed. A pair of casual shoes, then underwear and finally a couple of polo shirts. "They want us taking more time off so we can travel and spend more of our money."

"How will we spend more money if we're making less of it?" Yue Tao asks. She stops and turns to Zhihong. "Will they do the same to yours?"

"How would I know?"

"You know what this means, right?" Yue Tao says, now staring directly at him.

She doesn't usually stare dead on. She finds distractions, something other than the person she's speaking to because her left eye deviates outward, a defect that forced her to endure endless taunts when she was a child. Zhihong understands the psychology behind her reluctance to make eye contact and has never made an issue of the habit. He also knows that the taunts meted out in her earlier years stiffened her resolve to succeed, to prove she's as worthy as anyone with the regular looks. When Yue Tao does look directly at him, or at anyone, the matter is urgent.

"We won't have enough for the down payment. Now we're going to have to look for a place that's further outside." She pauses. "We may need to start looking outside the Fifth Ring if we want something with a second bedroom."

Zhihong lays his toiletry bag on top of the clothes he's arranged in the suitcase. "If we need to go further out, we will," he says, quietly, measuring his words.

"Tian! We're getting shut out of the housing market and you don't seem to care," she snaps.

Zhihong doesn't respond because Yue Tao has made this accusation many times. He doesn't care.

Yue Tao approaches him with clenched fists braced uselessly by her sides. "It doesn't seem to matter to you, does it?"

"It doesn't. No."

Zhihong looks at her left eye, her vulnerability, and then back down at his packing.

"It doesn't matter to me at the moment. The studio said they're not interested in my film anymore. They got their mini-series deal with CCTV and now they're not interested in the film, which makes me a fool. This is what matters to me right now."

Yue Tao looks at him silently and Zhihong doesn't know whether to hope for a renewed attack or for her to stand down. Standing on a precipice, where the mix of fear and vertigo scrambles rationality and makes free fall look like relief, he's lost the ability to modulate emotion. This might be the moment that ends their marriage.

"What?"

Zhihong doesn't answer. Having to say it again will only intensify the pain he's trying to kill. He turns back to his suitcase to finish organizing its contents. He closes it and starts pulling the zipper around. It gets stuck around the third corner where the items are protruding most. With his teeth clenched, Zhihong tugs and yanks at the zipper. Yue Tao moves toward him and he fears that, if she mentions anything about apartments or bonuses or careers, all of the exertion that he's putting into the stuck zipper will all at once be redirected at his wife. So he stops yanking the zipper to calm himself.

Yue Tao bends down and puts her hands in the suitcase to shift some of the items towards the centre of the bag. She then pushes down on the corner and nods at Zhihong. He pulls the zipper around to the end of its track and feels his temperature drop by a degree.

Hao le," he says. Good.

He puts the suitcase on the floor and rolls it out of the bedroom, leaving it by the front door. Yue Tao follows him.

"There aren't any others interested?" Yue Tao asks as she throws an orange and a sweet bun into a small plastic bag.

Zhihong shakes his head as he removes the slippers and slides his feet into a pair of fake leather shoes. "All of the scripts I have are worthless. They could make great films but they don't follow the formula everyone is using now." He takes a file out of his satchel, from which he pulls the screenplays, and brings them over to a garbage can. Yue Tao stops him from dropping them. She takes them and puts them back in the folder which she slides back into his satchel.

"Tastes are always changing," she says. "Keep them. Maybe they'll be more welcome a year or two from now." She hands Zhihong the plastic bag with the orange and the bun.

"Eat this at the airport," she says. "The food there is expensive and lousy."

In a cab, stuck in traffic on the east Fourth Ring, Zhihong isn't thinking much about the meetings he and his colleagues have scheduled in Hong Kong. They'll be reviewing storyboards and concepts and Zhihong will hate all of them. The trip will be meaningless until they hop on the ferry for a night of gambling in Macau where he'll see Dawei again.

Zhihong tells himself to forget about films and get behind his wife's plan to buy an apartment with a spare bedroom for a child. Artistic pursuits seem as futile as his parents warned. "Artists starve," they said, when, as a primary school student, he'd bring home a drawing from school. He knew the drawings were good. He saw it in the faces of his teachers who looked puzzled when he worked on them. They'd lift the paper to see if Zhihong was tracing something underneath. They'd tell him that he's talented but said it in an almost pitying tone. When Zhihong told his parents and grandparents what his teacher said, they only had one thing to say. "Artists starve." And they said it in the same distant tone his teachers used when they remarked on his abilities, as if everyone around him was genetically imprinted with the ability to provide only one response to any discussion of art. He also got the same response when he told them he wanted to apply to the Beijing Film Academy for his university education.

What is the value of art anyway? DVDs, regardless of the quality of the films burned into them, regardless of the years the screenwriter had spent, the sacrifices actors made to pursue an impossible career, all are available for next to nothing on any street corner of any city in China. Artists starve and property owners eat. And now that apartment prices are rising by 30 percent a year, property ownership is the new social imperative. Salary increases don't keep pace so, the longer buyers wait, the more difficult it becomes to get into the market.

Every weekend, Yue Tao drags Zhihong to see residential developments hitting the market throughout Beijing. Enchanted by the clean and efficient layouts on display at the presentation centres, she doesn't see any risk or downside.

She loved the last one they visited, about a week earlier. Yue Tao brought it up every evening since they visited. The sales agent, a woman in her twenties wearing what looked like a flight attendant uniform, led them into a model unit in the first of six buildings still in varying stages of construction. A five minute walk from the subway stop under the Third Ring road, southeast of central Beijing, the location would allow both of them to get to work within 30 minutes. Zhihong could feel Yue Tao's approval even before entering the unit. The corridors were carpeted and wallpapered, which deadened the sound. The silence made their own building feel, by comparison, too public, too institutional, like a hospital or an office building. The lock on the show unit clicked quietly and cool air carrying the scent of newness greeted them as the door opened. The agent remarked on the door, weighty but fluid in the way it swung open, made of solid wood. The kitchen was open to the living and dining area, making the apartment feel spacious, and its fixtures and appliances, still coated in blue-tinted plastic, were integrated seamlessly with each other. Some kind of mechanism on the cabinets and drawers prevented them from slamming. They glided slowly into position.

"The floors are made of a very durable wood-grain laminate that's easy to clean," the sales agent said flatly as she tapped out a text message on her phone. Yue Tao agreed and went to inspect the two bedrooms, lingering in the smaller one.

"Most of the south-facing units are gone so, if you want one of those, you'll need to secure one with a down payment soon," the agent said. "You can speak to representatives from our finance department on your way out."

Yue Tao stood in the middle of the air-conditioned living room as she looked out the floor-to-ceiling window to survey the east side of Beijing baking under hazy sunshine. "Do you hear that?" she asked, directing the question to no one.

Double-glazed windows completely muted the honking below and construction noise from the surrounding buildings, leaving a gentle hum from the air conditioning unit as the only sound.   "What do you hear?" Zhihong asked.

"I hear comfort," Yue Tao said with a satisfied smile. "This is what comfort sounds like. This is what beauty sounds like."

Zhihong is now sitting in an airport lounge with colleagues from his department, thinking about his wife's infatuation with the comfortable, cool silence of modern residential living. By the time they had decided to put down a deposit, the developer raised the price. The down payment requirement doubled as a result of a central bank directive aimed at rooting out bad loans.

Yue Tao now wants a child and Zhihong is thinking, almost spitefully, that it might be a good idea. If he doesn't fall in with the plan, she may never have either. She doesn't deserve that. They had been there for each other in many ways. Their awkward natures brought them together in university and a friendship born from their need to fit in grew into an assumed engagement followed by marriage.

Zhihong decides that he'll get some of those blue wei-ge pills in Hong Kong. The ones that make anyone's dick hard. Perhaps a child will help him put the fantasies of a life in film production to rest. This dream must end, he tells himself.

Waiting to board his flight to Hong Kong, Zhihong is sitting at the gate with his colleagues who are discussing how they'll manage to steal a night in Macau. "Three to a room," one says. "Then we'll just need two rooms and, if we eat cheap, we'll have enough to get us back to Beijing."

Another is fiddling with a new cell phone, a Canadian-made device called Blackberry which allows him to check his email. Zhihong lets them sort out the logistics.

Leaning away from the group, he looks across the tarmac and watches earthmovers at work on the site of a new terminal that the government promises will make Beijing's airport Asia's largest. The air outside is so thick with a brownish-yellow haze that it's possible to stare directly at the gauzy rising sun, which blends with the sky. The construction vehicles are clearing an area so large that it dissolves into the distance at both ends. Yellow dust kicked up by the activity makes the crawling machines ghostly and indistinct, creating a scene that looks like a giant impressionist oil painting.

Zhihong wants to disappear in the dust but knows that, just like mist and dreams, there's no way to inhabit particulate matter.

These thoughts commingle like spoiled stew. They push Zhihong to acknowledge that his dream to be involved in film projects has caused nothing but frustration. How could his wife's plan cause more anguish? The more he thinks about a child – his child – the more he's willing to see his wife's plan as the solution. He won't let his child make the mistake of chasing unrealistic dreams. He'll talk softly to his child as he cradles her in the landscaped garden of whichever development they wind up living in. They all look the same with their groves of saplings and patches of impossibly green grass. He will tell his child that artists starve.

In the meantime, he longs to sit with Dawei by the water and to let the salt air heal his battered spirits just like the first time they met, after he got the first rejection from a production company that once seemed interested in the script. It was a terse message, similar to the one he just received this morning. Remembering how drunk he was that night, Zhihong feels a debt of gratitude for the way Dawei stayed with him instead of bundling him into a cab. Dawei, this naïve fool with artistic aspirations, this muse who is one pay envelope away from starvation, wouldn't even accept 100 kuai. Without the right connections, Dawei's lot is where the creative land. Zhihong will see Dawei again in a couple of days but it may be the last time they'll meet.

Dawei looks up whenever someone walks through the entrance. Dishes are piling up in the kitchen because he's spending more time busing and setting up tables so he can look out for Zhihong who hasn't been back for two months. "Dawei," the restaurant manager barks, "get back to the sink."

Taking a last look toward the entrance, Dawei turns and heads to the kitchen with a half-full basin of tableware. Time has warped his memory of Zhihong's face he laments while scraping abandoned vegetables and noodles into a garbage container. He then places the plates in a plastic rack and douses them with steaming water shot from a nozzle hanging over the sink. When Dawei tries to picture Zhihong, he now sees Yiming, his uncle in Harbin, whom Dawei hasn't seen in more than a decade.

Dawei lashes out at the dishes and silverware with a blast of steaming water. He loads a rack with dripping flatware and shoves it so hard against the end of the steel basin that two of the plates break. It's the peak of the evening with orders coming in so quickly that the cooks and waiters don't react. Dawei grabs the broken pieces and throws them into a garbage bin before the restaurant manager, who is taking orders out on the floor, comes back in. He turns back to the sink, releasing another blast of hot water.

Counting cash, the manager ambles with a slightly uneven, arthritic gait over to the corner of the kitchen where Dawei is stacking plastic racks of tableware. "A friend is out there asking for you," he says.

Dawei looks at his boss to be sure he heard correctly. Then, catching himself, he looks at the floor.

"Ok, thanks," he says, gathering a few stray pieces of silverware which he drowns in lukewarm, soapy water and throws into the rack. When the boss walks away, Dawei unties his apron, pulls it off slowly and throws it into a hamper. He looks at the oyster sauce stains on his white shirt and brushes at them, uselessly.

"Our meetings ran late," Zhihong says apologetically as they walk under the streetlights along the embankment. "The others went directly to gamble. I told them I had a headache." He smiles at Dawei.

The sound of hammering from the construction sites in Zhuhai, glimmering in hazy light across the inlet, continues even though it's after midnight. Autumn on the Mainland has brought cool breezes down to the Pearl River Delta, giving Dawei relief from the constant shock he feels as he shuttles dishes between the restaurant's chilled dining room and its sweltering kitchen. He glances at Zhihong, noticing the distinctions between his face and his Uncle Yiming's and resolving to keep the image clear in his head.

"It's becoming more difficult to get over here after our Hong Kong meetings," Zhihong explains. "They look at our expenses more closely."

Dawei wants to thank Zhihong for returning every couple of months, to tell him that he's happy to see him, to explain how he finds himself looking at the calendar, wondering when they'll get together again. But, he keeps this inside.

"Hong," Dawei says. "I'm stuck here and I need to get out. Can I come to Beijing and stay with you for a while?"

Zhihong looks down.

"I know they're making more films in Beijing now. I...I was thinking maybe you could help get me a job in one of the studios," Dawei blurts out, hoping to change whatever thought is causing Zhihong's expression.

"Dawei, I'm not very high up in my division," Zhihong says apologetically. "Besides, even if I tried, there would be a lot of questions about my connection to you."

Dawei thinks. "Okay. I could get a job myself. I hear there are so many restaurants opening up there now. If I just had a place to stay, I could start saving some money."

Zhihong stops and rubs his chin while he stares at the ground. He's trying to put his words together. Dawei starts to regret bringing the subject up.

"Dawei, I'm married."

They look at each other for a moment.

"What?"

"I said I'm married."

Dawei doesn't understand. They've shared so much about their backgrounds. He knows how Zhihong wound up studying political philosophy instead of film production, how he detests his work, how much he likes to sit quietly and look at the ocean to clear away his frustrations while his colleagues gamble. Dawei thought he'd heard about the most important moments of Zhihong's life but the wife never came up.

The light from a convenience store across from them switches off. Dawei feels a flush of anger and then a familiar wave of hopelessness. Injured, he sits down, dangling his legs over the embankment. Zhihong crouches beside him.

"Dawei, I'm as trapped as you are," he says, punching his chest, each impact producing a hollow thud. "I'm sorry I didn't tell you earlier. How could it be any other way for me? I'd never get anywhere at the bureau if I wasn't married by this point. It's painful for me to talk about it, especially with you, here, where I feel like I'm removed from everything that's wrong with my life.

Zhihong hangs his head. I wish I could help you, Dawei, but I'm as stuck as you are." Zhihong turns away and wipes his face.

His mannerisms and the pain in his expression blunt Dawei's anger. He's not sure what right he has to feel so disappointed, or jealous or possessive, for that matter. They've shared more with each other than with anyone else in their lives but there's no word for what they are to each other.

They resume walking in an awkward silence which Dawei breaks after a minute or two because he's afraid this void will cut their connection permanently.

"Do you have a child?" he asks.

"Not yet but we may in the next year or two. My wife wants one before she turns thirty-five, and that's two years away."

Dawei thinks to ask for the woman's name but decides to wait to see if Zhihong volunteers the information. Knowing her name would give him something the wife doesn't have and the balance would be in Dawei's favour. She doesn't know he exists, let alone his name. But Zhihong remains silent.

Approaching the end of the promenade, they sit on a bench.

"Who knows? With a child to feed, I might move higher in my bureau. The married ones with a kid always get more respect," Zhihong says. "Maybe I'll wind up in a place that will allow me to help you."

Maybe, Dawei thinks, but probably not. He tries not to be cynical. Married or not, Zhihong is still his only connection to a world he dreams about. They've spent hours sharing their stories and, within that time, they inhabit a world free of desperation, a place he's not ready to vacate even if Zhihong has a wife. He knows the space he shares with her can't possibly be as happy.

Zhihong continues.

"In the meantime..."

He reaches into his satchel and pulls out a document encased in a clear, plastic folder. He hands it to Dawei who looks puzzled. Zhihong doesn't offer an explanation, just a wry smile. Dawei takes the document out of the folder. The text centred on the front page is sparse, leaving room for what appears at first to be abstract illustrations which fill most of the empty space. Looking at them more closely, Dawei sees the drawings reveal themselves as human characters surrounded by mathematical formulae rendered in an undulating, cursive script. The numbers emerge from celestial clouds and encircle the characters. In the lower right-hand corner, there's a poem in highly stylized calligraphy with numbers and characters alternating in a way that Dawei has never seen.

He begins flipping through more of the document, finding on random pages more calligraphy and drawings in the wide margins. Dawei recognizes the text as dialogue but he can read only some of the characters.

"Is this some kind of comic book?" Dawei asks, as he looks up.

Zhihong lights two cigarettes and hands one to Dawei. "It's a screenplay," he says.

Dawei flips through a few more pages, carefully, as though it's an ancient text from an airtight vault. A bit of ash drops from Dawei's cigarette and lands on the page. They both wipe it away.

"Don't worry. I'm afraid it's not very valuable," Zhihong says with a mournful smile.

Dawei looks puzzled. "Has it been made into a movie?"

"No. I've tried to convince producers in Hong Kong that this author's stories would make great movies but they've turned me down," Zhihong says, exhaling a stream of smoke. His smile vanishes. "It's too late now, anyway."

"What's so special about this story?" Dawei asks.

Zhihong pauses. No one has ever bothered to ask him this question. Producers want to know whether it's action, drama or comedy. Have any big names expressed interest? People in the industry ask the practical questions, the ones that ensure Chinese films are always the same, just like Hollywood.

"Well, first off, the author is a theoretical physicist," Zhihong says, realizing as his words come out that Dawei won't understand. "I mean, the writer is a scientist."

"Why would a scientist write a screenplay?"

"She has a very interesting idea. She's a professor at Tsinghua University. She studies a type of particle that moves faster than light. You know, it's difficult to imagine anything moving faster than light, right? A lot of scientists believe this kind of particle exists although no one has been able to decect one."

Dawei looks confused.

"Because these particles move faster than light," Zhijong continues, "they can also move through time. You see, time and space start to blend when you reach a certain speed. Scientists of today are still trying to understand how this works. Anyway, this writer's story is about two scientists living in the future, many years from now. They're part of a privileged group working on technologies that will allow the people to travel through time by transmitting their consciousness on streams of these special, hyper-fast particles."

"Is that possible?"

"All of this stuff is theoretical, meaning that some people think it might be the case but can't be sure. That's what science fiction is all about. You've seen movies about people travelling to other planets, right?"

"Yes."

"Well, we haven't been able to send a human to the surface of another planet yet but we know it's theoretically possible. This story is the same thing. We've never been able to send messages through time, but this author believes such a thing is possible."

"So what happens in the story?"

"They live in a world where technology has eliminated all forms of art. Poetry, fiction, dance, music. These things don't exist in their world and when they manage to beam their awareness to earlier ages, they fall in love with the beauty that humankind has created."

Dawei thinks for a moment and then looks at Zhihong.

"Let me guess," he says. "These two fall in love because they both have this experience that others don't understand."

The comment strikes Zhihong for its perceptiveness, and then saddens him. It shows the depth of Dawei's intellect, a strength he was never given the chance to develop like a sapling deprived of sunlight and water. Dawei shouldn't be scrubbing pots but what can he do? For the moment, Zhihong can only tell a story that may help Dawei forget about the hot kitchen.

"Anyway, these characters eventually come to learn that the authorities plan to use the technology they're working on to alter past events in a way that would eliminate their enemies. They begin to understand this plot just as they're figuring out how to live the lives of artists by beaming their consciousness into a couple that lived in Shanghai in the 1930s. The couple loves each other and respects each other for the sacrifices they've made for their art. The man is a painter blending traditional Chinese landscape styles with a new style of abstract painting that was becoming popular in Europe at the time. The woman is a dancer developing new forms of movement, perhaps the first attempt to bring a new creative expression to the very rigid forms of Chinese dance."

"What do the scientists do?"

Dawei's curiosity lifts Zhihong's spirits, a new vitality that changes the whole meaning of the screenplay, as if the entertainment it provides to this audience of one makes Zhihong's efforts worthwhile.

"Well, they need to make a choice. Continue spending much of their time living as artists in the twentieth century or foil the evil plot."

"And?"

"They start to send warnings in the form of dreams to the people the authorities are trying to eliminate by tampering with the past. They send the same message, delivered to everyone in the future who would be affected, warning them of what's happening and how they can avoid their revised fate."

"Does it work?"

"The scientists know it will work but they also figure out that the most effective way to foil the evil plot will eliminate one of them. One of them won't be born."

Zhihong's revelation lands like a chord changing the direction of a scene. Dawei scratches his chin as he thinks through the implications.

"So what happens in the end?"

Zhihong smiles as he takes a drag.

"Don't you want to read the ending yourself?"

"Um…"

The wonder in Dawei's gaze turns to something less discernible. Zhihong sees that he's pulled Dawei out of the story and realizes that reading is a challenge for him. He wants to pull the comment back and stamp it out. This gift he's giving Dawei is meant to uplift and, until a moment ago, it was doing more than that. He had brought the story to life, giving it the respect it deserves. And more importantly, he had created a small world where they were closer than they had ever been.

"So here's what happens," Zhihong continues, opening his hands to play up the drama, to sweep away Dawei's frustration and draw him back into the story. "Sensing that they have no options in the face of a harsh sentence that will separate them forever, the lovers figure out a way to transmit their consciousness, essentially their souls, into the dreams of other people at different times."

"Really? And they can live together like that?"

"Have you ever had a dream that seemed so real that you were emotional when you woke up?"

"Yes," Dawei says enthusiastically. "Sometimes the d…d… dreams are so bad that I'm actually happy to wake up. And sometimes dreams are so good all I want to do is dive back into them. Sometimes w…waking up is the worst thing."

"Those dreams felt exactly like real life, right?"

Dawei nods his head.

"Well, these two characters have lives together that are just as real."

Dawei gazes out over the water as though he's looking for signs of ethereal transmissions between beings living in other eras.

"I would love to see this film," he says.

It's always the closest relations – best friends, brothers and sisters, lovers – who say these things. Pragmatists should treat such praise as though it has no more value than the air that produces the sound. The truly ambitious should only tune into the criticism. But Zhihong can't help feeling certain that Dawei's comment is, if anything, an understatement and would have given him an extra burst of motivation to bring the project to life. If only it wasn't too late.

Dawei would love to see this film. Indeed. Zhihong would like for him to see it on a big screen, in a modern, air-conditioned cinema. Instead, he'll need to see the story in his head, based on Zhihong's words and gestures.

"I wanted you to have this because movies mean so much to you."

"Is the author still writing?" Dawei asks.

Zhihong shakes his head quietly. "She died earlier this year. I feel like I let her down. I came close to getting one into production, but..." He pauses and looks away. "But, it's not going to happen. It's all about calculations...return on investment and capital commitment guarantees."

Dawei doesn't know what capital commitments are but is sure that it somehow involves money. And that Zhihong has given up hope trying to get this movie made.

He notices that a low ebb tide has exposed a small beach on one side of the rocks. Nimble crabs dart back and forth across the sand, nabbing bits of seaweed and other aquatic detritus that leave an odour of maritime decay in the heavy air.

"I can't accept this," Dawei says, returning the script to its folder and then handing it back.

Zhihong refuses to take it. "I'm telling you, the only value this has is sentimental. You would be the kind of person she'd write about. I'm sure she would want you to have it. You have the iron will of a hero and you don't give up, Dawei."

The word hero resonates with Dawei. It gives him hope that the scenes he conjures up in his head aren't fantasies.

Dawei grabs Zhihong's cigarette and throws it into the water. There's no longer any point in restraining himself. He lunges at Zhihong, grabs the back of his head and kisses him. Zhihong pulls back, his focus darting between both of Dawei's eyes as the meaning of this moment and all the time they've spent together so far sinks in. Zhihong grabs Dawei's hand and stands up, pulling Dawei with him. The two of them move urgently towards the end of the embankment, each step releasing in Dawei a higher level of exhilaration, until they pass the last streetlight. They clamour down the sea wall and find their way onto a boulder where they kiss so violently, in a frantic embrace, that Dawei tastes blood.

Dawei is lying on top of Zhihong, both of them sweaty and lifeless except for the slow expansion and contraction of their torsos. All of the evening's exertion, physical and mental, make it impossible for Dawei to want to say or do anything other than hold Zhihong and listen to the water lapping up against the sea wall.

Macau is still and silent; the only sound is the distant clattering of construction sites across the causeway in Zhuhai, too far away to disturb them. Dawei must concentrate on every detail of this moment to keep away the thought that he'll be back in the restaurant kitchen in a few hours and Zhihong will be on a ferry back to Hong Kong to catch a flight to his home, and his wife, in Beijing.

THURSDAY, March 28, 2007

The incoming call is from Washington, DC. It can only be Kendra. Jake excuses himself from a meeting, explaining that the call is from a source.

"Hi, what have you heard?"

"It's not good."

The response triggers an anger that Jake quells by reminding himself that she's only the messenger, that she's on his side. No one would have a better read on the situation than Kendra and he clings to this thought in order to stay calm.

"I was at least hoping for a good-news-bad-news scenario."

"The problem is that he's been detained by officers on the municipal level, not the national level," Kendra says.

"Why is that a problem?"

"Because they answer to people on the national government level and they never want to look like fools. If they've gone through the trouble of investigating and detaining, they'll be inclined to follow through regardless of what the evidence says."

So now someone's life hangs in the balance because of paranoia and incompetence.

"What do you recommend we do now?"

"We need to make noise about this. I can start that here in DC."

"Ok, tell me more."

FRIDAY, March 29, 2008

Diane arrives at Jake's apartment at 9:45 p.m. She's about an hour and a half late because, as she's explained in a series of text messages, the flight from Shanghai was delayed. Her knock at the door, soft and small, seems to lighten the load he's been carrying. Jake jumps up, tucks in his shirt and heads to the door.

Diane is smiling as the door opens. There's no sign of frustration over the flight delay or the traffic in Shanghai and Beijing, not to mention the disappearance of her only sibling. She has Qiang's large eyes, as well as his rounded nose and small mouth. The resemblance fills Jake with hope and makes him want to hug her.

She has someone with her. A fair-skinned white guy with flushed cheeks and dirty blonde hair that's thinning on top. He looks just like Prince William.

"Jake?" Diane asks, unsure.

"Diane, thank you so much for making it here," Jake says in Mandarin.

A hug might be appropriate but Jake isn't sure how acquainted she is with Western customs. They shake hands.

"Jake, no, I must thank you," Diane answers in English with barely a hint of a Chinese accent. "This is Benjamin. He's a friend of Qiang's who's just flown in from San Francisco."

"Ben," he says, offering his hand. "Pleased to meet you, Jake."

Diane is petite, about two inches shorter than Jake, even in mid-high heels. Her hair falls just above her shoulders, parted on the side and swept away from her face in a feathered cut. Subtle, professional and feminine. Thin maroon piping along the edges of her black jacket and pencil skirt is even and precise.

Having lived in Shanghai for years, working in finance, Diane wouldn't likely outfit herself with the usual mismatched combinations that skew either too gaudy or utilitarian. But still, Jake didn't expect her to look Parisian. He also didn't expect her to show up with someone else.

"Wow. The family resemblance is really apparent," Jake says, switching to English. "Welcome to Beijing. I just wish this was under different circumstances."

"It's great to meet you and to know that my brother has such a good friend here," Diane says.

"You two must be starved," Jake says as he rolls Diane's bag into the living room. "I had dumplings for dinner earlier and got extra for you, Diane. But there should be enough for both of you."

Diane puts a hand on Jake's shoulder to stop him from going into the kitchen. "That's so nice of you, Jake, but I ate a full dinner at the airport in Shanghai just before I got on the flight," Diane says.

"Are you sure?"

"I'm serious, Jake. Really, I've had enough to eat. I'm not just being polite. I'm not just being Chinese polite if you know what I mean," Diane says.

"And you, Ben?"

Ben flashes the palm of one hand. "I've had twenty-four hours of airline food going into me," he says in a booming voice. "What I really need to do is empty myself, not to fill my stomach. Could I use your washroom?"

The resonance and volume Ben uses to describe the state of his digestion takes Jake off guard. Personalities usually reveal themselves over time but Ben has just established himself, fully formed, as a man who doesn't edit himself.

"Well, that is a lot of information, Ben. The powder room is right next to you."

"Thank you, my friend," Ben says as he lets go of the handle of his luggage, drops his shoulder bag and ducks into the bathroom.

"Um. Diane, come in and have a seat," Jake says, trying to move them away from the powder room as quickly as possible. "At least have something to drink. We have coffee, tea, juice.... Also, I have a bottle of red open."

Diane sits at the dining room table, laptop open, looking at a spreadsheet. Jake sets out Dragon Well tea in a simple clay pot from Yixing, a gift from one of his teachers and one of the few items he has kept from his years as a student in Anhui Province. He puts a small cup that came with the set in front of Diane.

"Charming," Diane says as she looks up from the screen and examines the teapot. "Most tourists to Yixing go for the most elaborate teapots but you chose a very fine and classic one."

"Actually, I didn't choose it," Jake says. "The set was a gift from one of my teachers. Something they gave me as I was leaving. It's one of the few things I've kept with me as I've moved around."

Made of dark purplish-brown clay, the tea set has a slightly coarse, unfinished texture meant to absorb the essential oils of fine tea. It reminds Jake of his first stint in China, when he went on his own to qualify later for a more prestigious language program. His primary instructor at the university in Anhui, a thirty-something woman he knew only as Teacher Zhou, seemed to understand how bewildered Jake was. She and her husband, an affable engineering professor, looked after Jake, inviting him for dinner every few weeks.

Jake found some of their food unappetizing, particularly the preserved eggs which were the colour of gangrene and tasted rotten, but eventually adjusted to the dishes that more closely resembled standards served in the U.S.: fried rice, sesame chicken, barbecued spare ribs. The generous quantites of freshly chopped ginger and garlic Teacher Zhou used in her cooking made dishes like stir-fried vegetables and tofu – something Jake would never order in the U.S. – tasty.

Teacher Zhou showed more concern for Jake than he was accustomed to. She made sure he had enough blankets in his dorm when he arrived and requested a new desk for him after seeing that the inside of one of the drawers had rotted. She brought him to the local clinic when he came down with a fever, and then ensured he got chicken soup with ginseng and goji berries every day until he recovered. Jake's mother usually didn't acknowledge health issues unless blood had spilled.

When the three-month program ended, Jake had nothing with him from the U.S. to leave with Teacher Zhou and her husband but a few cassette tapes he wasn't sure they'd like. He eventually selected the most accessible ones: *Technique* by New Order, *Like a Prayer* by Madonna and *Rumours* by Fleetwood Mac. They tried to refuse the gifts, as is customary. When Jake followed through with the customary persistence, they seemed genuinely happy with the tapes.

When Teacher Zhou and her husband saw him to the train station for his trip to Shanghai where he'd board his flight back to the U.S., they presented him with the tea set that Jake's using now to bridge the cultural gap he supposed might separate him from Qiang's sister.

"Well then," Diane says as Jake begins to pour the tea, "you deserve credit for your recognition of quality."

The precise enunciation and word choice make Diane sound English.

"*Na li,*" Jake says. Nonsense.

With the formal interplay of courtesy over, they turn their attention to the spreadsheet. The first tab is a list of police stations closest to Qiang's apartment, those that Diane plans to visit tomorrow to start making inquiries. Her phone rings as she starts explaining her strategy.

"Jake," she says apologetically. "I know it's rude but this is my husband calling to make sure I've arrived at your place safely. Do you mind if I take the call?"

"Diane, please. It's not rude."

Jake glances at the spreadsheets and schedules on Diane's screen as she starts talking to her husband about what to do to get their daughter to sleep. The methodical instructions and the organization of Diane's documents reminds Jake of Qiang's habits, how he can't work unless everything on his desk is aligned and orderly. After working with Qiang, the importance of order had influenced Jake. He would clean up his own desk in the newsroom throwing away stacks of press releases and conference agendas and resolve to keep order intact, only to let the clutter build up again and, then, he would clear the mess again a few weeks later, always resolving to never let the mess overtake him again.

Jake fell for Qiang before he even met him, two years earlier. A former classmate now living in San Francisco emailed Jake to let him know about a friend who had just left a position as chief marketing officer with a firm that developed programmatic ad buying services.

"He's the smartest guy I know and the most down to earth," his friend said in the note. "Oh, and I may as well let you know that he's very easy on the eyes. You can't get a better combination."

The email continued with more details about Qiang, more than necessary for an introduction. Through these details, Jake saw the sense of loss his classmate was feeling because of Qiang's departure. After reading the email a few times, an infatuation with Qiang began to grow like vines climbing tree bark.

Jake took to Qiang when they first met over drinks at a bar in the neighbourhood about an hour before the party on Pierre's rooftop terrace. He thought Qiang would appreciate a before party briefing on who's who and a champagne toast to celebrate a new beginning in Beijing. They might then get to know each other better during the ten-minute stroll to Pierre's.

Qiang had arrived in Beijing from San Francisco less than 24 hours earlier but showed no sign of the sleep interruption that comes with a trans-Pacific flight. Wearing a navy-blue hoodie over a black t-shirt with faded blue jeans and converse running shoes, Qiang looked very Californian, like a photographer keen to fade into the background and not at all interested in making much of an impression. While no one arrived at Pierre's parties looking flashy, most sported some kind of personifying element to get a conversation started. An element that no one else at the party would possibly have: a beret here, a studded leather belt there, a psychedelic patch sewn onto a pair of jeans. Jake's flourishes that evening were the bright orange racing stripes down each sleeve of an olive drab Junya Watanabe jacket which he wore over a grey t-shirt and jeans.

Unlike an American, Qiang arrived with a gift. A tube of *Tom's of Maine* brand natural toothpaste, the sort of specialty item that hadn't yet caught on in China and was available nowhere in the country. It was a token of his appreciation, Qiang said, for Jake making some time for him on a Saturday night and including him in an important social event.

"I know toothpaste is a little unusual," he said. "But this is good stuff and it's something I'm sure you'll use regularly. I have an American friend in Shanghai who always asks for this stuff."

Jake looked at the box and let out a small laugh. Not because he thought the gift was inappropriate or trite. Toothpaste made with natural ingredients was more than a token. There was real spearmint oil in this product. The packaging was understated, featuring a seal certifying that its ingredients were organic, a counterpoint to every other consumer product in China. Reports of unhealthy or counterfeit items filtering through the consumer markets had just started to make headlines in the domestic media. Jake and one of his colleagues were following the story also. Unable to discern real from fake or contaminated from clean, Jake had subconsciously buried the issue and hoped whatever he was consuming or brushing his teeth with would not inflict any lasting damage on him. Part of Jake wanted to go back to his apartment immediately and brush his teeth. If nothing else went his way that evening, Jake thought, he could end it in the early morning hours by falling asleep with a minty fresh mouth. Perhaps the fragrance of the genuine essential oils would last until he woke the next day.

"Oh my God, I…" Jake started to say.

"Sorry, I'm really the worst when it comes to picking out gifts."

"Oh no, please. You don't understand," Jake continued. "I love this. You're absolutely right, Qiang. It's something I'll be able to use every day for the next month or two and it's like a little piece of what's good about the U.S., right? You don't see so much of this kind of thing here."

"Well, not yet. It's coming, I'm sure," Qiang replied. "I stuffed one of my bags with these tubes so I'll give you a few more later."

"Please, that's not necessary. This is kind enough," Jake said while holding up the toothpaste box. "Now tell me about what you'll be getting up to here. I hear you'll be shooting documentaries."

The conversation flowed better than Jake had expected, mostly due to Qiang's curiosity about Beijing. How much had Jake's neighbourhood changed in the decade he'd been in the city? What kind of live music options are there at 798, the old munitions factory district which had gradually transformed into an artist colony? What sorts of barriers had Jake come up against in his news reporting?

By the time crumpled cocktail napkins began to accumulate and the empty wine bottles started to outnumber the unopened ones, Jake realized he had been sticking by Qiang's side since they arrived, even as they merged into and out of small groups of guests keen to introduce themselves to the new arrival. Qiang gave no hint that he'd had enough of Jake's company. But, Jake thought after introducing him to a couple of other journalists, wouldn't anyone with good social graces stick with their escort in this situation? This question then set off a recap of the evening to that point. Who had benefitted more from the before-party de-brief and the champagne toast, not to mention the leisurely stroll to the party? Jake suddenly saw through his own self-deception. Was his attachment to Qiang throughout the evening predatory – a bid to mark territory – or selfless? Which way had Qiang seen it? Was Qiang just too polite to extricate himself from this game? Once this possibility became clear to Jake, he scanned the venue for another island of social interaction on which he could beach himself. He spotted a friend of Pierre's who had just returned from a holiday, someone tedious but worth a few minutes of droll conversation for the opportunity of a smooth transition away from Qiang.

"Hey, sorry to interrupt," Jake said as he tuned back into the conversation Qiang and a few others were having about a new railroad to Tibet. He put a hand on Qiang's shoulder. "You seem pretty established here, Qiang. I need to chat with a couple of friends over yonder," Jake said, gesturing across the terrace. "If, for some reason, I don't find you before I leave, you have my number and email, right?"

"Oh, sure," Qiang said, looking a bit confused, just as Jake wanted it. "Don't worry, I'll look for you before I go," he added.

"You never know who might sweep you off your feet at one of Pierre's parties, Qiang. Pierre's not happy unless there's plenty of gossip about what happens here. Anyway, we'll get together sometime soon if I don't see you later. Drop me a line whenever you want."

As he walked away, Jake felt as though he had played his hand like an expert. He exchanged the possibility of a fast romance, however remote, for assurance that he wasn't a loser, at least not in this particular case. Dignity is healthier than speculative pursuit and, anyway, time would tell whether something more exciting could develop between him and Qiang. With this achievement of discipline over emotion, Jake had found it easier to keep his thoughts about Qiang confined.

Over the next couple of weeks, the few times when the two of them met for lunch or drinks, their conversations rarely strayed from impersonal subjects like their shared hatred for warmongering Republicans in Washington, DC or American films, which Jake was able to keep up with thanks to Beijing's many bootlegged DVD shops.

Qiang might occasionally mention others in Pierre's circle who invited him for dinner and Jake would clench his teeth but reveal only a casual interest.

"Oh, yeah? What did you say?"

"It was awkward," Qiang said several times, always to Jake's relief. "My work is my only focus right now."

Jake would then say something like, "You'd think that message would have sunk in by now."

Knowing that Qiang batted away propositions like cold marketing calls helped Jake accept the distance he would have to keep. At least he was a confidante of sorts, enjoying a proximity to Qiang that no one else in Beijing had. It wasn't like being chosen last for the sports team or the sting from the dozen rejection letters Jake got back from the prestigious colleges he should not have bothered applying to.

But this resignation didn't last. Just as water has a way of infiltrating the strongest of barriers, Jake's feelings broke through their constraints when he saw a hidden dimension to Qiang's kindness.

A mid-week dinner party organized by Pierre added fuel to Jake's attraction. Pierre wanted to do something special for an old friend in town on business for just a few nights. He called it for 8:30 p.m., which really meant 9:00 p.m., to accommodate the work-related crises that seemed to be part and parcel of expat jobs as home offices in New York or London sent impossible requests. Only ten guests, including Jake and Qiang, probably, Jake thought, because Pierre wanted to get closer to the fresh arrival. Place cards with names scrawled out in Pierre's handwriting supported his theory. Four on each side of the table's length. Pierre at one end and his out-of-towner friend at the other. Jake and Qiang at opposite corners and, of course, Qiang was to share a corner with Pierre.

As the guests unwound with gin drinks and wine around the piano in Pierre's living room, munching on cashews and nori, Jake moved his place card, switching himself with the guest seated on Qiang's immediate left.

When the guests gathered at the table, each taking positions behind their designated seats, Pierre gave Jake an inquisitive look. Eager to bat away an awkward exchange, Jake opened his arms in a gesture that drew attention to the table. Fine silver and crystal. Two bottles of Veuve, each planted in ice-filled tureens, and several bottles of well-aged Bourdeaux. Pierre's dinner party guests were always forbidden from bringing their own wine. Pierre would explain that he ordered too much of his own but everyone knew he simply didn't trust the tastes of his guests and no one begrudged the opportunity of an immaculate meal without even having to drop 100 kuai.

"Impeccable taste, as always, Pierre," Jake said. "Thanks very much for inviting ... me."

Jake almost said 'us', stopping himself at the last moment when he realized 'us' might be taken to mean him and Qiang, an implication that might be risky.

The dinner was prepared by the sous chef at one of Beijing's most prestigious Western restaurants. The meal consisted of eight courses including a starter of tuna tataki served with wasabi mayo and red quinoa and a main course of pan-seared lamb chops, broccoli rabe, rosemary fingerling potatoes and parsley butter.

Pierre played the role of a Western banker well. The most financially well-endowed expats in Beijing usually flaunted their ability to live a life removed from the local environment in every respect - nutritionally, linguistically and vertically.

After a fourth course of garlicky escargot, the chef's two servers brought out a very pale sorbet served in martini glasses. Confused, Jake looked at what he thought was dessert.

"I…"

As he began to speak, Qiang put a hand on his knee and clenched. The effect was much like a jockey pulling his reins to stop a horse from trotting.

"Wow," Qiang said, interrupting Jake and turning to Pierre. He kept his hand on Jake's knee. "You've gone as far as to have us cleanse our palettes. I guess the main course is coming next."

With a hand on Jake's knee and compliment to the host, Qiang had saved him from the kind of embarrassment he dreaded most. He had no idea how common it was for the cultured classes to "cleanse their palettes" with sorbet during a meal. Was this something they did at family dinners or was it only reserved for fine dining? Jake had been to many high-end restaurants. He had picked up a taste for things like fig marmalade with hard cheese on water crackers, an oddity for someone who had only ever eaten preserves. Jelly to him went with peanut butter on pre-sliced white bread or an English muffin if things were fancy. How is water the featured ingredient in any food product anyway? How had he not yet come across this custom of cleansing one's palette with bland sorbet before the main course?

As these questions darted through his mind, he remembered to finish the sentence he started.

"I… have never seen the cleanse served in martini glasses."

Jake couldn't be sure that the sorbet wasn't usually served in martini glasses, so he clarified.

"I mean I haven't seen it served in such nice martini glasses."

The other guests had already dug into their sorbet, some of them continuing with their conversations, so Jake's ignorance remained concealed.

But the relief he felt - this infusion of warmth, reassurance, bliss and confidence - vaporized into memory when Qiang took his hand from Jake's knee and put it back on the table.

How, Jake wondered, did Qiang know what he was about to ask? His kindness had sprung into play like a reflex, giving Jake more insight into Qiang's intelligence.

Jake pulled Qiang aside after they left Pierre's to ask him.

"Oh, that" he said, as if he had completely forgotten the incident. "I was there once before. The first time I got sorbet in the middle of a meal, I had no idea what it was. It's not a common thing as far as I know. Anyway, I kind of sensed what you were about to say. Don't worry, that kind of thing is only for extreme foodies."

Qiang laughed away any residual embarrassment Jake had felt as though they were in on a joke together.

As Jake rode home in a cab, he wondered if he would have made the same protective move on behalf of another guest. He wasn't sure. Or maybe he was sure but didn't want to acknowledge what would have transpired. When you're so conscientious about what other people think, you're not inclined to pass up a chance to look smarter. Qiang had no interest in this kind of opportunity.

"...and I'll be home in a week, hopefully with Qiang," Jake hears Diane say as she ends the phone call.

A loud flush from the powder room followed by a rush of water from the faucet helps to break the spell. Ben emerges and walks into the dining room. He's shed his overcoat, showing him to be thinner than he appeared at first. Or perhaps his odd introduction made him seem bigger. He wears a black leather blazer over a t-shirt with an image of Mao Zedong standing next to Whitney Houston.

"That was cathartic," Ben says.

"You're just an open book, aren't you, Ben?" Jake says. "We're having some tea but I also have some red wine on offer."

"Yes, Qiang told me you love your red," Ben says as he opens his suitcase and rummages through it. He pulls out a bottle of wine with an appropriately faded label full of French text. Côtes du Rhône, several cuts above Australian varieties Jake usually buys in Beijing. Ben hands it to Jake.

"And for all of us...," Ben says as he digs further through a mass of clothing he didn't bother to fold properly. He pulls out a bottle of precious-looking whiskey and holds it up like a trophy with one hand and points at Jake with the other.

"You, my friend, are from Kentucky, so I got the best Bourbon available in Bluegrass Country!" he says.

Jake tries to place Ben's accent which sounds like the midwestern broadcast standard, except for his slightly long pronunciation of "grass," which suggests either an elite, New England upbringing or a significant chunk of time spent in the UK.

Jake recognizes the label. "Basil Heyden's. You know bourbon."

"Basil Heyden's! Spicy like rye but smoother," Ben announces like a spokesman for the product.

Jake doesn't like bourbon, or anything from Kentucky for that matter. And no one from Kentucky drinks Basil Heyden. Jake sees it more for people who pride themselves on cultural intelligence. Proclamations of love for Kentucky bourbon, particularly when you're not from the state, confer high and low-brow credentials simultaneously. One needs a thorough understanding of Scotch, including the subtleties of highland peat moss, in order to make the conscious decision to like the version of whiskey developed in North America, the kind descended from the stills of Appalachian hillbillies.

None of this matters to Jake as much as the fact that this complete stranger knows how much he likes red wine. In fact, everything so far feels wrong. Teapots, bourbon, cathartic defecation and the generally light tone all seem at odds with the situation facing them. But Jake chooses to be a diplomat.

"This is too kind of you, Ben," Jake says as he scans the wine bottle's label. "I have a few questions for you, like how do you know about my greatest weakness, but we should probably save that for later."

"Let's all just have a sip of bourbon and we'll get into it," Ben says. "Where are your glasses, mate?"

Fatigue catches up with Jake as soon as they're sitting around his dining room table, Jake with red wine, Diane with tea and Ben with his high-end bourbon.

"You know," Jake says as he takes off his glasses and rubs his eyes, "Qiang has a contact in Washington who may be able to start what we call, in English, some back-channel chatter about your brother. This would make it clear to whoever's holding Qiang that his disappearance will become something China's Foreign Ministry will eventually need to manage if the issue drags out. It would be a warning, delivered respectfully, allowing the Foreign Ministry to keep face.

"Friends in Washington? No, I don't think it's the time for that," Diane says.

"Have you thought about when the time will come for us to reach out to our connections in Washington?" Jake asks. "I'm not proposing that we go to the media at this point. We just want the authorities to know that Qiang's disappearance hasn't gone unnoticed."

"I understand," Diane says, this time looking at Jake directly. "I understand and appreciate that but I don't think it's an appropriate time yet."

"So, you're planning to visit the Public Security Bureau tomorrow? What kind of strategy are you going there with and what do you hope to accomplish?" Jake asks as suspicions about Diane begin to worry him. Whose side is she on?

Diane sighs. "Jake, you sent me an email two days ago. We've spoken about this on the phone several times, right? I booked a flight to Beijing."

"Yes, but I think it's going to take more than that to get your brother released," Jake says.

"Of course it is. I'm not suggesting we stop here."

"Then what are you suggesting? I think we may be looking at a serious fucking situation. And I'd like to know how you think the PSB will help."

Then Jake looks at Ben. "I don't mean any disrespect, Ben, but who are you anyway, apart from some American guy who knows whiskey?"

Ben pauses and then massages his temples.

"I was married to Qiang for five years."

The comment silences Jake. Diane doesn't react. This isn't news to her.

"We may be separated but I still love him. He's still a huge part of my life, even if the feeling isn't mutual at the moment, and I'm going to do whatever I can here to help."

Ben speaks in a steady tone, without blinking. The levity he had brought to the room is gone. Ben is now a completely different person. Unwelcome. Uninvited. Jake takes a gulp of wine to help him swallow the marriage revelation.

"Well, this is a surprise to me," Jake says as he feels the wine's tannins dry his throat.

"Jake, do you think I'm the only one who read that email?" Diane asks. "Do you think I was the only person you were talking to on the phone? You're a foreign journalist here. Of course you'll know how to get in touch with people in Washington."

"Diane, just tell me what you're thinking. We've been sitting here a long time and I still don't have a clue."

"I'm saying this: they already know that you're likely to make that move at some point. If they haven't figured that out from our correspondence and phone calls, I'm sure they know now."

Diane looks around the room, directing her gaze toward two corners of the ceiling as she says this. Then back at Jake.

Jake has never been sure how far the Foreign Ministry goes in keeping tabs on Western journalists. Working for a financial news network, he had never faced the kind of interference that some of his peers have, those who follow the political stories: Dissidents, Uighur uprisings in Xinjiang, Factory worker riots in Guangdong, Harvesting of organs at secret concentration camps in the northeast where the government puts Falun Gong followers.

The political reporters in Beijing swap stories about their phone calls being cut off. They talk of emails that never reach the intended recipients. One even had a CD mailed to her, a recording of her at a bar talking to someone about her husband and how he no longer satisfied her sexually. How she had started meeting a mutual friend, a man married to one of her other friends, for afternoon trysts. Someone sitting next to her at a bar must have been recording the conversation.

After so many years covering China, he's never been close to any stories about dissidents so he's unsure of whether his apartment is bugged.

"You, me and Ben here are all very well connected people," Diane continues. "We're all here in Beijing, obviously very concerned about what's happened to my little brother. And we're going to give the authorities the distance and time they need to figure out that they've made a mistake. They've simply misunderstand my brother's intentions. I know he'd never be unfair in the way he treats his subject matter. I think they will figure that out as they talk to him and investigate whatever it is they're looking for."

Bound up in suspicion, Jake can't formulate an intelligent counter argument. He looks away for a moment, bouncing one leg, and then turns to Ben, hoping that a change in direction will help him regain the upper hand.

"Can I ask what it is you do that makes you so well connected?"

"Well, Diane's estimation of me and my position might be a bit exaggerated."

"He's the program director at the CSAIL lab at MIT," Diane says, interrupting. "He works with some of the world's most well-respected computer scientists and researchers."

"Very impressive," Jake says. "But I don't know how that gives us leverage."

"Ben has many connections in the scientific community," Diane says. "You have connections in the media and with politicians in Washington. I have connections in the world of finance. I would say the three of our networks, put together, would give us leverage if we needed it. But we're not going to use this leverage, at least not yet."

The way she looks at Jake, with sincerity, with focus and without blinking or flinching, signals the end of discussion. Just like Qiang, she directs the scene to a kind of closure that Jake must accept.

"Let's try being cooperative. There are laws and procedures in this country. It's in no one's interest, particularly not ours, to start a conflict over this."

Jake wants to argue his side but remembers Diane's quiet reference to the bugs that may or may not be picking up their conversation. So he nods and sips his wine.

"Okay," he then says. "Let's not start a fight. Let's just get this resolved peacefully."

Diane closes her laptop as though, for the moment, she's shutting the door that leads to her brother's predicament.

Ben reaches across the table and grabs Jake's wrist. "Hey, I know this has been very stressful for you these past few days," he says just above a whisper. "Let's just work together on this. I don't pretend to know what's right or wrong here but I'm sure that it won't help Qiang if we're at odds with each other."

The contact and the softly spoken words are meant to reassure. But Ben doesn't know how Jake feels about Qiang.

SATURDAY, March 30, 2007
8:45 a.m.

Diane unclasps her messenger bag, a John Woodbridge made of vegetable-tanned leather, a purchase she made during a trip to her company's Geneva office. The bag's natural grain clashes with the cheap veneers and fluorescent light of the police station. She pulls a plastic folder with several papers neatly clipped together from the bag.

"Good morning," Diane says to a female officer behind the counter.

Getting no response, she places the papers on the counter, in front of the officer who's filling out a form on a clipboard. On the first sheet, a blurry image of Qiang's face. A copy of his identification card, which expired three years earlier. Diane spreads the papers out. Underneath, a copy of the deed to the apartment she and Qiang bought for their parents in Chongqing and a copy of the deed to his Beijing apartment.

Diane unbuttons the Burberry raincoat she's wearing over a pinstriped blouse and olive-coloured slacks while she waits for the officer to acknowledge her and the matter she's presenting.

"My brother is missing. He lives in this district," she says in a louder but still respectful tone. "He owns a condo in Progress Park."

"Just a minute," says the uniformed woman who doesn't look up as she transcribes information from a computer printout onto the clipboard sheet. "Please have a seat."

Another female officer sits at a desk set back a couple of metres from the counter, also processing paperwork. Two male officers button their jackets and make small talk as they come out from a room behind the woman at the desk and leave the station through an exit behind the counter, for PSB staff only.

The room is flooded with white fluorescence. White vinyl floor tiles full of black scuff marks, white vinyl walls marred by the backs of six chairs lined up against the far side of the office. There's a four-seat bench with cushions, upholstered in rough black polyester, built on a gray metal frame that's meant to be bolted to the floor. Diane looks at the chairs and notices the blanks on the bottom of the seating frame where there should be bolts holding the set in place. She then looks down at the paperwork that the officer seems intent on finishing before she'll consider giving Diane any of her attention.

"I believe my brother's been detained."

The female officer looks up at Diane, puts her pen down and then picks up the paper with the blurry image of Qiang's ID.

"You need to wait a bit," she says, squinting as she inspects the paper. "Go have a seat."

"Thank you," Diane says while she refastens the straps on her bag.

She turns and walks to the set of tandem seats. After taking another glance at the papers, the officer rolls her chair back and converses with her colleague in a voice too low for Diane to hear what's said. Diane watches as she centres her bag on her lap.

Without looking back at Diane, the officer behind the counter walks through the entrance to a room next to her desk, holding the papers with the blurred image of Qiang.

Diane saves the spreadsheet she's been working on and glances up at a clock on the station's wall. It's 10:17 a.m. She checks her watch: 10:22. Several groups have come and gone, lodging complaints with the female officer who's taken over for the one who's disappeared with the documents Diane brought. One married couple reported the loss of some inventory at an electronics store they own. They suspect an employee who hasn't turned up for work for two days. An elderly man came in to complain about several black Audis that have been parking in the alley behind his building. They have official plates which, he said, shows how municipal officials take their privileges too far. No one else has the right to park there. The old man dictated the numbers to the officer and asked what the PSB will do about it. "We'll look into it," said one of the officers. "You said the same thing a week ago," the old man retorted.

It's been quiet for the past twenty minutes. Diane shuts her laptop and slides it into her briefcase. She approaches the counter to find the officer tapping out a text message on her Nokia phone.

"Sorry to trouble you," Diane says. "It's just that I've been waiting here for more than two hours."

"What's the problem?"

"I've mentioned it already to your colleague. My brother has been missing for nearly a week. I think he's been detained and I'm here to get this matter sorted out."

The officer doesn't look up.

"He owns an apartment in Progress Park," Diane continues. "That's part of this station's district, right?"

"We don't know anything about this matter. You'll need to come back tomorrow morning. There may be someone here then who will know something about this.

May, 2005

Zhihong's workplace lies beyond an immense pedestrian bridge. A giant oval spread out over an intersection with too many lanes and signals to allow anyone to cross on street level. Backed-up traffic on Chang'an Avenue, corralled into order by a uniformed officer on a pedestal, crawls obediently under the sprawling bridge splayed across an area so wide that the access ramps on the opposite corner fade into brown haze. The officer wears a crisp, green uniform with a peaked cap, red insignia over the visor and aviator sunglasses.

At each corner, pedestrians climb the stairs that ascend at an angle low enough to allow those with bicycles to push them up ramps alongside the steps and join the slow-motion circumambulation of people over the steady procession of black sedans, red taxis and blue pick-up trucks.

Zhihong had once described the location of the government department where he works so, keeping the details in mind, Dawei found the building on a tourist map one of the patrons at his restaurant had abandoned along with an empty water bottle and a ferry receipt. Like most of the government buildings in Beijing, the State Administration of Radio, Television and Film is a large compound, contained within a perimeter fence, just southwest of Chang'an Avenue and the Second Ring. Dawei knows the characters for state, television, and of course, for film.

Dawei realizes he may have arrived at the building too late. From the railway station, he asked a passerby to point him to Chang'an Avenue, then toward Tiananmen Square, which he has seen countless times on television. The direction was easy, but the scale of Beijing threw him off. The map made it seem as though the television bureau wasn't more than 10 or 15 minutes from the railway station. In fact, it took that much time just to traverse the square. After walking for what seemed like more than a half an hour passing monolithic buildings, Dawei had to ask someone for confirmation that he was going the right way.

It's now sometime past 6:00 p.m., after most people leave their offices and head home. Dawei will wait, if he must, until tomorrow.

A security officer rouses Dawei from sleep by poking him in the side with a baton. Startled, Dawei grasps for bearings on where he is and why. He props himself up with one elbow and the light jacket he had draped over himself falls to the ground. Looking at the officer and remembering the long journey to this bench, Dawei rights himself to a sitting position and then leans down to gather up his jacket.

"Move on," the officer says.

There's no sign of daylight. In the silence, Dawei hears his stomach growl. He routes in his bag for the last of four preserved eggs that he pilfered from the restaurant before catching a bus to Zhuhai, where he then boarded a train for the two-day trip to Beijing. The eggs, along with some dried fish and other scraps from the plates he carted back to his washing station, sustained him for the trip. Now he's down to a few foil packets of preserved vegetables, usually stirred into watery rice. Dawei rips one open and digs out the stringy bits of radish and cabbage. The briny taste whets his appetite for something more. He imagines a steamed pork bun or a plate of fried noodles, which makes him salivate. Even the leftover scraps of Macanese food, with the curry taste that took time for him to find palatable, would be a treat right now. Dawei pulls the foil apart so he can lick the residue.

Noticing a lighter shade of bluish-grey over the buildings he's facing, Dawei wonders if the glow is coming from the Square or the approaching dawn. He doesn't want to look for another bench in the same neighbourhood so he wanders toward the light. Back to Chang'an Avenue.

The International Bank of China's headquarters comes into view. Just the night before leaving Macau, Dawei overheard some of the restaurant patrons talk about how much the bank's chairman had spent on the building. The executive has been criticized for the high cost and there's talk of an investigation. The building was designed by the relatives of a Chinese-American architect who is world famous, the one who designed the International Bank of China's tower in the heart of Hong Kong's financial district.

Dawei thinks the building looks ordinary. Just a low-slung, boxy structure with a large glass dome cantilevered over an entrance at one corner. He heads closer for a better look into the atrium, which rises to the roofline ten-storeys above, and sees a bamboo grove planted around an angular koi pond made of black marble.

From inside the International Bank of China atrium, a security guard trains his eyes on Dawei who backs away and moves toward the sidewalk.

More new buildings sit across the street. Clad in glass and metal and other reflective surfaces, they glow and Dawei can't discern whether the illumination comes from inside or out. Just as impressive, maybe more so, than anything he'd seen in TV broadcasts from Hong Kong or Tokyo or New York City.

By the time morning rush hour traffic begins to build, Dawei has positioned himself outside the Ministry's west security gate, back far enough so that the security guards won't become suspicious of him. There's also an entrance on the east side of the complex so Dawei has a fifty-fifty chance of seeing Zhihong go in here.

The procession of people builds. Larger groups descend from the buses stopping across the street. The men all look similar, with their dark jackets and dark slacks, and carrying satchels. Dawei wonders how much money these government workers make as they keep the business of media regulated and running. They file in between 8:00 and 9:00 a.m. and then leave sometime well before 6:00 p.m. They only work five days a week, giving them two whole days to rest or visit a park or watch movies. And they probably all make enough to buy an apartment.

As Dawei ponders the privilege of civil servants, he notices that the flow of workers heading into the Television Bureau has started to dwindle and his thoughts darken. Why did he make the trip here? Why did he use all of the cash he's been stashing away to visit a married man? He had to tell the restaurant manager that his mother is sick and has no assurance that his job will be there when he returns. If he returns.

The day passes slowly. Only a few workers at the bureau file out for lunch. Zhihong is frugal and has probably brought a meal packed by his wife, or maybe he prepared lunch for both of them. He knows nothing about how they order their lives so he fills in the details, always casting Zhihong as an unhappy participant who's desperate to escape. Dawei starts walking southeast, away from the centre of Beijing with its ministries and embassies and tourist draws, to find cheaper food.

Having settled his growling stomach with two ears of boiled corn that a vendor sold for the price of one, Dawei continues walking around the quieter neighbourhoods outside of the Fourth Ring. He walks slowly to conserve energy and because he's tired from a lack of sleep, but he must keep walking. If he rests, he might sleep right into evening and miss Zhihong again.

After a few more hours, Dawei positions himself against a steel pedestrian bridge support not far from the east-side security post, watching another procession of civil servants file out. With all of the corn's energy absorbed by the long walk, Dawei feels pangs of hunger return. But they disappear as soon as he sees someone with a familiar gait. The man's head is turned toward two others he's walking with. Dawei remembers one of them from the night he met Zhihong. He went gambling with the rest of the group that left Zhihong, alone and drunk, to settle the bill. Dawei recalls how he felt sorry for Zhihong in that moment. The man with the gait reveals himself as Zhihong as soon as he faces forward, filling Dawei with equal parts hope and dread.

Zhihong stops to check a message on his phone. He nods to the others who continue walking east towards the Second Ring. Most of the other employees head in the same direction. Some climb a pedestrian bridge to the residential blocks across the street where Dawei was evicted from a bench sometime before dawn.

His stomach churning with the acids of hunger, Dawei approaches Zhihong who's tapping out a message as people rush around them. He is oblivious to the physiological reaction that his mere presence has triggered.

"It's been almost half a y...y...year."

Zhihong looks up.

"Dawei! What..." He looks back in the direction of his two colleagues who are no longer in sight. He looks at Dawei again, confused, and then scans the crowd as if they'll help to clarify what he's seeing, as if he needs confirmation that he's in Beijing and not Macau. "Dawei, what are you doing here?"

Dawei knew his presence would be a shock but he had hoped for some hint of joy. A smile, at least. Something positive. Instead, he feels like he's been punched in the chest, making it impossible to summon the breath for the obvious reply. To find you. To see you. To talk to you. "It's been half a year."

"It hasn't..." Zhihong looks again at the people around them and then at the security post he's just walked through.

Knowing exactly how many days have passed since the last time Zhihong visited him in Macau, Dawei wants to spit out the exact count. But again, the mixture of confusion and frustration in Zhihong's stare creates an emotional front that Dawei doesn't know how to breach.

Zhihong grabs Dawei's wrist and tries to lead him away. Dawei doesn't move. He just looks at Zhihong while grounding himself onto the pavement under the soles of his worn-out shoes. He wants something, anything, from Zhihong before he will budge.

"I waited for hours here yesterday and d...d...didn't see you," Dawei says, drawing strength from the ground he has secured.

Zhihong clenches his fists and looks around again at the minions in motion, the security post, the commuters trotting to the street who are hailing cabs and those checking text messages as they head toward the subway station.

"Dawei, I'm sorry it's been so long." He pauses. "You think I don't care at all?" Zhihong stands, hands open, palms facing the sky to somehow prove his impotence.

The question Zhihong asks doesn't need an answer. It comes out full of anger directed at circumstance, not at Dawei, which gives him a sense of hope. But Dawei still wants more before he will budge.

"I can explain what's happened," Zhihong says. "My department has been cracking down on expenses. They check everything. I can't even steal an extra few hours to get over to see you."

In the silence that follows, Zhihong continues looking at Dawei. People walk around the two of them in the afternoon rush hour throngs. Zhihong seemed threatened by them before but now seems too lost in anguish, too tired and resigned, to care about who might bump into them.

"Every time I go, I think I'll make it over but I never get the chance. I understand this hurts you but you need to know that I'm just as hurt."

The anger drains from Zhihong's expression, leaving only the sorrow that Dawei saw so often when they shared with each other the details and disappointments of their lives. Sorrow is their bond and, as long as the bond remains, this trip isn't a waste of his time. He'd gladly return immediately to Macau if he could get some kind of commitment from Zhihong that they'll be in each other's lives somehow. The embankment, which now only reminds him of Zhihong, won't sadden him as much if he knows that they will meet there again. For the first time since he stuffed his backpack and departed Macau, Dawei sees the possibility of a positive outcome. This is why movies have happy endings. They reflect life. People endure hardships and challenges, their faith is tested, and then they're rewarded. No one can expect to arrive at his destination without knowing hunger or fatigue along the way.

"Wh...wh...when do you think you'll make it back to..."

"Eh! Zhihong." The voice cuts through the rough clatter of traffic and movement.

A man who's just passed through the bureau's security gate, who is somewhere in his 50s and wearing a suit that looks sharper than the other bureaucrats, hurries up to Zhihong and grabs his shoulder. The gruff voice reminds

Dawei of his father.

"Eh, Zhihong, Where were you this afternoon? I was looking all over for you."

Zhihong turns to face the man with a smile and puts a hand on the man's upper arm. The face-to-face positioning leaves Dawei blocked out of the interaction and he sees discomfort behind Zhihong's smile.

"Don't worry, Gao Hua spoke to me about it. I'll have the details for you tomorrow," Zhihong says, scratching his brow.

"Morning or afternoon?" the man asks as he pulls a pack of cigarettes out of the inner pocket of his suit jacket. "I have a meeting with the division head in the afternoon so I need it early, ok?" He offers Zhihong a cigarette and Zhihong declines.

"No problem." Zhihong says, keeping his back to Dawei.

"Ok, see you tomorrow," the man says as he turns to leave.

Zhihong bids him farewell and then looks at the ground, rubbing the back of his neck. His phone rings and he pulls it out of the holster attached to his belt to look at the display.

"Hey. Yes. In a few minutes. Yes, I'll pick some up."

Zhihong puts the phone back into the holster. Slowly. And he doesn't look up at Dawei.

This isn't like the movies. The silence is too drawn out. Characters should know what to say to each other. Or, in the middle of a sidewalk on a busy street in Beijing, they could at least smile. They shouldn't miss a beat, let alone stand through an endless stretch of time during which dozens of people pass and Dawei becomes aware that the sun has moved behind the trees that line the street. The air is colder in the shade.

"Dawei." Zhihong breathes in and then sighs. Something about the exhale adds to the chill of the shadows.

"Dawei, we can't see each other in Beijing. Why did you come here?"

That question again. Full circle. As if nothing in between had happened.

Still looking at the ground, just inches from the spot that Dawei had claimed for himself, Zhihong reaches into his back pocket and takes out his wallet, grabbing several 100 kuai bills, the red ones, with Mao's face beaming like it does in the portrait above the Forbidden City.

"You need to go back to Macau. I can't see you here."

"But wh…wh…when?"

"Dawei, here's 500 kuai. Get yourself back to Macau. I don't know when I'll get there."

SUNDAY, April 1, 2007

The female officer recognizes Diane. She's the same one who took the copy of Qiang's expired ID card and disappeared into the back room of the PSB station the day before.

In the morning sunlight flooding in through the windows, a janitor sweeps a couple of crushed cigarette packages and some small bits of detritus from the previous day into a pile.

"Good morning," Diane says. "I'm following up on the matter of my brother. Do you still have the documents I gave you yesterday?"

"Please have a seat."

She steps into the back room. Diane sits and pulls her laptop from her briefcase, resuming work on a spreadsheet. The officer comes back out and takes her seat behind the counter.

The morning rush hour traffic outside has slowed to a crawl and the agitated honking drowns out the buzzing tone of the fluorescent tubes that provide no more light than what's coming through the windows. Three men wearing suits enter from the street entrance and approach Diane, two of them taking seats on either side of her. The third man, holding a fake leather file folder, stands. Their suits are dark. Two grey and one navy blue. No ties, plain shirts open at the collar like most other businessmen in the city.

"Can I ask what it is you're doing here?" asks the one on her left, a wiry man in his late thirties.

"I've been trying to find out where my brother is. He's been missing for a week and I think he's been detained by the authorities."

"What makes you think that? Perhaps he's gone away on a trip."

"I'm his sister. If he was going away for two weeks, he would have told me. And I'm not stupid. Are you with the PSB?"

"I have access to some information."

Diane sits quietly, staring at the wiry man for a moment.

"Ok. I understand and I'd appreciate it if you could help me confirm what's happened to my brother."

She reaches into her briefcase and pulls out another set of the copies she gave to the officer behind the counter and hands them over.

"I gave these to your, well, I gave the same documents to the officers behind the counter yesterday. They haven't been able to help me yet."

The man looks at the paperwork and then hands it over to the standing man who slides the documents into his file folder.

"Come back tomorrow morning. I may know more about this then."

The three men wait until Diane leaves before they walk behind the station's service counter and continue through the door on the back wall that leads to a conference room.

"She's going to continue with her inquiries," the wiry man explains to the two others who are seated at a table. "The American journalist I told you about is communicating with another American journalist, one who was previously based here in Beijing and now lives in Washington, DC. This woman in Washington knows the system here fairly well and she's advising him to make noise about this."

SATURDAY, April 7, 2007

From Pierre's balcony, the lights below dance like reflections on the surface of an endless lake. A front of southern heat and humidity mixes with the cool remnants of winter still in the ground, all refracted by dense particulate matter that's been accumulating for several days. The Australian Merlot Jake has been drinking more quickly than he should helps to bring another layer of ethereality to the cityscape.

The wine could use an ice cube but Jake won't throw one in. It would mark him as the imposter he often feels he is, as telling as the rusting appliances in the front yard where he grew up or the old Pontiac Maverick that he inherited from an uncle who lost his driver's license. The car's transmission broke just a few months after he got it registered in his name and Jake left the vehicle to rot when he slipped away from Magnet Hill, Kentucky to attend university in Bloomington, Indiana. Under an ashtray full of squashed cigarette butts, he left a note for his mother and her boyfriend who were, at midday, sleeping off a hangover. In the note he let them know that he was off to college and would call once he got settled. Fifteen years on, he still hasn't been in touch.

From Pierre's terrace, Jake can survey the distance he's put between himself and the Kentucky bourbon, the watery Coor's beer and the frozen TV dinners that would never be seen served at parties thrown by Pierre. From here he can see the headquarters of some of the companies and ministries he writes about and he can tell himself that he's earned his position. He was happy to start covering finance and economics to escape Kentucky and ensure that he'll never need to crawl back there. It's not that Jake is ashamed of where he's from. It's more that he did nothing in particular, at least in terms of academic achievements or award-winning news reports, to secure his position in Beijing's foreign press corps. Nothing that would explain the quick transition from Kentucky to parties attended by international business strategists and intellectual misfits from Oxford and Cambridge, versed in thinkers from Herodotus to Habernas.

Instead, he charmed his way into this milieu. With a custom-tailored tweed jacket and a crisp oxford shirt, Jake drove 16 hours straight from Indiana for an interview with the administrator of a Princeton University study-in-Beijing program. He started by talking about the few months he spent studying in Anhui and how he cherished the tea pot his teachers gave him. Moving on, Jake explained how Kung Fu classes helped him cope with the homophobia, alcoholism, xenophobia and general bigotry of his hometown. The Princeton administrator was an academic, somewhere in his late 40s, who had spent years studying Eastern languages and philosophy. Sporting a bracelet of sandalwood beads and a small metal spike through his earlobe – and absent a wedding ring – he seemed to Jake as though he'd be open to possibilities. Throughout the interview, Jake played up his accent but was mindful of his vocabulary, referring to "life in more rural townships" and not "out in the country", casting himself as the outsider who deserved a chance. He managed to get through all 800 pages of Jonathan Spence's *In Search of Modern China* in order to show a degree of historical fluency.

The other applicants, he bet, were all from the Ivy League and wouldn't bother spending an afternoon, or even 15 minutes, stopping by the office to introduce themselves in person. With memories of the Tiananmen Square crackdown still fresh, American students weren't clamouring to study in China in the early 1990s. For Jake, though, it was the most obvious place to go to reinvent himself.

To help seal his acceptance, Jake used the word that academics love. Epistemology. After listening closely for an opening during the interview at Princeton, Jake dropped an idea about the "epistemological limits to cross-cultural understanding" and knew immediately from the administrator's satisfied smile that he was on his way to Beijing.

Jake learned other, simple linguistic tricks. Don't say "What?" Say "sorry?" Say it with courtesy by raising the pitch at the word's second syllable. Say it with a smile and with the mouth closed. He reminded himself that he doesn't have "co- workers". He has "colleagues".

And Jake had one final strategy to ensure his induction into a small corner of the Ivy League. He held eye contact with the administrator a beat longer than what would normally be appropriate, pairing the look with a slightly crooked smile, a stare that was at once challenging and inviting. Challenging as in: "Are you really going to kill my best option to get out of the Midwest?" Inviting as in: "Wanna fuck?"

A few months later, Jake Bradley of Magnet Hill, Kentucky was studying Mandarin in the Middle Kingdom. The administrator added a handwritten note on the acceptance letter: "Hey Jake, *yi lu shun feng*. May the wind be at your back. Call me when you're back in Indiana."

But he hasn't been back to the Midwest since.

Jake had spent years resenting his mother's indifference towards him. She had laughed when, at eight or nine, Jake said he wanted to learn figure skating. Only girls and fags learn to spin on ice like idiots. She mocked the British New Wave music he liked as an early adolescent. Duran Duran, Spandau Ballet, Culture Club. To his mother, the only British bands worth listening to were Led Zeppelin and Jethro Tull. Nothing compared to good old American Southern Rock, though. Tom Petty, Allman Brothers and Lynyrd Skynyrd sang the background to Jake's childhood. His mother played their albums on all occasions, anything from Christmas, when Jake might get a Tom Petty t-shirt as his gift, to the breakups with a series of her boyfriends, many of them accompanied by police officers responding to complaints from neighbours about his mother's shrieks as she ordered another man out of the house.

Jake never wore the t-shirts he got as gifts from Mom, something else that set him apart from the others in his school and neighbourhood. He couldn't bring himself to wear them. This resistance had limits, though. He'd never broadcast his love for Duran Duran, on a t-shirt or otherwise, even though he couldn't get enough of their 1983 album Rio. U2 and Pink Floyd worked, though. Loud and guitar-driven, these bands also clicked with the rest of Magnet Hill's adolescents. His Aunt Tracy brought him t-shirts from the bands' concerts and

Jake wore them until they frayed.

After many years, the sight of frozen dinners and the sound of Lynyrd Skynyrd no longer make Jake tense. He realizes that the frustrations of his early years fed his determination to go far. There's always a limitation somewhere, though. Decades ago it was the Duran Duran t-shirt. Now it's the ice cube he wants to drop into his wine.

Most of the other guests at Pierre's party are sipping champagne, chardonnay or cocktails mixed with vodka and one of the freshly squeezed fruit juices that Pierre's housekeeper had laid out on a table on one side of his enormous terrace. Not a moment passes without the sloshing sound of a bottle pulled from a sweating tureen full of ice.

Inside, Pierre has double-high ceilings over a living and dining room area furnished with contemporary Italian furniture. A twelve-seater dining table consisting of a pane of glass supported by double-stitched, black leather straps supported internally by steel. It is elegant and simple, without any mechanism allowing it to contract because that would weaken the design. In a penthouse apartment, you don't need to conserve space.   Other guests are folding smoked salmon onto water crackers and Scandinavian rye crisps arranged artfully amid at least eight varieties of cheese, a balanced selection of hard, crumbly and soft.

A grand piano sits by the picture window that looks out on the terrace. Having vowed to relearn the basics, Pierre has a young instructor whom he describes as 'very cute'. Pierre offers such details with an arched eyebrow and a crooked grin, a tip-off to anyone paying attention that the piano lessons probably wind up in the master bedroom, up the stairs and behind one of the doors along a mezzanine lined with steel wire bannisters. It's the highest point, atop the tallest apartment building in the neighbourhood of the China World Centre, where partygoers lucky enough to get onto the guest list assemble once every season – laughing, drinking, flirting and dishing.

Jake sees Sugimoto-san step out onto the terrace. A logistics manager of some sort for Japan Airlines who arrived in Beijing two weeks earlier, Sugimoto is the evening's sacrificial lamb, offered up by a few acquaintances at the fringes of Pierre's social circle as a way to stay on his guest list. For anyone in the know, it's basic social capital calculus: give Pierre first dibs on the new arrival and get regular invites to an event offering many more hook-up opportunities as, well as every other sort of networking from career development to hash connections.

This is how Jake became friends with Pierre. He showed up as a plus-one with someone he's since lost touch with. A few minutes after arriving, Jake pulled Pierre aside and told him about a newcomer to Beijing he met at Drag-on the previous night. "He's cute, horny and into white guys. Would it be okay if I invited him up?" The transaction proceeded and turned into the longest re-lationship Pierre had since he moved to Beijing. It lasted nearly a week. Since then, Jake has had license to invite whomever he wants to Pierre's parties.

Jake has already met Sugimoto once, as part of a Thursday evening out at a new Brazilian restaurant, during the newcomer's first weekend in town. They exchanged business cards but haven't called each other yet. Jake will make that move eventually. For now, Sugimoto is earmarked for Pierre, who's descending from the mezzanine with two flutes filled with sparkling wine. Jake knows the glasses are full of Krug, which Pierre keeps chilled in his bedroom. He'll bring one to Sugimoto and toast him privately to welcome the newcomer to Beijing. Pierre will also let him know what he's drinking and that there's more upstairs for later. As someone who got the same welcome reception from Pierre when he arrived in Beijing, Jake knows the tactic well.

Jake retreats to the edge of the terrace and looks down on the foundations of new buildings taking shape around China World where worker housing blocks had stood just a few months ago. The pounding of steel fills the vacu-um between Pierre's building and the China World Towers. But Jake can only observe. Even the former residents of those buildings, thoroughly Chinese and well connected enough to live in a favoured locale, only had a few months' notice of their move to some new suburb outside the Fifth Ring. That notice was delivered in the form of the character sprayed in red paint on their walls. Demolish.

The residents protested by means of a feeble procession orchestrated just before the Lunar New Year when they figured too many of the authorities would be in transit to clamp down. They carried banners that avoided any di-rect demands and no specific target for their anger. The banners, saying "Guo Mao residents looking forward to a joyous New Year," were ironic, written in red characters and evoked the spirit of the season.

Jake saw the protest from his newsroom and decided to take some notes and gather quotes for Qiang. But in the fifteen minutes it took him to ride the elevator down and walk over to the streets that no longer exist, the protest had vanished. Jake didn't look for them because his editors were waiting for a story about the newly-appointed deputy governor of the People's International Bank of China.

Jake looks at his phone to see if Diane has sent any texts. She's supposed to be at the party by now and Jake is anxious about whatever news she will bring. Face-to-face is the only way to communicate with her because new rules implemented by the Telecommunications Ministry make it impossible for anyone to buy a SIM card anonymously.

Knowing they're all tracked closely, Jake has decided that the Public Security Bureau will get one message clearly. Several foreign correspondents are regulars at Pierre's parties. Always eager for a story, they would want to follow Qiang's detention. It's the kind of story that plays well among audiences in North America and Europe, one that the authorities won't be able to ignore once more than one news outlet starts covering it. Bringing Diane into this community, introducing Qiang's closest relative to the foreign press corps, means some of the control in this scenario rests with Jake.

"Nice ass," Ben says, breaking the spell as he approaches Jake from behind. Under his black leather blazer, Ben wears a white t-shirt with a black silhouette of a hand brandishing a middle finger. His jeans and Converse All-Star sneakers completes the punk, hostage-taker chic. A grey scarf draped around his neck softens the look.

"The scarf's a good idea," Jake says as he shakes Ben's hand and then kisses one of his cheeks. "Really, you need a French accent somewhere if you're going to come here and drink the Veuve."

Diane isn't with him. Something about Ben's expression confirms the obvious and Jake tenses up.

"She felt very uneasy about showing up in this crowd," Ben says.

All that's required of her is her presence, Jake thinks. He wonders again whose side she's on. If not on her brother's side, she would have trouble taking this seriously because, well, because people just get plowed under if they stand in front of earthmovers. That's why the protesters in the streets of the Guo Mao district scattered and never showed up again. They knew the endgame.

Why didn't Qiang see the futility of this project? As smart as he is, he couldn't figure out where to stop? Where did he think this documentary project would lead him, doing interview after interview with controversial figures. It was just a matter of time before he was taken away. Now he's just another blip of dissent. Deleted. And Diane's just another one among 1.3 billion people who, in the end, respect the momentum of authority. Putting Diane in a box labelled "Chinese," Jake has clarity on this now, giving part of him a sense of relief. Diane's exactly the person he suspected she might be. But psychoanalytic accuracy won't change Jake's inability to do anything about Qiang.

"She called me," Ben continues. "She's not ready to start talking about the situation. She thinks she might be getting somewhere with the PSB."

"How. In what way?" Jake shoots back.

"Another one of the officers she's been talking to acknowledged the detention."

"That's progress? We've known that for two fucking weeks now. Thanks Diane, wherever the fuck you are tonight," Jake says, gesturing outwards over the balustrade.

"Hey," Ben says. "Chill."

Jake pauses to take a sip of champagne and then leans in to Ben.

"It's almost two weeks since he disappeared, Ben, and nothing. Doesn't that lend some credence to what Kendra said? That they're just going to string her along. Isn't this exactly what they're doing?"

"Jake, you know Diane's been visiting the PSB every day since she's been here, right?"

"I only know what she says. I know nothing about what she's doing."

"Jake," Ben begins in a calm tone, "if she wanted to do nothing, she'd be in Shanghai working, taking care of her three-year-old daughter and not jeopardizing her career. She's taken an extended leave. Not easy for someone in her position. And she's away from her family. Why would she do that if she didn't think she was making progress? That's why I'm willing to give her a little more time."

Ben's tone makes him sound like a therapist. The psychoanalytical approach has the opposite result. Jake sees it as condescending.

"Well, I'm not," Jake says, pointing to a group of guests congregating in one corner. "Maybe I'll march over to Regine from Trask News over there and give her the download."

"Do you think you know more than Diane about how this place works?" Ben asks.

Jake puts his wine glass on the balustrade. He knows his threat to go to other reporters draws on spite and probably went too far. But the audacity of the threat doesn't compare to what Ben is suggesting, so thick with irony that Jake doesn't know where to start.

"And what the fuck do you know, Ben? How long have you been here now? What has it been, five days?"

"I know that I'm concerned enough about this to put my life on pause to come over here, to help where I can."

"You know what Ben?" Jake says, pointing a finger close to his face. "I don't care how you're dressed. You remind me of every American CEO who decides to invest in China. They show up quoting Confucious or Laozi, making some connection between ancient Chinese wisdom and their own business strategy. And you know what happens to most of them? You know what happens to their investments here? They get their asses kicked. And do you know why they get their asses kicked? Because they don't know shit about China. Just...

like... you."

Jake pokes Ben in the shoulder. Ben swats Jake's hand away, sending it into the wine glass which flies outward and then down toward the construction site. They freeze for a moment and then lean over to watch the glass spin and roll and disappear into the abyss of construction lights illuminating patches of grey concrete shot through with steel beams and spindles of rebar. Jake can barely make out the yellow dots, hard hats thankfully, moving below the glare of the construction lights.

"Dude," Ben says. "The question wasn't meant to be a challenge. I'm just trying to figure out what's the most logical course of action."

Ben can't possibly know how many things about him disturb Jake. The history with Qiang. The privileged New England upbringing and Ivy League education that Jake had pieced together through Ben's LinkedIn profile and other sources he'd turned up through Google. Nothing of Ben's background should matter. Most importantly, he seems to be close with Diane. It won't help to give them the impression that he's unstable and he tries to lighten the mood.

"Yep, I get it," Jake says, beginning to calm himself. "It's been a tough couple of weeks as you can imagine."

A moment passes as they study the bustling topography below. In the silence between them, Jake realizes he's gone too far.

"I probably owe you an apology," he says.

Ben shakes his head. "That's silly. If anything, I should be thanking you for your concern about Qiang."

Jake doesn't want to hear this. If Ben was more of a jerk, Jake could handle the situation in his own way.

"Well, you can thank me by getting me another glass of wine."

Ben chuckles and puts his arm around Jake's shoulder. A purely platonic move, but the embrace still sends an invigorating buzz through Jake. He wonders whether he's attracted to Ben or just hard up for sex since he hasn't had any since Qiang disappeared.

Emerging from the crowd, one of the guests sidles up next to Jake and peers over the edge.

"What's the attraction down there?"

"Greg, hi," Jake says, forcing a smile. He needs to stifle the anger. "This is Ben. He's a friend of a friend, just in Beijing for a few days."

"Pleased to meet you, Ben. Are you also a reporter?"

Greg would want to know. Journalists, PR account managers, and industry analysts must all know each other. Their objectives are at once distinct and overlapping. They exist in a self-sustaining ecosystem like fish, plants, algae and bottom feeders in an aquarium.

"Ben, this is Gregory Nell. He runs Greater China for Whitewash Communications," Jake says.

Smirking, Greg holds his hand out. "I never get tired of that joke, Jake."

"Pleased to meet you," Greg says as he shakes Ben's hand. "The firm is actually called Whiteboard Communications. And, yes, I'm what's known to some as a spin doctor." Looking back at Jake, Greg enunciates the term, eviscerating it.

"Thanks for getting me on the guest list," Greg says to Jake.

"Reward me by lining me up with a CEO who can talk about something other than his love for shareholders."

"Ah, that little gem keeps everyone out of trouble," Greg says.

"Seriously, Greg, you guys are getting so good at your job there's almost no point in interviewing anyone here anymore. No one can even confirm the time of day anymore."

"Jake, these companies are now listed in Hong Kong and New York, or aiming to be," Greg says. "You know this, mate."

"I get that, but now it's worse here than in Hong Kong and New York," Jake says. "You guys are instructing them to say nothing to any Western reporters."

"It's not about them or me," Greg replies. "It's about you. You and Trask News and TRADEWIRE and all the others are under more pressure than ever to move share prices. Do you know how many corrections I've had to ask for because of reporters playing fast and loose with comments made by my clients? These guys need a bit of protection."

"You've never needed a correction from us," Jake says.

"Remember what I said last week, Jake," Greg says. "If you can't beat us, join us. Come to the dark side. You could be in a senior position in less than a year."

Greg has made the offer before and Jake has always waved him off. At first, Jake stuck with journalism because of a genuine interest in China and the adventure reporting trips provided. He just happened to finish his language training in China when the newswires were clamouring for stories from the country, so he stayed in the country he had grown accustomed to, where nothing is stagnant, where it's so easy to ride the rapids of transformation to something more exciting and where nothing is like it was in Kentucky or Indiana.

Journalism also offered Jake something else that made his life easier: a degree of social protection. Moving into finance, as many of his classmates in Beijing did, meant he wouldn't need to come up with false stories of women in his life. Jake never wants to get into frat boy banter about tight pussies. The only ones he ever saw were in the magazines his father left lying around the house to use as coasters. Currency and bond traders don't like cock unless it's their own. The press corps was generally more open-minded about anything, including sexuality, than the testosterone-addled members of the finance industry.

Greg's line of work might not be as stridently masculine as finance but PR managers need to work closely with clients, often treating them to meals and drinks, creating lots of space filled with conversation about family and living arrangements, territory that a semi-closeted gay man in Asia can't easily meander through. Jake knows Greg wants to bring him on board for the optics. A youngish, Mandarin-speaking American vaguely reminiscent of Robert Redford, familiar with the do's and don'ts of China could help Greg attract more business from American multinationals as well as publicly traded Chinese companies. But he's not sure that Greg, knowing Jake is gay, has thought through all of the implications. The idea had enticed him at one time, just ahead of his ten-year mark as a reporter, when he wondered how much longer he would stay with a career that didn't inspire him and thought about how nice it would be to turn left when boarding a plane and have a flute full of champagne waiting for him as he sits.

Such thoughts had ceased, though, when Qiang arrived in Beijing. As he became friends with Qiang and learned how to size up the quality of sources, Jake recommitted himself to journalism. He helped subtitle the interviews Qiang shot for his film and the work had been a constant reminder of the importance of good reporting. It pushed Jake to work his sources for better quotes. The key to a good story isn't just the information or the particular action, he had learned. What motivates decisions? What motivates action? Such details can turn the most mundane story, something one might feel they need to read, into something one wants to read. A year of friendship and work with Qiang helped Jake evolve from a lightweight reporter who covered press conferences, wrote up announcements, "scrummed" and "doorstepped" government officials to a mid-weight. He hadn't turned into a Pulitzer Prize candidate, but at least he had become someone who could pull together decent feature stories, some worthy of a front page. Perhaps, he thought, he was making a difference somehow. Throughout this evolution, Greg's attempts to recruit Jake had become more amusing than enticing.

But now, confronted by how little control he has over Qiang's predicament, Jake re-evaluates the importance of his work. Curiosity turned to cynicism and cynicism has become apathy. Is it really worth the trouble? Most journalists either fade away as they climb the ranks of news organizations, taking up roles behind the scenes as senior editors, or they wind up in public relations, twisting objectivity towards sales objectives and keeping the vast machinery of economic growth intact.

Or, like Qiang, they wind up missing.

"So tell me, Greg," Jake says, finally, "how dark is the dark side, really?"

Ben returns with a glass of red wine, which he gives to Jake.

"Truce?"

*****

The guests have coalesced into distinctive groups under a canopy of bossa nova lounge music playing through Pierre's invisible sound system, a network of overhead speakers integrated into lamps at four corners of the rooftop terrace. Worn down by the confrontation with Ben, Jake takes in bits of conversation around him. Gwen Stefani will play in Tokyo. The sad state of "millennial" foreign students flooding into Beijing who are more interested in Facebook than exploring the city. Then again, Beijing's most interesting corners are now construction sites so adventures are more difficult to find. Anecdotal evidence that HIV rates are rising because too many local gay guys think they won't be infected as long as they don't fuck foreigners. The Bird's Nest, the Water Cube and other Olympic venues are almost ready and worth checking out even if you only get to see the tops of them behind construction barriers.

Having lost count of the number of glasses of wine he's consumed, Jake disengages from a group of a few others talking about how Turkish Airlines has great deals on flights from Beijing to Muscat. It's the new must-see place and, with the opportunity to make Istanbul part of the trip, who wouldn't go for it?

The good wine now gone, Jake rinses an abandoned rocks glass with a splash of San Pellegrino and then pours in some Johnny Walker. And then some more. Greg has vanished. Sugimoto and Pierre are no longer present. Jake will find out tomorrow if that transaction closed.

"Hey Jake, I got some news for you," says a familiar voice approaching from behind. "Make sure you have plenty of whiskey in that glass."

Regine speaks in her precise South African accent, smooth as honey and all the more magnificent through the filter of peak buzz in the heart of Saturday night. Regine and Jake have spent hours together in hotel lobbies and other venues waiting for Chinese Central Bank and Finance Ministry officials. Eventually they forged a somewhat co-operative relationship, agreeing to "truce" when it looks like the chances of a comment are slim and sharing notes with each other to make sure they got the story right.

A self-labelled "rice tart," Regine only dates Chinese men. With long, strawberry blonde hair, blue eyes and fair skin, Regine is a dead ringer for Nicole Kidman.

"News?" Jake says. "Regine, I don't do news. What time is it?" He looks at his bare wrist, confused, before remembering that he left his watch in a hotel room in Dalian a week ago. The second one lost in as many years, so now he uses his cell phone display as a replacement. One less thing to keep track of.

"Well, I'll tell you anyway because you need to know this," she says, smiling and grabbing Jake's watch-less wrist. "The Foreign Ministry is watching you."

The comment doesn't register immediately. It's as if Regine is talking about someone else. They keep tabs on all foreign reporters anyway. Jake then pictures the connections between himself and Qiang's documentary and the guy Qiang was interviewing, laid out like a graphic element in a news report. His heart rate picks up, snapping him out of his buzz like a sudden wind clearing smoke. Jake runs several scenarios through his head, the worst of which involves a knock on the door late at night.

"How does a financial news reporter like you get on the Foreign Ministry's radar?" she asks.

The question is a form of respect, posed as much to congratulate him for stirring up shit as it is out of curiosity. With too many thoughts in his head, Jake can't respond and Regine's expression changes from playful to concerned.

"Jake, does it have something to do with your friend and his documentary? Qiang, right? Are you helping him with that?"

"Subtitles," he says. "I'm just doing subtitles. Where did you hear that they're watching me?"

Regine leads Jake to a quiet corner of the terrace.

"I'll tell you but, Jake, you can't mention anything about this."

"Of course."

"I'm telling you this because I'm concerned about you. If you talk to anyone else about this, or how I know this, someone else will get into a lot more trouble than anything you would ever face here."

"Regine, I understand. I swear I won't say anything."

"One of your Chinese reporters was asked about the stories you're working on. You know, in the regular meetings that we're not supposed to know anything about. I'm pretty tight with my assistant. She told me this came up. Some questions about whether Toeler News was getting into political reporting."

The spies among us, Jake thinks. Foreign news outlets in China must source local assistants through the Diplomatic Service Bureau and everyone knows why. Not that anyone cares anymore. Cell phone interception and improved surveillance technology now give the authorities a direct line into the lives of journalists. Most of the Mainland Chinese newsroom assistants just want to be in a profession that allows them to use their foreign language skills. DSB-appointed assistants aren't supposed to do more than arrange interviews and translate but, in practice, many of them report and write stories from top to bottom. Some even get bylines. The DSB hasn't cracked down, at least since anyone can remember. Regine is obviously tight with her Chinese colleague, showing how the system has holes and moles.

Regine looks around. "Where is Qiang, anyway? He's usually at these soirees, right?"

Jake stands silently but wide-eyed, like a hostage trying to communicate over the shoulder of his captor. Regine pulls a pack of cigarettes out of a small purse made of a colourful Yunnan batik fabric. She shakes the pack until two sticks protrude, offering one.

"Jake, has Qiang been detained?"

"I've promised not to mention anything about what your colleague told you," Jake says as he takes the cigarette. "So, I need you to keep what I'm about to tell you under wraps, at least until I say it's time to report this."

Jake urinates into the stainless steel trough that runs the width of the men's room at Destination. Purple lights and black walls intensify his buzz and the delirium of physical relief. He had needed to piss when he left Pierre's party, but Ben was close to the bathroom and he didn't see any way into a casual conversation. Music from the bar pounds through the wall and the smell of urine rises from the trough, mixing with gin and tobacco fumes.

Jake sees the guy next to him in his peripheral vision. His head is cocked slightly as he checks out Jake's dick. Equally blatant, Jake looks down at his neighbour's business. In the low purplish light, the piss is translucent, glowing with the colour of cigarette smoke. Their streams resound where they strike the metal, emanating at slightly different keys.

As the force of the streams wane, Jake looks up, meets the guy's stare and smiles. Somewhere in his 30s, the guy has a very fair complexion and a strong jawline, classically northern Chinese. The guy smiles back and then looks down again.

"*Hao kan*," he says. Good looking.

Jake isn't sure if the guy is referring only to his penis or if he thinks the whole package is hao kan. Not that he cares too much either way. This is going well enough to help him bury the frustration and fear that has built up throughout the week, the sort of irresponsible and reckless activity that one must engage in, Jake thinks, when nothing else is working out.

The flow of piss stops for both of them and they're now doing the shake, for longer than necessary. And the shakes become strokes.

Two other guys stagger up to the trough on Jake's left side. As they fumble with their zippers, the one closest to Jake almost falls backwards and adjusts his stance to regain balance. Once their dicks are out, the unstable one notices the stroking. He leans forward to get a better view of the display, teeters a bit and puts a hand on the trough's rim, covered in droplets of urine and moist pubic hairs, to steady himself. Jake moves closer to his playmate on the right and turns to face him, close enough to smell vodka on his breath.

Turned on and completely erect, Jake wraps his fingers around the guy's penis and strokes it. He then works the guy's jeans lower and feels his scrotum, only vaguely aware of others around them, some lingering and giggling out comments too slang for Jake to understand. The guy is completely hard as Jake brings his hand out and handles his penis again. Jake then brings his hand to his nose and mouth to breathe in the guy's essence. Organic, like damp leaves in autumn. The guy grabs Jake's dick. Spurred by the smell of booze and saliva and sex and the perversity of the setting, Jake moves in and begins kissing him, scissoring jaws and wrestling tongues, one hand massaging the back of the guy's head and the other continuing the slow masturbation.

"*Wo men yi qi hui qu, hao ba?*" Jake says. Let's leave together.

"My boyfriend is outside," the guy whispers in accented English.

"Nice," Jake says. "Bring him along and we'll take turns fucking you."

The idea of a threesome excites Jake so much that he feels a surge of energy that could trigger an orgasm, so he backs his hips away.

"He do not…" the guy says before exhaling a quick moan as Jake fondles the head of his penis. "He do not like foreigners," he finally explains.

From the bar just outside the men's room, Jake hears shouting though a megaphone. Everyone begins stuffing their dicks back into their pants. The stern voice pierces the pulsing dance music which then stops abruptly.

"Fine then, we can take turns fucking him."

In the sudden silence, Jake's voice booms. Bright light from the bar area floods the restroom and several men walk in as the voice from outside barks orders. Jake's playmate withdraws like he'd been electrocuted. He turns towards the wall to do up his pants.

The sudden rush of fear and confusion concentrates the energy that had been building in Jake. Two of the men who had just entered wear uniforms. Two others wear polo-style shirts and dark slacks. The moment Jake realizes this is a bust, the escape instinct morphs, uncontrollably, into the first pulses of an orgasm. Fighting for control, Jake turns to the wall to shove his dick into his pants but the sensation of his own hand against the head of his penis combined with nervous energy in the disorienting haze of purple light causes the eruption that sends white gobs into the urinal trough. Jake arches his back and puts a hand on the wall to steady himself.

The uniformed men and the plain-clothed officers push the others, including Jake's playmate, out into the bar area.

Jake shudders. The spasms abate and he turns around. There's only one officer left in the bathroom, holding a video camera pointed at him.

"Jie-ke Bu-la-de-li," the law enforcer says as he closes the viewfinder. They know his name. "*Ni waiguoren keyi zou.*" You foreigners can leave.

In the cross currents of post-orgasmic release, shame and paranoia, Jake walks out through to the bar area where police officers are checking ID cards. Some are singled out and sent toward the exit where Jake is heading.

Jake understands most of the comments the police are barking. The Mainland Chinese are in for drug tests and some might also be charged with *liumang zui.* Hooliganism.

Jake looks at the lineup one last time and sees the guy he was fondling just a couple of minutes earlier held next to the police officer barking out orders. The guy looks up at Jake. They might as well be on opposite sides of an ocean. Jake can only look back with an expression meant to show solidarity but probably looks like stupidity to the one who's now facing a night in jail and an embarrassing new entry in whatever dossier they had on him.

May, 2005

Dawei sees people coming out of the restaurant in a row of storefronts across the street from China World Center. A China Construction Bank branch on one side; on the other, a florist selling flowers he's never seen before. Huge ones with petals too large to be real and stamens glistening with nectar. He knows the restaurant is expensive because the lights are dim, lit by fixtures with countless pieces of dangling glass shrouding bulbs that throw very little light. Western people seem to like dim places. Now many Chinese too, especially the rich ones.

Dawei has practiced his speech so that he won't stutter. But he won't go in until he knows more about the place.

Two young Western women exit together and stand just outside the door, one of them licking white rivulets running down her ice cream cone. They wear t-shirts and athletic pants. Both have some kind of mat rolled up and slung over their shoulders like they're going camping. Even the wealthiest Westerners wear casual clothes which makes it difficult to figure out how important they are.

The two women start giggling, as though the ice cream makes them deliriously happy. Ice cream is cheap and available everywhere now. Why would anyone order it in such a place? A dim restaurant that caters to Westerners is where they usually serve large slabs of red meat in individual portions, each with a bowl of uncooked lettuce and vegetables that they call sha-la.

Everything used to be dim. And dim used to mean ordinary and cheap but now it means expensive. How ironic.

The bare light bulbs in his home in Yongfu burned dimly enough to see every detail of their glowing filaments. He hated those light bulbs once he saw how everyone in the big cities had as much light as they wanted.

During those few months when he lived with Auntie and Uncle in Harbin, it was possible to do homework at night. Everyone said that would help Dawei catch up with the local kids but, for Dawei, it only illuminated the gap between himself and the others. Auntie scolded him. She said he couldn't keep blaming his grades on the poor conditions of Yongfu, especially since he had the chance to make something more of his future while the kids of Yongfu could only expect a hard life growing corn or soybeans.

Now there's plenty of light everywhere. All of the new grocery stores and building lobbies have fluorescent tubes so bright they turn windows into mirrors when it's dark outside. Bright, pure light is everywhere. It's become so common that the special places are the ones that seem to have gone dim, like the one he's looking into. The boss of the restaurant in Macau wants to replace the fluorescent tubes with something that gives the place more qi fen. Ambiance. He's talked to electricians but only ends up arguing with them over how much that would cost. Something about "co-ordination" and the need to replace everything, including the menu. So the bright lights remain in the dining room, the same ones that light his washing station and the rest of the kitchen, though the boss keeps some of the ones in the dining room turned off.

The bright places now are where you work and do ordinary things and the dim places are special. So why are people coming out of such a nice, dimly lit restaurant with ice cream?

The women finally stroll away and Dawei approaches the window for a better look. He's so hungry that he would even eat sha-la, the raw lettuce and carrots and other vegetables that Westerners serve with their hunks of beef. Not ice cream, though. He knows how sweets can make an empty stomach hurt. Since he arrived the night before, he's only had an orange he found on the ground at a night market and a handful of roasted chestnuts.

The late afternoon sun has moved behind China World, cutting the glare enough to see more clearly inside. Customers linger in front of a large case in the front of the restaurant which displays twenty or so different flavours of ice cream. There's a dining area just as pristine as some of the best restaurants he's seen in Macau, with carpeting and tables surrounded by upholstered chairs. Those seated wear jeans. One has a collared, short-sleeve shirt with a small insignia over the heart; another has a hooded jacket. Clothes that now cost so much more than the suits and button-up shirts that Zhihong wears.

The women have handbags with metal bangles hanging off their hinges, the ones that can cost thousands of kuai in the new shops of the expensive shopping malls near the Forbidden City. They're also available in some street markets for less than 100 kuai.

In the dining area, everyone's dish has ice cream arranged artistically, topped with bits of twisted chocolate and fruit Dawei doesn't recognize. There are no proper meals on any of the tables, even for Westerners - no seafood or meat or sha-la. Also, no one is drinking wine or beer or even baijiu. Why would the owner of this restaurant take the risk of serving only ice cream in such a well-furnished setting at such an expensive address? And ice cream drips everywhere.

The customers in front of the display case study the options as though they're choosing jewellery. The attendant hands some of them tiny plastic spoons, each with a small quantity of ice cream. Dawei wonders how much each of the small scoops cost because some of the customers get two or three. He strains to see the price list. The cheapest option is eighteen kuai. That could cover him for two days in Beijing or Macau, a week if he still lived in Yongfu.

The prices go all the way up to 260 kuai, which makes Dawei wonder what else could be included besides ice cream.

Dawei steps back to look at the name of the restaurant. Two words, in what looks like English, with a hyphen between them. He learned to recognize what's English and what's Russian when he lived in Harbin. He recognizes the letter that starts the English alphabet. The letter A. There's a few of them in the name.

As Dawei leans backward trying to make sense of the name, the employee from behind the ice cream counter opens the door and leans outside.

"Hey, are you looking to make trouble here?" he snaps, holding the door open. He makes a sweeping motion with his free hand.

The question puts Dawei off balance. He doesn't know what he's done wrong. There's nothing secret about what's going on inside. If there was, why would they have such a big window? The attendant must be the manager. Otherwise, he wouldn't care so much about what Dawei is doing outside.

"B...but I...I...I...,"

The manager glances at Dawei's canvas running shoes, now wearing through near the base of both big toes.

"But, I wanted to ask for a job here. I...I...I've been working in a restaurant in M...M...Macau for..."

"Just move on or I'll call security," the manager says as he looks back towards the counter. Two groups of diners are waiting to pay.

The other attendant behind the counter looks harried, prompting the manager to trot back. The door closes gently, pushing out cool, vanilla-scented air.

SUNDAY, April 8, 2007

The Latin jazz is audible from the street, discordant against the mechanised female voice, stern and direct, emanating from buses plying the north Second Ring Road. "Attention, attention…"

A double column of soldiers on the north side of Dongzhimen rounds the corner, marching in perfect synchronicity into the embassy district. The light green of new leaves on the massive oak trees that line the streets of diplomatic compounds had created a refuge until groups of North Korean defectors began rushing the gates of several embassies a few years earlier. Once an oasis for expats looking for a quick escape from the churning construction noise and bleakness of wide, monumental avenues, the neighbourhood wound up in news reports worldwide in the form of images of refugees climbing walls and hurling themselves through entrances guarded by security personnel unable to cope with the chaos.

The Chinese government responded by erecting banks of extra fences around all of the buildings and stationing pairs of army cadets on every corner. Jake and Pierre continued to patronize the few restaurants in the district and would sometimes wink and smile at the cadets to see what kind of reaction they'd get. But Jake will keep the looks to himself now that the authorities have footage of him climaxing in the bathroom of a Beijing gay bar. Thoughts about where or when that footage might emerge interrupted his sleep three times overnight.

Jake opens the door to Beijing's first Cuban restaurant and bar. The syncopated rhythms and fairy lights strung through the fronds of fake palm trees on each side of the bar manages to create an air of Caribbean warmth even though it's pure pastiche. Two women of some kind of mixed ethnicity step back and forth, shaking maracas, adding texture to the tunes played by three black men seated on stools behind them. The décor is a better attempt than most in Beijing. At least the lights glow in   uniform amber rather than the usual blinking variety in every colour of the spectrum.

The tables are mostly full, occupied by a roughly even split between foreigners and Chinese. Scanning the bar, Jake spots Ben and starts weaving his way through the tables. As he approaches from behind, just a few feet away, he hears Ben talking to the bartender in Mandarin. Jake then stops and turns so that his back is to Ben, close enough to hear the conversation, and brings his cell phone up to his ear, nodding his head as though he's having a conversation. He doesn't want the bartender to acknowledge him.

Ben's Mandarin is fluent, probably more so than Jake's. They're discussing Beijing's transformation in recent years.

"The embassy district just outside is about the only area in this part of town that looks as it did when I was a child," Ben says in perfect intonation. The Beijing accent is just prominent enough to endear him to the locals and not enough to interfere with the clarity of his speech.

Jake remembers Ben telling him, just a few days ago, that he first visited China with Qiang and had only been in the country one other time. A quick calculation puts that timeframe of those visits within the past eight or so years.

"Things were bound to change quickly," the bartender says as he muddles mint leaves in a tall glass. "But the Olympics have really changed the scale and the pace of the development. No one can afford to fall down in this effort. That would bring them too much trouble."

"*Kai tian pi di,*" Ben says.

"Right. You're absolutely right," the bartender says as Jake hears him finish stirring the drink and plant it in front of Ben.

Ben has thrown out an idiom that Jake's never heard. There are only about five or six that he knows well enough to throw into a conversation as a natural rejoinder. Idioms separate the fluent from the merely proficient and Jake is stuck somewhere in between. Intensive language study in a tier-three city in Anhui Province, away from the English-speaking world and a self-imposed exile of sorts, helped Jake learn the language faster than he had expected. The immersion prepared Jake to conduct interviews in Chinese as soon as he started working as a journalist. It gave him an advantage over many other *laowai*s in the gay bars. It helped him make China home for however long he wanted. As long as the conversation wasn't philosophical or technical, Jake felt confident enough.

But some foreigners speak with native fluency. They studied Mandarin for many years or had lived in China or Taiwan as youngsters. Some just had a knack for languages. Ben's Mandarin puts him in this group. His grasp of the language is too natural for him to have picked it up from a lover in California and a couple of trips to Beijing.

After listening for another minute, Jake moves back towards the restaurant's entrance, keeping Ben in his peripheral vision to make sure he's not seen. He steps outside and waits a few moments before re-entering. Once back inside, he moves quickly towards the bar, walking directly up to Ben.

"Hey," he says, taking a seat next to Ben.

"Hey dude, how's it going," Ben says, putting a hand on Jake's shoulder before turning to the bartender. "We're going to move to a table. Can I move the bill to the table," he asks in English.

"*Mei wenti*," the bartender says. No problem.

Ben jumps up and leads the way to an open table furthest from the bar and the band. No tip. Another sign of his familiarity with local customs.

"So, where did you disappear to last night," Ben asks with a smile as he slaps both of his hands on the table in front of him. The spread of his elbows opens his blazer, revealing an elaborate Jefferson Airplane tie-dye underneath. He hunches forward over his hands and forearms, waiting for the answer intently, as if whatever Jake says will be the most entertaining thing he's heard in years.

"Sorry about not saying goodbye," Jake says, leaning back in his chair. "I can lose my manners when I've had a few too many."

"Say no more," Ben says, putting a hand up. "Wherever you wound up, I hope you got a chance to blow off some steam. This whole thing is too stressful and I'm sure Qiang wouldn't want everyone to be cloistered in fear and anguish."

Blow off steam. Don't be cloistered. Jake doesn't like the tone of Ben's suggestion. The comments are just a shade away from something overtly sexual like, "I hope you're getting out and fucking around." It would probably reassure Ben to think that only a small part of Jake's life revolves around Qiang. That the matter they're trying to resolve can be compartmentalized, left to Ben and Diane as the plot thickens and, of course, left to them when it's resolved. So Jake lies.

"Nope. I just went home."

"Right." Ben just nods and then looks around the restaurant as if he might find in the crowd another subject to keep the conversation flowing.

"So, how are you finding Beijing," Jake asks. "I suppose it's not easy to get around if you don't speak the language."

"Well, I can speak a little bit. Qiang taught me some."

Ben runs a hand from his forehead to the back of his head, the kind of move that probably became a habit when he had a full head of hair, wild and grown out. The kind of look consistent with Ben's personality and dress code.

"Ah, good. Like enough to tell a cab driver where to go, or..."

"Oh, just the basics," Ben says as he leans forward again. "Look, I just wanted to meet up to make sure we're ok."

Subject changed. Jake can't help but get stuck on how he doesn't want to talk about language skills.

"We're okay, Ben."

As the words come out, Jake realizes they're short and sarcastic. He doesn't mean for his answer to sound like that. Or maybe that's exactly what he means. He just doesn't know what level of his consciousness is driving his response.

Looking away, Ben nods his head in a knowing way that suggests he heard more the insincerity and less the words.

"You know what, Jake? I get it."

"Get what?"

"You're in love with Qiang."

Jake clenches his jaw and looks over at the Latin jazz band, noting the fluid precision of the women stepping back and forth, hips jutting to the beat as a way to detach himself from the conversation.

Jake likes to think of Ivy League types as people who aren't necessarily smarter than anyone else. They benefit from circumstances they never created, most of them nurtured in intellectually stimulating environments, not just in the classrooms of the best schools but also in museum galleries and on tours abroad, all funded by inexhaustible deposits of wealth. Jake knows this is a generalization but nurtures the idea just the same because, he feels, his background gives him license to do so. Rich fuckers have the judicial system, the financial system and the tax code on their side. People born to white trash should be allowed to hate them indiscriminately if it provides some comfort. So Jake doesn't want to be confronted by a member of the elite who's genuinely perceptive and intelligent, who would have probably excelled regardless of his background. He won't give Ben any satisfaction. So Jake will lie again.

"Love is kind of a strong word, Ben. I like him a lot. I have, on occasion, wanted to get into his pants, of course. But love?"

"Ok, fair enough. I just want you to know that I'm not here to undermine whatever it is you two have. I also want you to know that I think we can be friends. You seem like an interesting guy. From Kentucky to Beijing. A journalist covering some crazy stories, I'm sure. Let's just say I admire you. I admire your guts and ambition. I just…"

Ben pauses. These comments take Jake off guard and he doesn't know how to respond to them. He wants to apologize but it seems impossible, as though some part of his mind refuses to allow his mouth form the words. Apologies create vulnerability.

"Jake, I just don't think it helps any of us, not you, not me, certainly not Qiang, if we're not supporting each other."

Enough, Jake thinks. He doesn't want to be confronted with the injustice of his own thoughts.

"Ben, sometimes…" He stops and takes a breath. "Sometimes I just don't know how to let my guard down."

A smile spreads slowly across Ben's face. "That's the spirit, my friend," Ben yells above the music and the chatter from the tables around them. "Let's get some mojitos. They're every bit as authentic here as they are in Cuba."

"Wait, how does an American get to Cuba?"

For a moment, Ben seems at a loss for words. "Ah, good question."

Ben puts one hand up to the side of his mouth and looks from side to side in a hammy, overly theatrical move. "I also have a Canadian passport," Ben says, winking conspiratorially.

This additional detail about Ben's background brings Jake back to the question surrounding his perfect Mandarin but he holds it aside.

"I've only ever been to the tropics once. A trip to Indonesia." Jake says.

"*Bisa bicara Bahasa Indonesia*?" Ben asks. Can you speak Indonesian? One of the few bits of language Jake managed to retain from the basics he learned on a recent trip to Bali.

"No way. You speak Indonesian also?"

"I like languages," Ben says. "And I like the tropics. Indonesia has some of the best dive sites in the world. And such amazingly friendly people. I spent a month there and made it a point to learn as much of the language as possible."

"I study it in my spare time because… well, I guess part of me wants to move there sometime."

A waitress comes around and Ben orders two mojitos, in English.

"You're a bit of a mystery, aren't you, Ben?"

"Well, if I seem mysterious, there's one thing I want to make completely clear. I will do whatever is necessary to help get Qiang out of this spot he's in."

"Then I guess we should get back to the matter at hand. I wanted to let you and Diane know that I'm going to have access to a U.S. representative who's coming here as part of a trade delegation from North Carolina where all of the textile mills have been put out of business. His name's Blake McKee. McKee's tight with the administration and my friend in Washington tells me he's a direct line to Condi Rice. Just imagine what kind of influence we'll have if the Secretary of State gets invested in this."

"How can I help?"

"Just let Diane know that I'm not going to let this opportunity pass by. I know she doesn't want any publicity but I fail to see how being quiet is going to help."

"You can tell her yourself," Ben says.

"I would, but when would I ever get the chance? She didn't show last night. I don't want to discuss this over the phone and…"

"She's right behind you," Ben says with a smile.

Jake turns around to see Diane approaching the table. He looks back at Ben, puzzled.

"I think you'll appreciate what she has to say.

Diane is seated between Jake and Ben with her hands wrapped around a mojito. "My approach isn't working," she says. "I've come directly from the PSB. My fifth trip. I've come, how do you say it in English, full circle."

Looking tired, she speaks in a monotone, a kind of deadpan delivery that Jake recognizes as a way to keep the emotions from pulling her apart the way a small leak in the thickest dam can turn into a torrent that tears apart the entire structure.

"I thought I was making progress with the first group of people I talked to. I told them that I'd keep quiet and I'd make sure that all of Qiang's friends here remain quiet. They've acknowledged that Qiang is under investigation. They didn't use the word "detention" or "arrest" but I didn't expect that much. It was enough to have a discussion that allowed me to show the authorities some respect. But the tone has shifted. Qiang, they now tell me, has been in regular contact with dissident groups outside of China, many connected to foreign governments. The details change each time I talk to someone different and never is a shred of evidence presented."

Ben puts a hand on Diane's shoulder and Jake looks down. A waitress brings their meals of roasted pork with black beans on rice.

"I know my insistence on complete silence has caused you to doubt me, Jake. It's caused you to doubt my intentions. I'm sorry that I insisted on this. I had no right to do that."

Jake puts a hand on Diane's forearm.

"We don't know, none of us knows, what the best course of action is, Diane."

"Hey," Ben says. "Let's pick up the mood here! We're three smart people. Well connected. We're going to crack this one way or another. You both might think I'm crazy but I just know that we're going to see Qiang again soon."

Ben hails a waitress. As he orders the shots, Jake feels a psychological reprieve. Stress has a way of burning itself out, at least temporarily. Jake has a theory based on absolutely no knowledge or evidence that when his nerves become worn and need a rest, all of the synaptic energy that fuels stress and worry will cease. Ben's words, and the promise of a tequila buzz, have led him to this point.

"You know, Qiang and I aren't so different. We were both drawn to the U.S. by the silliest of things," Diane says.

Ben laughs. "I know this story." He begins to sing in a rich tenor, full of vibrato.

"If you're gooooing to Saaaan Fraaaanciscooo..."

Diane puts a hand to her mouth and laughs. She smacks Ben's shoulder with her other hand.

"Stop," she says. "You need to let me tell the story!" She looks at Jake. "You know the song, right?"

"I would sing the next few bars," Jake says, "but my voice is so bad you'd both cringe. Believe it or not, I didn't hear the song until I was in university in Indiana. It's not the kind of song that gets much play in Kentucky. My dad used to call San Francisco a place full of faggots and freaks. But I remember the first time I heard it playing from a dorm room down the hall from me. I wound up introducing myself to the student playing it just to find out the name of the artist."

"C'mon blondie," Ben shouts. "Let's hear you sing!"

"In the streee-eets of Saaaan Fraaaancisco, gentle people with flowers in their haaaaairrrr."

The people at the table next to them smile and clap. Grinning, Jake bows his head in appreciation.

"So, the song was one of the few American cultural exports that made it into China in the 1980s. It was on a bootlegged cassette tape with other songs by The Carpenters and other artists that I learned later are seen as corny."

She begins singing. "There's a whole generaaaatioooon with a new explanatioooon. People in motioooon; people in moootioooon."

"Bravo!" Ben yells, making Diane and Jake laugh.

"There was something in those lines that...that...moved me," Diane said. "Especially set within such a beautiful melody and sung by a man with such a beautiful voice. Anyway, one year, during the New Year break, I brought the cassette home. Qiang and I listened to the song endlessly. The whole attitude of the song was so much the opposite, the polar opposite, of everything we knew in China where all the messages were about struggle and fighting the enemy."

Diane's smile disappears. "And then, a few months later, we got word of what was happening in Tiananmen Square. We wanted to join the students but we felt compelled to stick with our classes until the end of the semester. Qiang and I were both at Nankai University in Tianjin. I was a year ahead of him. As the older sibling, it was up to me to keep him in class. I reminded him how much our parents sacrificed to help us get into a good university."

"I hope you don't regret that," Ben says.

"Well, when classes ended, Qiang and I began preparing to join the other students in the Square. But they started limiting the number of buses and trains heading to Beijing. By the time we found a way to get in, by pretending to be workers, news of the crackdown started to reach us. Many people killed. And then we heard hundreds of people killed." She pauses. "And then there was complete silence and we knew things were very bad. Next, we decided to apply to graduate programs in California, you know, the place where, as the song says, gentle people walk with flowers in their hair."

"So, a terrible tragedy and a beautiful song led you both to California," Ben says.

"It's just so ironic how things went from there," Diane says. "I mean, we kind of grew apart. I wound up going back to China to pursue a career in finance while Qiang ended up sticking with his ideals. I think, deep down, Qiang resented me for convincing him not to join the demonstrations in 1989."

Diane looks as if she's re-examining the outcome. Jake can almost see her thoughts, the irony that Qiang was destined to be detained at some point. He doesn't know whether it would be helpful to point this out or if it would add to the scorn Diane has heaped on herself for letting her brother out of sight.

"There's one thing I forgot as I chased my career," she says. "The fact that I'm the older sibling," Diane says. "I'm his older sister. I know his disposition. I should have been looking out for him more closely. I've failed many times when it comes to this responsibility."

"How do you mean?" Jake asks. "You stopped him from going to Tiananmen Square, right?"

"I'll give you an example," Diane says as she rearranges the condiments and the salt and pepper shakers in the center of the table. "Qiang and I had some of the same classes in grade school. In one of them, the teacher made a mistake on the chalk board. An incorrect character. The teacher was old, starting to lose his bearings. Qiang raised his hand to point out the mistake. I knew what he wanted to do. I sat next to him but didn't grab his arm in time."

"So what happened?"

"The teacher didn't see the error. Qiang got up and walked to the chalk board to point it out, and the other kids began to laugh at the teacher." Diane stops and fiddles with her phone. Jake can see that she's holding back tears.

"Qiang wasn't laughing, though," she says. "He just wanted the error corrected. He felt compelled. He couldn't help himself. He in no way intended to embarrass the teacher. He just wanted everyone to be clear. The others were immature, or at least not nearly as mature as Qiang. Their laughter infuriated the teacher and Qiang paid for that for the rest of the school year."

"And you blamed yourself for this?"

"The truth is, I just don't know anymore what the right thing to do is," Diane says as she lowers her head and begins to cry.

"You said it yourself, Diane," Jake says as he grips Diane's wrist more tightly. "Qiang needed to make things clear. That's what he's been doing with the documentary film. How could you have stopped this? None of us could stop him. I knew this was risky. The more I reminded him, the less he wanted to listen."

Diane pulls a tissue from her handbag and dabs her eyes, tracing the underside of her eyeliner.

"So what do you think we should do now?" she asks as she crushes the damp tissue into a ball and tucks it into her bag.

"All I know is that we need to do more than listen obediently," Jake says.

"I agree, and I have something for you," Diane says. She reaches into her bag, pulls out a thumbnail drive and puts it in front of Jake. "Pass this to one of your friends in the foreign press corps," Diane says. "I don't recommend that you publish anything on this."

"What's on this," Jake asks. "And why can't I do anything with it."

"It's a paper trail of payments made by Beijing Capital Land to one of the members of the International Olympic Committee. Ben helped me connect the dots."

"Shit," Jake says, looking at the USB and then back up at Diane. "But..."

"We want this information to have some impact but not too much yet," Ben says. "Bribing one IOC member wouldn't have handed Beijing the win against the other cities. We think we can find paper trails for remittances from China to other IOC members but that's going to take some time and the three of us are going to have to work together."

"So," Diane continues, "we can't let the authorities know that you have anything to do with this story. That's why you can't publish it. We need someone else to publish it so they don't suspect us."

"Even if you find more, what difference will it make?" Jake asks. "Didn't the U.S. bribe IOC officials to get the Salt Lake City Olympics, what, just few years ago?"

"We don't know what effect it will have. Whether or not the U.S. played the same tricks, Beijing's not going to want this getting out. We want this to be a warning shot, something that will make the Foreign Ministry uneasy," Ben says. "Later, when the time is right, if necessary, we let them know where this story is coming from."

Jake wonders how long Diane and Ben have been working together to produce the information on the USB stick. The thought then makes Jake confront his own poor judgment about them. Diane, in particular. How easily he threw her into a category and tagged her as someone willing to acquiesce completely to the authorities. It was in the midst of anger, Jake realizes, that he formed his opinion and refused to reconsider it.

"When you're covering the trade talks with Congressman McKee, I'm assuming you'll be working next to other reporters," Diane says.

"Yes. I will be able to pass this stuff to my friend Regine at Trask News. My main objective was to get your letter and the documents about Qiang to McKee and I was kind of hoping that McKee would help get this all resolved."

"He might," Ben says. "But he might not. That's why we need a plan B and a plan C."

"So details about IOC bribes is plan B. What's plan C?" Jake asks

"Let's not go there yet," Ben says.

Jake pauses. "Ok, then I just have one more question."

"Shoot."

"Can you both forgive me for being such an asshole?"

May, 2005

The first direct rays of sunlight over a building across the street wake Dawei from another troubling dream.

He's in large apartment. Modern, like the lobbies of so many of the new buildings he's passed in Beijing, spaces with objects that don't define themselves clearly and where he can't figure out what's artwork and what's a seat. Or where uniformed security guards stand awkwardly against clean white emptiness. Dawei is looking for something that he needs to give to his parents in Yongfu. He doesn't know what he's looking for, only that he'll know when he comes across it. But in a space full of strange objects, all Dawei knows is that he's an intruder and he's likely to be discovered by someone who knows he doesn't belong. Dawei runs for the exit but can't figure out which door will let him out. None of the doors has a knob, just keypads like on a phone, and none of them will open without the correct number. Dawei's only option is to turn and fight off the attacker.

When Dawei used to wake from a bad dream in Yongfu village, his mother would calm him by explaining matter-of-factly that bad dreams never become reality. Bad dreams have one benefit. Whatever they depict hasn't happened and won't happen.

Dawei has had many troubling dreams since he left Macau a week ago. Dozing on park benches doesn't let him descend to the depths of sound sleep. Hard work makes one too tired for bad dreams, his father used to say. And Dawei hasn't been working. Instead, he's been wandering aimlessly, trying to figure out where he might be able to work.

He rights himself into a sitting position and looks around for one of the vendors that sell roasted chestnuts. One of them is from a village in northern Heilongjiang Province not far from Yongfu. Dawei recognized the accent and started a conversation. The vendor gave him some extra chestnuts yesterday but must be elsewhere this morning.

As he cracks one of the few remaining chestnuts, Dawei eyes a travel agency across the street. He ties up the plastic bag with the rest of the chestnuts and puts it under everything else in his backpack: an extra t-shirt and pair of socks that need laundering. A separate plastic bag with a bar of soap, a toothbrush and a small tube of toothpaste. A manila envelope holding several photos of him with his parents and with Auntie and Uncle. Also, the plastic folder containing the screenplay that Zhihong gave him. He's tried to read it a few times but always ends up getting lost in the illustrations that the author drew in the margins, some of which snake around the lines of dialogue.

He's in an older neighbourhood, further away from the city centre, where the surroundings look like the area where Auntie and Uncle live in Harbin, where the stores are more familiar to him. He finds a main thoroughfare lined with mature trees that spread out and provide the whole area with shade and flanked by bicycle lanes separated from the vehicles by wide dividers.

He opens the screenplay again and descends into the story to pass the time until the travel agency opens.

Standing in the shade in front of a display window, Dawei eyes a giant model of an airplane with Air China livery that sits at a slightly upward angle on a stand in the window. The plane, more than a metre long, is banked to one side as though it's really in flight. Dawei's never seen a passenger jet in such detail. He's only seen them as tiny pellets in the sky, trailed by white lines and moving so slowly he wonders why they don't fall out of the sky. The chestnut vendor told Dawei that many people take airplanes because prices have fallen. Some travel agents can't find enough people to deliver tickets. He said his nephew in Harbin is making good money delivering tickets on his bicycle and is saving enough to open his own travel agency in the next couple of years. Some travellers are too busy to go to the airline office or to a travel agent themselves. They order tickets over the phone, pay with the numbers on their credit card and expect the ticket to be delivered within hours. Sometimes even within the same hour.

Dawei enters. There are no customers and the four chairs in front of the counter, just a few steps away, are empty. But Dawei doesn't draw any attention from the two women who sit behind the counter, each talking on their phones, mechanically quoting prices and schedules.

Several smaller airplane models sit on the counter. China Eastern Airlines, Hainan Airlines, another one has English words on it and what looks like the solid red circle on the rear fin, the Japanese flag. A small, plastic oscillating fan buzzes back and forth on the left side of the counter causing the smaller model to rattle.

The younger of the two women wears a pink blouse with a drawstring around the neckline and the older one, somewhere in her 40s, is in a dark blue blazer over a t-shirt with a foreign word spelled out in shiny round dots. D-K-N-Y. Both women fixate on their computer screens as they continue rattling off numbers and airline names. It doesn't seem to matter that no customers are present and that the four chairs in front of the counter are empty. A third phone, in between the two women, starts to ring. They both ignore it.

Dawei approaches the chair in front of the younger woman but doesn't sit. He leans in to see the front of the computer screen. He's never seen one so thin. They look like the televisions he's seen in the lobbies of expensive buildings, hanging like paintings.

Without moving her head, the younger woman looks up at Dawei. They lock stares for a split second and then she scans Dawei down to his waist. Dawei knows what she's trying to determine with the small sliver of attention she's giving him while she exchanges information with the client at the other end of her phone line. The client apparently needs to be on the earliest flight to Shanghai tomorrow but doesn't want to pay more than 500 kuai. She seems to know that Dawei's not going to buy an air ticket, though, and so Dawei needs to speak up quickly. And he mustn't stutter.

"I...I...want to know if you need anyone to deliver tickets," Dawei says.

The woman points to her colleague and her eyes focus again on her screen. The middle phone continues to ring. The other woman, probably the owner or at least the manager, is talking about flights to Hong Kong.

"Twenty-eight hundred, if you want the first flight out tomorrow. There's only one airport in Hong Kong," she says impatiently. The boss glances at Dawei much the same way as the younger one and looks back at her screen.

"If you want cheaper, you can fly to Shenzhen and take a bus or a train over the border. For twenty-two hundred. Hello?"

She drops the receiver into its cradle and picks up the middle phone which has been ringing nonstop since Dawei walked in.

"Yes? Shenyang? When are you going?"

He feels his cheeks flush. Every interaction like this cuts him down by another centimetre. This one is so pathetic he'll lose half of his height. If he doesn't learn to stand his ground now, he will become too small for anyone to see. "Give up and you'll wind up washing dishes here or sorting soybeans back in Yongfu," Auntie used to say before the explosion that sent him from Harbin. That's how she and Uncle left northern Heilongjiang to become engineers in Harbin. Dawei's own parents, who spent their school years on communes reading Mao, never had a chance to escape.

They recounted the story of Auntie and Uncle's accomplishments, how they forfeited sleep and drove themselves to the limits of exhaustion to study for the university entrance exams. Dawei knew the stories were meant to motivate him to work harder in school but they began to have the opposite effect every time he had trouble understanding what was on the blackboard. Once they found a way to get Dawei to Harbin for his last two years of high school, after paying bribes and forging papers, Auntie continued the motivational efforts that often tipped into harassment. "Don't give up or you'll be back to washing dishes."

"I...I...just want to know if you need anyone to deliver tickets," Dawei says, loud enough to interrupt the boss.

"Hang on a moment," she says to the customer on the other end of the line. She points at Dawei, sending a jolt down his spine as he starts to shift his weight to turn and leave.

"Do you have a bicycle?" she asks without a note of offense or aggression. Dawei nods.

"No. Not you," she says into the phone. "You think I'd suggest you ride a bike to Shenyang? Hang on a second."

She raises her head, chin forward, signaling to Dawei.

"Sit down. I'll be with you soon."

Dawei looks at the row of bikes under a canopy of corrugated metal between two residential buildings in a neighbourhood marked by the character 拆, a character that he now knows means demolish. A breeze blowing the leaves of the mature oak trees nearly drowns out the hum of traffic on the east Fourth Ring. He sees parents returning from work, walking quickly with plastic bags in hand and elderly residents watching their grandchildren chase each other around broken benches and clamouring around a derelict water feature of rocks sloping down into a basin that looks like it's been dry for a decade.

There are more than 100 bicycles, a jumble of colours muted by a uniform tinge of brownish grime. Some of them stand out because they've been wiped clean. Or maybe they're just new. Most are the ordinary one-speed variety with built-on locks that loop through the back wheel. Pressed together, they form a kind of giant industrial python. He knows he can snap any of the locks on the one-speed bikes by bracing the back tire between his legs and ramming the lock with the heel of his palm. He saw Uncle do it to Auntie's bike when she lost the key. The canopy will block the view of anyone looking down from the old brick buildings. To be sure, though, he'll come back at 2:00 or 3:00 a.m. He won't steal a new bike or an expensive one. Even if he wanted to, they have newer locks of metal braids encased in plastic. He notices that several of them look abandoned, covered with a layer of particulate matter so thick that it masks all colour and detail. Dawei will take one of them.

MONDAY, April 9, 2007
7:52 p.m.

The PSB investigator searches her database for Gregory Nell's cell phone number. She's received a report that Nell is with the American journalist, Jake Bradley, who is having a drink at the bar in Aria. Part of the sprawling China World complex, the bar and restaurant is popular with expats. Various national security bureaus station operatives at Aria to gather intelligence on foreign companies, on which banks are negotiating debt deals or structured loans with which manufacturers, on which UN officers are meeting with which NGO's and which diplomats are chummy with each other.

A mobile technician notified the PSB investigator that the American journalist's microphone isn't accessible. He's probably taken the battery out, though he's not likely to suspect that the PSB knows who he's with or that they can tap Greg Nell's phone.

Happy hour at Aria has been a habit for Jake since the place opened, a refuge of candlelight and jazz, like what he imagines night spots are like on New York's Upper West Side. Jake usually looks for many of the same associations that the intelligence officers are there to note, at least until his third glass of wine, at which point he no longer cares.

Contemporary, earth-toned velvet chairs are arranged in random clusters around coffee tables with inlaid geometric designs. Some of the larger clusters have love seats that well-dressed patrons recline into as they sip red wine and frothy beer. In front of the windows looking onto an east Third Ring fly-over jammed with traffic, a woman with bleached blonde hair sings "Stormy

Weather" in a deep, tobacco-leavened voice. Wearing a deep purple, baby doll dress under a black leather petticoat, she's backed by her pianist, a black man wearing a fedora and a crisp, white shirt.

Jake sees Greg come out of the dining room, dressed in a grey suit and carrying his weathered leather briefcase. One curl of his wavy hair hangs down over his forehead interrupting the square-jawed symmetry of his face, like Superman. Jake wonders if he checks periodically throughout the day to make sure it's hanging correctly. How often does Greg re-shape it? What time is it anyway? Jake's been nursing his third or fourth glass of merlot since last call for happy hour. Maybe the fifth?

"What client were you dining with and what news can you divulge?" Jake asks as Greg sits next to him.

"Such a warm salutation. It's good to see you too, Jake. Sometimes I wonder why I keep pushing you to go into PR."

"Fuck you."

"Ah, the charm never stops."

"Oh Greg, you put up with me because I turn more of your PR pitches into real stories than anyone else in this city. Do you know how many fights I've been in with editors over stories you've pitched."

"Indeed." Greg summons the bartender. "I'll have the *Bunnahabhain Islay* twelve year and, please, give this gentleman another of whatever he's having."

Greg reaches for the finger bowl of bar mix from which Jake has picked out all of the pretzels and almonds, leaving only barbecue-flavored corn chips which Jake believes intensifies dehydration. "Ok Mr. Bradley, since you're so keen to cut to the chase, two things. First. Are you interested in joining us? There's a position opening in Hong Kong that pays probably double what you're making now."

Double? Close to a quarter million a year? The number clears Jake's mind of all other thoughts like a gunshot in the woods silences birds. With this money, Jake could become, several years from now, a real New Yorker and not someone who simply imagines what life is like in New York. Magnet Hill, Kentucky would no longer be a place he is from. Kentucky would become nothing more that a place where he was merely born. It would become a place where all the taunts and indignities he suffered could be placed, like cheap objects, in an imaginary box that he can toss into some dark corner of his mind.

"Double? Really?"

"Well, almost," Greg says as the bartender sets down their drinks.

Jake now has nearly an entire bottle of wine in him, on a stomach that's empty save for a few salty snacks. This makes it difficult to pair the random thoughts racing through his head with any values. He sees images of modern, open-concept Manhattan apartments with blonde wood flooring and stainless steel kitchens, spaces as pristine as those in Architectural Digest. These images compete with the dark of the room that Qiang might be occupying. Or the cell. Or the grave. Perhaps there's nothing he can do and he'll need the uncomplicated luxury of a pristine condo to finally give him the gratification that's always seemed so elusive.

"You know, you could make an argument for double," Greg says. "The company is desperate for Mandarin-speakers with strong ties to the financial press."

"Um, it's not so much about the money."

Greg looks perplexed.

"I mean, the timing is kind of bad," Jake says.

"Mate, the timing couldn't be better."

"Except that…" Jake sorts through the set of possible answers, everything from 'I'll send you my CV tomorrow' to 'I'd make a terrible PR manager and you know it.' All of them right and all of them wrong, depending on what lens he uses. All of them vulnerable to defeat.

Greg leans in towards Jake with a curious expression.

"I'm trying to help a friend who's been detained."

"Oh yes, that," Greg says as he takes a sip of his scotch.

"That? You know about that?"

"There's some talk going around about that. Your friend the documentary film-maker, right?"

Jake looks at Greg, trying to process the way he has reduced Qiang and the horror he's living through to one syllable – "that" – thrown into the conversation like he's clearing his throat.

"How do you know about that?"

"Mate, please. You know it's my job to know all of the reporters here. It's a group that's quite aware of what's happening in this town, especially if it involves one of their own."

"Right," Jake says before taking a big sip of wine. There's obviously more to PR than just spewing spin. The information-gathering part of the work might be just as rigorous as it is for journalists. And then there's corporate filter, the fractious and conflicting interplay of legal, marketing and finance. What is factual isn't necessarily in the interest of the paymaster. What isn't factual might become so with the right qualifiers. Something to keep in mind.

"So, what are you doing about this? How does your job help you resolve this problem?"

"Let's just say I'm working to create some leverage that might make it more difficult for the authorities to hold him. It will be easier to do this in my current job."

"How so?"
Jake shakes his head. "I don't want to jinx things."

The PSB investigator searches "jinks…jincks…jinx." She then begins writing a report for the file around Qiang's case.

The American journalist, Jacob Bradley, [passport #655293884, work permit: VR-345-7554] is preparing activities that will put pressure on authorities within the PRC government to release Sun Qiang. No details about these activities were divulged in the conversation.

Surveillance facilitated via China Mobile directive issued by PSB, Beijing, Chaoyang district, RWS-5766-32445-dd

A detailed transcript of the conversation he had [09-04-2007; 19:52 — 20:03] with Gregory Nell [UK passport #QR-6884-931] at Aria, a restaurant at the China World Hotel, follows:

MAY, 2005

Jake wakes for the third time.

He was up earlier, stumbling through the inadequate dawn light towards the bathroom to wash down an Advil with handfuls of water from the tap. The bottle of mineral water next to the basin was empty and he didn't want to bother navigating to the kitchen for more. That would have required him to walk all the way around the bed, a path littered with clothing, a couple of used condoms, and a semen-encrusted rag. Besides, there's only a very small chance, he'd once heard, that a glass of water direct from the tap would make someone sick. The local treatment system takes most of the contaminants out. With his head pounding, Jake only wanted to fall back to sleep as quickly as possible, letting the Advil's chemical properties soothe the pressure and hoping that the half-pint of raw Beijing water he'd consumed didn't contain anything that would spark a bout of the shits.

An hour later, Jake was woken again by the shifting of weight on the mattress, the clinking of a belt buckle, the padding of bare feet on the wooden parquet floor, the splash of urine followed by a flush. Jake pretended to sleep through all of it, through the moment of silence after his guest, a Malaysian Chinese called Tommy or Dickey or perhaps Harry, stepped out of the bathroom. The guy was standing by the bed, probably deliberating whether to bid Jake farewell and suggest an exchange of numbers. Jake kept his eyes closed and breathed with a hint of a snore, hoping a deep-sleep act would drive Kenny, or Timmy, away. Nice ass and abs, Jake thought, but the cigarette breath was a problem. The guest, whose now-dry semen glued together some of the hair on one side of Jake's chest, left the bedroom and made his way through the living room. He slipped into his shoes, closed the front door and Jake fell back to sleep.

With the third awakening, a start to the day is possible. Jake's headache has now mostly subsided and the thin slices of sky he sees through the blinds are blue. That can only mean that a cool front has moved through, pushing the smog east, and would explain why he feels chilly even under a sheet and blanket. He rolls out of bed and tugs the blinds open to reveal a clear sky above the towers, eight of them laid out in two rows of four, surrounding a large grassy courtyard with a tennis court on one side and a small playground taking up the corner closest to Jake's building. A wall, which helps keep the grass healthy and the walkways free of litter, and two guarded entrances surround the entire complex. Surrounded by an oasis of green, a couple of grandparents stand behind a toddler on the playground's swing set, alternating pushes. The kid sits on the middle swing, inanimate as a doll.

Jake flicks off the air conditioning and opens some windows.

Pierre messages.

```
weather amazing … brunch? … i'm going to get a table
at the greek place in second embassy district.>

perfect … i will b there in 30.>
```

Jake fills the electric kettle, smacks the boil button and trots over to the bathroom. He jumps in the shower where he shampoos the gooey build-up of styling paste out of his hair. After drying off, he digs out a fresh blob of paste which he works around his hair into what Pierre calls the "just-fucked" look and pulls on a fresh pair of jeans and a t-shirt. Back in the kitchen, Jake grabs a pinch of Dragon Well tea leaves from a canister next to the stove, throws them into a mug and pours in the boiled water with enough force to make the leaves swirl around and settle quickly to the bottom. Jake watches, hypnotized, as the leaves unfold and turn the water a pale greenish-yellow. In this quiet space, Jake wonders how much longer he'll stay in China. Will it be a matter of months, years or decades?

Jake blows on his cup to cool the tea and takes a few sips to clear the clouds in his head. He pulls on a denim jacket and shoves a wad of cash into his front pocket before stepping out and locking the door behind him.

A young couple steps out of the elevator on Jake's floor and the doors shut behind them before Jake can hit the call button. "Thanks a lot, assholes" he mutters.

One of the two elevators is permanently on service because people are still moving into his building, the last one to be completed in his development. It will be another two or three minutes before the operational one comes back. He pounds the call button again, uselessly.

The couple is out of sight, around a corner. Keys rattle and Jake hears one of them say something about how many *laowais* live in the development.

"Fuckers," Jake says under his breath.

Throughout his first years in China, he couldn't walk anywhere without hearing *laowai*. Outsider. Foreigner. Some Chinese insist it's a term of endearment. "Foreign friend," they say. But Jake's been in China long enough to know. No one has ever called him a *laowai* to his face. It's only used when those who say it think he's out of earshot or that he won't understand. He's heard Chinese people use the term in places like Paris, Washington and Sydney to refer to the locals. That, he's convinced, shows that the word, whether those who use it realize this or not, doesn't mean "foreigner." It means: "he who is not of us."

Some of Jake's Chinese friends agree that the term might be rude but only depending on the inflection and tone. Most never think about it, though. They just say it. "The *laowai* wants a haircut." "The *laowai* wants the check." "The *laowais* don't understand." And Jake can no longer hear the word without clenching his teeth and his fists.

The elevator finally arrives. Jake steps in, catching the eye of the only other person inside: a young man leaning into one of the back corners. The strap of a navy blue satchel is draped over one shoulder and the bag rests on his opposite hip.

"*Zao shang hao*," Good morning, Jake says, giving him a friendly smile with a slight bow. The greeting is more angry provocation than greeting. Strangers here don't address each other in an elevator. He knows it makes locals uncomfortable. Occasionally though, if the stare remains locked after the initial exchange, or if intuition gives him a green light, Jake turns his expression into a smile. A practiced look with subtle gradations of urgency and intent. But the sneer isn't yielding the response Jake wants. The young man in the elevator is neither switching off nor signaling that he's open to a chat. He just looks confused.

Cute, Jake thinks as he turns around to lean against the back wall and looks up at the floor indicator. High cheekbones and a prominent Adam's apple. Jake loves that combination on Asian guys. But there's no point trying to push this one any further.

The doors close and he sees in his peripheral vision that the guy is still looking at him. Another second ticks by, the elevator begins to descend and the stranger continues to stare. Jake doesn't get it. Foreigners have lost their mystique to all but tourists from the interior, construction workers and other labourers. None of them would be in this elevator on a Sunday morning. This dude's dressed like an urbanite: a t-shirt with a neon green beverage logo splashed on the front and a pair of baggy shorts. Cross trainers, badly worn and scuffed with one of his big toes nearly breaking through. But cross trainers nonetheless, instead of the usual all-purpose fake leather dress shoes.

Jake looks again at the curious stranger who appears to be somewhere in his late twenties. A uniform buzz cut nearly to the scalp suggests that he's just been released from an army boot camp, jail or a Buddhist monastery. He looks shell shocked and something about the stare intensifies the headache that has returned since the Advil Jake took at dawn has worn off.

Jake has spent years being stared at and called a *laowai*, every time trying to ignore the slight or to swallow it and move on, even though each swallow enlarges a tumor of anger somewhere in his gut. A figurative tumor for now but, Jake often wonders, how long will it take for this anger to combine with the dense particulate matter in Beijing's air and petrochemical-coated food to produce a real one?

Jake now wants to shove this guy against the wall, hard enough to pass the anger on. He wants to deliver a shock that will leave an impression that the stranger has probably never imagined he'd get from a *laowai*. Jake would pin him against the wall, hands above his head, fingers entwined, and continue to press his body up against this guy. Chest-to-chest, groin-to-groin. He would place his mouth just over the stranger's ear and ask, in a slow whisper, "What would you like to know about me? I can tell you anything you want to know. I can tell you everything I like to do. I can tell you what I'd like to do to you. Then, you can tell me what you'd like to do to me." Jake's mouth would linger by the stranger's ear, so close that he could feel the folds of skin on his lips, close enough to let his hot breath communicate the intent. Then, as they would both breathe heavily, he'd bite the stranger's ear lobe, hard enough to make him want to bite back as the only defense because his hands are pinned against the cold metal of the elevator's walls.

The elevator stops. The door opens and no one's in sight. Jake smacks the close-door button. He wonders whether his thoughts were audible. They echo in his own head with the energy real enough to possibly have a life of their own. Real enough to have been uttered. Isn't this how insanity starts? How unfair is it to connect this stranger to everything that Jake decides is wrong about an entire country?

The stranger shifts his weight and opens the flap of his satchel, looking at its contents as though the papers inside are children.

Frightened by the flash of anger that has just welled up in himself, Jake decides to strike up a conversation. A friendly exchange to tame the chaos of his thoughts. So he looks back at the stranger, meeting his stare again, this time with no intent.

"You live here?" Jake asks, using a thick, gravelly Beijing accent.

The stranger looks down, his eyes darting between several spots in what appears to be an effort to think of a response. Strange that he would have to. Beijing folk are rarely at a loss for words even when they don't want to talk.

Jake looks up to see how much longer the trip to the ground floor will take. 9... 8... 7...

"I'm delivering an air ticket." The voice is muffled and he's still looking at the elevator's floor, making him sound as though he's trying to take back the words as he speaks.

"Huh, you deliver on Sundays?" Jake says.

The stranger responds with a quick nod as he puts a hand on his satchel in which he probably has several more tickets destined for other travellers in the neighbourhood. His gaze remains fixed to the floor.

Of course. People book last minute all of the time now. How quickly that change had crept up. Just a couple of years ago, securing an air ticket was almost as bureaucratic as applying for a visa. Passport, work permit, residence permit and maybe a few other documents were necessary to satisfy the sleepy staff at the CAAC office. After filling out lots of forms, you'd get a ticket with an itinerary that you'd need to plan around. Few options. High prices. Payment in foreign exchange certificates.

How much that's changed. Flight times are now seemingly limitless. Tickets can be delivered to your door within an hour or two, even on a Sunday morning apparently.

Jake looks at the floor indicator again and thinks about what he'll order at the restaurant with Pierre. He's all but forgotten the stranger he was fantasizing about just a few seconds ago. 4... 3... 2...

The doors open and Jake steps out. As he turns toward the exit, he hears the stranger speak up.

"Do you live here?"

Jake stops and turns around. "Yes. Just upstairs."

Jake wonders how much to engage. He doesn't want to be rude but his hunger has turned from a generalized feeling into audible stomach churns.

"I really like this location. It's very convenient to where I work."

The stranger gives him a very fleeting smile. Jake senses that it's forced but he appreciates what has obviously taken some nerve.

"Are you from Beijing?"

"I'm f... f... from the northeast, originally. I've been here for just a short time."

Jake nods, unsure of how he should follow up. He offers his hand. "My name is Jie-ke," he says, using the transliteration of his Western name as he holds his hand out.

He no longer uses the Chinese name which his teacher, impressed by a pledge Jake made at the time, gave him many years ago. He's been doing this a lot lately, the gradual abandonment of the name, Ben-de, which means "source of rightness." The name is one of the last connections he has to his first years in China when the country was a different place and Jake was a different person. Back when Jake would take two-day train trips to far away, during which he'd chat all day with passengers who gave him watermelon seeds and boiled eggs and wanted nothing but his stories in return. They just wanted to know about the details of an ordinary life in the U.S. Whether his family owned a car. Is it true that Western parents make their children leave home when they are teenagers?

"Y... y... your Chinese is pretty good," the stranger says, taking Jake's hand uneasily, varying the strength of his grip like he's trying to find balance.

The stutter probably explains why this guy is so timid. He doesn't say Harbin or Shenyang, the industrial cities that anchor the region, just "the northeast" which is as much a condition as a physical delineation, much like "the midwest" to Americans. The northeast means corn, soybeans and isolated farming hamlets that haven't changed much since 1949.

"I've been in China for quite a few years," Jake says. "I should be able to speak the language after so much time, right?"

The stranger doesn't answer. He looks at the security guard standing by the door in an ill-fitting, drab olive uniform. He then looks at a young woman sitting on a bench in the lobby, a stark three-storey space with solid white walls and a floor of gray slate. The stranger then looks up at a sculpture of metal strips painted red, pink and orange, with some sections twisted randomly and others where the strips are woven together to look like fabric under a microscope, angs from the ceiling on steel wires.

The woman sits impatiently on the edge of the bench, which is made of the same gray slate as the floor. Dressed in black slacks and a crisp white blouse, she keeps one hand on a binder at her side. A cell phone rings and she reaches into her purse, a colourful designer piece with a chain link strap, to answer it.

"What? No. I told you this was a waste of time," she snaps at the person on the other end. "They're going with a unit in Season's Park. Why didn't they say they wanted the Second Ring? No. Just forget about it. I'm not wasting any more time on this!"

Her voice echoes, amplifying the sculpture's tension. The woman shoves the phone back into her purse, mumbling a stream of incomprehensible accusations in one angry exhale. She stands, adjusts her purse and walks toward the door. The clicking of her glossy black heels on the slate floor echoes throughout the lobby, sharp and unrestrained like angry punctuation.

Jake doesn't know where this is going. He's hungry and his Sunday is, as usual, slipping away too quickly. In another few hours the dark clouds of Monday, threatening another deluge of acquisition and interest rate rumours, will be on the horizon. But the idea of ending the exchange seems wrong, like walking away from an injured cat.

"So, what's your name?"

"Dawei."

Dawei is now looking directly at Jake, no longer needing to focus on the ground. Jake doesn't sense that Dawei is looking to practice English or sell calligraphy or promote a cousin's moving company and, all at once, he remembers what it's like to feel diminished by unfamiliar surroundings. Back when he was a "source of rightness," Jake would have made time for this guy. It might, in some small way, help him address the pledge he made to repay the kindness that delivered him to the gates of Anhui Normal University in Wuhu so many years ago. The pledge moved his teacher to give Jake the auspicious name that amuses many other Chinese because, they say, it sounds quaint and antiquated.

Wuhu, after the start of the reform and the opening up, and before email, was typical of hundreds of small cities whose residents had seen foreigners only in newspapers and television broadcasts. The place wasn't what Jake expected while he was in Indiana waiting for his visa to study in China. No plum blossom groves. No limestone peaks poking through tufts of pure-white mist.

When Jake stepped off the train in Wuhu, he moved within a sea of chattering passengers through dim tunnels under the tracks leading to the main concourse. Coal was everywhere, stamped into round bricks piled up in the corners of the passageway and scattered about in crumbs crushed into black dirt underfoot. Wafts of sulphur mixed with cigarette smoke gave the air an acrid weight. The train station's main hall was a bustling hive of simultaneous construction and demolition. Groups of people dressed in worn Mao-style suits sat on large bundles, camped out like refugees. The men smoked and the women peeled oranges.

Outside, dented minibuses struggled for traction along the unfinished station plaza while young men hung halfway out of the vehicles' doors calling destinations. The stares from everyone around Jake made him feel like a gravitational force.

"*Laowai*," he heard everywhere. *Laowai* this. *Laowai* that.

Jake walked slowly, hearing the rumble of a locomotive pulling a train out of the station, and wondered how he would get to his school.

He approached a man wearing an ill-fitting suit, no tie and his pant legs rolled up for no apparent reason. Jake used the only greeting he knew which was probably too formal. He then said the name of the school. Surprised and amused to see a foreigner, the man stopped and responded but Jake couldn't understand.

Then Jake asked a woman wearing a Mao jacket and gray slacks and a frayed canvas sack slung over one shoulder and toddler in tow. She stood stunned at first and Jake repeated the name of his intended destination. Anhui Normal University, "an-hui shi-fan da-xue."

"Ah," she said, repeating the name in the abbreviated form which drops the second character of each word. "*An shi da*!"

"*Dui*!" Jake said. Yes!

The woman put a hand to her chin as her child, a girl wearing a dark blue jacket and pants made of the same material as her mother's, giggled and imitated Jake.

"*Dui! Dui!*" the mother said.

A random group of people surrounded Jake and the woman. Some of them inspected the clips and zippers on his backpack, making comments that Jake didn't understand apart from the word *laowai*. Another pointed first to Jake's hair and then to a wisp of light-coloured chest hair poking up from his denim shirt. Another squatted by Jake's side and unfastened the Velcro straps on his hiking boots.

The woman pointed to one of the buses while she rattled off some instructions. Again, too rapid and accented for Jake to understand any of it except that he'd have to change buses at some point. Jake sighed and began looking beyond the crowd. The buses churned in seemingly random directions through loose dirt as construction workers waved them around sections of freshly poured concrete.

One of the men on the edge of the crowd, older than the rest with deep wrinkles that radiated out from his eyes, pushed his way towards Jake and took him by the wrist as he addressed everyone present in a scolding tone. Jake pulled his arm back at first but the man held tightly while he continued barking at the crowd. The man then chatted with the mother. She nodded, pulled her daughter up into her arms and said something to Jake which he guessed from the warmth in her eyes to be a good luck wish.

The man shook two cigarettes from a crumpled pack, handed one to Jake and lit them.

"*Lai*," he said. Come.

Jake choked after his first inhale but then the nicotine kicked in. He felt the chemicals calm him as they coursed through his bloodstream, eventually making their way to the tip of his fingers. Something about the slow gait of the old man and the reassurance of nicotine allowed Jake to relax for the first time since he lifted off from Chicago several days earlier.

On his first day of class at Anhui Normal, Jake told his teacher the story of the old man who spent half a day escorting him to the campus. When his teacher tried to think of a Chinese name for Jake, she asked what he had most recently wished for. Jake said he'd like to find the old man, to know if he had a grandchild or a relative who dreamed of studying in the U.S. Jake wanted to help the old man's relative apply, to meet him or her on the ground in the U.S. and take them to their school, to make sure they found the right building.

And here stands a young man, perhaps just slightly older than Jake was when he arrived a decade earlier in Wuhu. Dawei's stare triggers these memories and reminds Jake that he has never fulfilled his pledge. In recent years, he's done the opposite: always trying to measure out and compartmentalize his relationships with anyone local, those who always ask whether he's married. So he doesn't want to provide any information and that requires distance. Jake has perfected the art of distance.

It occurs to Jake, while he's conversing with this young guy named Dawei, how far he's drifted from the language student who enjoyed splitting watermelon seeds between his teeth for hours with Chinese families who would adopt him, at least temporarily, as their train snaked through river valleys and dusty towns. Back when he used to listen and appreciate. Back when he didn't need distance.

Jake exhales slowly. "So, do you deliver tickets in this area often?"

Dawei furrows his brow, looking around the space again.

"I'm not sure. This is just my first day."

"You look a bit confused. You're not very familiar with Beijing?"

"Um. I'm g... g... getting to know it."

They chatted for a few more minutes. Dawei asked about Jake's work.

Whether he owned or rented his apartment.

"Rent. I don't plan to live here long."

How much does he get paid?

"Not enough for the trouble they give me."

Shaking his head and laughing, Jake responds before Dawei finishes asking because he knows the question is coming. Jake sees that the laughter puts Dawei at ease, the stutter now undetectable. Jake asks whether he has any family in Beijing.

"No." And with that answer, Dawei feels his satchel and looks into it. "I should get back to work."

"Sure. I'm actually very late already to meet a friend for lunch."

But Dawei stands still, scratching his forehead, and Jake doesn't know how to interpret the body language. Jake wants to bid farewell but his pledge to repay the kindness of the old man in Wuhu becomes a force lording over him like a parent goading a child to say please and thank you.

"So, how about I give you my cell number? Give me a call if you're in the neighbourhood again."

Dawei looks down. "I don't have a cell phone."

Jake takes a name card out of his wallet and a pen out of his backpack. He scrawls his unit number on the Chinese side of the card and gives it to Dawei. "Stop by anytime then."

TUESDAY, April 10, 2007

Jake recognizes his target as soon as he walks into to hotel lobby. The hair, parted on the side and perfectly styled with a slightly wet finish, gives him away. Republicans are nothing if not immaculately groomed. The representative's top aide, a legislative director, wears a navy blue suit with a red paisley tie fastened with a clip against his white oxford shirt. Simultaneously amused and nauseated, Jake needs a moment to digest the symbolism as he wonders how such ideological dickheads take themselves seriously.

Jake is wearing a forest green corduroy blazer with brown suede patches on the elbows. Purchased from Banana Republic sometime in the late 90s, it's one size too large. Underneath, he has on a light blue oxford shirt, without a tie. It's evening, after all, but Jake wonders if he should run back to his room to put one on.

Ross Andrews, the legislative director, is clicking away on his Blackberry keyboard. As the top aide to a Representative of the House Committee on Foreign Affairs who's just landed in enemy territory, Andrews probably has dozens of emails to answer. Jake looks over at the bar. He'll need a drink.

Jake is in Tianjin to cover two days of trade talks meant to address U.S. grievances over the yuan's exchange rate and complaints from Beijing about congressional reviews of proposed takeovers of U.S. companies by Chinese state-owned firms. Both issues, each side charges, are politically motivated acts that impede market rationality. In recent months, they've boiled over into threats of retaliatory measures. Punitive tariffs are in the works, U.S. congressional committees say. Cooperation with the U.S. on many international issues will be difficult, China's Foreign Ministry spokesman says. And so it's been since Jake began covering the trade relationship, an issue that sparks diplomatic rhetoric so repetitive the biggest challenge in writing about it lies in finding alternate words to explain the same boiling points. The only difference being the names of the latest U.S. politicians looking to score political points by piling on.

While Jake's in Tianjin to cover recycled arguments about trade deficits, he has a much more urgent personal agenda. To fortify himself for the mission, he orders a gin and tonic. He's learned to avoid the red wine served in fully state-owned hotels. It will taste like vinegar.

As he approaches the aide, Jake wonders whether to call him Ross or Mr. Andrews. He appears to be the same age as Jake. Someone of a similar rank in China must be addressed by putting his title together with the family name —director, chairman or some such manager. At the very least, an honorific. Separated from the U.S. for so long, Jake's not sure about protocol in this case.

"Mr. Andrews, right?" he says, playing it safe.

Andrews looks up. "You must be Jake Bradley," Andrews says before turning back to his device to finish his response.

"Yes, thanks for taking the time to meet with me. How are the preparations for the meeting going?"

Andrews offers Jake his hand and they shake. "Your associate in Washington, what's her name again?"

"Kendra."

"Yes, Kendra. She said you wouldn't be asking me about the talks until after they wrap up."

"Sorry. Just a habit. I'm here now to let you know about the filmmaker who's disappeared."

"Right. Kendra gave me the details and we're interested in following this."

Of course you are, Jake thinks. McKee needs an issue to make the public forget what he's known for. Re-elected by the skin of his teeth in the midterms, he nearly lost to a Democrat in a Republican stronghold state. McKee had also been one of the most fervent supporters of the war in Iraq, which he's silent about now. Jake has followed McKee's ups and downs because the congressman has been one of the most outspoken critics of same-sex civil unions. He's compared gay sex to bestiality, something Jake was used to hearing from drunken uncles and cousins in Kentucky.

Jake pulls copies that Diane prepared for him from his backpack, the same ones she submitted to the PSB.

"So, you know he has a Haas MBA with a green card and has lived in the

U.S. for almost a decade?"

"Yes. Haas," Andrews says. "That's Berkeley, right?"

Yes, asshole. *The left* coast to you, Jake thinks.

"Yes, that's Berkeley. Look, his sister doesn't have a copy of his green card but I'm assuming your staff can get that information. And…" Jake pulls out a manila envelope. "inside is a letter from his sister Diane to the Secretary of State, asking her to bring the matter up with the Chinese Foreign Minister."

Jake hesitates. This whole mission suddenly seems naïve. Think like an American, he tells himself. Make this a negotiation. Make Qiang's predicament an asset to be traded.

"Mr. Andrews, I don't mean to be mistrustful but can you let me know if Mr. McKee will take this issue up? I need to know whether I should be spreading this around to other congressmen."

"I can't guarantee anything but you know Mr. McKee's position on China. He doesn't take kindly to the illegal detention of people the U.S. has deemed worthy of a green card. Let's put it this way, I'm pretty sure he'll take this up. If not, I'll let your friend Kendra know."

Jake hands over the documents. He wonders if it makes sense to point out how much an issue like this could help his boss. How much it would deflect attention from positions that have weakened McKee's standing among the good people of North Carolina. This is an even exchange of favours. McKee gets to own a unique issue; Jake gets Qiang back. But then again, they've thought of this already. Otherwise, Jake wouldn't be having this conversation. He doesn't want to overplay his hand.

"Thank you, Mr. Andrews, I appreciate it. And I'm sure your constituents will find the story interesting."

Andrews looks at the documents.

"So, how do you know this guy, um, Kee-ang?"

There it is, Jake thinks. Andrews wants as much information as possible to compile the dossier he'll deliver to McKee. He's fishing for some details. He can't know much about Jake beyond the basic facts: Originally from a reliably Republican, red neck jurisdiction; went to university in a liberal, Democratic stronghold; works for a news service that can't be pegged as either; stories with his byline wouldn't give any indication.

"Chee-ang. The Q is pronounced kind of like C-H."

"Well, that's silly. If they're using English letters, why don't they just use C-H instead of a Q?"

"The C-H is used to make the same sound it does in English. Q is for a more clipped version of the C-H sound."

Andrews shakes his head.

"Crazy, just like their policies, right?" he says with a laugh.

Jake sees nothing crazy about it. Two sounds. Two different Romanizations. But he smiles anyway to keep the deal on track and to squelch the anger he feels towards this foot soldier in the war on decency and common sense.

"How do I know Qiang?" Jake says. "Well, we're friends."

THURSDAY, April 12, 2007

Sitting in a makeshift press room, Jake gives his story a final edit. He's been running between this room and scrums with Chinese trade officials for 13 hours. At this point, the story makes complete sense and none at all. Hopefully the editors in Washington will iron out the rough spots. He sits next to Regine, who's on the phone with her editors in London, clarifying a few final points. The reporters for Dow Jones, AP and Kyodo have left. Outside of the room, in the hotel's lower concourse, a maze of function rooms where deep pile carpet deadens the sound and light from baroque lamps and wall sconces barely reaches the furthest corners, it could be any time of the day in any month in any year in any city.

"Are they letting you go now?" Jake asks Regine as she hangs up.

"Yes, and I'm knackered."

"Nightcap somewhere?"

"I wish I had the energy, darling. I need to go to my room, call my boyfriend and collapse into the deepest sleep imaginable."

"Sure, go ahead and abandon me."

Jake curls his lower lip down into an exaggerated pout.

"Oh please. You need to check out the bars while you're here and I'd be a liability."

Regine closes her laptop and slides it into a shoulder bag. She gives Jake a pat on the shoulder. "You heading back to the Jing tomorrow morning or later in the day?"

"Depends on how late I'm out tonight."

Jake pauses and looks around the room. The few remaining reporters are out of earshot.

"Hey Regine, remember you were asking me about my friend, Qiang?"

"Yes." Regine pulls out the seat next to Jake and sits.

"He's still detained," Jake says.

"Okay. What more can you tell me about this? Are you going to report what's going on?"

"You know Toeler News. We're all about business."

"So, Jake, can you give me the details so I can get them out?"

Regine asks the question like a police officer trying to convince a criminal to hand over his gun and Jake pauses to think, to remember the strategy he's worked out with Diane and Ben.

"No. We're playing it safe for now."

"Ok, so…."

"So, here's a story that I think will make the authorities here squirm," Jake says as he hands Regine the thumbnail drive. "It has nothing to do with Qiang, for now at least."

"So, how does it…"

Jake puts his hand up and then leans toward Regine.

"Let's make a deal. Don't ask me questions about what's going on with Qiang or the strategy we're taking to resolve this and I promise to let you know about any new developments before anyone else."

It's close to 10:00 p.m. at one of a few discreet gay bars popping up around downtown Tianjin. After throwing back a double gin and tonic, Jake finds his target. A Chinese man in his early thirties sitting by himself at the bar, tapping out a text message. His shiny hair is trimmed short on the sides and left spiky up top. He wears glasses with dark maroon frames that match his striped maroon and orange shirt that he has tucked into a pair of jeans. Jake moves closer. The shoes look like Kenneth Cole or Ben Sherman. These brands aren't in Beijing yet, let alone Tianjin, but Jake is sure the guy is from the Mainland. Guys from Tokyo or Seoul or Hong Kong in a gay bar on a Thursday night would be in t-shirts and running shoes. So the guy travels.

"*Ni de yanjing hen shuai,*" Jake says, leaning into the bar. Your glasses are very cool.

The guy looks up from his Nokia phone. "Thanks."

As he smiles, Jake clenches his teeth to flex his jaw muscles, making his face look more chiseled. He's aiming for maximum impact to get the conversation going. The faster this transaction goes, the easier it is to keep second-guesses away.

"*Wo jiao Jie-ke,*" Jake says, holding out his hand.

"I'm George," the guy says as they shake. He over-enunciates the R to a degree that confirms him as China born and bred.

"*Hen gaoxing renshi ni, George. Ni zhongwen mingzi jiao shenme?*" Pleased to meet you, George. What's your Chinese name?

"Cao Zhi, but it's fine to just call me George."

"*Jiao ni Cao Zhi shi mei you wenti de,*" Jake says, making sure to play up the Beijing accent. It's no problem to call you Cao Zhi

"Your Mandarin is pretty good. Where did you study?" George says in English.

Jake relents. It's more important to keep the conversation flowing. He delivers the standard, self-deprecating introductory blather. He's said it a thousand times. "I've been in China too long to speak Mandarin as badly as I do. Anyway, I studied in Beijing and Anhui," Jake says in English.

George says something about a relative who's from Anhui's provincial capital, Hefei.

"Really?" Jake replies. "I spent two nights in Hefei visiting the family of my favourite teacher. They fed me so well, I probably gained five pounds that day."

None of this is true but Jake knows that stories like this play well. It makes him more of a *zhongguo tong* – a relative of China, an endearing term that can help speed up the ceremonial positioning but which still keeps the outsider at a certain distance. Better than *laowai*.

George laughs. "I can tell you really understand Chinese culture."

"Oh, just the surface really," Jake replies. "There's still so little I understand here. *Nimen de wenhua zhen fuza.*" Your culture is so complex.

"*Ni tai qianxu,*" George says. You're too modest.

By turning the conversation back to Mandarin, Jake wins the opening round and now wants to see how far he can push.

"*Xiang bu xiang gen wo yi qi hui qu wo de fangzi?*" Want to go back to my room?

"Wow, that was fast," George laughs. "Maybe, sometime."

This might take more than an hour, Jake thinks, but no one else in the bar turns him on as much as George. So he sticks with it.

"Hmmm, sometime. I don't know if you're shooting me down or just playing with me."

"If I said no, would you try your luck elsewhere?"

"No, because you're the hottest guy in this bar. I can't take my eyes off of you so I'm going to double down, as we say in English."

George smiles and nods.

"So," Jake continues. "Can I buy you a drink?"

"How about I buy you a drink, Jake?"

"Sure."

"You probably do pretty well in gay bars all over Asia," George says. "Blond hair and blues eyes go a long way in this part of the world."

"Is that a compliment or a reproach?"

"It's whatever you want it to be. I'm just not attracted to white guys."

Sticky rice. There's more of it around these days. Jake looks around the bar again and tells himself in consolation that there's no other white guy around who could close this transaction.

"Right. I appreciate the honesty," Jake says. "Do I still get a drink as a concession?"

"You get a drink and that's all."

"I've had worse disappointments in my life," Jake says in his best attempt to appear unscathed. "Ones that don't come with a gin and tonic as a concession."

Gulping the remainder of his third drink and reaching for his jacket, Jake watches George chat with another guy at the end of the bar. Karmic retribution. How does the hook-up expedition square with the effort to free someone he cares about so deeply?

As he heads towards the door, Jake sees a white guy wearing a baseball cap and a hooded sweatshirt enter the bar. He looks like he's mistaken the establishment for a sports bar. The guy also wears a pair of glasses with thick, black frames. As the new arrival scans the bar, Jake recognizes the slightly flattened nose and slight underbite. Another moment and Jake realizes the guy is Ross Andrews, McKee's legislative director, and freezes. This should be an opportunity but something tells him to hold back. That something, he knows, is the unspoken understanding among gay men to maintain a discreet distance unless the social context assumes recognition is okay. The reflection on Andrews' glasses obscures the direction of his focus but Jake can feel the eye contact the way dogs sense fear. Andrews casually turns towards the bar and pulls out his Blackberry as he settles onto a stool in front of it.

Jake decides to break the unwritten rules and kill two birds. He can use this as an opportunity for more leverage. If he plays this well, Jake will also get to fuck a war-mongering, hypocritical, self-loathing gay man. There's something so perverse about swapping spit with the ideological enemy that Jake can't acknowledge the risk he's about to take.

"Howdy partner," Jake says as he takes the stool next to Andrews who drops his head and lets out a quick chuckle.

"Hello, Jake Bradley. Fancy meeting you here."

"Indeed. I'm guessing you didn't wander in here by mistake."

"I doubt you're dumb enough to believe that. As you can imagine, I'm not out." His tone once again serious, Andrew looks at his device.

"Guess what? I'm not either. My career would be over if anyone knew. It would be tough to build sources here."

Not entirely true, but Jake needs to exaggerate his own vulnerability as part of the plan. In the distorted world Andrews inhabits, it's probably believable that being gay would end a career.

"So we're not here to socialize, are we Ross? We're here on the prowl, right?"

"Yep," Ross says, now finally looking directly at Jake.

"So let's get out of here."

In the dim light of the hotel room, Andrews is on his back. Jake slides his briefs down, letting Andrews' dick spring out and smack against his lower abdomen with the strength of a sucker punch. Jake slides one foot between his guest's legs to work the underwear completely off and then pushes the briefs onto the floor. He spits into his hand, begins stroking the shaft and rolls the palm of his hand around the head, making Andrews arch his back and moan. Jake crouches down like a cat and licks his Adam's apple, then makes his way around to Andrews' ear.

"You're so fucking hot," he whispers into it. "Hungry?"

"Oh, yesssssss." Andrews breathes the words and then puts his forearm over his mouth.

As Jake wraps his mouth around Andrews' dick, a flash lights up the room. At first, he thinks the light is some optical effect caused by the excitement. He remembers when he discovered masturbation in his early teens, his vision would sometimes white out and he'd get a sharp pain in his head at the moment of climax. At the time, he fretted that it was an indication of a brain tumour or some sort of hormonal imbalance. The problem dissipated after a couple of months and he forgot about it. Until now. This must be the same kind of phenomenon.

But Andrews jerks himself upright. He's seen the flash also.

"What the fuck was that?"

Jake looks up and another flash lights up the room. This time, Jake sees that it's come from a mirror that's hung on the wall like a painting. As he looks toward the source, several more flashes burst from behind the mirror.

Shock sets in as Jake figures out what's happening. The implications freeze him and he can't move until Andrews kicks himself off the bed and scrambles for the briefs that Jake had sent to the floor a few minutes earlier.

"Holy fuck," Jake says, still looking toward a mirror that continues squeezing off shots. "They're getting photos of me to use as blackmail," Jake says in a stunned whisper as though Andrews is no longer in the room.

Without thinking to put his briefs on, he picks up the room's desk chair and walks toward the mirror. By the time he gets there, though, he realizes how dangerous it would be to escalate the situation with a vandalism charge. In any case, the images are already on some server far away from this hotel room. He drops the chair.

Andrews looks anxiously back and forth between Jake and the mirror.

"This is about your friend Kee-ang, right?" he says. "Or is this some kind of set up? Are you trying to bring me down with this? Are you trying to bring McKee down with this, you twisted fuck?"

Too stunned as he realizes how these photos, this chaos, may have undermined the effort to get Qiang released, Jake doesn't answer.

"Hey!" Andrews shouts. "Answer me!

"My only motive, my whole life at this point, is about getting Qiang released," Jake says, his voice trailing off as a sob wells up unexpectedly.

Jake swallows and shakes his head to push his emotions back down into the bile of his stomach, to dissolve them. This is not the time to appear weak. "My friend is gone, Ross. Why would I make this shit up? The letters. The documents. Think about it."

Andrews is silent for a moment and Jake can see him thinking about all of the elements, putting them together and undermining the logic of his suspicion.

"Well, whatever's happening here, now I'm wrapped up in it," Andrews says, standing against the wall, next to the mirror. "Do you fucking understand?"

"I don't know what to tell you, Ross," Jake says as he slides his boxer shorts up and then steps into his jeans. "But don't you see, this is what we're up against."

Andrews hastily pulls his coat on while he steps into his shoes.

"So what do you suggest I do about this?" he says to Jake in a hushed but angry tone as though he's trying to stay below the audio threshold of whatever recording device is monitoring the room. His brow is contorted into an angry stare. "You want my help and you get me into this shit?"

"What, do you think I planned this?" Jake spits back loudly, not caring who hears what.

Andrews just stares, mouth open and shaking his head, as though he's about to lob more accusations but can't get his thoughts together. "I don't know what to think. I just gotta get the fuck out of here. Out of this room. Out of this city. Out of this fucking, fucked up country."

He leaves without tying his shoes. The door slams, leaving Jake in half light and dead quiet, except for the sound of his breathing.

Halfway through a wad of Uyghur hash packed into a ceramic bowl, Jake sees the music pumping through his headphones. Pink Floyd's "Sheep". His head lolls from side to side along with the rhythmic bass line that carries the intro of rambling keyboard notes. When the song shifts into its frenetic violence, the sounds assemble into a scene and Jake slowly closes his eyes. Above a herd of terrified sheep running for their lives, a cartoon-animated Roger Waters descends like a surfer on a wave, carried by the sound of David Gilmour's searing guitar riff. Brandishing a jagged knife, Waters falls onto the back of one of the animals with a scream. He rips open its throat just as Gilmour's guitar slams out the first of the song's cacophonic chords. Waters' shriek breaks into hysterical, wide-eyed laughter as blood spews from twisted and severed arteries, splattering the singer's victim and the other wooly white sheep running next to it, now more terrified than ever as the mortally wounded sheep stumbles and trips up the animals behind it. Continuing to laugh, Waters pulls above the herd, ready to repeat the kill.

A bloodletting of sorts, Jake sometimes sinks into hash-fueled ritual if he's feeling bruised by a day in the newsroom and doesn't have the energy to go out with friends. "Bodies" by Smashing Pumpkins, "Whichever Way the Wind Blows" by Bob Mould, "*Come*" by Fleetwood Mac. Voices and guitars unrestrained, with a fuck-everything approach that provides Jake with a release of the poison that builds up as his editors in Washington bear down on him like Roger Waters descending on sheep. Every currency policy rumour left unanalyzed is reason for punishment, even if the rumour is the same one that's bubbled up twenty times in the past month.

The violence that's meted out in these musically driven visions is more therapeutic than complaining to friends. They transport Jake as far away as he can get from everything he wants to escape. Away from the cadence of corporate spokesmen. Away from Hello Kitty and the hundreds of other smiling, massive-eyed anime characters the Chinese idolize as a subconscious escape from the disarray of a world in flux. Away from the demands for straightforward clarity in putting inherently irrational market sentiment into context, as if the context wasn't vicious and incomprehensible enough. Away from government officials who regard Jake and all other foreign reporters as spies trying to spark a neo-liberal counter-revolution. Away from the constant construction noise that's supposed to end by midnight but doesn't because no one has the stamina to fight the interests backing redevelopment. And even further away from the Bible retreats, faggot jokes and appliance-strewn front lawns of Magnet Hill, Kentucky. An hour or so of smooth hash, a fine red win, and masterful classic rock is usually all Jake needs to slip away from all of these troubles.

Someone knocks but Jake doesn't hear it right away. He's constructing the final moments of carnage on the animated farm that John Waters is terrorizing. The music fades enough for Jake to hear the knock. His muscles lock. He wants to keep quiet because he's not likely to know the person on the other side of the door. Anyone he knows would have sent a text message before showing up. The only tricks with his correct number are the ones Jake would be happy to have as a repeat. No one he'd want to see just shows up. Perhaps it's building security. The public security bureau? But why?

Jake rises, scoops up the bowl, lighter and ashtray. Thinking whoever is knocking might still just go away, he tiptoes toward his bedroom.

The tapping on his door resumes. The bowl slides off the edge of the ashtray Jake is carrying and, slowed by the effect of the hash, he can only watch, in vivid slow motion, as the object falls to the floor and shatters into many pieces.

"Shit," he whispers to himself as his heart revs.

He opens a drawer in the bureau next to him and drops in the baggie of hash and the ashtray. He then gathers up as many of the bowl pieces as he can with a few sweeps of his hand, walks to the kitchen and throws all of the broken ceramic mixed with bits of ash into a trash bin under the sink.

"*Deng yi xia*," he yells. Just a minute. "*Shi shei?*" Who is it?

"Dawei," says the voice on the other side of the door.

Jake is relieved. Of course. He should know by now who's going to show up unannounced. The only person he knows without a cell phone. And he doesn't need to worry about the smell. Dawei probably wouldn't know what hash is, let alone care.

Maybe this time it will happen, Jake thinks as he grabs a wine glass for Dawei who had visited twice since they met in the elevator a month earlier. Hash heightens everything about sex. The hash has Jake feeling intensely horny and bereft of all inhibitions. He has enough wits about him to know that he may behave badly, but not enough to tell Dawei, politely, that he's under the weather and that Dawei should probably come back another time.

Jake puts the odds on Dawei being gay at about fifty-fifty. There's no outward indication other than the interest Dawei took in a complete stranger of the same sex at a time when foreigners were no longer a novelty on the streets of Beijing. Enough interest to show up for no apparent reason.

When Dawei arrived unannounced for the first time, Jake had just got out of the shower and was wearing a towel, an unplanned setup straight out of bad porn without Jake even trying to engineer it. So he decided not to change into clothes right away. With his hair damp and beads of water still on his skin, Jake gave Dawei a tour of his apartment. Dawei was quiet, except for questions at a few points, like when Jake showed him the guest room.

"Whose room is this?" Dawei asked.

"Just for friends who visit from out of town."

"So most of the time, no one stays in here?"

"Correct."

When he looked into Jake's computer room, Dawei asked why his work equipment is in his home and Jake had to explain the difference between his own personal computer and the one he uses in the office he goes to every day in one of the two China World Centre towers.

The tour continued in the last room, the master bedroom, and Jake's heart raced in anticipation of how the next few minutes would play out. Would Dawei be easy to talk into bed? Would he play coy like the Chinese who are still conflicted, the ones who seek out white guys for sex because that puts the entire scenario in a different context and makes it easier to think of the experience as a form of curiosity playing out in a world that doesn't exist to anyone else they'd know.

Or maybe Jake is just dead wrong about this Dawei guy. The uncertainty makes things interesting and exciting because the encounter could end in a confrontation.

Once in the master bedroom, as Jake was ready to change, Dawei asked the last question of the tour.

"Don't you have a wife?"

"I don't have a wife and I don't have a girlfriend," Jake said as he casually removed his towel.

He looked away from Dawei to make his intent less obvious. Chinese don't have the same hangups that Americans have about nudity but a dead-on stare might have been too much. Just as his arousal was beginning to show, Jake turned and rummaged around his underwear drawer and Dawei stepped into the bathroom.

"You have a shower on one side and a tub on the other," Dawei said, his voice echoing off the glass and tile of the enclosed space. "Isn't that kind of strange?"

"Um...I never use the tub," Jake said, not really answering the question.

Then silence settled in, as he looked in the drawer at a stack of neatly folded Marks & Spencer boxer briefs he buys in Hong Kong and wondered what the next move should be.

"How much is your rent?" Dawei asked, souring the moment with one of those income-related questions that Mainland Chinese will always ask prematurely.

"I don't know," Jake replied. "My company pays for it."

This is a lie Jake tells to avoid further discussion of money.

"Your company pays your rent?"

"Correct."

And the seduction died there.

Jake was fully clothed when Dawei visited a second time, on a rainy Sunday evening, carrying his satchel full of delivery receipts. Jake had spent much of that day in bed with someone he had picked up at Destination the night before so he didn't bother trying to engineer a move to the bedroom. The two settled in on the couch, Dawei sitting stiffly as he looked around the room and Jake looking directly at Dawei with his feet up, arms wrapped around his legs and chin resting on his knee.

"Do you go back to the Northeast often?" Jake asked.

"It's difficult for me to get there," Dawei said.

Not really, Jake thought. There are scores of flights now to anywhere from anywhere in China. Trains too, some with seats that cost less than 100 kuai from Beijing.

"Do you at least get back there for the Lunar New Year?"

Dawei shook his head and then focused on the Singapore Airlines amenity kit sitting on Jake's coffee table.

"It's what they give you on long-haul flights," Jake said as he reached for the kit. He turned a small metal notch on the front to open it only to find half of its contents gone. The travel-sized toothpaste was on his bathroom counter, a stop-gap to get him through to the next shopping trip. The earplugs were sitting on Jake's bedside table, caked with wax. The only items that remained in the kit were a pair of fuzzy socks, a small tin of breath mints and a stick of lip balm which Jake pulled out.

"This keeps your lips…umm…" Jake didn't know the words for "moist" or "balm." These are words that separate language mastery from mere proficiency.

"You put this on your lips when the air is dry. It makes your lips not too dry," Jake said in slightly mangled Mandarin.

Jake took the lid off the lip balm and reached over to apply some on Dawei's lower lip. Dawei drew back.

"Sorry," Jake said. "It won't hurt you."

He then handed the tube to Dawei.

"Is it like lipstick?"

Jake laughed. "There's no colour in it. It's only meant to protect your lips from the dry air," Jake moved his hand around his lips to show Dawei how to apply the balm.

Looking at Jake, Dawei dabbed his lower lip tentatively with the end of the stick and then handed it back. Jake put the cap on, dropped the balm back in the bag and refastened the clip. He then got up and trotted into his bedroom.

"Just a second and I'll get you one with all of the contents," he said as he disappeared into the darkness of the room. "I have a lot of these," he said as he re-emerged and handed another kit to Dawei.

Dawei drew back. "Oh no. I can't accept that."

"Don't be so polite," Jake said. "I have so many of these, they usually end up in the garbage. Just take it. It's really nothing."

"I was just curious. I d…d…don't want it. You're too generous. I really can't take that."

Jake sighed. This tiresome test of manners, trying enough for the culturally indoctrinated, could have gone on endlessly.

"Just take it, Dawei. It doesn't mean anything."

Dawei was good enough to thank Jake and let the issue lay. They made more small talk before the conversation trailed off into details so small that Jake had to stretch and yawn and then explain apologetically that he needed to call his editors in New York.

That was a few days ago. Or maybe weeks. And here Dawei is again, showing up for a third time, even though the previous two visits had never established any kind of rapport that would explain the need for more. Jake dwells on this. There must be something that keeps Dawei coming back. For Jake, the unspoken meaning behind their meetings hangs over them both, enveloping them in a suffocating and deafening silence. Perhaps Dawei feels this also. The hash-induced rush of sexual desire pushes aside the possibility that Dawei's visits might be about something other than sexual gratification. But Dawei is hot and Jake wants to bust through the wall of culture and etiquette that separates them. One of them needs to do something to bring air back into the room. Dawei is the guest so Jake must make the move. This will require alcohol. Not wine this time. Tequila shots.

Seated next to Dawei on his couch, Jake is leaning over his coffee table slicing into a lime that sits on a wooden cutting board. First in half, then quarters, then eighths. As Jake pours the tequila into two shot glasses, Dawei is rummaging through his delivery bag. He pulls out a well-scuffed plastic file folder containing some documents and photos.

"Could I ask a favour of you?" Dawei says.

His tone is more serious, inappropriate for an onslaught of depravity, and suddenly the chances that Jake's plan will work out seem to evaporate.

"Sure," Jake says as he holds up the two shot glasses full of amber liquid. He says it with an eye roll and a note of sarcasm that he knows Dawei won't recognize.

Here it comes, Jake thinks. Dawei wants an introduction to someone in his company or English lessons every weekend in a language exchange. Perhaps he has a sister who's applying to college in the U.S. anad needs help with the application. In his head, Jake begins lining up the excuses and defenses, the little exaggerations and outright lies about this and that which will limit the extent to which he's able to help with whatever Dawei is about to ask for.

Dawei rips open the Velcro fastener on the folder and pulls out a thick document with sparse text and hand-drawn figures enveloped in streams of numbers and poetry. Characters in Tang-era costumes mingle with what appear to be Chinese zodiac animals.

"What's this?" Jake asks.

"It's a s...s...screenplay. A gift from a friend who works in the m...m... movie industry."

Jake starts laughing. This one will be easy to swat away, he thinks.

"You might be mistaken about my job. I work in the news business, not film," he says. "I don't know anyone who could look at this and get it produced."

Dawei looks confused for a moment.

"No, I just want to keep this here. The places I stay aren't very safe and this is important to me. Once I'm settled in a better place, I'll pick this up again."

With the hallucinogens still coursing through his system, Jake stares at the drawings, transfixed by the characters' expressions. He can see the dramatic interplay between characters from an earlier age confronted by those wearing modern dress.

"Jie-ke?"

Jake shakes his head and looks up at Dawei.

"Um, sure," Jake says, confused about how to follow up.

Something about the division between these characters of different eras makes Jake think about the difference between himself and Dawei. They exist on separate planes and were brought together because of some wrinkle in the fabric of space-time. He sees more clearly how mistaken he was to expect a sleazy, carefree hookup.

Acting on its own will, Jake's mind begins to surface ideas about cultural divisions and time travel. He sees the difference between himself now and the person he was a decade earlier, before the amount of his salary wasn't as thrilling as the fact that he had a salary at all. The separation allows Jake to see the Jake who took long-distance train rides through China's hinterland, enjoying the company of fellow travellers and drifting to sleep in the top bunk of a hard sleeper car, in clear focus as a character distinct from who he is now. The Jake who used to drop a few kuai into the baskets of elderly beggars, the ones with dirt ground into their sunburned and leathery faces, wasting away on the streets of Beijing. They're no longer as visible since the government cracked down on anything that sullied the image of the city. It is just as well because the Jake that used to drop money doesn't exist anymore either.

Jake had read somewhere that every cell in a human body is replaced over the course of seven years. Not only had every cell from a decade ago turned to methane but every experience since then had changed his outlook. But if all of this is true, why does this being that looks out from Jake's eyes feel just as alienated, just as detached from everyone else, as he ever had? The question makes Jake dizzy. He shakes his head to make these thoughts go away.

Dawei reaches into the folder as Jake mulls over the dilemma and pulls out a laminated sheet encasing a maple leaf and a pressed lotus flower against a white page with the word Friends in English, French and Chinese. It's clear to Jake that the item is some piece of diplomatic propaganda produced for some Sino-Canadian function.

"I know that maple leaves are a symbol of North America. I want you to have this because you've been a good friend," Dawei says. "It sort of represents our friendship. The maple leaf represents America and the lotus flower represents China."

Jake smiles, as much for the thoughtfulness of Dawei's gesture as he does for the fact that Dawei feels the need to explain the representation. The mood no longer bodes well for a seduction. Dawei's circumstances are tougher than what Jake had imagined. Any sex to be had, were that to happen, would be two completely different experiences and Jake would never know for sure if Dawei wasn't giving himself up out of desperation. Sex can feel empty enough once the orgasmic shudders subside. Knowing that someone's putting out for anything other than physical pleasure makes the aftermath twice as wretched. What's worse, Jake would feel more obliged to help this character who's just looking for a safe place to sleep.

FRIDAY, April 13, 2007

"This was recorded on the morning of Monday, March 25, at 9:43 a.m.," the young PSB officer tells the others before she hits play. "I have a transcript with a translation."

She hands the set of papers to her division head.

"I'm just torn up about this, Qiang," says a woman speaking American accented English, her S's clipped by a poor phone connection degraded further by the recording.

"So, what are the chances that interview will show up sooner than you planned?"

"I don't know, Qiang, if I had known Zhao was going to reveal anything that explosive, I wouldn't have given the network access to it. I can trust most of them. I just don't know all of them. And as I said before, I don't know that his story is accurate. But whatever happens, I can assure you this guy wants the message out. He sought out the ones I'm working with, specifically to tell this story."

"But, you know, I promised him that none of this would be seen until the twenty-year anniversary of June 4th. He's expecting to be dead and buried by then."

"I know," the woman says, "And what's got me worried just as much is that you're still there. How much longer will you be doing interviews for your film?"

"I'm going to my last one now. Once I get this guy, I'll have enough to assemble a rough cut."

The American woman sighs. "I may have let you both down."

"We don't know that yet," he says.

"Just hurry up with your project, Qiang, so you're not there if the interview gets leaked," the American woman says. "In the meantime, I'll do my best to make sure those who have the footage understand that lives are at stake and to keep it under wraps until the documentary runs."

The division head scans the transcript as the file plays.

"How," he begins. "How did we get this recording?"

"It was triggered when one of the subjects said 'June 4th'. It's a new voice recognition technology that the mobile providers have started using. The transcript was turned over to us and a team over in Division 53 crossed referenced the name and the date with the files on your case."

May, 2005

Dawei counts the signed receipts as he waits for the travel agency manager to arrive and open the shop. He's not sure if she's the owner or part-owner. She doesn't speak to him much, leaving all of the details of the ticket deliveries to her assistant. At least she seems like an assistant.

Dawei will get eight kuai for each receipt, bringing the total to 120. If he keeps up this pace, he'll be able to get a dorm bed or some kind of accommodation, even if it's somewhere outside of the Fifth Ring. There are so many new subway lines under construction that it will be easy to get around town even from the fringes.

Something has changed now that Dawei has a friend in Beijing. The American, Jie-ke, who lives in the nice apartment just outside of the Third Ring. It was very strange to talk to him after they got out of the elevator that day a couple of weeks ago and it still feels strange every time he sees him.

They never talk about anything that leads anywhere. Not like the conversations with Zhihong which went on for hours. But his relationship with Zhihong isn't normal. Maybe, Dawei thinks, maybe his conversations with Jie-ke feel strange because he's never had any normal friends. He moved from Yongfu Village to Harbin, where the other teenagers saw him as a hayseed. Then he shuffled from place to place until arriving in Macau. All the while, Dawei realizes, he never had a real friend. How strange to go from having so few friends to having a foreign friend. What else could he consider Jie-ke to be? He's not a blood relative or a co-worker or a boss. Friends can be as important as family,

Dawei thinks. That must be what's giving him this feeling of confidence about starting a new life in Beijing.

New friends and a new job mean a new life. He takes a breath, pulling fresh air in so deeply he feels it in his hands and feet, as though the oxygen is clearing the bad luck from the deepest recesses of his body.

Refreshed and feeling lighter, Dawei rehearses in his head how he will ask for more work. How many couriers in Beijing can handle fifteen deliveries in one day? He's familiar enough now with the city's layout to maximize the efficiency of his routes. Maybe the manager and her assistant would be willing to bring him on as a regular employee. They seem to have enough business. They have more ringing phones than they can answer. He's been in the office, waiting for his pay, while some phones just ring non-stop. If they'd allow him to answer the phones and show him what to do on the computer to print out tickets, he'd strive to excel as well as he does delivering tickets. Dawei recognizes the characters for most cities and, of course, numbers are easy. He watched his father calculate payments for the wheat and soybeans they'd deliver to the markets.

As he watches Beijing's morning rush hour traffic build, Dawei sees that he won't need to return to Macau where the little bit he's able to save seems to disappear every time he wants to treat himself to a magazine or two.

The manager approaches, wearing a colourful jacket, dark slacks and shiny high heels. She's talking on her phone about the price of a kitchen countertop, too involved in haggling as she unlocks the travel agency's door to acknowledge Dawei. She walks inside and Dawei follows her.

"Not good enough," she snaps and closes her clamshell phone.

She looks at Dawei as though this is the first time she's seen him.

"I'm here with the receipts from yesterday," Dawei says, digging in his bag for a bunch of papers held together with a paperclip which he removes and drops back into the bag. "F...f... fifteen of them all together."

He hands them over. The manager takes the papers and begins flipping through them.

"Oh God, I don't know why she quoted such low prices on these," she says, talking to herself. Then she looks up at Dawei.

"You see! This is why I fired her."

Dawei doesn't see. He stands, frozen. The manager's anger seems directed at him, which makes no sense. Shifting uncomfortably, he looks around for the other employee, the one who sent him out with 15 tickets to deliver the day before. She's probably the one who's been fired.

"I d...d...don't know anything about the prices," he says.

"I should have fired her long ago," the manager says, walking behind the counter and taking her seat. She clips receipts together, opens the drawer closest to her, drops the papers in and shuts the drawer. She then pulls out a key and locks the drawer and 120 kuai disappears with the click of a latch.

"But I'm supposed to get eight kuai for each one of those receipts," Dawei says.

"I don't know what you're talking about. I never authorized these sales, so there's no commission, for her or for you."

The manager switches on her computer and the fan on her desk, which sends some of the papers fluttering to the ground. Muttering under her breath, she bends down to gather them.

The game can't be over that fast, Dawei thinks, not before he's even had a chance to play. Not just this exchange of words between himself and a woman who's swindled him out of 120 kuai but the whole idea he had in his head about living independently, sleeping in his own bed every night and, maybe eventually, saving enough to open a small restaurant in Beijing. Why didn't he hold onto the receipts until she gave him the cash? He must think of some other way to keep this game going because he's not going to walk out of the travel agency empty handed. The woman will expect him to storm out or threaten to contact the PSB, knowing that the police would never consider his complaint. He needs a smarter strategy. Perhaps he could sympathize with her.

"I'm sorry that your colleague tricked you like that," Dawei says, keeping his anger hidden. "You j...j...just can't trust anyone these days," he says.

The manager only lets out a guttural laugh while she taps on her keyboard. She doesn't make eye contact. She wants him to leave but he won't. The more he thinks about her trick, the more determined he is to stay.

"Anyway," Dawei continues. "I value this job and your decency in giving it to me so I don't mind just getting on with today's deliveries."

"There's no more deliveries, or at least not enough to keep you around," she says.

"What?"

The manager shakes her head, obviously annoyed by the continued distraction of Dawei's presence. Every time he tries to get ahead of the revelations the manager lobs at him like grenades, he falls further behind, as though this woman understands his strategy.

"E-tickets," she says.

"What are e-tickets?" Dawei asks.

"People are booking online now and then printing the tickets out themselves."

WEDNESDAY, April 18, 2007

The swinging door opens with a thud and a bang. Mr. Ong walks briskly through the kitchen, heading for his office while he argues with a vendor who's following. Something about prices for prawns sourced in Vietnam now being lower than those from Thailand. Dawei now knows enough Cantonese to recognize the subject matter, if not the details.

"Dawei, someone out there looking for you," Mr. Ong snaps as he passes, keeping his eyes fixed on the crumpled invoices he's brandishing like a weapon as he walks by the cooks. They're subjected to Mr. Ong's diatribes every day, a continuous one-man show of strength meant to beat back the constant encroachment of costs. The vendor has his own set of papers. He holds them up with one hand and wags the index finger of the other at the top sheet as he argues back, something about price fluctuations. The arguments and gestures are lost on each other, absorbed into the activity of the kitchen. The details are as relevant as the guts being pulled out of the fish and tossed into a large plastic bin that Dawei will need to haul outside once he's finished washing up the dishes from lunch.

This rant is different, though, because Mr. Ong has told Dawei that someone is looking for him. There's only one person that could be.

In an alley behind the restaurant, just wide enough for one car to pass, Dawei stands against the yellow wall streaked with black mold. Avoiding Zhihong's stare, he's looking into a window fitted with security bars on the opposite wall. He hears someone inside watching a local news report in Cantonese, the animated vocal flourishes, the drawn-out "ahhhs" and "wahhhhs" added like punctuation.

Zhihong takes a pack of Triple Fives and a lighter out of the pocket of his maroon polo shirt and shakes two cigarettes out. He hands one to Dawei who takes it hesitantly. Zhihong flicks the lighter's strike wheel three or four times without getting a flame. He shakes the lighter and tries again. Dawei grabs it and flicks more forcefully. A tiny flame blooms. He then lights his cigarette, lets the flame disappear and hands the lighter back.

"I know I've been away for too long," Zhihong says with the unlit cigarette in his mouth, as he flicks the lighter several times without effect.

"These crackdowns on spending," he says. "I've told you. There's no extra time or money. My colleagues won't take the chance to come over here any more."

A breeze pushes away the wafts of Macanese curry and garlic mixed with touches of disinfectant and garbage. Dawei looks out towards the end of the alley, beyond the traffic roundabout, for a glimpse of ocean through the trees that line the embankment he visits every night. The same embankment where he's fallen asleep several times with Zhihong by his side.

"I told them I'm really sick. That's the only way I could get over here today and why I need to get back before evening."

Dawei remains silent.

"Dawei, I'm a middle-aged bureaucrat. What else can I do at this point? I'm always thinking about how I can change things but…"

Dawei finally looks up at Zhihong. "How's your wife?"

Zhihong stands still and his face flushes. He raises his hand and throws the lighter to the ground, not far from their feet. Dawei doesn't blink or look down. Zhihong folds his arms in front of his chest.

"You know, I was here just a week after you showed up in Beijing. I came all the way here to apologize. Where were you?"

Dawei takes a drag from his cigarette. "I found work in Beijing," he says as he exhales into a breeze that carries the smoke further into the alley.

Zhihong looks at him quizzically.

"Remember how you told me that I never should have tried to find you there, in Beijing, and how we could never see each other there?"

Zhihong doesn't respond.

"I decided right there that I never wanted to see you again, ever, in any city," Dawei continues, looking towards the end of the alley. "So I figured if I lived there, I wouldn't ever have to see you again."

Zhihong lets his arms fall to his side. He bends forward as if he's lost the energy to stand, hands sliding down the front of his thighs and resting on his knees for support. Head down, he looks out in the direction of Dawei's gaze. A loud command from the chef in the kitchen behind them followed by chatter from the other workers reminds Dawei that the dirty cookware is probably accumulating.

"But I wasn't in Beijing long. The work dried up within a few weeks and it gets pretty cold there, so I made my way back down here while there was still time to get my job back."

Dawei takes another drag and exhales quickly. He draws his arm around his chest as though he feels the chill of the northeast.

"I'm sorry," Zhihong says, slowly bringing himself upright.

"Good. Now leave."

Dawei takes a last drag, flicks his cigarette away and turns toward the kitchen door. Zhihong tries to stop him by putting a hand on his shoulder but Dawei shakes loose. Zhihong jumps in front of Dawei to stop him and Dawei body checks him against the moldy wall.

"At least give me one minute to tell you something that I know you'll want to hear."

Reaching for the door handle, Dawei ignores him.

"You have something that's now worth a lot of money."

Dawei stops.

"You won't need to wash dishes again," Zhihong says.

Dawei turns and looks at him.

"Autumn Truce," Zhihong says.

"The movie? What about it?"

"It's the hottest film right now. In Hong Kong and on the Mainland."

"So?"

"Dai Xiaohui wrote it. The same one who wrote the screenplay I gave you two years ago."

The kitchen door opens abruptly and one of the kitchen hands, also dressed in greasy whites, sticks his head out.

"Eh," he grunts. "Stuff piling up in the sink. Get in here."

His stare now fixed on Zhihong, Dawei doesn't react to the order.

"That script is worth a lot of money," Zhihong says.

Several seconds pass and the kitchen hand looks out again.

"Eh, you deaf?"

The embankment looks different now. Dawei's never seen it in the golden glow of late afternoon. The sun, hanging low over the construction projects across the causeway in China, is enlarged and muted by the sulphuric haze over

Zhuhai. Dawei is usually only out here after the last of the pots are scrubbed and the kitchen floor is mopped. By that time, the world consists of only what the streetlights reveal.

As he faces Zhihong, contemplating the possibility of changed circumstances, Dawei can't help but feel unfamiliar pangs of appreciation for whatever forces create the palette of oranges, reds and pinks before him. Released from the kitchen, possibly for good, Dawei feels he's now part of this world. He leans on the railing which provides the balance he needs while the earth below him seems to shift. After putting some of these thoughts in order, Dawei can look at Zhihong who's explaining why the screenplay is suddenly so valuable. The late afternoon light brings more definition to Zhihong's face, which seems to have aged more than the year or so since they last met.

"She wasn't known as a screenwriter so no one knew how to find her scripts," Zhihong says. "They went through all of her files. There are only hard copies. Only three, as far as anyone knows. Autumn Truce and two others. You have one of those two."

"What about the other one?"

"Her son. He's asking one of the studios for two million kuai. Crazy. But, I think they'll cough up half of that."

The number is as strange and alluring as the light that bathes everything around them in pastels. This number would set him free, an idea so powerful it sends his thoughts, again, into disarray. Will this wash away the mistakes of his past? What would it cost to open his own restaurant? Who's manning the sink? The pots and pans are probably too numerous now to even reach the drain stopper. Mr. Ong might not even let him back into the kitchen. Does any of this matter now? How can he trust that Zhihong is right? He's let Dawei down before, after all. More than that, Zhihong had just about left him for dead.

Dawei drops his head onto his forearms, which are folded on top of the railing. A wave of anger rushes over him. He looks up at Zhihong. "You think they'll pay a million? You s...s...say you think? You can't say things like this unless you're s...s...sure!"

Zhihong looks away. Dawei rises from the railing, grabs the front of Zhihong's polo shirt into his fist and they're face to face. Zhihong doesn't flinch as Dawei looks into his eyes, focusing on one and then the other, and then back again.

"You thought you'd be here every month! You th...th...thought I was the only person you could talk to and that y...y...you'd do anything to make sure of that."

Dawei's aggression captures the attention of some passers-by. A few of them, Mainland tourists wearing tour group sun visors, look over at the couple. One stops a few feet from Zhihong and Dawei, only to move on slowly after a few seconds.

"Why would they pay that much?"

"They want a follow-up to *Autumn Truce* as soon as possible," Zhihong says. "They want all of her scripts. They want to make her material into a franchise. They've already started raising money."

"Can't they j…just make one up and say it's hers?"

"I'm sure they'll do that if they can't get the script," Zhihong snaps back, his tone changing from remorse to anger. "Maybe they're already putting that plan together. I don't know. But, you know those drawings that are all over the script?"

Of course, Dawei knows the drawings. He had lost himself in them when he took the train from Macau to Beijing to find Zhihong a year ago and countless times since to distract himself from boredom and despair. The drawings, along with Zhihong's explanation, helped Dawei to follow the arc of the story.

"Some of the producers believe that the drawings have imbued her scripts with luck," Zhihong says. "You know how they are down here with the superstitions."

Dawei knows this too. He's seen how particular Mr. Ong is about replacing the fruit and burning incense on the shrine up high in the corner of the restaurant's dining room. On the small red shelf stands the porcelain incarnation of Guanyin, who's supposed to protect his business. Dawei is aware that Guanyin is good. He's seen characters in movies mention her, pray to her. The shrines are everywhere in Macau, their red lights glowing in otherwise darkened apartments and shop spaces, ensuring that bad, unlucky energy doesn't accumulate.

Something must be responsible for the wealth that permeates Macau. Something other than ports and factories. Maybe it's Guanyin and the other gods that appear on the shrines with the red lights. These spirits don't let people down. Why else would everyone around here have such respect and veneration for them? Maybe that's why life on the Mainland is so bitter. There are no benevolent beings watching from the corners, righting wrongs and helping the mistreated. Guanyin has seen Dawei's troubles and has influenced the course of events. She's seen him toiling over his sink night and day, his skin red from the steam, his hands rough from the detergent. And Guanyin knows that he's been wronged. She's making things right.

"Don't question this," Zhihong says. "They're interested but they won't be interested forever. You never know when the next big hit will divert their attention. Get me the script. You'll get half of the payment."

A million kuai. The number is almost three times what Uncle Yiming in Harbin made a year. In Yongfu Village, his parents only got several hundred kuai for the corn they coaxed from the ground all summer and dried under the sun on tarps laid out around their home.

In that restaurant Dawei will open with the money, he will set up a shrine for Guanyin. He will burn real sandalwood incense and every day he will place the most perfect pears and oranges for her.

He looks at Zhihong, squinting to see deeper inside as an extra measure of assurance that he's not kidding, that this isn't some ruse that will end in another disappointment. Noticing the fine lines around Zhihong's eyes, signs of age that emerged in the short time since he saw him last, Dawei sees a kind of sincerity that he can't doubt.

"I'll get you the script. But, how do I know you'll get that half million kuai to me?"

Zhihong smiles and shakes his head. His eyes seem to search for something, perhaps some bit of the connection they had shared when the screenplay didn't matter.

"It's funny," Zhihong says. "You'd think that with age comes wisdom but that's not the case. I thought it would be easier for both of us if we stayed apart. I wondered how we would repair the damage that we'd cause by trying to live together. Romance flares and dies quickly, doesn't it? And where would that leave us? We'd be left with pain and no prospects."

Zhihong pauses and Dawei takes a step back from him. The comment about age strikes Dawei. Did Zhihong hear his thoughts?

"But, I've come to realize that maybe I misjudged how close we are. Or were. At least I still feel as strongly for you as I did when we first met. So, just as I've become wiser, I've somehow managed to lose you."

The words and the defeated expression temper Dawei's anger.

"This half a million kuai won't be enough to regain your trust," Zhihong says. "I would give you the full million in a second if I thought it would get us some kind of a life together. But that much probably wouldn't do it either."

He bows his head and begins to laugh, the saddest laugh Dawei has ever heard.

"So, I'm left with the life that I will live with my wife and the child she's carrying now. Half a million kuai might make that life livable. And the other half might make your life better. And I'll learn to be happy enough with that."

THE WOUNDED MUSE

*****

The edge of a manila envelope catches Jake's eye as he walks by the mailbox vestibule next to the elevators, his IBM ThinkPad bag slung across one shoulder and a gym bag hanging off the other. The postal worker had to fold the envelope in half to get the document into the slot, making it visible without even opening the box. Otherwise, Jake wouldn't have bothered to open the box. He uses his newsroom address for his cell phone bill and his home utilities are covered in his rent.

Feeling uneasy, Jake fumbles in his pocket to find his keys. His taxes are deducted automatically from his pay. All correspondence with friends goes through email or his phone. He's arranged all official matters so that he'd never need to bother opening a physical mailbox.

The lock sticks and he jiggles the key to get it to turn. The door opens with a squeak and Jake pulls the envelope out. It's addressed to Jake using his English and Chinese names, with the street address in Chinese. There's no return address.

"Oh, God," he whispers to himself as he opens the envelope and sees photos inside. Before he even sees them clearly, Jake knows what's on them. The Tianjin incident and stills from the video taken in the bathroom of Destination a week or so earlier. The Beijing postmark is the only indication of its origin. Jake can only look at the first two photos. He shoves the photos back into the manila folder as a woman steps into the vestibule to get her mail.

He calls Ben.

The late afternoon light in Ritan Park is fading but the lamp posts haven't yet switched on. There's barely enough light for Ben, sitting next to Jake on a bench, to see clearly what's happening in the photos.

"This is just a scare tactic," he says. "Pathetic."

Ben seems more certain about this than he has been about anything they've been grappling with so far but Jake won't let himself breathe easier. Perhaps, he thinks, Ben is just delivering the obvious response. Why would anyone offer anything but reassurance? He's certainly not going to say: "Wow. You're fucked".

"Jake, how do you think this would play if foreigners suddenly had to worry about surveillance in their hotel rooms when they're visiting China?"

With this, Ben does have a point, especially considering how the government is trying to put forward the most welcoming face ahead of the Olympics. The arguments for concern and reassurance compete in Jake's mind. He thinks about how these images, with captions that include his name, would look in some public forum. He's always shocked at what shows up on Facebook profiles, which everyone seems to be tuning into these days. Maybe they would end up in a newspaper. He imagines the photos on page three of one of the Mainland-based Hong Kong tabloids as part of a feature on the sordid lives of Westerners in China.

The photos expose Jake in more than a purely graphic sense. He feels bludgeoned and paralysed, unable to fight back as his attackers close in for the kill.

"I can't look at these anymore," Ben says as he reaches for his crotch and shifts his sitting position. "They're turning me on."

The line catches Jake off guard and he chuckles reflexively. Ben's perfect comedic timing chases away some of his tension. It takes a certain kind of intelligence to pull a laugh out of a miasma of despair and Jake wonders where Ben gets this ability. This audacity. In another time, Jake would have dwelt on the privilege and the enlightened environment Ben must have come from to be so free with his comments, to not muzzle his thoughts. But what's the point in turning every interaction into some sociological polemic? And perhaps he should just be grateful that Ben is thoughtful enough to deliver a laugh. They're on the same team in more ways than one.

"Well," Jake says. "I guess I have other career options if journalism doesn't work out."

"Or just make it a part-time job to start," Ben replies in a dead pan.

"This is probably not the most ideal time to ask you this, Ben, but how is it that you speak perfect Mandarin?"

Ben furrows his brow and looks at Jake with a curious squint.

"At Cubana last week," Jake says.

Ben scratches his chin and Jake sees that he's holding back.

"*Kai tian pi di*," Jake says, shaking his head. "The idiom you threw out at the bartender. I overhead it. I had to look it up. I've studied and used Mandarin for a few years and don't have the ability to drop idioms like that. Where do you get that skill?"

Finally, Ben drops his head and laughs. "You're a better reporter than I thought."

"I don't know about that but I do know that you couldn't have learned Mandarin that well living in the U.S., even if Qiang was teaching you the language."

"Yep."

"So, how is it that you know Mandarin so well and why have you been keeping this a secret?"

"You know," Ben says, drawing the words out as though he's carefully constructing a response. "The irony is that I was about to tell you."

Jake leans closer to Ben. "I'm all ears."

"I'm working with Diane on a plan that will give us enough ammunition to resolve Qiang's predicament. And our plan would probably bury this issue also," Ben says as he waves the manila folder full of photos. "But we need your help."

The talk of ammunition makes no sense. They are three people against countless. How large does a stash of ammunition need to be in order to subdue an opponent so strong that every Western country bows to it?

"Give me your phone for a second," Ben says.

Jake hands the device over. Ben takes it, removes its battery and then hands it back.

"You know," Ben says as he pulls the battery out of his own phone, "the paper trail to the IOC member?"

Jake stares at his now-powerless phone and then looks back at Ben.

"Oh yeah, there are now ways to turn phones into transmitters even when you don't have an open line. Some of this stuff has been under development at my lab for a couple of years. So, keep that in mind when you're talking. Even if we're outside of our apartments, sitting here in a park, they might have the ability to listen in."

"That's seems crazy. And you think the authorities here have this technology?"

"I know the authorities here have this technology. At least they have the code for a lot of it. Whether they've deployed it, and who's using it here, I don't know. But it's better to be safe."

"How do you know they have the code?"

"I'll tell you that later. Right now, I need to tell you how we're going to get Qiang back."

"Right. And it involves the story I delivered to Trask News?"

"Yes. Diane and I were able to put the trail together because she had access to some records when she worked at International Bank of China."

"It's going to look bad for China when that story is published, if it's published, but I don't see that it's enough to help us."

"No. It's not, but we might be able to find several more if we can get access to remittance records back to 2001."

"And where do I come in?"

"Get an interview with anyone at the IBOC and bring me in as your assistant," Ben says.

"You can pull records just by being physically present in the building?"

"The technology that can turn your phone into a transmitter. It's related to technology that can capture data running from cordless keyboards to computers. Much of it has been developed in one of the programs I'm part of at CSAIL. If I'm in close enough proximity, I can capture logins and passwords. Once I have login credentials for people in the right departments, Diane and I can figure out where to search in the bank's database."

The park's lamps grow brighter as the last bit of daylight fades, throwing an amber glow on the concrete walkway. Slogans about next year's Olympic Games hang from the light posts. "One World, One Dream." "China Welcomes the World." "Everyone Benefits From Olympic Glory." As he reads the slogans, Jake realizes how damaging these paper trails could be. But only if they can find enough of them.

Policy lending, Jake thinks. That's what would get him an interview quickly. He's seen an uptick in announcements by the government about loans for projects in China's Western provinces, all of which go ignored by the foreign media. The disparity between economic growth in the hinterland and the booming cities on the east coast has been a source of concern for government planners. The imbalances has prompted people in the countryside to look for better prospects in the eastern cities, where many of them end up on the street. Living on the margins, these migrants pose a threat not only to China's image but also to the country's stability. The government has launched countless initiatives to channel more wealth to the west but the disparity only continues to grow.

With each initiative, the foreign reporters show less interest because there's nothing at stake for foreign investors, even when the government tries to talk up the opportunities. Jake could take the bait. He could feign interest and explain to the IBOC's spokesman that he's planning to write a feature on China's policy lending in the west. More publicity about this might attract the attention of foreign investors and lenders. That's what he'll dangle in front of the IBOC's communications director who wouldn't suspect that he's the one being baited.

"How much dirt do you think we'll be able to turn up?" Jake asks.

"Your guess is as good as mine, my friend."

"Once we've turned the tide against them, these photos will become our ammunition, not theirs."

*****

The email arrives with a ping as Jake sits, exhausted after a long day, in front of his monitor.

TO: jfb4543@yahoo.com
FROM: kmonahan597@yahoo.com
Wednesday, April 18, 2007, 13:14

Jake, I'm getting nowhere with McKee's office. Andrews won't take any of my calls so I visited the
office in person and had to wait for him to leave
the office for his lunch break to be able to talk.
Here's all he had to say when I followed him to the
elevator:

"This issue isn't a priority for us."
When I asked him why he went from such strong interest to this complete stone wall, he said you might
have an idea.

So, what happened? (!!!)
Kendra

Jake wonders how to explain what went wrong in Tianjin. The strategy seemed
foolproof at the time. But hindsight clarifies the wisdom of his decision. Really, how else would a closeted Republican react to the sort of desire his world
requires him to detest? Even without the shock of flash photography from
behind a mirror, would he have remembered the experience fondly? No. Jake
only needs to think about how he feels about most of the guys he sleeps with.
He wants them gone, preferably before the first light of day. And that has nothing to do with his career or position.

Andrews lives at the centre of American politics. He's probably been working on the blueprints for his path to power for years and none of the points
along that road would have involved gay sex in Red China.

Disgusted with himself, Jake slides the last of his untraceable SIM cards into
his phone and calls Kendra with the news.

As he dials, Jake notices the time stamp on the email. Kendra sent the message at 1:14 p.m. DC time. That's 1:14 a.m. Beijing time. This message was
sent almost twenty-four hours ago yet it arrived in his inbox just a few minutes
earlier.

THURSDAY, April 19, 2007

Payment from Chinese Property Developer to IOC Member Raises Questions

By Gustave Risolli and Regine Taylor

GENEVA, April 19 — Remittances totaling $7.5 million from a Chinese state-owned property developer to a company tied to the relatives of an International Olympic Committee member are raising questions about whether China bought the committee's decision to award Beijing the 2008 Summer Games.

According to documents seen by Trask News, Vegrette Holdings Ltd., a shell company based in Cyprus, received three payments of $2.5 million each from another shell company, Tidebreak International, based in the British Virgin Islands, a month before the IOC's decision was announced. Tidebreak received $7.75 million from Beijing Land and Property 10 days earlier, according to another set of documents. Vegrette's owners, Gwendolyn Barsha and Gabriel Barsha, are, respectively, the sister and nephew of IOC member Julian Segre.

"We will investigate these remittances if the documents we've been sent prove to be authentic," an IOC spokesman said about the remittances when contacted by phone for an interview.

The possibility that at least one IOC member was bribed adds to scandals that Beijing is already struggling to manage. The city's Deputy Mayor, Liu Zhihua, was recently purged following revelations that he funneled millions of dollars from projects related to the Summer Games slated for next year.

Beijing Weifang Law Offices, based in China's capital city, filed Tidebreak's registration papers.
Tidebreak's ownership isn't disclosed.

*****

2:30 p.m.

Jiang Yu, the Foreign Ministry Spokesperson, wears a Hillary Clinton-esque pantsuit with stiff power lapels. Hillary has always been popular here. Boot-legged copies of her memoir, *Living History,* translated into Chinese had turned up on the blankets of hawkers throughout Beijing shortly after the tome was published a few years earlier and are still available even though no domestic publishers can print it legally. The prohibition probably enhanced Hillary's influence in China.

Regine's news report, which ran just an hour before the press conference, will surely dominate the questions Ms. Jiang will field as she faces foreign reporters from behind the lectern that stands just below a map of the world featuring China dead centre.

"Thank you. Is the Foreign Ministry investigating the allegations in the Trask News report? The one suggesting that Beijing Land and Property may have tried to influence a member of the International Olympic Committee?" asks a female reporter, who then hands the microphone back to one of the event hosts.

She's seated several rows ahead of Jake. He doesn't recognize the voice and she hasn't given her name or press affiliation. She must be new to Beijing's foreign press corps.

"I'm not aware of the report you're asking about but I can tell you that there have been many attempts to smear China's image within the context of next year's Olympic Games."

Expressionless, Jiang speaks with the clear, formal cadence used by all high-ranking officials in formal settings. The delivery at these Foreign Ministry press events never changes, regardless of how challenging the questions are. Their speech is like a uniform, triple stitched along every seam.

Jake doesn't normally cover the regular Foreign Ministry briefings but had to race over once he read Regine's report online. This is the first time he's happy to see a competing newswire run an exclusive story that has the entire foreign press corps asking questions. He looks around the auditorium and sees Regine ahead of him, in the second row.

"The report is very specific about payments made by Beijing Capital Land to a shell company with Chinese connections, followed by a similar amount of money going from that shell company to another one tied to one of the IOC members. Is this something that you think will warrant an investigation?" asks another reporter.

"China's government will investigate any and all matters that involve corruption, assuming the allegations are credible. Are there any other questions?"

Another reporter asks about negotiations with Japan about visits to the Diaoyu Islands, an exchange that becomes background noise as Jake considers what he's done. Jiang's voice took on a harder edge as she dodged the last question about Regine's story. Jake has made the government sweat, which invigorates him some but terrifies him more. His heart races as he wonders if there's any way the story could be traced back to him. He mentally runs through the precautions he took. Then a deep breath. He made sure Regine understood not to call, email or text him any questions about the story. The documentation would speak for itself. Any indication that he or Diane have a connection to the production of the Trask News story would make it impossible to dig further.

FRIDAY, April 20, 2007
6:09 a.m.

Dawei's train pulls into Beijing's main railway station after a 36-hour trip from Guangzhou. Eyes half open, he waits for the jostling of the other passengers to die down before retrieving his jacket and backpack from the overhead rack. Once on his feet, Dawei is pushed out onto the platform and into a thicket of travellers carrying trunks and bundles held together with tape and rope. A woman's voice rings out from loudspeakers. She's saying something about ticket inspection but Dawei doesn't understand because the vast space turns the anxious chatter of hundreds and the hum of machinery into a sea of echoes that swallow her words. He massages his neck to work out the stiffness that set in during a fitful sleep leaning against the carriage wall. His feet shuffle within a procession of hundreds of other pairs towards the station's exit gates.

Dawei zips up the blue-hooded jacket he found in a dumpster in Macau. The jacket, in near perfect condition except for some darkening around the cuffs and the bottom corners where the zipper connects, was probably discarded by someone who didn't want to be burdened with such a heavy article of clothing in the subtropical climate of Macau. When he salvaged the jacket, Dawei felt a wad of folded paper in one of the inside pockets. He remembers the sting he felt when the paper turned out to be a restaurant receipt instead of cash. He could read the characters for Shanghai, several of the dishes ordered and the number of patrons. More than 3,000 kuai spent on a dinner for five. And then another receipt in a different pocket, this one for the coat itself, purchased just a few months earlier for 2,600 kuai. Echoes of wealth, the receipt and the jacket itself.

A gust of wind whips up a cylone of Sytrofoam and bits of plastic wrapping just outside the station's exit. An overnight storm has left large puddles for Dawei to walk around as he makes his way across the train station's front plaza. His tennis shoes won't keep the water out and a new pair would cost more than half of the cash that he carries in his front pocket, cash that he checks for every few minutes.

He must find the American journalist. Once he does, he'll have more cash than he can fit in all of his pockets. How high, Dawei wonders, will a stack of thousands of 100 kuai bills stand? Would they fit in his backpack? Will he need to buy another bag just to carry the money?

He won't need to carry it for long. He will go to a bank, wearing a Western-style suit jacket, a clean shirt and new shoes. The security guard won't look at him suspiciously as he walks to the counter with his money and the woman behind the glass will call him "Sir" after she sees how much money he has. The scene plays out for Dawei in slow motion, like he's seen in movies when the hero is rewarded for upholding justice. When the righteous warrior vanquishes the scheming regents. When the guy gets the girl.

He'll open his own restaurant. No more unheated quarters on construction sites. No more overnight dishwashing shifts in the bowels of hotels and casinos where people leave meals on the plush carpet outside their doors, unfinished and abandoned.

Most importantly though, this money will put him on an even keel, able to make amends for the actions that left him homeless in Harbin and unable to return to Yongfu Village.

The front of the train station faces north. He'll need to keep walking in that direction until he gets to Chang An Avenue which forms the east-west axis of the city. Once on Chang An, he'll need to head east and keep walking until he gets to the apartment complex somewhere to the east of the Third Ring Road. He will need to rely on his sense of distance because he doesn't remember exactly what the American's building looks like.

Standing on Chang'an Avenue, Dawei notices that many of his landmarks have been replaced by oddly shaped glass towers. The weather front that left the puddles and the chilly gusts has blown away the city's usual blanket of haze, leaving the air clear enough to see details in the Western hills now illuminated by the sunrise. He stops and wonders how he never noticed them the last time he was in Beijing before. He turns and starts walking away from them.

*****

```
TO: jfb4543@yahoo.com
FROM: kmonahan597@yahoo.com

Wednesday, April 18, 2007, 13:14
Jake, I'm heading to Adams Morgan for some inter-
views so I'll be tied up until about 11:00 p.m. my
time.

Kendra
```

Jake subracts 90 minutes from the time Kendra mentioned - 9:30 a.m. Beijing time. He can be outside then. "Adams Morgan" means he needs to use the number ending in "66".

*****

Diane has been staring at the blank MySpace field for half an hour, assigning risk levels to every word she's about to write and evaluating probable outcomes. She takes a deep breath and starts typing.

```
China is a just country and this is why I have hope
for my dear brother, Qiang, who was detained three
weeks ago for working on a project that only sought
to create harmony between developers and ordinary
citizens who comprise ideal communities. I appreci-
ate the way the authorities are taking their time
investigating him because it's only through careful
consideration that they'll understand what a patri-
ot Qiang is.
```

Pacing back and forth amid the lunchtime crowd in front of the China World towers, Jake listens for the remaining value on his pre-paid account. After half a standard promotional message about upgrading to a mobile plan, the auto-mated voice finally divulges the information he wants. Just twenty-three kuai left. Jake ends the call as the voice starts in with some offer he'll never need and a call rings in showing a number from Washington.

"Kendra, hi."

"Good time to chat?"

"Sure. Let's just keep it short 'cos the minutes remaining on my unregistered account are ticking down."

"Ok, long story short: McKee's not going to do anything."

Jake clenches the phone. Perhaps if he throttles it, a different message might come through.

"So I guess Andrews is too scared about the photos."

"Guess what, Jake. Andrews is no longer working for McKee. He's been fired."

"No."

"Yes."

"How?"

"I don't know, Jake. Maybe he divulged the details of your night with him in Tianjin, or maybe those photos were sent to McKee's office, or maybe this is all a coincidence. McKee's office is in turmoil because of Iraq and everything else, right? All we know for sure is that we don't have an advocate in Congress now."

Standing between the China World Towers, looking helplessly at a proces-sion of suited professionals filing into a Haagen Dazs outlet, Jake wants to knock them all over like bowling pins. Or just stand in place and scream. Any-thing to release the anger and shame that's sloshing through his gut like bile from a ruptured appendix.

"I fucked everything up, didn't I?" He says in a voice that starts to crack as it morphs into something closer to a sob.

"Too early to say. Do you know if Diane is going to make this public? Be-cause that's our only hope now."

Jake takes a deep breath. Falling apart never solves a problem, he reminds himself. One of the few useful pieces of advice he heard his mother say on a near-daily basis as he was growing up. The words served her like a crutch when boyfriends disappeared or when bills arrived that she didn't know how to pay.

"She said she's going to."

"Good. Now we need to use that to start a shit storm. I've got a few irons in the fire but I'm not going to go into detail about them because we can't afford to run down your pre-paid accounts. I'll check back with you tomorrow. How much time is left on this account?"

"Maybe fifteen minutes as long as the call is incoming. Three minutes tops if I need to call you."

"Right. Obviously, I need to call you."

"Yes, keep using Adam's Morgan. Once this is drained, I have one left, which we'll use when I mention *Georgetown.*"

*****

"His sister is ready to talk. She's setting up a blog," Jake tells Gavin, a Tokyo-based managing editor at Toeler, as he cradles his cell phone between his shoulder and ear.

Previously a London-based bond trader, Gavin moved up quickly through the editorial ranks by covering bond markets with more accuracy than anyone else on his team. Jake heard the backstory even before HR sent the email around, chatter he picked up while covering events with reporters from other regions. Word had it that Gavin got market-moving tips from his former colleagues, the sort of activity that might lead to disciplinary action by market regulators if it were ever discovered.

"Her blog will get a lot of attention," Jake adds, dangling the prospect of a hot story.

After Gavin racked up enough bond market reporting wins, he wanted to – as he put it in his first conversation with Jake – "experience the Orient". Single, thirty-something, and looking for adventures that will mainly play out in bars, bedrooms and brothels, Gavin is everything Jake dislikes about expats. Someone who's made a living trading bonds in London can't make decisions about what constitutes news in Asia, especially one who refers to the region as 'the Orient'.

"How does this differ from any other dissident story that we *don't* cover?" Gavin asks in a snarky tone.

Jake fumbles with his keys and wants to groan but can only roll his eyes. He enters his apartment, lets the backpack slung around one shoulder and his laptop bag on the other drop one by one and switches on the lights. He leans against the foyer wall with the bags by his feet.

"Because this guy has an interesting backstory, Gavin. A Silicon Valley whiz originally from Chongqing who got scholarships at good schools in the U.S., got a green card and now he's missing."

"Sounds like pure tabloid junk to me. What else is there about this story that's so interesting to you?"

The question sounds like an accusation. It's not just that the story is personal and, therefore, would need a finer editorial filter. This dissident case is killing Jake. Does Gavin know about his relationship with Qiang? He's aware that others in his social orbit know about this but can't believe the information would have surfaced in Tokyo. Perhaps Gavin does have a knack for news.

"Let's talk about it again next week," Gavin says.

"Right, thanks," Jake says just before cutting off the call.

He looks down at the full laptop bag. It has an IBM ThinkPad, a digital voice recorder, extra batteries and lists of questions he'll lob at the Chinese Central Bank governor from the sidelines of a conference he's covering tomorrow in Zhengzhou. He'll need to leave the apartment in less than five hours to catch the flight and he hasn't eaten dinner because he had to file a series of templated stories that cover each of the Central Bank governor's likely comments.

Hungry and tired, Jake lacks the energy to metabolize the anger he feels towards Gavin. He needs to redirect these feelings into something more constructive, a strategy to get the story about Qiang written, a story that the editors in Washington won't want to spike.

As he reaches for a bottle of wine from the refrigerator, Jake starts thinking about other publications, ones that will recognize what's at stake politically and not be bothered that it has zero market relevance. Now that Diane plans to start blogging, he's free to make noise. Perhaps he will write the story that creates enough interest, and enough pressure, to get Qiang out. How would that change things between them? He plays with that thought for a moment and then tries to suffocate it. Love doesn't grow out of gratitude.

Jake needs to pack for tomorrow but clothes from the last trip a few days earlier, carrying the pungent stink of frayed nerves and deodorant gone sour, still occupy his luggage. He'll need to put all of it in the washer and stay up long enough to throw them in the dryer. The collision of mortal urgencies and mundane tasks leaves Jake stuck, staring at nothing. He empties his pockets of a wallet and a few bent name cards, his own mixed with those of government and corporate spokespeople. Then one of several coins he drops on the table rolls onto the floor and under a bureau. The silence that ensues after the coin settles hypnotizes him. He wonders how much damage he'd cause if he just got on another flight – to Auckland or New Delhi or Johannesburg – and started a new life. Do Diane and Ben really need him? Do the stories he writes make any difference? He could just resurface in a few days, in a different city, and tell his employer that his parents died in car crash or some similar tragedy. Or he could just tell the truth. His psychological tethers snapped and he followed the rapids. And wound up in Buenos Aires.

A knock at the door breaks the spell. Jake looks at the display on his cell phone. 11:29 p.m. He hasn't had unannounced visitors since that guy kept showing up two or three years earlier. He forgets his name.

He doesn't want to answer the door. It could only be someone who's been to his place and doesn't have his number, a particular category of people who don't have his number for a reason.

"Jie-ke," says the voice on the other side of the door. "Is that you, Jie-ke? I am Dawei."

Dawei waits on the couch while Jake puts a load of clothes into the wash. Jake has set him up with a cup of tea and McVitie's digestive wafers. As he waits for the water to start sloshing into the machine, Jake takes a sip of wine, wondering what might unfold between him and Dawei who looks exhausted. Sitting with his backpack on his lap, Dawei wears a blue hoodie with brownish grime around the pockets. The drawstring is missing.

"So, how long has it been?" Jake asks as he comes back into the room. "At least two years, maybe three?"

"Yes, something like that," Dawei says.

"Are you still delivering air tickets?"

"No. I lost that work after only a few w…w…weeks because people started getting tickets through their computers."

The stutter reminds Jake of how awkward their connection had been.

"So, did you get other work?"

"No, I had to go back to my job at the restaurant in Macau. I used the rest of my m…m…money to get back there."

Dawei seems anxious. He's looking around. Not so much out of curiosity like during the first visit. The washing machine fills the silence by clicking into the steady whir of the first spin cycle, changing over from the periodic swish of agitation. Jake doesn't want to ask what's brought Dawei back to Beijing. There's something about the fatigue and anxiousness Dawei projects that suggests a long story.

"I've been in Beijing for some time now. It took me a while to figure out which building is yours and then which unit is yours."

"Yeah, they all look the same, don't they? Sometimes when it's late and I'm tired, I walk to the wrong–"

"Do you remember that script I gave you when we saw each other last?" Dawei asks, cutting Jake off and looking at him directly. A fixed stare that prompts Jake to put his glass down. Dawei had only ever made eye contact through split-second glances.

Jake remembers that Dawei left a few items in a folder, including a memento of Sino-Canadian diplomatic relations in the form of a maple leaf and a lotus flower, flattened and encased in clear laminate. He doesn't remember exactly where that folder is, so he doesn't answer straight away. He scratches his chin.

"Um, yes I think I remember."

Dawei focuses on Jake intently, his eyes now so wide and searching that Jake moves a few inches away. Moving slowly, like a cat fixing on a kill, Dawei puts his backpack on the floor. He then stands up, looking over into the computer room and then back at Jake. The stare demands action, or at least some kind of movement. This visit clearly isn't a reunion. There will be no small talk or exploration of roads not taken when they hung out years earlier.

Prompted by Dawei's apparent desperation, Jake walks into the computer room and flips on the light. Two of the room's walls are lined with shelves full of file boxes and stacks of binders, folders and files. Workbooks from his courses in China, tote bags full of material from the dozens of conferences he's covered, some books that he's read, some untouched. Abandoned GMAT study guides, brochures from attractions like Xian's Terracotta Soldiers.

With his hand still on his chin, Jake eyes the shelves. It occurs to him that he's thrown some things out. Could Dawei's folder have been among them? He remembers that Dawei's mementos were somewhere in the various heaps but years have passed and, with them, any obligation he'd felt to keep the items safe. They probably got tossed amid various attempts to restore order on his shelves. Dawei stands behind Jake as he surveys the banks of shelving stacked with file boxes.

Jake can't bring himself to tell Dawei that his items are probably gone.

"Dawei, I can't look through all of this right now and I need to leave for a work trip early tomorrow. Actually, in just a few hours. I can go through this when I come back and call you if I find what you're looking for."

Dawei continues looking at the shelves as though he hasn't heard anything Jake has said. The more Jake thinks about it, the more likely it seems that he's ditched Dawei's mementos. He's aware that Chinese place more importance on thoughtful gestures than the always-too-casual *laowais* but Dawei's concern for what's happened to these items seems to go far beyond sentimentality.

"I can go through these boxes myself," Dawei says, his stare still fixed on the disarray in front of them.

Jake wants to ask why Dawei feels so strongly about the things he's trying to retrieve but knows how such a question might come across as callous and flippant. It would seem reasonable at this point to ask why Dawei would have left these items in his place for so long if they were so important. A few months, yes. A few years? That doesn't make sense, especially since they hadn't established much of a friendship.

"That's not a good idea," Jake says. "Besides, I've moved many of my things around. I've moved some things to my office here in Beijing and even some things back home to the U.S."

He puts a hand on Dawei's shoulder and Dawei steps away.

"Dawei," Jake says firmly. "I need to get ready to leave and I'm not going to find your items before I do. I understand that you want these things back and I'll do my best to get them. Please don't give me any trouble about this."

Jake puts his hand on Dawei's shoulder again and leads him out of his office. Once they're in the foyer, Jake grabs a post-it note and scrawls his cell phone number onto it.

"Here, if it's so important for you to have these things, call me on this number in a week. That's when I'll be back and can look through all of my things more thoroughly."

By the time Jake gets Dawei out his front door, he's issued at least a dozen assurances that he'll find the screenplay. He had started by saying that he'd jin liang, try his hardest, but Dawei wouldn't reach for his bag or motion that he's ready to leave until Jake started using more definitive language.

"*Wo hui zhao dao*," Jake says. I will find it.

"What time is best to stop by?" Dawei says as Jake grips the door handle.

"You have my cell number," Jake replies. "Just call me and we'll set a time."

He remembers that Dawei doesn't have a cell phone.

"Oh, right. Here," Jake says as he pulls his wallet from his back pocket and lifts a 100 kuai note from the bills inside. "I know you don't have a cell phone so you can use this to call from a public phone."

SATURDAY, April 21, 2007

TO: jbradley@toelernews.net
FROM: KendraEMonahan@gmail.com
Saturday, April 21, 2007,

Jake, my op-ed in tomorrow's World Chronicle…

I'm pasting it below in case they're jamming this link in China.

THE WOUNDED MUSE

This is what I didn't have time to tell you about on the phone yesterday. Note the link to the translations I'm doing for her. Spread the word.

Kendra

Shattering the China Dream: Unlawful Detentions Undermine Respect for Beijing
By Kendra Monahan, Sunday, April 22, 2007; A25

On Feb. 16, Sun Qiang, an independent filmmaker and U.S. permanent resident, became another victim of Chinese state kidnapping. It is unclear why state agents abducted Qiang (his given name) on March 25, but his friends think it may be related to his work on a documentary about the redevelopment of neighbourhoods in Beijing, and attempts to keep at least some residents in the newly redeveloped communities.

Qiang's ordeal involved no courts, arrest warrants, official paperwork, police stations or jails. While his captors work for China's State Security Bureau, what happened can only be described as a kidnapping. The extra-legality and the lack of official records make it impossible to count such cases. Human rights organizations try to keep count, but the outside world generally hears about only those victims whose friends and family manage to overcome police pressure to stay quiet and who are also well connected or savvy enough to get the story out somehow.

Qiang turned 34 this week. He personifies a generation of urban Chinese who have flourished thanks to the Communist Party's embrace of market-style capitalism and greater cultural openness. He and his sister, Diane Sun, who works in finance and lives a comfortable middle-class life in Shanghai, have enjoyed freedoms of expression, travel, lifestyle, and career choice that their parents could never have dreamed of. They are proof of how U.S. economic engagement with China has been overwhelmingly good for many Chinese.

Problem is, the Chinese Dream can be shattered quickly if you step over a line that is not clearly drawn — a line that is kept deliberately vague and that shifts frequently with the political tides. Those who were told by the Chinese media that they have constitutional and legal rights are painfully disabused of such fantasies when they seek to shed light on social and religious issues the state prefers to keep in the dark.

Since Qiang's detention, Diane has spent countless hours pleading with police officers for information about his case, location, and condition. After a month of getting nowhere, she's just started to chronicle her ordeal on a Chinese-language blog at http://spaces.msn.com/sunqiang. It is a heartbreaking account of how China's regime eats its young. In her first entry she holds out hope: "China is a just country, and this is why I have hope for my dear brother, Qiang, who was detained one month ago for working on a project that only sought to create harmony between developers and ordinary citizens who comprise ideal communities."

Diane also describes her disillusionment: "the people I dealt with never showed police credentials (despite repeated requests), and never called each other by name. I was angry at myself for my political naiveté, and angry at this place that displayed the police insignia but did not actually 'Serve the People.' "

With an ever-increasing interdependence with China

in terms of trade and investment, Americans need to re-asses this relationship. What is this country to think? On the one hand Qiang's government has raised the living standards of millions of its citizens with economic reform and international trade. On the other hand, his underlings trample shamelessly on his people's basic human rights.

The careers of some politicians in both countries — not to mention military budgets — would no doubt benefit if our two nations became enemies. As an American who lived and worked in China for more than a decade, however, I continue to believe that peaceful engagement between the United States and China is in the best interest of both nations' people.

But we have a serious problem that won't go away: How can Americans respect or trust a regime that kidnaps our friends?

*****

In the press room in Zhengzhou, Jake sends Kendra's opinion piece to the printer. Twenty copies. He walks it over to where Regine is seated and slides it in front of her.

"I thought you'd find this interesting," he says. "The link is now blocked unless you have a VPN."

Regine's eyes open wide after reading a few lines. "Oh my God, I heard about this piece and tried searching. You know, they're really jamming the websites now, aren't they?"

Jake scrawls a phone number on the left margin. "Here's Diane's cell number if you need more info for your story."

"Darling, you're a star," Regine says, drawing out the last word as she scans the document.

"I'm still fighting with one of my regional editors to write this," Jake says. "You know us. If it's not going to make someone money, it's not news. I'm going to put copies of this all over the press room later today to be sure the story gets out."

"Are you going to provide Diane's cell to everyone?" Regine asks.

"That's only for you. You get the head start and direct access to Diane. You now owe me a drink," Jake says as he pulls his laptop bag strap around one shoulder.

SUNDAY, April 22, 2007

The signal on the monitor set to GlobeCast, one of several screens high on the newsroom wall, cuts out. Something has bothered the censors. They have seven seconds to react to the foreign satellite feeds, those available only in five-star international hotels and grade-A office complexes. The authorities have been intervening more on these conduits to the outside world lately. Jake hadn't thought much about it. The years he's spent in China wore down any sensitivity to these controls which had become both obvious and meaningless. But this time, amid the stress of recent events, in the silence of a vacant newsroom, the dead signal draws Jake's attention.

Jake is tempted to check out the GlobeCast website, to see if he can find whatever story has tripped the wire but stops himself before he reaches for the mouse. It's Sunday and he doesn't want to be in the newsroom any longer than necessary to finish a story he got on the sidelines of the conference earlier in the day. He's even turned down the volume on all of the monitors to concentrate on bringing his story to a close. The GlobeCast signal resumes, just at the start of a report featuring chaos in the aftermath of another explosion in Baghdad.

And then the BBC monitor goes black. They generally don't tamper with BBC as much, at least not lately, since relations with the UK have been on an even keel. Jake now won't be able to focus on his story until he finds out what new story is bothering the powers that be. He clicks on the BBC website and one headline captures his attention.

Interview Footage of Former China Leader Suggests Beijing Let Top Reformer Die in 1989.

Jake reads on to learn that the interview excerpt by an unidentified documentarian in China surfaced on a Taiwanese television network. The footage was obtained, the report says, by mainland Chinese dissidents living abroad. Jake clicks on the video but it won't play so he skims the story and sees a still from the video. The image shows a frail, old man with a serious expression. The lighting is harsh and the framing awkward. According to the report, the interviewee claims the CCP party leadership withheld medical care to Hu Yao-bang, the reformer whose death sparked the pro-democracy demonstrations in Tiananmen Square in 1989. Hu suffered a heart attack and, the report alleges, the hardliners let him die.

Jake refreshes the screen to get the embedded video working and this sends the load-wait circle into motion. Frustrated, he clicks over to his Firefox browser and calls up BBC only to see the same. When he clicks back to the default browser, he sees that BBC has timed out. And the same on Firefox. The censors have cut access to BBC.

"Dammit," Jake mutters. There's only so much room for China in the global headlines. The interview story might knock Kendra's op-ed piece, and all the other stories about Qiang, below the fold. He'll check in with Regine to see when she plans to publish her story.

Don't overreact, Jake tells himself. Less than a year away, the Olympics Games have stoked interest in China. Maybe the two stories will build traction for each other.

Jake takes his glasses off and rubs his eyes, trying again to focus on his story, and realizes he needs a diversion. He stands, stretches out the fatigue of the past few days and heads through the reception area. The glass door slides open when Jake waves his badge in front of the security box and he walks down the corridor to the men's room. From 43 stories up, he looks at the sun hovering just above the Fragrant Hills as he empties his bladder. All he needs to do is add an ending to his report and he'll be able to have the last few hours of the weekend to himself.

On his way back to the office, Jake notices a shadow moving in the reception area and wonders which of his colleagues has come in. Strange. According to the schedule, Jake is the only one working this weekend. The government often drops important news outside of business hours when they think journalists won't be paying attention. But if something big was announced, an editor would have alerted him.

Once he's in front of the door, swiping his badge to open it, Jake sees Dawei standing next to the modern, white leather couch, scanning the magazines on the coffee table. His disheveled appearance clashes with the clean order of the Toeler News reception area which is framed in with large, off-white panels. Dawei must have been waiting in the corridor, just out of sight, or perhaps around a corner, for the newsroom's door to slide open. It takes a few seconds for the glass pane to slide shut again. It occurs to Jake just then that he handed his name card over to Dawei when they had first met. Had Dawei kept it all of this time? Or maybe Dawei followed him from Jake's apartment, where he stopped briefly to drop his luggage and change into a t-shirt and jeans.

Dawei looks up at Jake when he hears the door slide.

"Did you find that screenplay?"

The invasion infuriates Jake. Dawei is now more than a nuisance. He's a threat. Jake told him clearly that he was going to be away for several more days and would look when he returned. Dawei staked him out anyway. There's now no trust between them so there's no point in any civility.

"How did you get in here? Do you know you're..." Jake doesn't know the word for "trespassing" in Chinese so he switches to simpler language. "Do you know you're not allowed to be in here?"

"Did you find the script? I need that script," Dawei says, slapping the back of the seat next to him, the sharp sound announcing his occupation of the entire space.

Jake wants to grab Dawei by the throat and throw him out of the office but the surveillance camera will pick all of this up. If this turns into a physical altercation, there's no telling where this matter will end up. Security guards? The PSB? Courts? It's not worth it.

"I left Beijing shortly after you came by my place on Friday night. I just got back and came here to get some work done. You saw how many things I need to go through to find some document you gave me, what, two, three years ago."

Dawei stands. "Y...y...you need to find that screenplay. Please find that screenplay."

Dawei's tone shifts from anger to desperation and he uses the polite form of the second person. Maybe he realizes that he's overstepped his bounds. Nevertheless, Jake feels responsible for the unauthorized entry of a stranger into this workplace. Someone unhinged and possibly violent.

Jake picks up the phone that sits on the reception desk.

"You need to leave. If you don't, I'm calling security downstairs and I'll tell them to look at the video that shows how you got in here."

Dawei is silent. Jake has neutralized him but knows this is only a temporary reprieve. He knows he'll never find this document that's become so vitally important. And that's the problem. Dawei has nothing, which is perhaps what's driving this delusional pursuit of something, the one thing besides the clothes on his back and whatever other items take up room in his backpack. This is tragic, Jake tells himself, but not his fault.

"I tried calling you y...y...yesterday and today. You didn't answer."

Jake now remembers getting a few calls from numbers he didn't recognize. At the time, he had forgotten that he asked Dawei to call. Other events weighed more heavily on him, of course, like conferences to cover, stories to file. All the while trying to manage the dissemination of news that will free someone he can't stop thinking about. This lost screenplay business can't possibly be a real problem for anyone.

"I was in transit. I was probably in the airplane at the time. I'm on the ground now. I'll answer."

Dawei knows that the answer is bullshit and Jake doesn't care. Anything to make this obsessive lunatic go away.

Dawei heads towards the exit and then stands still in front of it. Jake swipes his badge over the security box. The glass pane slides open and Dawei, head down and muttering something Jake can't understand, leaves.

*****

Sparks fly from the top of another steel structure that's been rising from what was, until less than a year ago, several blocks of decaying worker housing. Jake watches as a crane fastened to the side of the building lowers a rectangular piece of glass panel cladding that swings like a pendulum. He hears the voices of the construction workers shout out shrill warnings. "Careful! Watch out." Several workers on the ground pull cables fastened to either side of the glass panel, bringing it under control.

Construction is supposed to stop by this hour but everyone knows the edicts to finish all major projects before the Olympics start trump the regulations. The soldering and fastening will continue through the night, just like it does at all of the construction sites along the Avenue of Everlasting Peace. Having decided to walk home to clear the drama of the weekend from his head, Jake now realizes it would have been more peaceful inside a cab.

He feels his phone vibrate and he looks at the display. It's a text message from Regine.

No luck getting a hold of Qiang's sis. The phone is switched off. U sure you gave me the correct number?>

Jake dials Diane's number and it connects to nothing. He throws up him arm, looking to hail a cab. "Fuck," he mutters as he sees all of the traffic at a standstill. He then tightens the straps on his backpack and breaks into a jog towards Qiang's apartment building.

Jake faces the door with the same fear he felt just a few weeks earlier. There will be silence when he knocks. Jake hates this fucking door which had only ever led him to frustration before the detention and dread since. He has no choice but to knock. He pounds on the door with the meaty side of his fist. No response. He pounds again and listens more closely. This time hears the silence on the other side broken by the sound of footsteps approaching the door. Hope and dread collide as Jake wonders who will open it. He stands frozen. The light through the fisheye peephole disappears as a person on the other side of the door looks through. The lock clicks and the door swings open. Diane stands there looking at Jake with bloodshot eyes. She's been crying.

"Come in."

"What..."

"Did you know that Qiang was working on some documentary about 1989? About Hu Yaobang?" she asks. "They played me a recording of a phone conversation he had with that...that... American woman in Washington, the one who's caused so much of this trouble."

It can't be, Jake thinks. This can't be about the interview footage that the BBC is running. He would have known if Qiang was working on something so sensitive. In any case, Qiang always had nuanced views about 1989 and never seemed interested enough in the events that led to the crackdown. How would he have gotten involved in such a project? He can't swallow this revelation that Diane has thrown out like a grenade.

"This is completely out of my control now, Jake. Qiang's work was more involved than I thought. 1989? Hu Yaobang? What was he thinking?"

Bewildered, Jake puts both hands on his forehead and looks around the apartment for some bearing on the situation. "Qiang never said anything to me about working on a Tiananmen Square project," he says. "How do you know this evidence isn't just something trumped up by the PSB?"

"They showed me footage of an interview Qiang shot with the same official, in the same setting, with material about the redevelopment of properties in Beijing. Qiang was sometimes in shot and his voice is asking questions."

Jake feels like he's stuck in quicksand. Everything Diane has said adds up to the fact that Qiang was working on some piece about 1989 in addition to the one about redevelopment. Anything he says now to try to refute this will be meaningless. If Diane is giving up, there's no hope.

"Even if that interview was shot by Qiang," he says, "does that give the authorities the right to erase him? He's your brother, for God's sake, Diane. What about all that stuff you said before about...about filial piety? Where is your sense of filial duty now? Was that just bullshit?"

"Don't you see, Jake? This just shows there's no way I can look out for him. Not when he can't see when he's gone too far. Whether or not you think that line shouldn't exist doesn't matter. And it doesn't matter whether or not I think he went too far. The fact is that he should have known how sensitive that subject is here."

Jake stares out the window, unable to look at Diane because she has just turned into another obstacle between him and Qiang. She is now exactly the person his first impression suggested. Completely willing to submit to authority when she should be fighting.

"Listen to me, Jake," Diane says as she grabs Jake's hand with both of hers. "You need to just forget about all of this."

As he moves to push her away, Jake feels Diane trying to work something into his hand. A small, round object.

"Qiang is certain to be charged with something soon," she continues as she closes Jake's hand around the paper. "I will make sure that he has some kind of legal representation but there's nothing more I can do."

Diane holds his hand shut and squeezes them with more strength than Jake would have expected from her petite arms. The covert delivery, like sudden reinforcements in a hopeless gun fight, shifts the moment back to hope. Knowing the authorities are listening in, Jake searches for something natural enough to say, something about resignation and submission. Something that might make sense for this performance. Something vague, because he doesn't know what circumstances now prevail. The note in his sweating palm will provide the answers.

"What can I say?" Jake says as he withdraws from Diane, keeping his hand with the note clenched. "You're saying our only option is to hope that this evidence turns out to be false?"

He backs further away from her. "Or maybe all I can do is hope that this is all some bad dream?"

They stand in silence for a few moments.

"Just go back to your job and your life and maybe this will one day get resolved," Diane says. "I will do as much as I can for Qiang but I need to work within the system. I also need to refocus on my work. I'll be no help at all if I'm out of a job. I have some work meetings lined up tomorrow and then I'll need to head back to Shanghai."

Jake slides his hand into his pocket and leaves the note inside.

"I don't know how to swallow any of this, Diane. I've been completely powerless and I don't see that changing anytime soon," Jake says, shaking his head. "I guess this is in your hands."

Diane nods, like a director prompting an actor, signaling that Jake has nailed the scene.

Back at his apartment, Jake shuts the bathroom door and pulls the note out. He puts the toilet seat down and then sits as he unrolls the note, written in perfectly clear block lettering.

Jake, I was detained by the PSB for the past day. Long story short,: the video with the party official who made revelations about 1989 has made it very unlikely that they'll release Qiang. They're look- ing for the sources of funding for his projects. They suspect that I might be part of that network. They don't seem to know that you have helped out on some of Qiang's work (subtitling, I think). If they find that out, they'll drag you into this. I need to shake the PSB enough to carry out the plans we've made with Ben. If they think I'm going to agitate things further, I'd still be in detention. Ben is now staying elsewhere and has his phone switched off but please call him later today, (outside of your apartment, using the untraceable number), to final- ize your plan to interview people at IBOC tomorrow. He should receive the ID we talked about. It's vi- tally important that we get him into the building. I have a meeting at NICB tomorrow afternoon and Ben will be with me for that.

MONDAY, April 23, 2007
8:40 a.m.

Jake stares down at the atrium's granite koi ponds lined with bamboo trees sprouting from beds of river rock. As the woman behind the information desk takes down their details and prepares badges for himself and Ben, he falls into a trance. The odds seem long for what he and Ben are about to attempt and Jake has trouble believing it could be so easy to steal data from such a secure environment. To keep calm, he projects his concerns into the gurgling water.

The koi ponds are arranged in a series of steps, each with a notch that allows water to flow down from the altar-like information desk where Jake and Ben are being processed, down to the atrium's street-level entrance. The morning sun reflects off one of the twin towers of grey-tinted glass soaring above them, sending a cascade of geometric reflections throughout the atrium's cream-coloured marble.

Taking a deep breath, Jake looks back at the woman behind the desk who writes their names with deliberate precision, cross-checking each letter against those on the IDs in what seems like an elementary school lesson. Jake needs to get Ben settled while the bank's employees are logging in. There's no Chinese version of the name on the business card Ben has handed over so she struggles to transcribe the characters. It has the name of a Toeler News journalist based in Kuala Lumpur, someone who recently left the company. Jake figures there's no chance the former reporter, Thomas Jantzen, will suffer any repercussions. Ben had a colleague at his workplace create a fake ID with Jantzen's name and it arrived yesterday afternoon, just in time. It will be clear soon enough that Jantzen was in no way responsible. In the whirlwind of recent events, the boundaries of right and wrong aren't very clear.

When the elevator door opens on the thirty-eighth floor, a Chinese woman in her early thirties is waiting for Jake and Ben. She wears a plain white blouse and a navy blue skirt. Her shiny hair is pulled back into a bun.

A set of rosewood furniture takes up most of the reception area, ornate and uncomfortable as possible because no one will expect to feel at ease here. A long bench sits against the wall with two chairs on each side of a low table, all arranged under a large tapestry of the Great Wall snaking over hills of autumnal foliage. On the opposite wall, east-facing, floor-to-ceiling windows provide an expansive view of sunlight-tinted smog with only the closest buildings visible as silhouettes.

"You must be Jake and Thomas," the woman says in Mandarin-accented English, approaching them with an outstretched hand. "I'm Director Liu's assistant. Please call me Anna.

They enter a conference room where Director Liu is waiting. Liu is pale and plump, probably the result of a regular schedule of dinners with central government officials whom the man must court.

"Director Liu," Anna says. "We are welcoming two journalists from the financial news company Toeler News."

"Please come in. Please sit," Liu says, offering his card to Jake with both hands. Jake knows the card is useless but takes it graciously with both hands and offers his in return.

"Thank you, Director Liu, for your time," Jake begins in Chinese. "We're very grateful."

"You're too polite," Liu says. "Please sit anywhere you like."

"Thank you, Director Liu. My colleague here, Tuo-ma-si, is based in Kuala

Lumpur but we're hoping to transfer him here to Beijing because he speaks Mandarin. He'll just be taking some notes."

Jake moves away from the head of the table where Liu will inevitably sit. Rummaging in his bag for his recorder and note pad, Jake moves to a seat at the side of the table, closest to Liu. He places the items on the table and arranges them while waiting for Liu to settle into his chair.

"Welcome," Liu says.

"Thank you, Director Liu," Ben says obediently.

"I'm glad Toeler News is taking an interest in our operations in a way that's not negative," Liu says with an ingratiating smile.

Liu claims the head of the table and bids Jake, again, to sit. Jake nods respectfully and thanks Liu once again. He moves slowly as he positions himself between his chair and the table, allowing Liu to sink into his chair first. Jake then sits and hits a button on his voice recorder.

Ben puts his laptop on the table, in front of the seat next to Jake. He opens it, plugs a device into its USB portal, and begins typing. In his peripheral vision, Jake sees a cascade of data pouring down a screen.

"Director Liu, many foreign investors are interested in the policy lending you're directing in the Western provinces and we are grateful that you have granted us this opportunity to better understand the opportunities for foreign banks."

With his left hand, Ben begins to tap his pinky, signaling to Jake that the search for user names and passwords is just starting. They had worked out the signals the day before, on a subway ride, with their phones powerless. Ben will tap with his ring finger when the data pull is underway and stable. Jake needs to keep the interview going until he sees the thumb tap, which means that he's reached the point of diminishing returns and can stop the data pull.

Jake gradually works through a list of ten questions, stopping for clarification of details he'll never need and looking at the time display on his phone. Every five minutes that he thinks has passed turns out to be only one or two.

Twenty-five minutes into the interview, as Ben is still tapping his middle finger on the table, Jake asks the last question he had prepared. They only have thirty minutes with Director Liu and Anna, who's sitting across from Jake, starts checking her watch.

Liu is explaining how the high-speed rail system, now under construction throughout the country, will make investments in the Western provinces more viable because enterprises there will have better access to markets.

"And, more importantly, people will be more willing to live in cities like Xining and Chengdu," Liu says. "People are the key. An industry can't run without qualified engineers and researchers. We're financing so many projects, like high-speed rails, to make these places more attractive to people with the skills to make enterprises competitive."

Jake is no longer taking notes. Every additional second that Ben spends tapping his middle finger ratchets up an alarm that's sounding in Jake's head, making it impossible to concentrate on Liu's answers.

"Frankly speaking," Liu continues, "we can't afford to let the Western provinces fall any further behind the east coast. The government is earmarking billions in the west and we're increasing our lending there at the same pace. From that perspective alone, foreign banks should feel more confident about lending to industries there."

Ben starts tapping his index finger and Jake exhales. Ben had told him he would probably have enough login credentials by the time he's on the fourth finger, although Jake should keep things going until he's tapping his thumb just to be sure.

"Director Liu," Jake says. "I'm so very grateful for your answers. Could I ask just one follow-up question?"

"I'm afraid that Director Liu's schedule is very busy today," Anna says, interrupting. She repeats this in English, giving Jake time to think of a question to lob.

"Just very quickly, Director Liu, could you let me know which hinterland industries will get the most lending from International Bank of China this year?"

Looking first at Anna and then back at Jake, Director Liu smiles.

"I'm afraid I can't answer that question. All I can tell you about that is that we're looking at a wide variety of industries."

Ben begins tapping his thumb.

"Thank you, Director Liu. Thank you, Anna."

*****

3:50 p.m.

Twenty minutes into the meeting Diane set up at NICB and Ben is still tapping his pinky. At the same time, Diane has been taking a small group of policy lending directors at the bank through a deck of case studies. Five case studies in all and she's nearly through number four. The group is led by Director Zhang, a senior vice president somewhere in his mid-fifties.

"As you can see, this one shows the problems that we experience when we don't get all of the documentation we request. Our overall net return when joining the domestic banks in policy loan syndication is on the rise. But this is what happens when we bypass certain requirements in the due diligence phase."

Diane traces one of three lines in a chart. One line, rendered in green, shows revenue assumptions provided by the company in question. Another, in blue, shows repayment obligations on the syndicated loan that Diane's bank helped to arrange. The last line, bright red and thicker than the others, shows actual revenue. That line starts out on par with the green line, begins descending shortly after the mark labeled 'loan initiation' and then drops precipitously over the next several months shown on the horizontal axis. Less than one year into the life of the loan in question, the red line falls below the blue line. The lines turn from solid to dotted once they pass March, 2007 with the red line continuing its plunge until it runs into a question mark.

"So, you can see why we need to insist on audited numbers for every metric used in our modeling," Diane says. "Our policy is tightening up here, not just in China but worldwide. There's some growing concern about commercial paper exposure in North America. We all know that China is a different story but we're under pressure to lower our exposure to risky assets everywhere."

The red line mirrors the tension caused by Ben's lack of progress. His pinky is still tapping. Diane decides to spin her talk into more positive territory in order to keep her hosts engaged.

"I intend to keep our plan to increase our engagement in syndicated policy lendin, but I'd like to ask that you steer us towards companies that will be able to provide the audited numbers so that we have some recourse to the collateral."

Diane notices the white roots of Director Zhang's otherwise jet-black hair, roots that reveal the effort that so many mature Mainland Chinese men go through to look like the country's leaders. Two managers in Zhang's department sit on either side of him, expressionless and deferential. One is a woman who looks to be about the same age Diane was when she worked at NICB. The woman, of course, is taking the notes. Zhang just rubs his chin as he ponders Diane's presentation.

"Your request is reasonable," he says. "And, in fact, we're implementing the same restrictions on our end."

Ben is now tapping all of the fingers on his left hand at once. Diane looks at his hand and winces. This means he's stuck and they need to do anything possible to get to a different part of the building.

"I really appreciate your understanding, Director Zhang," Diane says, looking back up at her counterparts. "Since we're proposing to work more closely together, I thought we should share with you some of the data we've been tracking here."

"Charles, can you pull that up for us," Diane says to Ben, whom she introduced to their NICB counterparts as a Frankfurt-based colleague. To cover the lie, Diane had told them Charles forgot to bring his business cards. As a former NICB employee, she was able to get Ben in without ID.

"I'm so sorry, all of you," Ben says in perfect Mandarin as he looks at his screen and taps out bogus commands. "I can only access the data through our secure network and the mobile signal in this room isn't strong enough. Sometimes it's just a matter of moving down the hallway. I wonder if I could trouble someone to lead me somewhere else in the building. We may not need to go far."

"I'm sorry about this," Diane says to the NICB directors. "This is sensitive information that I can only show you on our screens because we're not supposed to be showing it to anyone outside of the institution. I'm legally bound and our system will detect when something gets printed. Otherwise I'd give you all a copy."

"We understand," Zhang says as he taps a few numbers on the conference phone that sits in the middle of the table. "Xiao Tang, can you come in and lead one of our guests to one of the conference rooms on the east wing?"

"If you don't mind, I'd like to use the washroom," Diane says as the administrative assistant, a young woman in a charcoal pantsuit paired with a white blouse, steps in. "Is it okay if we take a quick break?"

"Sure, I can get someone else to lead you..." Zhang says.

"Oh, no need, Director Zhang," I'll just go with Xiao Tang and Charles and stop into the washroom on the way back.

"Is there a washroom on the way back?" Diane asks the woman, who nods back.

"So what's the problem? Are you going to be able to pull the data?" Diane asks Ben in English as they follow Xiao Tang down the hall.

"All I can say is that I'm hoping for better luck wherever we're going," Ben says, tight-lipped.

Seated again in front of the NICB team, Diane finds herself stammering and repeating the same point several times as she makes her way through the final case study in her deck. She's drawn it out for 15 minutes, more than three times the amount of time she would normally spend on this material with barely enough meat to draw out more than a couple of high-level insights. Concern about Ben's progress trips up her thoughts further. She wonders if Ben is getting the credentials he needs. It's close to the end of the workday. More employees would be logging out than in. What if they get nothing? Would the data they get from IBOC provide enough ammunition?

"So, um, you can see that it took a longer time for the, um, reality of this revenue scenario to become clear," Diane says, pointing to another line chart.

The director sitting next to Zhang looks at his watch, prompting Zhang to look at his own. Feeling nauseous, Diane glances up at the door, trying to pull Ben back in through the sheer force of her will.

"Despite all of this, um, I believe we're much clearer on what leads to these scenarios and I'd like to propose we move ahead more aggressively," Diane says.

The comment revives her audience's interest. She's bought a few more minutes but the bullish message she's put out, disingenuously, deepens the pit in her stomach. She'll never get such clearance from her bank and will eventually need to back away from these promises, possibly putting her employer in a bad light, not to mention the risk to her career. But like a kayaker paddling through rapids, her only choice is to follow through. The fate of her brother, Diane reminds herself, might be hanging on this bid to pull login credentials from wireless signals coursing through the NICB's headquarters.

A light knock comes through the conference room's door and Diane stops talking.

"Excuse me, Director Zhang," Xiao Tang says. "Your guest is back."

Ben enters the room, expressionless.

"Sorry if I've caused any delay," Ben says, taking his seat. "I've pulled the documents we want to show you."

He strides into the room and gives Diane a nod. She exhales. Ben takes his seat and opens his laptop. Diane looks at his left hand as he begins pulling up a presentation they threw together the previous day.

He begins tapping his index finger.

*****

4:30 p.m.

INTERNAL INVESTIGATION:

The Public Security Bureau, Beijing Municipality, is currently investigating revenue sources for one or more documentary films about sensitive political

subjects, including events around counter-revolu-
tionary activities in Beijing in 1989. These film
projects distort historical facts and should be
considered subversive activities that potentially
threaten social stability and order. Our department has been asked to support the investigation
into these matters by scrutinizing the producers
we advise in the Hong Kong Special Administrative
Region.

Details of the case now under investigation are included in the attachments to this file.

Please ask your contacts in Hong Kong whether they're
aware of any effort to fund documentaries about the
property development in Beijing or events surrounding Tiananmen Square in 1989. Your immediate supervisor will notify you about when a meeting will be
called to discuss intelligence gathered about this
matter.

In accordance with Section 34.6.12 of the National
Intelligence Act of the People's Republic of China,
all of the information surrounding this matter must
be kept confidential. Any violation of this confidence will be dealt with in the strictest measures.

Zhihong scans page after page of documents related to the investigation of Sun
Qiang, a Chinese national with an American green card. It seems strange that
someone who claimed to have worked in the technology sector in California
would give up such a promising career to work in an industry that rarely pays
well. Qiang is a homosexual who has apparently never tried to hide this fact.
Zhihong can't help but have mixed feelings about this fool. Driven apparently
in equal parts by bravery and stupidity, Qiang has pursued dreams that Zhihong has never had the guts to chase. Zhihong himself has flirted with escape
plans for years. This guy Qiang put his plans into action and look what's happened to him.

Why dredge up an issue like 1989? Why not focus on a cause that matters
now? At least he would have been detained for something worthwhile. Zhi-

hong knows the Chinese government can be thuggish. They stifle so many forms of expression and expect a nation of 1.3 billion people to spout the same drivel, to contribute to a 'harmonious society' that's neither harmonious nor civil. Washington can be just as bad, if not worse. With their senseless war in Iraq and their constant meddling, talking about democracy out of one side of their mouths and then supporting fascist policies through the other. They're either propping up dictators or toppling them. It keeps their military in business. If the US government really acted in defense of its ideals, the world might be a better place and China might have no choice but to stop cracking down on people like Qiang. But instead, both countries waste lives and money.

The only real difference is the degree to which ordinary Americans fool themselves. No one in China talks seriously of harmony. They know it's just a slogan, useful only as a reminder of the presence of a massive bureaucracy that will, at least, keep 1.3 billion people from killing each other. Americans, it would seem, believe the rhetoric of their leaders. Qiang seems to believe it also.

Zhihong reads further into the file, about Qiang's friends, Chinese and American friends, trying to help him. One is an American journalist, a Mandarin speaker credentialed to work in Beijing. Jake Bradley has been in the country since the early 1990s when he was a student. Also gay. Qiang has a sister, a wealthy woman in a successful career with a European financial group. There's another American, named Benjamin, but the details about him are redacted. Strange. There's another character somehow involved with the American journalist. His name is Chen Dawei.

Zhihong sits stunned for a moment. He reads the name again. Chen Dawei is a common name. This couldn't be the same person. How many people named Chen Dawei live in Beijing? There are probably thousands. But just as this thought starts to settle him, Zhihong remembers Dawei telling him that he left the screenplay with an American journalist. How many people named Dawei could be friends with an American journalist? The number would probably shrink by 99%.

The PSB hasn't figured out how this Dawei character is involved. There are only theories so far. He's been seen sleeping on park benches and doesn't have a cell phone. It's very unusual, the report says, for an itinerant to be friends with a foreign journalist. Perhaps the lack of an address and phone helps to keep his role under wraps. He might be acting as a courier of money or information. Recordings from the American's apartment suggest that the two have had some kind of relationship for the past two years.

"*Wo de tian*," Zhihong says to himself. Oh my God.

8:00 p.m.

Dawei pounds on Jake's door. It's been more than a day since the confrontation in the American's workplace at China World. That's more than enough time to find the screenplay. He wouldn't have just thrown something like that away. The idea that Jake could have been so insensitive, that the time they spent sharing stories with each other meant nothing and that the screenplay and the other items Dawei put in his care were thrown out like month-old newspapers, is too intolerable. Dawei pounds on the door again, and the silence that follows seems louder than the knocks.

The person knocking at the door, Jake knows, is either Dawei or someone from the PSB. He remains seated on the couch, his knees drawn up to his chest. If it's the former, the knocking will stop. Otherwise, someone will surely open the door with the assistance of the building's management office and Jake will face questioning about how much work he's been doing to support Qiang. Or perhaps the PSB will have found it suspicious that Ben has accompanied Diane and himself, separately, in meetings with two of China's biggest banks. It seems like an obvious red flag but perhaps Diane has thrown the authorities off their trail with her act.

If Dawei continues to wait, if he decides to sleep in the corridor, Jake will need to confront him. Ben and Diane are expecting Jake to be in his newsroom to confirm some information that will complete the evidence they're compiling - the last, crucial step needed to produce a bargaining chip.

After at least five rounds of knocks over several minutes, each knock louder than the last, Jake hears the person outside walk away. As the footsteps fade and the elevator dings, Jake wishes he could help. He wishes he hadn't tossed the folder with the screenplay and the photos and the little card with the maple leaf, that charming symbol of friendship. To keep the shame at bay, Jake reminds himself, again, that more than two years have passed. This stretch of time should absolve anyone of such a responsibility. He finds more reasons to assuage his guilt. With the way rent has been rising over the past year, Jake, like so many others in Beijing, might have moved already. Nothing in Beijing is fixed anymore, at least outside of the cluster of monumental structures and compounds at the centre of the city. Those structures of past and present power, whose permanence only becomes more deeply entrenched as the pace of change everywhere else in the country speeds up. No one stays put, physically, psychologically, economically, spiritually or otherwise. Jake might even have given up and left the country, like many others forced out by the deafening roar of opportunity and change. How could anyone keep track of sentimental trinkets offered by mere acquaintances in the chaos of a perpetual earthquake?

After several minutes pass, Jake tiptoes to the front door and puts his ear against it, listening out for any sign that Dawei is still waiting. Hearing nothing but the hum of the building punctuated by an elevator ding, Jake heads to the den to grab his backpack and picks up a baseball cap on the way out of the door. He slides his last unregistered SIM card into the slot on the back of his phone.

*****

Ben feeds four data sets into the CSAIL analytics platform, one of many similar projects kicked off in the wake of 9/11. There are IBOC and NICB remittance records, European clearinghouse data, transaction records from the two European banks Diane has worked for and a list of IOC member names.

The CSAIL platform, still without a name for security reasons, uses a complex set of algorithms to create connections within a defined area of online activity. Working backwards and forwards, the advanced cognitive technology should work up a list of companies with connections to the IOC members. The technology is still experimental, its algorithms still being tweaked by researchers at MIT, but early results have proven so encouraging that CSAIL has already registered a company that will be used to market the platform commercially. Ben has helped to steer the patent process and negotiations over how much MIT will own of the product that will eventually emerge for intelligence-gathering purposes.

At Diane's suggestion, Ben tweaks his query, changing a few ors to ands and vice-versas, and adjusts the timeframe to end a month after the announcement made on July 13, 2001. Their cell phones sit on the table, batteries removed.

```
Beijing Baisheng Co. Ltd. to Auriele Holdings,
$650,000, August, 2001.
          Intermediaries: International Bank of China
(Luxembourg) S.A., UBS.
          Details


Beijing TongChang Agricultural to Trehaus Group,
$785,000, June 2001.
          Intermediaries: International Bank of China
(Hungary) Close Ltd. Details
```

Beijing NuanFeng to Simsek International $1.2M, May
2001.
      Intermediaries: PT NICB Indonesia, Citibank.
Details

Beijing RuiJia Biomedical Co. Ltd. to Bradshaw Ltd.,
$1.4M, June 2001
      Intermediaries: International Bank of China
(Middle East) Dubai Ltd.
      Details

Beijing JinSui Industries to Anotansov Bright & As-
soc, $1.6M, July 2001
      Intermediaries: NICB Abu Dhabi, ING. Details
...

And the list goes on. Forty-three transactions caught by the query Ben generated for the trove of data from IBOC, NICB, and the two European financial
institutions Diane has worked for, one in Switzerland and another in London,
bringing the total to 31.8 million.

"I guess they wanted to be sure the votes went their way before remitting, at
least for some of them," Ben says.

"There might have been a lag. The orders might have gone through right
before the vote. Just seems like a real last-minute push. How do you say, elev-
enth-hour effort?" Diane says.

Several earlier queries turned up only a few transactions, which wouldn't
have given them the evidence they need. A few more tweaks to the query and
perhaps they'll find more.

A waitress approaches their table.

"Pardon me, but we're closing soon. I need to trouble you to please settle
your bill now," she says, dropping the slip of paper onto the table.

The restaurant has helped to cloak Diane and Ben's activities, located as it
is next to NICB's headquarters. Running an analysis of bank transaction data
won't look out of place through the NICB wifi signal that Ben has hacked into.
They're not sure this measure is necessary but decided to take it anyway. Diane
had made the final call, saying, if nothing else, the feeling of cover would help
her concentrate better.

"We'll be gone in five minutes," Diane tells the waitress as she pulls out her wallet.

They need to run a few more queries to be sure they've caught all of the most obvious, and damaging, transactions. Then they'll call Jake using an unregistered SIM card to feed him the foreign company names.

Jake will use Toeler News' database to verify the owners of each of the overseas companies and cross-reference them against a list of IOC members.

TUESDAY, April 24, 2007
8:47 a.m.

Zhihong waits outside his supervisor's office in a corridor running the length of the ministry's east wing, a dividing line between those in classroom-like offices who work in open-plan clusters and those who work independently, who in turn answer to those occupying quieter corridors on higher floors. Zhihong should be on this side of the corridor by now, in his own office, at least according to the expectations of his wife and in-laws. The longer he languishes in the clusters across the hall, the more likely he is to stay there until it's too awkward to continue working in Beijing. His only opportunities for advancement will be to move with the ministry to another city, where he'd have another chance to prove his value. Beijing always seeks to spread loyal ambition throughout the country.

How quickly a loss of momentum in one's career can affect so much of the future, like sitting inattentively in a train car that diverts to another track. Focus too much on the scenery outside instead of the track you're on, and suddenly you're just part of the scenery and nothing more. The dreams about producing films led Zhihong astray, they sent him down the wrong track. They kept him from socializing with the right people in the ministry and angling for work on the right projects. They kept him out of the office suites he's now sitting outside of, waiting to get more information that he hopes will not be about the Dawei he knows. Zhihong stands to lose either way. He hasn't thought through what he'll say if the homeless character in the PSB report turns out to be his ex-lover. He may provide useful information but the ministry won't reward a gay man who was apparently using his connections as a government bureaucrat to shop screenplays to producers he's meant to be advising. Everyone's running some kind of hustle but Zhihong's not in a position to make his inconsequential. All of this will come out if the Chen Dawei in the reports and the one from Macau are the same.

The Dawei in this mess of a situation involving the documentary filmmaker might turn out to be someone completely different, the whole situation a complete coincidence. If so, Zhihong is just pestering his superiors for classified information and offering nothing in return, another useless interaction that will undercut any chance to move up in the hierarchy.

Zhihong taps his fingers on the armrest of the bench while he checks the time on his cell phone display.

"Executive hours," Zhihong mutters to himself as he sees the time tick past 9:00 a.m. The section chief might not be in for another fifteen or twenty minutes.

The muscles in Zhihong's stomach and legs begin to tense up as a voice inside, activated by a sense of practicality and self-preservation, pipes up. He needs to stand up and walk away. But another thought keeps him in place. Dawei couldn't possibly be involved in a documentary about social causes. He wouldn't even know anything about 1989 let alone want to make some kind of revisionist history about it.

"Eh, Zhihong," Changxing says as he approaches, flipping through the keys on a chain he's just pulled out of his front pocket. "What's going on?"

At somewhere around 1.8 metres tall, Changxing makes Zhihong feel small physically as well as functionally. The extra height his boss has over most people in their section probably helped him gain the edge he needed to get his office. This isn't just something Zhihong tells himself. He's heard the same from intoxicated colleagues in conversations everyone knows must stay off the record and on occasions no one is supposed to mention, like the unauthorized trips to Macau.

"I wanted to get a few more details on the investigation we're running around the documentary filmmaker," Zhihong says.

"Do your contacts know something about this?" Changxing asks, looking up from his set of keys.

"No. None of my contacts are aware of such projects being funded from Hong Kong."

"So why would you need more information?"

"It's the itinerant. The guy without a phone or address. I think I've heard his name before. I'm not sure of the context. Maybe it was in some conversations I've had with producers."

Changxing thinks for a moment and then looks down at his keys, pulling one from the bunch. He seems unsure about whether to provide any more details.

Zhihong decides he needs to be less keen on the request, as though this is a routine step that everyone should be taking. A box to check. "It's probably nothing," Zhihong says. "I just wanted to be sure. I thought maybe if there's a photo, I could…"

"Let me see if there's any more information available to us," Changxing says in a tone that signals the end of their conversation.

Zhihong holds his position, hoping for some indication of how or when this might happen. Changxing opens his office door and flicks a light switch just inside. Stepping inside his office, he looks back at Zhihong.

"I'll let you know as soon as anything else comes in," he says. "In the meantime, keep polling your contacts in Hong Kong for any information on this or any other documentary films currently in production."

9:45 a.m.

Jake slides the USB key into the port on his computer before the courier dispatched by Diane is barely two steps back towards the reception area. He'll need a couple of hours at least to compile the information Diane and Ben need. This puts him on edge because of the laws of bad timing when it comes to breaking news. The likelihood of big news on Jake's beat increases in direct proportion to the degree to which he's preoccupied with other matters.

As a safeguard, he's alerted the editors that he'll be busy conducting an interview for the rest of the morning. To keep the plan airtight, he's also thought of an explanation for why this interview will never surface in any of his stories, just in case he's questioned later. The interviewee will be fired, making the information unreliable. It's a small fiction but part of a web of lies that's becoming larger and, therefore, more of a threat if he gets caught up in it.

Using the Toeler database, Jake calls up each of the companies on the list that Diane and Ben have compiled. He needs to clarify the connection between the IOC members who voted for Beijing and the companies that received funds remitted from the city, 65 in all. Diane and Ben's CSAIL analysis turned up forty-three connections and Jake needs to confirm them. A few are obvious. Privately held Auriele Holdings' Board Director, Fausto Torace, voted for Beijing. They won't all be this easy, though, and Jake must confirm connections to at least half of the 56 entities to make it clear that the decision was bought.

9:56 a.m.

The junior PSB analyst on Qiang's case puts two photos together and sees a similarity. Taken the previous day, one photo shows Jake entering IBOC's headquarters and another shows Diane entering NICB. The American named

Ben is with both of them, wearing different outfits. In the earlier meeting, he's wearing an ill-fitting corduroy blazer with patches on the elbows, sunglasses and a baseball hat. In the afternoon meeting at NICB with Diane, Ben's hair is more slicked back and he wears a well-tailored suit.

The analyst pulls up supporting phone records and transcripts on Jake and Diane. Jake went to IBOC to conduct an interview about the bank's policy lending; Diane went to NICB for a business meeting.

Ben has a very close connection with Qiang. They even formed a "civil union," in the U.S., State of California. A marriage, essentially. California sanctions such relationships between members of the same sex.

It's understandable that Ben would want to be in Beijing to help Jake and Qiang's sister. Qiang and Ben have a history. They were a couple. Estranged now, according to the briefing documents, but perhaps they've maintained close ties. It makes no sense, though, that Ben would be attending meetings with both of them at the headquarters of two major commercial banks.

The instructions on these matters are clear. The analyst must be able to follow the subjects throughout the day, provide a description of their activities and explain the objectives of each of their activities, however mundane. All explanations need to be backed up with phone records, emails or transcripts of conversations picked up in phone calls or through recordings taken in apartments and offices.

Any questions surrounding the narrative that can't be explained through the documentation compiled by the PSB require further inquiry. These questions must be flagged for senior analysts.

The analyst reaches for his desk phone and begins dialing his supervisor.

11:49 a.m.

Jake, Boeing's doing a briefing with the Chinese media. They didn't...

Jake can only see the first line of the message.

"Fuck," he says to himself. "No."

The message interrupts Jake's search for the twenty-third connection between Beijing money and IOC member votes. A briefing by Boeing. The timing of this shit. How fucking typical.

The message comes from his company's Asia transportation industry team-leader who probably got a tip-off from a former Toeler News reporter who now works for a local PR company. A tactic PR types use to keep good relations with the media. There's a steady trickle of burned out reporters who drift to "the dark side," and so nothing is airtight in the nexus of people working on media and communications.

Jake hasn't clicked on the message yet. Once he does, the teamleader will see that he's read it. The first line tells Jake everything he needs to know.

Foreign companies operating in China often organize events for the local press, separate from those they arrange for the foreign media. The companies, or rather the PR firms working for the companies, provide "taxi money" in red packets for the Chinese reporters, usually well in excess of what's needed to get from one end of Beijing to another in the heaviest of rush hour traffic. The money comes with no strings but the message behind the exclusive "we're-giving-it-to-you-first" press events is clear. Foreign companies use the Chinese-only news briefing tactic in spite of their codes of ethics and best practice guidelines. They do it at arm's length. Boeing, BMW, PepsiCo and General Electric can blame the PR companies and then apologize to the foreign reporters, telling them there wasn't much news in the event anyway.

The only way to combat the practice is to know when the Chinese-only press briefings are taking place, get to them immediately and put the most critical spin possible on whatever message the company is trying to deliver. Of course, this has to happen today. The God of breaking news is a sadist.

The transportation team leader is no doubt waiting for a response from Jake who's wondering how to get out of this task. The other reporters are out covering other press events.

Jake feels the vibration of his cell phone before the call even comes through, like a forward echo. The team leader who has placed the call knows Jake is in the newsroom and logged into his system. The display on Jake's phone shows the number of the Tokyo newsroom.

```
11:49 a.m.

From: Anton Sutler/TOELER NEWS

Jake, Boeing's doing a briefing with the Chinese media.
They didn't invite any of the foreign press. You
know why, right? Can you get to the Kempinsky Hotel
ASAP
```

And he takes the call.

"I'm just reading your message now, Anton," Jake says as he connects. "The timing could not be any worse."

"Seriously, you can't go?" Anton asks.

"Anton, I swear this is really bad timing."

"What else is brewing that will give us an excuse to ignore news from a widely held company that's worth 100 billion?" Anton asks, reinforcing his point with the precision of his Swiss-German accent.

There's no way to argue with market capitalization. If Anton has got wind of this event, the other foreign financial wires might also know. It might just be a matter of minutes before the competition starts filing headlines from Beijing about Boeing.

"Yep," Jake says through clenched teeth. "You're right. I better get over there. I'll call you when I arrive."

The Boeing presser would keep Jake busy for the next three hours. He'll need to get there and find out what's being disclosed to the Chinese media. He'll need to file some headlines and a short first take to Anton. Then, he'll need to write a longer version of the story, possibly with commentary from analysts in the region. And then he'll need to get the full story through the editing gamut. All of which means he'll never make the appointed time with Diane and Ben.

Jake reaches for the untraceable SIM card in the small, front pocket on his backpack. He opens the SIM port on his cell phone to switch the cards but gets distracted by two of the newsroom's television screens. GlobeCast and BBC. They've cut to black again. They must be doing a follow-up on the Hu Yaobang death story which seems to be gaining momentum. Jake hasn't yet figured out how much this new development will complicate their effort. He hasn't had time to discuss it with Diane. There's no point in dwelling on this now. It's happened. The more immediate concern is the new task at hand: the cursor blinking on the exchange between him and Anton. The burning cursor that's produced an exchange that has obligated Jake to cover a press conference that will produce news of no value except for traders and the wealthy investors they work for. Just the kind of people who don't care about who's stuck in a dark room, wondering what their fate will be for nothing other than a film project meant to start a conversation. It's all about capital.

Jake pushes the SIM card port shut and dials Ben's number.

"Hello," Ben says tentatively, in a distant tone that confuses Jake.

"Ben, it's me Jake."

"Umm..."

The inarticulate tone conflicts with Ben's usual snappy delivery but Jake brushes this aside.

"Look," Jake says, standing up. "The good news is that I've confirmed a bunch of connections to the money from Beijing. The bad news is…"

"Um…" Ben says again, cutting Jake off.

"Ben, I don't have a lot of time. The bad news is that I need to run out for a press event, so I won't be able to meet up with you and Diane until…"

"Hello," Ben says. "Perhaps you have the wrong number?"

"Wrong number? You're Ben, right?"

The SIM card, Jake realizes. He pulled the unregistered card out and opened the SIM port on the phone before the dropped TV feeds distracted him. He remembers closing the port but did he switch the cards? How could he have forgotten that? Jake looks down and sees the unregistered card is still sitting on his desk, meaning the PSB is probably listening to every word he's just said. Whoever's monitoring will know the three of them are collaborating on something.

Jake hears Ben sigh.

"Let's talk later," Ben says before cutting the line. "*Di nomor lain ada instruksi.*"

Jake places his cell phone on the desk, sits and puts his hands on his forehead trying to stop the sensation of falling.

Di nomor lain ada instruksi. That's Indonesian. The other number has instructions.

Why?

The surge of anger at himself makes it difficult to think this through. Jake wants to pick up the phone on his desk, this block of solid plastic, and bash it against his forehead. He needs a concussion right now to take him away from everything he faces, to somehow erase the blundering error he's just made. To send himself spinning into the Land of Oz, away from shadowy PSB officers and censors, in the bowels of government buildings, listening to phone conversations and monitoring cable television feeds.

Except that a concussive exit would be cowardly. Jake's stomach growls audibly with hunger and dread. The PSB now has Ben's unregistered number. Jake lacerates himself with this thought. Stupid. How can I be so fucking stupid? The question bounces around in his head like an echo locked in a giant steel chamber. They'll be able to pull phone records on that number to see where the calls come from and they'll find that most of the calls come from the unregistered numbers Jake and Diane have been using. The pieces will fall into place.

They'll know that Ben, Diane and Jake are communicating through covert channels, which will prompt them to step up scrutiny. Perhaps worse. This might give the authorities pretext to detain all three of them for questioning before Ben can transmit the report that will embarrass Beijing.

Jake must get his data over to Ben and Diane immediately. He'll need to scrap the Boeing presser. That means he'll ignore direct orders. Desertion. Once the other foreign wires get the story, Jake will need an answer for why Toeler News doesn't have it. He can dwell on this or save Qiang.

As this stripped-down reality makes itself clear, Jake remembers the last thing Ben said to him on the phone call.

"Nomor lain ada instruksi." The other number has instructions.

Jake fishes the unregistered SIM card out of the front pocket of his backpack. He inserts it into his phone and waits for the signal. Three bars emerge and the phone buzzes with a text message.

> Diane did some laundry at your place. Please pick it
> up before you come to see us this afternoon.

Jake realizes they've moved somewhere safer than Qiang's apartment. If it's this obvious to him, it's probably just as obvious to whoever is monitoring them.

Indonesian? Jakes figures out that Ben used this language to buy a bit of extra time. It's not likely that the monitors listening in would know the language. They would need some time to find someone to figure out which language it is, a language that kind of looks and sounds like Spanish. Jake and Ben being American, and one of them living in California, it wouldn't be a stretch to assume that's their code. The effort to pull a Spanish speaker into the investigation would take just a few minutes. Another few to figure out the error and find someone who would know what language they're using and to translate. This whole process would probably buy five or ten minutes. That's all the time Jake needs to get to his place, if he runs.

12:26 p.m.

Holding the USB key with the data he's compiled, Jake exits the China World Tower II wondering whether to jump in a cab, head to the subway entrance just a few metres away or just make a run for it. About a mile away, Jake's apartment complex may as well be in another city when stuck in weekday traffic, even outside of rush hour. He's at the intersection of a jammed Jianguo Road and the equally slow East Third Ring, a major axis that routes traffic from China World through a gamut of u-turns and merge lanes. Jake knows how tense he'll feel every second he's sitting in the back of the cab, not moving.

He runs to the subway entrance and hesitates as he looks down the escalator. He then looks east, toward his apartment complex. The subway may take longer, especially if the doors shut, as they always seem to do, as soon as he makes it to the platform. Besides, the subway doesn't run frequently enough at midday and there's no cell phone signal. He remembers the last time the lack of a signal foiled him. That day a few weeks ago, when he didn't manage to get the address of the interview from which Qiang never returned.

Jake tightens the straps of his backpack so it won't jostle too much and begins running down Jianguo Road, heading east to get whatever instructions were left in his laundry.

The sun beats down as he tries to figure out whether to wait for the light to cross to the south side of the avenue or climb the pedestrian flyover about halfway between the China World intersection and his apartment building. His palms are sweaty so he puts the USB key into a small pocket on the side of his backpack. He then wipes his brow and continues running down the north side of Jianguo Road, making better time than the vehicles which are inching along.

Construction workers on the new buildings along the north side of Jianguo Road weld shiny steel window grids into place. Ahead, there's a crew jackhammering the sidewalk around the flyover. As Jake gets closer, he sees they've fashioned a makeshift footbridge of wooden planks flanked by orange construction netting over a gaping hole, in which workers clamour around pipes and new cables. Closer still, he sees they've blocked the stairs to the pedestrian flyover. The entire structure is for renovations. This throws Jake's calculations right off. He'll need to run to the next intersection, cross Jianguo Road and double back to his apartment building, adding another five minutes.

Jake looks at the traffic inching along in short bursts of acceleration followed by idling and impatient honking, four lanes going each direction separated by a fence topped with planters overflowing with red and yellow flowers. He takes a deep breath and steps onto the outside westbound lane, prompting a bout of honks from annoyed motorists. He dekes several cars and then runs toward the front of a long container truck which starts moving ahead. Jake stops and waits for the truck to pass so he can make it to the fence that divides the road. The honking horns get longer and louder as rear-view mirrors come within millimetres of Jake's waist.

Once at the fence, Jake finds an opening between the planters and wedges himself inside. Ignoring the honks and the occasional swearing from passing motorists, Jake works his way up so that he's sitting on the fence with one foot in a planter on each side, crushing some of the begonias. They've been watered recently, which has softened the soil so much his feet sink into the warm organic mush. He then swings his foot on the north side around so that he's facing south, wedged between two planters, a small space he uses as a safe spot from which to plot a path through the eastbound traffic.

He's dodged his last car on the south side of Jianguo Road and Jake begins sprinting to his apartment complex, leaving a wake of honks and curses.

"*Qing rang yi xia!*" "Please make way," he yells ahead to pedestrians walking several astride, taking up the width of the walkway.

12:40 p.m.

Zhihong's desk phone rings as he chews the last morsel of pork from the lunch that Yue Tao prepared. The display shows Changxing's name.

"Hey, just wanted to let you know that your guy, the itinerant Chen Dawei, isn't involved at all in the documentary business," Changxing says. "We got more transcripts in from the PSB."

"I see," Zhihong says.

This isn't the information he needs. He knows Dawei wouldn't have been involved in documentaries about 1989.

"Hey Changxing, any idea what he's doing with this American?"

"Um," he begins. Changxing seems uncertain at first about divulging anything further.

An instant later, though, he blurts out more details as if he's too busy for obfuscation and figures it will be easier to lob a few more details out.

"Something about a lost screenplay. He left it with the American a few years ago and wants it back. He's getting very aggressive about it. He might end up in trouble if he keeps pestering that American. The PSB don't want some other, unrelated situation getting in the way of a clean resolution to their problem."

Stunned, Zhihong stands quietly.

"Zhihong?"

"Um...yes, I'm here. Thanks," Zhihong says.

He places the receiver back in its cradle. The horror of what he's done hits him like a slap. As if it wasn't bad enough that he gave Dawei so many false expectations and then pushed him away with a few hundred kuai bills that were meant to get him back to Macau, back to the steaming sink in the kitchen of that smelly restaurant.

Zhihong picks up the receiver and dials Changxing's extension.

"Yes?"

"Changxing, I need the address of the American journalist."

"Why? What is your interest in this?"

Zhihong searches his imagination for something plausible. Say anything.

"You know, many of these foreign journalists live close to each other. If you're looking for connections between Hong Kong producers and foreign journalists living in China, we need to know where they're located."

Zhihong creates this flimsy rationale out of nothing. He needs to make it work, though, so he forges ahead without a filter, the words uttered as they're conceived, as though he's a medium channeling the spirit of a con artist.

"These journalists know they're under surveillance, right?" Zhihong continues. "If they're collaborating with Hong Kong producers, they'll be meeting in the bars or coffee shops in their neighbourhoods and not communicating through phones or email."

"Seems kind of a tenuous path to follow," Changxing says.

"You're probably right but it wouldn't hurt to know where the foreign journalists are spending time. If we have any suspicions about producers from Hong Kong or producers from anywhere..."

"You're proposing some kind of broader surveillance effort," Changxing says, cutting Zhihong off. "The PSB are just asking for assistance in this particular case," Changxing says dismissively.

"Ok. Look, just get me the American journalist's address," Zhihong says in a demanding tone that, he realizes, may be crossing a line. He softens his tone to keep Changxing engaged. "This is something I can take on as a side project. I won't need to spend much time on it. We may discover nothing. But maybe we'll discover something. At least we'll appear supportive. At least we'll look like we're taking some initiative."

"I'll see if I can get the address," Changxing says. "Just don't spend a lot of time on this. This is not our business."

12:42 p.m.

Sitting on the curb outside of Jake's apartment complex, Dawei is half asleep with his forehead resting on his knees, his arms wrapped around his shins.

"*Qing rang yi xia*" he hears someone yell in a foreign accent. Please make way.

He looks back and sees Jake running through the entry gate. Here's Jake in the middle of the day when he should be at work. This is odd. Maybe it's a sign, a gift from the heavens, he thinks. This is a sign that he must not give up. This is where his anguish must end. The American has eluded him too many times. He's given too many excuses. He has almost certainly looked at the screenplay and seen the name of the writer. *Autumn Truce* is playing everywhere. The writer's name is everywhere. Jie-ke must know how valuable the screenplay is now.

Dawei swings his backpack on and stands up, looking at the entry gate. The timing is good. There are many people walking through. The guard is paying only scant attention to each individual passing by.

12:44 p.m.

Jake finds the note under the first garment in a pile of freshly laundered clothes his housekeeper left on his bed.

> The authorities are closing in. We need to put the report together and send it ASAP. Come to the China World Hotel, room 712, but don't come directly. Go to your office first. Wait 30 minutes. Make sure no one is following you. Then go down to the lower concourse, remove the battery from your phone and make your way over to the hotel. Make sure you have the data.

As he repeats the number several times, Jake makes up a memory association for the numbers. Seven equals lucky. Twelve equals his age when he saw the film *Alien*. Jake then tears the note into dozens of pieces, throws it into the toilet and flushes.

Jake swings his backpack around one shoulder and heads for the door. As he turns the handle, he feels the door open toward him, automatically, and realizes someone on the other side is pushing it forcefully. Dawei emerges from the other side and is now facing him silently, scowling.

First, the unexpected news of the Boeing presser and now this. There must be, he thinks, some sadistic higher force determined to throw every obstacle possible at him.

"Get the fuck out of here," Jake says in English.

He doesn't have the split second it will take to translate the command in his head before saying it. His tone will make the meaning clear. Dawei pushes him aside and heads toward the dining room table. He begins rifling through the papers laid out not so neatly in stacks. Conference schedules, receipts he needs for expenses, research reports that he brings home to read even though he rarely gets to them.

"You're crazy," Jake says in Mandarin as he drops his backpack. "You're completely crazy."

Ignoring him, Dawei abandons the papers on the dining table and steps into the living room, his eyes locked on several stacks on the coffee table. As Dawei bends down to look through each document, Jake lunges for him and wraps his arms around Dawei's arms, just above the elbows. He clasps his fingers and tightens his embrace with all of his strength to immobilize the intruder.

"It's in here. I know it's in here," Dawei shouts. "You know it's valuable and you're keeping it from me."

Dawei drops down into a crouch, taking Jake off his balance, and twists suddenly. Once free, he turns to face Jake and delivers a punch to his stomach, taking the wind out of Jake.

"All of these papers and documents you have here," Dawei says as though the disorganization is as responsible as Jake for the loss of the screenplay. "Look at them. You're just too lazy to look through them. You have no idea how important this is to me. You want to keep it? You might as well take my life. I'm not going to let you do that."

Remembering that Diane and Ben are waiting for him, Jake straightens up. He's breathing heavily as he looks at Dawei, who's now even more of a threat to him, and to Qiang's survival, as any of the PSB officers or anyone else in the shadowy apparatus that decided Qiang is a threat to the state.

This isn't worth it, Jake thinks as he regains his breath. Let this psycho tear the place apart. Why should this delay him any further? Jake's already abandoned his post at work, heading down a path littered with consequences.

If Jake were to continue fighting, building security would show up. Then the police. Jake might be stuck in a police station filling out reports for the next 12 hours.

"Look for it all you want," Jake says. "You won't find what you're looking for."

Dawei stops. The sincerity of Jake's tone seems to have struck a nerve.

"You've hid it somewhere else? Maybe in your office? Or maybe..."

Dawei blanches, his skin now completely pale and all emotion gone from his face. He approaches Jake and stands face-to-face.

"Or maybe you really have lost it."

"I don't have your screenplay. I probably threw it out. I'm sorry but you disappeared — for a long time."

Dawei's mouth twists into something between a frown and a grimace brought on through physical pain. He walks slowly towards the door. He stops next to Jake's backpack and picks it up.

"Or maybe it's in this bag you always have with you."

Jake thinks only about the possibility that Dawei will run out with it, down the fire stairs, his smaller, wiry frame moving more quickly than Jake, down to the lobby and then out to anywhere in Beijing with the data needed to finish Diane and Ben's report.

Jake lunges, gathering a ton of force for every enemy and obstacle he's had to face since Qiang disappeared. The censors, the police, the PSB, the what's-his-name legislative assistant who abandoned the cause and now, worst of all, this insane drifter who's about to abscond with a set of data so carefully constructed. Information as worthless to Dawei as it is crucial for Qiang.

Jake's fury sparks a surge energy that feels super-human. In the second it takes for him to run into Dawei, he gathers enough force to send this foe, who is now everyone and everything he's clashed with for the past month, crashing backwards into the door. Dawei's head hits the solid metal surface with a crack and Jake sees his focus change, instantly, from a direct line on Jake to a stare into nothing. Then Dawei's eyes close as he slides down the door, the back of his head leaving a smear of blood, like a coarse calligraphy brush, all the way down.

Jake recoils. "Oh my God," he whispers to himself. "Oh my God. Oh my God. Oh my God. Dawei. Dawei!"

Jake crouches down and leans in to Dawei's face to check for his breathing. The breaths are erratic. Jake can't figure out if they're signs of life or just some spastic physiological response to trauma that will eventually kill him. As he realizes that he's breathing erratically himself, Jake also notices his vision going dark and blurry. He can't figure out which wall to lean on or even how to stand up.

Jake puts his hand on the foyer wall to regain his balance but the space spins and he has trouble gathering focus. He's drowning in too many thoughts.

The presence of Dawei, who's lingering somewhere between injury and death, makes Jake want to vomit. But with no food in his stomach, he can only turn away and wretch. It can't end here, he tells himself perhaps audibly, to clear away the thoughts and fears that have incapacitated him.

He feels his mobile phone vibrate with a text message. He looks at the display and sees the message is from Ben.

You need to get here NOW.>

Jake gathers his balance, grabs his backpack with the data files and runs.

Out in the corridor and unsure about why he's fleeing, Jake pushes open the door to the fire stairs opposite the elevators. The steel door explodes with a bang as it slams into the concrete block wall inside the stairwell and a dim light switches on, activated by a motion sensor. The sound of the impact reverberates up and down several floors.

Jake runs down one flight, wondering why he's in the stairwell. Of course, the elevators have security cameras. The instinct to avoid surveillance has brought him here. It directed his movements like an involuntary reflex, driving his legs even before the logic of this move was clear.

What does it matter though? The violence of the past few minutes, and every movement that follows, will end up reconstructed in reports and testimonies and judgments.

Jake knows he can't abandon Dawei in his unconscious state. He can't have murder on his conscience. But he can't stay in the building for another second. He needs distance from his deed to figure out what to do next.

As he sorts through each possible scenario, between scenes of incarceration and meetings with diplomats and lawyers, all the while seeing headlines about a bloody act carried out by unhinged American journalist, a plan, the only possible plan, begins to emerge.

In the dead air of the enclosed stairwell, Jake touches his ribs where Dawei punched him and feels a sharp pain. He pulls up his shirt, but the light is too dim to discern any bruising. It might be too early for the trauma to surface anyway. To be sure, he tightens his hand into a fist and bashes it on the same spot. Then he hits the spot again, and again, and again. The surge of pain, now throbbing, causes Jake to double over. After a minute, the throbbing stops and his laboured breathing begins to steady. As he rises, Jake looks at the concrete block wall and runs a hand along one of the mortar lines. He whips his head into the wall, pounding the ridge on the side of his forehead, just above his right eye. The pain sears him, stopping his breath as he crouches down and holds his left palm over the injury.

With his eyes shut, Jake imagines a world he can direct, one in which Qiang never existed and the insanity of the past few weeks dissolves. He recalls the moment, two years ago, when a friend asked if Jake wouldn't mind giving his guest room to a good friend who's moving back to China to shoot documentary films. In this newly reconstructed moment, Jake says no. He tells his friend that the room is taken. And then life proceeds as it had when his most pressing concerns were limited to the never-ending news churn and the race to send the first headline. Like a movie reel, Jake sees himself in scattered jump cuts, mingling with nameless, faceless people. Without the grounding of identifiable characters, every scene fades to black.

Crouching against the wall and breathing heavily, Jake hears the lights in the fire stairwell click off. A warm rivulet runs down his temple and he doesn't know if the liquid is blood or sweat. He opens his eyes and everything is as dark as the world he was trying to conjure up with his eyes closed.

Once the pain subsides, Jake begins running down the rest of the stairs, holding one palm against the swelling that's already beginning to disfigure his forehead. Jake takes two steps at a time, feeling as though he's just a moment away from losing his balance and tumbling to the next landing.

He bursts into the ground floor elevator lobby, startling a small group of people waiting.

"Unit 1510! Unit 1510!" Jake yells as he sprints toward the security guard standing by the building entrance. "An intruder! He attacked me! I hit him hard! He may still be after me!"

Jake doesn't wait for the glass doors, activated by motion, to slide open completely. He clips one as he passes though and pulls the door off its track with a loud crack. He hears a crash, the shattering of glass into thousands of pieces, and keeps running.

"Hey! Stop!" the security guard yells as Jake bounds down the steps leading to the entrance.

This is the only way, Jake tells himself. He keeps repeating this to himself to drown out the sound of the security guard behind him.

"Wait!" he shouts, and then yells something else that Jake doesn't understand as he runs at full speed through the gates of the apartment grounds.

Once the police arrive, Jake will already be underground, on the subway heading to the China World Hotel to give the data to Ben and Diane who are waiting to put the final pieces of their puzzle together and probably wondering where he is.

This is the only way, he thinks, to save Dawei and Qiang. Even if he winds up a felon in China, he won't have the weight of murder charges on him. He can live with aggravated assault on his conscience. Murder, he knows, will deal a psychological blow from which he's never likely to recover.

1:24 p.m.

Cool air blows down from a vent on the roof of the new subway car as Jake stares at the floor. It's his first time in one of the new carriages, a change he'd been waiting for since the news that Line Two would be completely revitalized before the Olympics.

These random thoughts and observations are the only things between Jake and the possibility that he's killed someone. He needs this wall of meaninglessness to finish what he's started. Otherwise, he will collapse under the weight of his guilt. And then two people might end up dead.

With his backpack resting on his lap, Jake sits crouched forward with his left palm covering the side of his forehead. The drying blood glues the skin of his palm to the wound.

When he pulls his hand away, he looks at the dark maroon stain on his hand and hears a woman sitting across from him make a comment about the blood. Something about a medical clinic or hospital. He moves to the end of the subway car where there are fewer passengers.

Jake thinks about the attention he'll attract by walking into a five-star hotel with a bloodied face. He reaches into his bag, rooting around the bottom for some sanitary wipes. He feels the rectangular foil packets and pulls three or four out.

The cold, astringent moisture stings the wound and the pain is too great for Jake to apply much pressure. He brings the tissue down to eye level and sees it's almost completely soiled with blood. He opens another packet. And another. And another. Finally, there's only a hint of red on the fifth wipe.

The doors open at the China World station and Jake steps out. He throws the soiled sanitary wipes and their foil wrappers into a garbage can attached to one of the station's pillars and heads toward the exit that leads to the China World Tower II.

1:32 p.m.

A chill takes hold. Cold so sharp Dawei can see it in the form of a translucent ice blue, so distinct he can trace this horrible sensation to the throbbing well of pain in the back of his head. He remembers the heat of the impact and then a sudden drop in the room temperature. This chill reminds him of Yongfu Village in the dead of winter, of the time he was face down in the snow, at least a lifetime ago, when his school collapsed. He remembers trying to save Xiao Bei. He doesn't remember anything about Xiao Bei after that time. She died, he thinks. He can't be sure. He wanted to tell Xiao Bei that he tried to save her. Not because he wanted any credit for this. He just wanted her to know that someone cared about what happened to her. She was so terrified by the deafening sounds of rending metal and cracking plaster. He can still see the terror in her face. Dawei can't conjure up memories of anything that happened afterwards. He doesn't know if he's been in this chilled state, in some kind of hibernation, since the school collapsed.

Something behind Dawei moves and the well of pain at the back of his head turns into a sharp spike. He hears voices. Gruff voices, like his father's. He doesn't remember the last time he saw his father or his mother.

This chill is now intolerable. He wants someone to wrap him in the heavy duvet he had on his bed in Yongfu, sometime yesterday, or maybe years ago, if ever.

2:03 p.m.

Diane whisks Jake into room 712 and guides the door as it shuts, preventing it from slamming. Ben, seated at the hotel room's desk, is tapping away at his laptop.

"Thank God, man. Do you have the data?" Ben asks, not looking up from his screen.

"Are you okay?" Diane asks, reaching for one of Jake's arms.

Jake doesn't answer. He expected her to be angry for taking so long to arrive. Instead, she's looking at him with a concerned, empathic gaze. She must see the horror in Jake's eyes, a wound even more apparent than the bruise on his forehead.

"Jake, are you okay?"

The more Jake searches for a response, the more difficult it becomes to answer. He wants to tell her everything that has transpired in the past hour but a rush of emotion welling up from his gut blocks his words and spill out in the form of a wrenching sob.

"Oh God," he says in a choked wail, followed by tears.

Jake's knees give out and he crumples onto the floor at the foot of the hotel room's king-sized bed. Diane kneels down and wraps both arms around Jake. The warmth of her embrace triggers another sob. The outpouring of emotion pulls Ben's attention away from his work. He walks over, crouches on one knee and puts a hand on Jake's shoulder.

"I've hurt someone very badly," Jake manages to say as he wipes the tears from his eyes. A strand of saliva drips from one side of his mouth. Diane stands up, grabs two tissues from a box on the bedside table and comes back to wipe his mouth.

"Jake, is it Dawei?" Ben asks.

Dawei? Coming from Ben, the name is out of place, like a well-known character from one movie showing up in another. Two movies with different themes and artistic direction merging incongruously. Jake rewinds through every interaction he's had with Ben. He's sure Dawei never came up. Or did he?

"How do know about Dawei?"

"I've been monitoring the PSB's database. I've found some files on this."

Jake looks at Ben, mouth agape, as he tries to absorb this newest revelation.

"You found some files? What...?" he says, shaking his head.

"It's the same way I got the banking records from IBOC and NICB," Ben says. "Look, you may as well know now, I spent years working as an agent, delivering technical specifications for artificial intelligence to the government here."

Ben's comment silences Jake's laboured breathing as he tries to understand where it came from.

"This is a really fucked up time to start joking around, Ben," Jake says.

"Ok, I'm joking," Ben replies as he stands and returns to his computer. "Anyway, let's just focus."

But he's not joking. There are too many details and not a shred of humour in the comment. Ben's intelligence includes immaculate comedic timing. Jake can also tell this from Ben's detachment. The way he moves away from the moment doesn't reflect a missed beat.

He's really a spy. Or was a spy. How might this change their circumstances? What kind of additional leverage does Ben have? Are there more reinforcements than what Ben and Diane had indicated?

"Oh my God, you're not kidding are you?" Jake says.

"I started doing it at the height of the Iraq war. I was so enraged about all of the lies and the bullshit. I learned my way around the networks while I was here."

Of course, Jake thinks. Ben is a project director of some kind at MIT's CSAIL lab. Computer networks and artificial intelligence. Jake hadn't thought much about what that meant when it first came up. He probably has access to everything there. And the Canadian passport. That would allow him to get in and out of China without the U.S. government knowing.

All of this would seem to coalesce into some form of hope. Except that the thought of Dawei extinguishes any optimistic thoughts before they have a chance to buoy him.

"Yes," Jake says weakly. "It's Dawei. I've hurt him badly. I...I may have...I may have..."

"Look, buddy, I know this is stressful," Ben says. "But I also know that they're looking for all of us right now and we need to put the data together and send all of this stuff to my people in the U.S. Let's get some perspective and get on with this."

"I'm swimming in perspectives, Ben. No. I'm, I'm fucking drowning in them," Jake yells.

The angry response comes out reflexively, as though some flash of wisdom rushes for freedom before the chaos of Jake's thoughts can trap it. Once out, the words help Jake face the questions that incapacitate him. Where did the violence come from? And what scares him more? Is it the consequence he faces for what he's just done to Dawei or is it an empathic reaction to the pain that Dawei is enduring? He can only hope that Dawei is enduring pain right now. Otherwise, he's dead. Jake doesn't know which weighs more or how to separate them and, because of this lack of clarity, he doesn't know who he is himself. Perhaps Qiang had figured this out. Perhaps he knew that Jake, on a fundamental level, lacks human decency.

Jake wants the floor to open up and swallow him but trying to escape would only undo everything Diane and Ben have accomplished so far. This pathetic emotional breakdown is nothing if not selfish. Every move he makes, it seems, puts their effort into greater jeopardy. He needs to make up for this. He needs to prove to himself that his fear isn't just about himself. It's not about being alone. It's not just about what will happen to him when this is over.

"Jake," Ben says. "We'll deal with the Dawei thing together as soon as we send off the data. As far as I could tell from the PSB correspondence, he's been stalking and harassing you. I have their records on this. Whatever happens, you have a case against this guy."

Jake shakes his head to regain his focus, reaches around to the side pocket of his backpack and pulls out the USB stick.

"Here it is. I was able to show twenty-nine connections."

"Brilliant, buddy," Ben says. "That should be enough to paint a pretty damning picture."

"Let's put this together," Diane says as she takes the USB stick and inserts it into Ben's laptop.

"How much time do we have?" Jake asks. "If they're already looking for us, won't they be here any second? You can't book a hotel room without ID."

"The room is booked under my colleague's name," Diane says as she searches some files. "I brought him up here from Shanghai for some client meetings. He'll be out until this evening. I have his extra key. We're safe here for now."

"Still," Ben interrupts, "the PSB will eventually get here once they figure out that we're trying to evade them. They'll search for any possibility. You and your colleagues stay here a lot, right?"

"Yes, my firm has a standing reservation."

"So it's just a matter of time before they arrive, no?"

3:45 p.m.

A knock on a door prompts Jake to sit bolt upright and sends his heartbeat surging. He was lying on the bed with his eyes closed, in and out of a fitful sleep, trying, again, to enter a world where he had never thrown Dawei's mementos into the garbage. A hundred times over, Jake has reconstructed that moment, rendering everything in it with such precision that the outcome he envisions might just become reality.

As Jake realizes the knock comes from across the corridor, his muscles relax. He hears someone greet a guest. They laugh. They exchange some pleasantries and then their voices trail off into the faintest of muffled vibrations as the guest enters the room and the door shuts.

There's no use in trying to rest so Jake slides off the bed and stands next to Ben, who's running commands on the computer he brought with him from Boston. PROPERTY OF MIT, says a label next to the power button.

Jake watches as the program constructs a multicoloured diagram on the screen. A list of dollar figures, some in the millions, on the left side connect with bank names and routing numbers, ultimately leading to names on the right side of the screen. Each name on the right is written over a photo and a date signifying the beginning of that person's term as an IOC member.

The lines are rendered in varying thicknesses and different grey-scale shades, signifying, as far as Jake can tell, the strength of the connection. The thickest and blackest lines lead to the individuals Jake found to be the easiest as he confirmed the role IOC members played in the companies and organizations that wound up with money that originated in China. Each line a takedown, a time bomb that will spray the connected individuals with shrapnel. The entire diagram may as well show a meteor heading for the centre of Beijing, threatening to vaporize the massive sporting venues nearly completed. Jake imagines this diagram on the front pages of every major newspaper in the world except, of course, for those published in China.

Ben saves some of the data onto a USB stick that he hands to Diane. She then prints out three sets of the diagrams on a portable printer she's brought with her.

"There's more evidence than we expected," Diane says as she hands a copy to Jake.

4:12 p.m.

Zhihong grabs his bag as soon as Changxing drops a scrap of paper with the American journalist's address on his desk. He closes all of the documents on his screen, files he's been parsing for the past six hours to see if he missed any references to Dawei. Maybe a footnote somewhere about where Dawei has been seen sleeping or where he goes for food.

"Thanks," Zhihong says, wondering what took so long. He can't ask. That will reveal the anger Zhihong feels about having to wait until the worst of rush hour traffic starts. The answer won't help anyway.

The value of the script now means nothing. Zhihong will give Dawei whatever he can to ensure he's safe and no longer needs to go back to washing dishes in Macau. He'll make up a story Yue Tao might believe, a story about a friend of his parents, a friend who helped shield his parents from the wrath of the Red Guards during the mid-1960s when anyone with a higher education became an enemy of the state and an enemy of the people. The people and the state, always one in the same. A friend whose son fell on hard times. Zhihong knows his parents went through hell during the Cultural Revolution. They never talk about that time of endless upheaval and the silence always made their anguish over that period in their lives clear. A repression that will work in Zhihong's favour because it fades and distorts the details of what happened.

Zhihong's parents are so old now that he needs to remind them of their neighbours' names. Reality for them is as malleable as it is for a toddler. It would be easy to construct a memory by melding it with some indisputable details. Zhihong could easily create a background for Dawei that would have roots in his parents' lives. Once that history sets, no one will question it. That will allow him to spare a few hundred kuai every month. Enough for Dawei to rent a room on the outskirts of the city. Somewhere outside the Fifth Ring.

Outside, surveying the stationary traffic, Zhihong wonders why he didn't come up with such a solution when Dawei showed up in Beijing two or three years earlier, looking for the companionship they had together next to the causeway in Macau. He now sees in sharp detail the damage he caused by breaking their bond. The strongest of bonds, free of family or career obligations, a connection that formed not in spite of their social distance but because of it. They had nothing to offer each other except an absence of judgment.

Then Zhihong detached himself when circumstances made their meetings more complicated but not impossible. He made a choice, turning off his feelings when he should have hatched a plan. The kind of plan he's conjuring up now. A plan to resuscitate the people they were when they shared their dreams and disappointments.

As Zhihong approaches the subway entrance, he sees a crowd meandering, confused, like a trail of ants interrupted and diverted into random movement by something that's fallen from above. From the chatter of angry commuters talking on their cell phones, he learns that the subway line is temporarily shut down. Work on the tracks, for the new subway cars meant to be running when the Olympics start, has caused some kind of power disruption.

"Tian!" he shouts.

"They're sending buses," says a woman next to him, picking up on his anger. "But how will they even get here in this traffic?"

Zhihong scratches his forehead as he looks east, surveying the countless stationary vehicles stretching into the distance and disappearing in the brown haze. He starts jogging.

5:47 p.m.

Grimacing, Ben cancels a third attempt to send the data through the VPN he's used to send earlier versions of their reports.

"Dammit," he hisses.

The outburst riles Jake. This is the first time Ben has shown anything other than confidence. Diane doesn't react. She's been spending more time with him. Perhaps she's seen him rattled before. Taking cues from Diane, Jake swallows his fear and sits still on the edge of the bed.

"They've probably figured out how to trace my VPN's," Ben says. "The protocols are associated with MIT."

"What can you do now?" Diane asks.

"I need to piggyback on another one."

Ben looks toward the door.

"There must be someone else in this hotel using a VPN," Ben says. "I need to find one."

"Can I do anything to help?" Jake asks.

Ben squints and rubs his eyes. He then looks at his and Diane's phones, which sit next to the television, their batteries removed. He picks them up, phones in one hand and batteries in the other.

"Take these," he says.

Diane starts shaking her head.

"Ben," she says. "He might already be in enough trouble."

Jake's heart begins pounding again.

"We have no choice," Ben says, looking at Diane. "I need more time. They're going to figure out where we are." He looks back at Jake. "Take these, I don't know, anywhere but here. As far as you can get in ten, maybe fifteen minutes. Put the batteries back in them and switch them on."

Diane looks out of the window, silently shaking her head again. A shake of resignation this time, not resistance. Jake sees in her expression the implications of Ben's request and accepts it. Now numb, Jake steps outside of himself to avoid the instinct of self-preservation and into the skin of some clone he's conjured up with his imagination, a more heroic version of himself. He takes the phones.

"And do the same with your phone when you get to wherever you're going."

Jake places the phones and batteries in the front pouch of his backpack.

"Wait," Diane says.

She hands one set of the documents she's printed out to Jake and another one to Ben.

"Each of us should have these documents on us," she continues. "It will show them, very clearly, what we know."

"It's damning, but it won't make any difference until I upload the data to my servers in the U.S.," Ben says.

"Then hurry up," she says.

6:15 p.m.

The sweat running down the centre of Zhihong's back makes the fabric of his shirt stick to his skin. The rough polyester fabric chafes. In the shade of the Third Ring's China World overpass, he stops jogging, removes his jacket, folds the garment and slides it into his briefcase.

He's covered well more than half the distance to the American journalist's apartment building. People file in and out of the China World subway entrance. The line must be running again but it won't help him now. He's only about a kilometre from his destination. It will take just as much time, if not more, to get down to the platform and then, once at the next stop, to figure out which exit leads most directly to the building he wants.

Zhihong's cell phone vibrates. The call is surely from Yue Tao who will be wondering where he is. It's dinnertime and they've agreed to eat at a new Korean restaurant in their neighbourhood, at least forty-five minutes away in the opposite direction. What could he possibly say? Another story he'll need to create. This is what it's like to live a lie. Constant fabrication and subterfuge. The need for total recall about alternate realities. Always teetering on the edge of being discovered. The luck will eventually run out. It's mathematically impossible to come out on the good side of the odds indefinitely. Even if he's lucky, he'll be exhausted.

As he lands on this conclusion, Zhihong decides he will come clean with Yue Tao. He will let the words "I'm a homosexual" drop like bombs, shattering the dream she's been trying to construct. There's no other way to deliver this message. He could try to ease the pain by telling her that he respects her too much to keep up the charade. He could try to shift some of the blame to her reluctance to entertain any other suitors. They needed to marry right after graduation from university and, it seemed, there were no other options for either of them. Why was that? Zhihong had no way to counter her determination.

But no. There's only the three words he will say. Any others will be meaningless. There's no way to plan for this crisis. People, no matter how well you know them, will surprise you with their reactions to life-changing circumstances. She might stand stoically and tell Zhihong that she knew all along. She might also shriek and demand that he never come home. So many possible outcomes but they will all be the same.

Yue Tao has been fretting about how their financial circumstances will keep them from their dream of an ideal home. She's about to confront a factor that's much more damaging.

Zhihong moves to take the call but the phone stops vibrating. The screen shows that she's already sent several texts.

6:28 p.m.

Ben finds a VPN signal on the fifth floor. Leaning against the wall, he sets in motion a series of commands that will access the keychain of the network's user.

"Come on, come on, come on," he whispers to himself as a gyroscope icon spins on his screen.

Ben hears a ping sound from the elevators at the centre of the corridor. He watches closely as two young Asian women carrying shopping bags emblazoned with fashion labels step out. Louis Vuitton, Chanel and Prada are the few he recognizes. Then another ping, this one very thin and tinny comes from his laptop, indicating Ben's successful VPN access.

Ben slides down the wall and places his laptop on his knees while he logs into his database.

6:31 p.m.

Jake keeps his head down, looking at his blank cell phone screen to avoid the surveillance cameras built into two opposite corners of the elevator's ceiling as he and the other passengers descend. He's planning to head back into the subway corridor and come out on the south side of Jianguo Road. He'll put the batteries back in the phones once he's in the Jianwai Soho development, a sprawling set of pure white towers that have been under construction, growing phase by phase for at least five years.

The elevator stops on the fifth floor and a group of eight or nine people pile in, yammering in southern-accented Mandarin about the restaurant they're heading to.

"Reasonably priced Peking Duck. Just inside the Fourth Ring. It's so frustrating," one says, "how difficult it is to get good Peking Duck in Wuhan."

The rest of them nod in agreement.

Jake feels protected by the mundane conversation among the crush of people around him. The elevator stops again on the third floor. A trio of Western tourists, parents in their fifties with a teenaged daughter, stare into the crowded car, unsure of whether to enter. The parents wear polo shirts – hers pink and his red – and khaki shorts. Americans, for sure. Jake wants them to enter. After a few seconds, they step away and the descent to the lobby continues.

Jake walks along the polished marble floors of the hotel's lobby towards the escalator down to the lower concourse, surrounded by soaring imperial red columns topped with gilded gold capitals, all designed as an homage to the Forbidden City. He sees a group of PSB officers coming through the giant, revolving door from the outside, at least six of them, and more officers are just outside, waiting for the next opening to swing through to the outside. To appear no different than a tourist, Jake looks away from them, up at the columns and the ornate, cross-hatched ceiling design. He then merges into a group of tourists leaving their bags in front of the concierge desk. Once he's in the middle of the group, Jake looks out to watch the officers as they proceed to the elevators. The next group of five or six officers head to the reception desk.

They're almost certainly here for Ben and Diane, Jake thinks. If he's right, there's no point in the diversionary tactic he's planning with the phones. Do they know what room? Should he try to get to room 712 before them? What would be the point? Should he just run? And run? And run? There's nowhere to hide. At least there's nowhere to hide for long.

6:32 p.m.

Several police officers mill around in front of the apartment building as a maintenance worker inspects a track embedded in the ground at the entrance. The worker operates a grouting tool that produces a deafening howl. A handwritten sign in Chinese, "MAINTENANCE IN PROGRESS", hangs on the right-side pane of glass, taped on a slight angle as if the person hanging it didn't bother to look twice. The left-side pane of glass is missing.

A security guard just inside stops Zhihong.

"I don't recognize you as a resident of this building," the guard says, yelling over the power tool's racket. "Do you live here?"

"Um. No. I'm visiting a friend."

The answer is lost in the noise. "What?"

"I said I'm visiting a friend," Zhihong says, yelling this time.

"Which friend? What unit?"

The stern tone rattles Zhihong. It occurs to him as he reaches into his pocket for the paper with the address that one of the units might be a crime scene. Could the police presence have something to do with Dawei and the journalist?

Zhihong leaves the paper in his pocket. He doesn't want the guard to snatch it. The power tool stops.

"Um. Oh right. I was supposed to call him when I arrive to find out which unit," Zhihong says apologetically.

"Sir, whom have you come here to see," the guard asks, this time more impatiently before looking over at two police officers who've just exited the elevator with a handful of men in plain suits. It's obvious to Zhihong from the way they interact that the men in suits are working in some branch of law enforcement or investigations.

Several more people enter the building and the security guard moves to stop them, most likely to ask for their IDs. One of the police officers asks the maintenance crew how long it will take to replace the broken door pane. In the flurry of interactions, Zhihong steps back outside. He continues walking down the path leading to the outer gates of the development and stops at a bench he feels is a safe distance from the journalist's building yet still with a line of sight to its entrance.

Zhihong's suspicion that the police activity somehow involves Dawei and the American solidifies into certainty. His phone rings again. It's Yue Tao. He connects and puts the phone to his ear.

"Hong? Hey, are you there?"

Zhihong waits a moment. "I'm here."

"Hong, where are you? What's wrong?"

"Um. It's a friend. He's hurt badly."

"Hong, you're scaring me. What friend?"

"Let me call you back."

6:33 p.m.

Prompted by a tour leader brandishing a travel agency flag, the group Jake was using as a form of shelter has decamped and swept, cluster by cluster, into the China World Hotel's giant revolving door entrance. They are now lining up to board a tour bus waiting outside, just beyond the police cars. Jake stands exposed in front of the tour group's bags, arranged in rows like cars in a parking lot. Several bellhops get to work lugging the bags to the bus.

Now vulnerable, Jake looks again towards the east side of the lobby, to the escalator that leads to the lower concourse, wondering whether it makes sense to flee.

Sooner or later he will be dragged out from whatever spot he manages to find. Why prolong the agony, he wonders? Just cut to the consequence instead of calculating what consequences await.

As he mulls the thought, three more police officers emerge from below. One looks at Jake and then down at a set of papers on a clipboard.

Jake looks away and starts walking towards the revolving door.

"*Bie dong!*" shouts one of the officers. Don't move!

6:35 p.m.

Someone knocks. Diane stands up, hoping it's Ben returning with a thumbs up but knowing it's more likely to be the police. Ben has a key card. Why would he knock? She hears the person on the other side of the door slide the magnetic card through the lock. She rolls her fingers into fists and then looks at the manila folder on the desk next to her printer. It appears that she will be the first one to lob the explosive material contained in the lists and diagrams. All of the waiting and placating that started with her first visit to the PSB almost a month ago will end as she pivots to face the authorities on her terms.

6:37 p.m.

Another ping comes from the elevators. Before the men inside even step out, Ben hears the harsh squawk of walkie talkies, "kksssshhhh-t", a crackling, disembodied voice barks an order, followed by another "kksssshhhh-t", and he realizes he's now facing the end of his gambit.

The progress bar on his screen is about three-quarters of the way to the end. It chugs across, pixel-by-pixel, and Ben stops breathing as he turns to see three police officers spot him and start approaching. Two other men in suits follow the police.

"*Cai-De, ni bie dong ni de dian nao xitong,*" one officer says, using Ben's Chinese name. Cease all operations on your computer system.

The progress bar, close to the end, stops.

"Fuck."

Ben hears some voices come from the room next to where he's standing, a couple of guests preparing to leave. They open the door and step outside, looking confused by the presence of police officers heading down the corridor. Ben puts his foot in the door, pushes it open, jumps inside and locks the door.

"Hey!" one of the guests shouts. "Xiao tou!" Thief!

A moment later the police begin pounding on the door. Ben refreshes the upload, restarting the progress bar which appears to be moving faster this time.

Through the door Ben hears the police calling assistance from management while two others continue to pound on the door. He hears the words "intrusion" and "criminal".

The progress bar is now halfway through to its finish. "C'mon, baby. Do this for me. C'mon."

Three quarters.

Four fifths.

The signal is stronger in this room.

Bing.

6:40 p.m.

Officers on either side of Jake grip his wrists as the elevator begins its ascent to the seventh floor. It stops on the third and, when the doors open, three officers escort Ben in, two on either side holding him by the wrists, and another behind. The two men in suits are the last to step into the car, one wiry with gray hair, somewhere in his fifties and another, thirty-something and stocky. They have identical crew cuts.

Jake begins speaking. "Did you..?"

"Zhu kou!" the officer not holding either of their wrists says. Shut up. He hands over the papers that Ben and Jake had in their pockets to the older man wearing a suit. The documents contain the maps of money from Beijing to IOC members.

Ben looks at Jake and nods his head.

6:42 p.m.

Zhihong watches the last of the police cars drive away from the front of the American journalist's building. The maintenance workers are maneuvering the large pane of glass into its tracks to make the entrance whole again.

They'd never fix things this quickly in Zhihong's building, he thinks. This is something Yue Tao would point out to him. This development is full of foreigners and the newly affluent Chinese. Not the super-rich Chinese, with their connections to the biggest state-owned firms. It's the kind of place that would be just within his and Yue Tao's reach if they somehow earned maybe fifteen or twenty percent more.

The security guard steps in to help when the workers have trouble balancing the large glass pane. Sensing an opening, Zhihong starts walking towards the building.

Once he arrives, a group of foreigners move in from behind him. They're dressed in jeans and t-shirts, laughing, two of them a couple, walking arm-in-arm.

With the security detail gone, the remaining guard on duty seems less interested in who's coming and going. Zhihong slips in with the foreigners.

6:45 p.m.

"This information is now sitting in isolated servers in the U.S.," Ben says, in perfect Mandarin, as the two men in suits examine the diagrams he and Diane constructed. "All of the connections have been verified. Copies of the data have been made and stored on standalone hard drives that your best hackers won't be able to find."

Some of the terms are lost on Jake but he figures out what Ben's saying through context.

"Thirty-four million dollars," he continues. "That's all it took for you to buy the decision from the IOC members? Imagine how often that number will be repeated as the opening ceremony starts here next year, not to mention every single day until then?"

"You think this means anything to us?" the officer asks as he waves the papers in front of him like he's about to throw them into a trash bin.

"I know you're with the Ministry of State Security and it might not mean too much to you. But there's also the Foreign Ministry, the Culture Ministry, the Olympics Committee. I could go on, but I suspect you have a better idea about whom you'll need to consult with before disregarding what we've done."

"It doesn't really matter what we think," Diane says. "What matters is what those above us think."

She enunciates "us," aligning herself, as far as Jake is concerned, with the Chinese side, all the way up to the Central Committee of the State Council. She's standing with China and against its leaders at the same time.

"I've set a mechanism in motion to have all of this data distributed to every news bureau worldwide unless I'm back in the U.S., with Sun Qiang, within forty-eight hours," Ben says. "My fingerprint and his simultaneously on a scanner in Boston is the only way to stop the countdown."

To Jake, this exchange is barely comprehensible. As long as he's been in the country, the authorities have the final word. There's no negotiation. No one dictates terms to anyone in power in China. He wants to chime in. He wants to reinforce the stakes they're playing with. He wants to remind the police that everything taking place in Beijing – the many billions of dollars spent on an urban transformation of unprecedented scale – has been for the Olympics. You can't walk more than 100 metres without a reminder about how important the Games are for the country. But Jake can't open his mouth because, once again, in the relative calm of this endgame, the thought of what transpired with Dawei deflates him. Whatever happens, Jake won't be a victor. Qiang is now closer to his freedom than anytime since he was detained.

What would Jake say to him now, anyway? "I left someone bleeding on the ground, unconscious, maybe dead, to save you." How is that heroic in Qiang's world? If Jake wasn't worthy of Qiang before, he's even less so now.

The younger of the two state security operatives grabs his walkie-talkie and steps outside, into the corridor. His speech is too fast and muffled for Jake to hear anything he says.

"Collect their equipment and all of their files," the older official tells two of the police officers. "And take them away, separately."

"Two more things you need to know as your higher ups confer about how to deal with this," Ben says.

"Nothing you say matters to me," the operative replies as he watches the police officers pack Ben's and Diane's laptops into a large reinforced metal briefcase.

"I will reveal my identity and my undercover work over the past ten years for the Chinese government and the identities of others doing the same work," Ben says.

With this threat, Jake understands how Ben is so fluent in Chinese. This also makes it clear how well he seems to be able to navigate the PSB's network, answering questions that reside in the shadows of the bigger problems they've faced over the past few weeks.

"You just need to know how much you have to lose by holding Qiang," he says as the police officers holding him lead him out to the corridor.

7:25 p.m.

"I know you see me as nothing more than a gangster now," Ben says, sitting across from two officers in a white room in the basement of a building with white and institutional blue corridors. He hasn't seen any daylight since the police escorted him to a windowless van. He doesn't know how long it's been. An hour already? Two?

"But consider how much I've done for China in the past few years."

The officers look at Ben, stone-faced.

"Do you know why Qiang left me?"

No response.

"He discovered what I was doing and he felt it was morally wrong. And he left me. Yes, he's known all this time and never said anything to anyone else. There's your proof that he's never been looking to harm the interests of this government, a government that all three of us have been serving."

The officers stop taking notes.

"I've sacrificed a lot for this government and all I ask is that you send Qiang to safety. This is so important to me that I'm willing to take myself down and suffer the biggest consequence if you don't.

They sit silently for a few moments.

"I'll be a criminal in both countries."

"We don't serve the same government anymore," one of the officers says, breaking the silence on their side.

Ben lets the comment fill the room.

"What if I did one more job for Beijing? What if I said I had the means to erase all evidence of the records we pulled for our report? It would be as if none of those payments ever took place."

7:40 p.m.

"Did you even review the footage that my brother shot for his documentaries?" Diane asks the officers sitting across from her, in a building to which she was driven in the back of a van with no windows. She could be anywhere in Beijing.

"We're asking the questions, not you," one of the officers says.

"I can't help but feel some optimism here because I know my brother is no enemy of the state. That must have become clear to anyone who's on this case."

"We're not finished with our questions, Ms. Sun," the other officer says. "Tell us, were we to release your brother, what guarantee do we have that someone, perhaps the American journalist or maybe someone else who's in possession of the data, won't release the report you've helped to construct?"

"You are both aware that I have a high-paying job in international finance. You also know I have a daughter. I love her very much. I've been kept from her for much of this past month and I don't want to lose another hour with her. I also have a husband. I want all of us to be together again."

"Of course, we know the details of your life, Ms. Sun," one officer says while the other takes notes.

"Well then. I'm your insurance. I have no intention of leaving this country. By all means, invalidate my passport. You have the power to do that. I suppose that measure has already been taken."

The officer continues taking notes.

"Despite all of this, I love my country," Diane says. "I want to go back to Shanghai and resume the life I had until you detained Qiang. If Jake or Ben or anyone else allowed someone to publish these records, you could take my life away. I trust them enough to know they won't let that happen to me."

7:50 p.m.

"If you've been monitoring all of my personal communications, you know I'm no American nationalist," Jake says to the officers across from him after recounting all of the details of his relationship with Ben, Diane and, of course, Qiang.

The officers speak perfect English. They don't want a language barrier interfering with the clarity of his answers.

"You also know that I'm no U.S. government operative. I'm just an idiot who fell into journalism and this is where I wound up. You must know by now that foreign news bureaus are your last place to look for spies or people trying to undermine the government. We gather intelligence all day, all of which you can monitor, and then we publish what we know on websites that you all read. Let's be honest. We don't write anything that would surprise you. The spies are probably the wives of investment bankers."

One of the two officers sitting across from Jake continues taking notes while the other one checks levels on the recording device.

Jake has more to say but doesn't know whether it will help. Something that will be awkward for him to hear in any setting, let alone a sterile PSB interrogation room. Given what he might be facing, Jake figures there's no point in holding anything back. Who knows how long he'll be interrogated, how many times he'll need to write out his side of the story. He may as well say everything exactly as it's happened.

"You also probably know that I fell in love with Qiang."

The officer taking notes stops and rubs his eyes. The other one, who's asking the questions, leans back in his chair.

"Assuming we let your friend Sun Qiang go, what will you do?"

Unsure how to answer, Jake hesitates.

"I think I'm in a lot more trouble than the others, right?"

The officers stare back, expressionless.

"Why would you be in more trouble than them?" one asks.

"Are you serious?"

"Of course we're serious. What sort of jokes do you think we're playing, Jake Bradley?" the other asks.

"I got into a fight with someone earlier today. I ran out of my building, screaming my unit number to the security guard. I broke the door as I left. The whole thing shattered behind me. Someone must have reported this. I think the individual I fought with was hurt very badly."

One of the officers flips through a few pages of the dossier in front of him.

"We know nothing about any such incident," he says. "Maybe whomever you got into a fight with must have got up and left."

Jake doesn't know whether to believe him. What if Dawei has been lying in his doorway, bleeding, for the past who-knows-how-many hours? Is that possible? He screamed out his unit number as clearly as he could. He left his door wide open. There's no way the security guard wouldn't have investigated.

The officers seem completely disinterested in this sudden confession. What about the bruise on the side of his forehead? Jake wonders if he should point it out as evidence of "the incident" but stops himself.

"Getting back to the matter at hand, you need to know that Qiang will be released this evening," the first officer says. "He'll be on a midnight flight out of the country."

The other officer picks up.

"We're releasing you now. We won't stop you from seeing Qiang before he leaves but you need to know that there will be consequences for you if you mention anything about what has transpired today. As for the report you, Ms. Sun and the other one prepared, we've been assured that it won't be published. If it is, you'll be agitating for the release of Ms. Sun and you won't get an outcome as good as you're getting now."

A female officer enters the room and places Jake's cell phone in front of him.

"Don't turn this on until you're back at your apartment," she says in Mandarin.

8:20 p.m.

The windowless van transporting Jake veers frequently between lanes as the siren screams. The motion induces a bout of nausea which reminds him that he hasn't eaten since sometime in the morning when he was sitting at his desk munching on a warm sesame biscuit while pulling data on companies connected to IOC members. He also hasn't showered since yesterday. All of the running around, releasing sweat infused with the pheromones of fear, has produced a stench that rises up from his armpits.

The van turns a corner and stops. Jake feels someone in the front of the van step out and hears him walk to the back of the vehicle. The doors swing open, and Jake recognizes a new residential tower rising above the trees in front of him. He's across from a police sub-station between Qiang's building and his own. Bathed in pale orange light from a setting sun, the building is nearly complete.

"Thank you," Jake says, not knowing why, to the officer as he steps onto the street.

Getting no response, he turns on his phone to check the time.

"Shit," he says, calculating back from midnight. Less than three hours before Qiang's flight out. He'll need to be on his way to the airport in less than half an hour. Maybe sooner. There's hardly any time to see him. But, Dawei. Their altercation has blended with the subsequent capture at the China World Hotel and the confusing interrogation at the police station into an otherworldly farce, as though all of it was a dream that would dissolve into nothing with a shake of his head, like sunshine disperses fog. But the bruise on his forehead reminds him otherwise.

Jake knows which direction to run, and it requires his full determination to start jogging towards his apartment and away from Qiang's building. The effort feels like shedding skin, each step transforming him further into someone else, someone who never longed for Qiang.

8:31 p.m.

Out of breath, Jake steps onto his floor. He dashes around the corner to his unit and stops. The door is shut. He gulps while reaching into his front pocket for his keys.

"Jake Bradley?"

The voice, speaking his name in a heavy Chinese accent, comes from behind him. Jake turns and sees a man somewhere about his own age. Pale but handsome in a boyish way and dressed in the kind of nondescript suit worn by everyone vaguely professional, the man looks like just another of the many undercover operatives he's been answering to all day. But why would he be by himself?

"Have you come to investigate something?" Jake asks.

"*Wo bu dong Yinwen,*" the man says. I don't speak English.

Jake repeats the question in Mandarin and the man lets out a small chuckle, full of fatigue and despair.

"This place was full of investigators—inside your unit, in the fire stairs, downstairs in the lobby," he says.

Jake looks at the door, wondering why the authorities are not still here looking for him, with handcuffs.

"Who are you?" Jake asks.

"I'm a friend of Dawei's."

Caught between his concern about what's behind the door and the time that's ticking down ahead of Qiang's flight, Jake doesn't know what to say. With nerves raw from weeks of overload followed by a day of madness and violence, he's only able to put his key in the lock and turn.

"I see."

"My name is Zhihong."

Jake can't continue this conversation until he knows what's behind the door. The tension silences both of them. Jake pushes it and nothing obstructs its arc. The lights inside are on. They weren't when he fled hours earlier. Jake steps inside. Zhihong follows.

Once inside, Jake looks at the door. There's no trail of blood. It's been wiped clean. Stepping into the dining room, Jake sees the papers that had been flung about the living room have been put back into neat piles. Everything on the coffee table has been restored to order.

He walks quietly into his bedroom where he notices how the covers have been pulled up and tucked under the pillows, a half-hearted attempt at making it properly. The clothing he left strewn on the floor from the previous night is still there, but pushed into a pile in the corner. In his bathroom, the toilet seat and cover are down. Jake always leaves them up.

In his den, Jake sees that his computer is powered off, something he never does. The screen is black when it usually has a screen saver animation building into geometric designs. Some of the file boxes on his shelves are out of alphabetical order. The lids are askew, like always, but at different angles. Nothing in the apartment, Jake thinks, is his anymore. Everything is tainted.

Jake walks back to the living room, where Zhihong stands, waiting patiently for answers. He sits on the couch and puts his face in his hands. Racked with equal parts terror and relief and dismay and bewilderment, he doesn't know which feeling to channel.

"I don't know where he is," Jake says finally. "We got into a fight. A very intense fight."

He wants to tell Zhihong, to confess how he snapped and released a torrent of fury at Dawei. He wants to tell him about the stakes Jake was facing, the operation that Dawei had put into jeopardy, but can't muster the words. He can't even figure out where he should start. The events of the past month now seem like a puzzle whose pieces are as scattered and disorganized as his clothes and file boxes in his apartment.

Zhihong crouches down to face Jake, eye-to-eye.

"What happened here? None of the investigators would say anything. One of the neighbours said someone was taken out in an unconscious state. They didn't put him on a stretcher. They just hastily removed him, two officers just dragging him into the ele–"

Zhihong puts a hand over his mouth to catch a sob and stands up. Jake feels his stare.

"What did you do? What happened here? Where is Dawei?" Zhihong yells.

Jake looks up and clasps his hands together in supplication.

"I need just a moment to…," Jake says, searching for words. He doesn't know how to say "collect my thoughts" but knows he got the meaning across.

He notices the clock on his DVD player. 8:45 p.m. Qiang might be getting ready to leave. He wonders if Qiang is expecting him. If Qiang wants to say goodbye. He can't imagine what he would say to Qiang. How would he express love to a man who's just stepped out of a cell? How could Jake put the weight of such a moment on the shoulders of someone weakened by endless anxiety? Who can express feelings of warmth and affection when they're still processing the difference between confinement and freedom? The line between life and death. And then a thought emerges that overshadows the others, manifesting itself, fully formed, as a counterpoint to everything Jake wants to do and say. He should be in Qiang's life only in the form of memories. He knows that Diane and Ben will speak well of him, decent people that they are. There's nothing more that Jake can say or do at this moment to help Qiang or bring them closer together. Maybe they'll see each other years from now, when Jake learns to face the emptiness that he always thought Qiang would fill. Detach from Qiang and learn to address the needs of someone else. The starting point is standing in front of him. This man, Zhihong, is in pain, perhaps even more pain than Jake had to endure. He obviously feels strongly for Dawei. Maybe they're lovers. Maybe they're best friends. In any case, this guy deserves to hear the whole story so Jake will need to start from the top. And that won't give Jake time to see Qiang.

9:15 p.m.

Qiang takes a final drag from a cigarette he bummed from one of the officers standing behind him as Ben loads two suitcases into the trunk of a taxi. He looks at the two police cars parked on the other side of the one-way street leading out of the Progress Park development and is unable to see through the darkened windows.

Standing next to Qiang, Diane sighs. "It took you so long to stop smoking," she says.

Ignoring the comment, Qiang flicks the butt into the street.

"I owe a lot to you both," he says as he watches the dying orange ember roll towards a sewer opening. "Kind of ironic that Ben's spying made me leave him and then became the bargaining chip that got me out."

He laughs in a way that shows a range of emotions, none of them amusement.

Diane sweeps Qiang's hair out of his face. "You smell of cigarettes," she says, picking up one of his hands to inspect the nicotine stains on the tips of his fingers. "I don't know whether to feel grateful or angry that they let you smoke so much."

Qiang looks at Diane and shrugs.

"You know, Jake helped us a lot," she says.

"I'd like to say goodbye to him," Qiang says.

"I thought he'd be here," Ben says, looking at the display on his phone. "Should I give him a call?"

"You two need to get out of here. You'll see Jake in the U.S. sometime."

Ben shuts the trunk and approaches Diane. He puts his arms around her.

"You're my brother-in-law, whatever happens between you and Qiang," she whispers into his ear. "Thanks for everything you've done."

"You're the real hero here. You really stepped up for your little brother. Thanks for everything you're doing."

Diane lets out a small laugh and wipes away a tear.

"Don't be ridiculous," she says. "Do me a favour and keep the cigarettes away from him."

9:28 p.m.

"He was ready to die for that document and I had to get out," Jake says, looking at Zhihong, pleading with him to understand. "Nothing else mattered for him and nothing else mattered for me."

Zhihong takes a final swig from a glass of scotch that Jake had poured for him. He puts it on the coffee table.

"My interrogators said they knew of no such incident at this apartment," Jake says.

Zhihong shakes his head.

"From the reports I saw, the authorities were concerned that your dispute with Dawei would somehow complicate your other situation. The one surrounding your filmmaker friend," Zhihong says. "He was just a complication. Something to be removed."

The last of daylight is gone. Jake looks at the time and goes numb. The minutes have ticked past any chance that he'll see Qiang. He feels incapacitated, weighed to the couch like a sack of flour, by the thought of Qiang being whisked to the airport in a cab with Ben.

"Zhihong," Jake says. "I know someone who should be able to find out what happened to Dawei. He's got some leverage on the authorities."

Hong Kong
June, 2007

Jake copies the bank account number from the email Zhihong has just sent from Beijing. It includes Dawei's name in Chinese and Romanised. He pastes it into a Word document which he sends to the printer.

"He's recovering well," Zhihong says in the email.

"Thanks for letting me know, Zhihong," Jake writes in his reply. "I still think it's best not to say anything about this arrangement. Maybe after some time, you both can come and visit me in Hong Kong. I would like to apologize personally. As you know, it's difficult for me to get to the Mainland. That may be the case for a while."

The street level noise dissolves into silence as the escalator conveys Jake into the belly of the HSBC building on Queen's Road Central, just a short walk from his new office in Pacific Place. Jake hears conversations in English and Cantonese, the tones muted by the empty space of an atrium that soars to top of the massive, skeletal structure. Jake had only seen the famous Norman Foster building in glossy coffee table books and advertisements, aware of its status as an icon of design. And now he's a customer of this international financial bohemoth, thanks to the advocacy of Greg Nell, his new boss.

Jake approaches the teller and presents an envelope of cash, several thousand Hong Kong dollars converted from renminbi in the account he closed in Beijing, as well as other documents he needed to open an account. The teller's grey suit, worn over a blue oxford shirt and a thin black tie, looks as though it was custom tailored, reminding Jake that he'll need to spend more than he ever did in Beijing to dress the part he'll be playing in this city.

Jake explains to the teller that his first pay will be remitted to the account in two weeks. He turns around and looks up at the shafts of light reflected into the atrium by banks of giant mirrors at the top of the building. Jake thinks about the effort behind the manipulation of sunlight, the challenges that architects and engineers overcame to bring natural illumination to everyone in the fifty-odd-storey building. The power of this massive composition of light, steel and glass catches Jake off guard. It prompts a realization that Jake should have arrived at two years earlier when Dawei showed up at his door looking for companionship. Dawei returned again, and again, and again. He wanted a safe place to store that document, that fucking screenplay. It was a simple request and it should have been clear to Jake, clear as the shafts of light beaming into HSBC's headquarters, that Dawei was looking for a friend. In many ways, they're the same person, one from rural Kentucky and one from China's rural northeast, both fighting for validation and security in a world that provides very little of either for those without the right credentials. They're the kind of people who can't afford missteps. The pivots and parries of Jake's path from Magnet Hill, Kentucky to a desk with a breathtaking view of Hong Kong's Victoria Harbour might have just as easily led him to the dead end that Dawei now faces.

They could have been friends but Jake didn't appreciate the friendship that arrived at his door because he was too determined to nurture a stillborn romance. And he nearly killed the gift that Dawei was.

A sob rises from Jake's gut, taking him off guard, and he breathes spastically for a moment.

"Sir," the teller says. "Are you okay?"

"Yes," Jake says as he presses a thumb and index finger to his eyes and then wipes away a tear. "Yes, I'm...I'm fine, thanks."

The teller goes back to processing Jake's data. The clicking of the keyboard hypnotizes Jake until he remembers Dawei and the account details Zhihong sent. He turns toward the teller.

"I need to initiate a standing instruction to send 5,000 yuan to this account every month until the remittances accumulate to a total of 500,000 yuan," he says.

Capelin Bay, Newfoundland
August, 2007

Qiang emerges from a grove of pine trees on a narrow trail that winds from the end of town. Large swells carried across the Atlantic crash against the broken sedimentary rocks just a few hundred metres in front of him and gusts of wind from the west carry scented air from the pine grove. The fragrance reminds Qiang of the Christmases he spent with Ben who would put essential oil of pine into an incense burner throughout the holiday to trick their guests into thinking their artificial tree was real. Thick tufts of green moss blanket the ground, cushioning each step so much that Qiang can't help but think he's walking on an alien landscape created in a Hollywood backlot.

A day that started in Boston ends here, on the rocky tip of a peninsula near the easternmost point of North America, after a transfer in Montreal and a few rides down-coast from Saint John's by generous "Newfies". Speaking in an Irish-sounding brogue, one of the drivers offered Qiang a cigarette. In exchange, Qiang gave the man one of his two small jars of Tiger Balm, which he explained is used to soothe sore muscles. It was a pure exchange and a welcome contrast to the politically driven give-and-take that had kept him busy for the past few months as a subject of intense media interest.

He had been barraged by reporters asking for details that would confirm the conclusions they'd already made about the Chinese government, looking to legitimise the positions they've taken on the subject. Dissidents, critics, academics, analysts, ingraciated themselves, most of them trying to back up their fellowship applications and speaking fees. Few of them willing to delve into the hypocrisy of the U.S. government or its Chamber of Commerce.

Qiang feels the cigarette tucked in a small pocket inside his windbreaker. He will save it for later. The sun has fallen below the ridge on the other side of Capelin Bay so he needs to find a spot to pitch his tent soon.

A few minutes later, Qiang fights the wind to get the last peg into the ground, allowing the tent to take its bulbous form. The top of the tent flutters but the foundation looks firm. After arranging the contents of his backpack inside the tent, he sits on an oversized clump of moss and eats the wild blueberries he collected from low bushes growing in clearings between the pine trees. The berries are smaller than those he's found in supermarkets but much sweeter. He savours each one as daylight dwindles into dusk and then to the pitch black of night. The wind, the sweetness of blueberry pulp, the sound of crashing waves and the scent of pine combine to create a sense of freedom for the first time since Qiang vacated his office in Silicon Valley a few years earlier. He didn't feel free when the authorities let him out of detention, nor was he free when he landed in San Francisco. He's been bombarded by that word lately, mostly by people who think they have freedom but don't, people who will never understand how viscerally it can be felt. The more the word has been used in the media to describe Qiang's condition, the more elusive it felt, which is why he's now disappeared into this wilderness between worlds.

By the time he finishes the berries and a ration of trail mix, the wind has died down enough for Qiang to remove his outer jacket. He lies on the soft vegetation and looks up. Perhaps he saw just as many stars as a child in rural Sichuan Province but the novelty of the night sky and the freedom of sleeping outdoors in a place of his own choosing gives the stars a renewed and awesome brilliance. As he tries to identify constellations, Qiang sees a hazy band arching across the night sky and realizes it's the Milky Way, a sight so majestic and profound he smiles, perhaps for the first time in months. Seeing this infinite array worlds so far away puts an equally infinite distance between Qiang and his recent trials.

He remembers the poem. The one he first heard in his university English class. It happened to be the poem that helped keep Qiang sane throughout the events he's come here to, finally, put into some perspective. *Sympathy* by Paul Laurence Dunbar.

I know what the caged bird feels, alas!
When the sun is bright on the upland slopes;
When the wind stirs soft through the springing grass,
And the river flows like a stream of glass;
When the first bird sings and the first bud opes,

And the faint perfume from its chalice steals —
I know what the caged bird feels!

The poem gave Qiang his first indication that English verse could be as profound as the classics he had learned over the years in Chinese. More specific on details, more modifiers, less of the ambiguity. But beautiful nonetheless. Qiang continues reciting the poem to the end. The breeze rushing by him is still strong enough to whip these words of wisdom up into the sky, across the Atlantic Ocean, and then across the great continent that separates him from so many people he's thinking about these days. Jake, in particular. And the young man who wound up injured as a result of Jake's efforts. These two characters, more than any others, need reassuring words.

Qiang watches them streaming up in the air currents blowing from the edge of North America. He inhabits these peaceful whispers, guiding them through the stratosphere and halfway around the globe. From these heights, Qiang can see London and Paris below. Then Moscow, with its concentric rings similar to Beijing. Then the amber sands of the Middle East and the green plains of Central Asia. When he watches the words finally descend on Jake and Dawei, he can sleep. And when he wakes, he'll resume his work.

Acknowledgments

The list of people whose contributions were vital to *The Wounded Muse* is long.

Susan Nanes steered me to the right books many years ago, including W. Somerset Maugham's The Razor's Edge, giving me my first appreciation for novels. Susan also provided some guidance on a few chapters early on.

Wayson Choy managed to tell me in a kind but firm manner to go back to the basics and to stop writing fiction like it's a news report. He sent me to Beth Kaplan's University of Toronto classroom, where I learned to take risks.

My mentors during a writing residency at the Banff Centre, Larissa Lai and M.A.C. Farrant, helped me develop my key characters and pay more attention to sentence structure.

My first writing group, which grew out of an online UofT class led by Michelle Berry, included Siobhan Jamison, whose poetic approach to prose inspires me constantly. Other members of this group – including Djamila Ibrahim, Charles Shamess, Alexandra Bednar, and Donna Hughes – helped me start to shape the narrative.

My second writers group, comprising everyone in yet another UofT class, this one led by Dennis Bock, was crucial in strengthening the story and the characters. These classmates – Joyce Wayne, Sandra Rosier, Terry Leeder, John Choi, and Leah Zaidi – helped me shape the story's characters. After a last pass through the manuscript, Joyce suggested some additions that turned out to be crucial.

Sam Hiyate convinced me to remove one central character, which required a thorough re-engineering of the story. That effort was like removing a dysfunctional kidney, unpleasant and messy but necessary to give the book a chance at life. Sam also provided great ideas that helped torque up the action.

And last but not least, my partner Klemens, who never complained when I needed time to write and whose editing skills I now take very seriously.

Many thanks to all of you.

Author Biography

Robert F. Delaney has been covering China as a journalist for media outlets including Dow Jones Newswires and Bloomberg News since 1995, and was recently appointed U.S. Bureau Chief for the *South China Morning Post*. He moved to China in 1992, when the government set in motion an economic reform programme, initially as a student and then spent many years covering the twists and turns of the country's transformation. In his spare time, Robert turned to focus on writing about the personal struggles of those in the middle of these changes. Many of the themes for *The Wounded Muse* were first developed in Route 1 to China, a collection of memoirs that won Robert first runner up in the University of Toronto – Penguin Random House Creative Writing Competition in 2012. Robert splits his time between New York City and Toronto.

Twitter: @RFDelaney